THE

EMPRESS'

JOURNEY

TIKL THE FIRST OF NEHEL

JOSEPH KOPEL

CONTENTS

GESHA   1

1. MOTHERS   3

2. CASAKANS   15

3. SARAK   26

4. ARCHMAGE   36

5. LAIMET   50

6. MANTID   63

7. SIEGE   75

8. VAGRANTS   94

9. YKARTE   108

10. KNIGHT   117

11. DALEHEL   133

12. MAGES   145

13. KORBA   152

14. JUNI   165

15. ENCOUNTERS   182

16. TROUBADOR   195

17. ANTEBELLUM   204

18. FEAST   223

19. JOUSTING   241

20. BLOOD   258

21. LAKIA   272

22. KORBEEN   283

23. PASS   297

24. METAMORPHOSIS   309

25. WALLS   322

26. ASCENCION   334

27. HEAD   348

28. CONVEYANCE   360

29. GREATSWORD   370

30. PLAINS   389

31. TREATY   400

32. HORDES   419

33. CORONATION   434

OUTCOMES   442

SAN LUIS POTOSI, MEXICO 1994   447

ACKNOWLEDGMENTS   452

GESHA

So many stories about the Gesha spread throughout Sankaris. Unfolded in different accounts, but the same culmination.

Though restricted to half a continent, the influence reached all over the world.

None of the four moons were visible that night as dark clouds gathered over the ailing Kingdom of Aranka.

A realm so cursed by the plague and the sudden death of two monarchs in a short time.

The thunderstorm came afterward.

A massive roar echoed from the clouds, even in distant places on three continents. The sound was too bizarre to be a rumble of thunder.

The blazing white lightning impossible to see fell to the ground somewhere in Aranka.

A burning reverberation resonated, shrieking.

The powerful earthquake trembled the underground.

Twisted and massive, rapid winds danced along with the fire.

It lasted a moment in time but seemed an eternity.

Then, void. Silence, darkness.

Without a trace, the clouds vanished, unveiling the night sky with the imposing moons of No Sak and No Nunn.

By the morning, when the sun arose, Aranka was no more.

Nothing.

All existence of a realm gone.

Life became dead.

Sand only sand.

Desert.

A kingdom obliterated.

Everyone knew the morning sensed strange.

A severed balance immutably maimed Sankaris.

I

MOTHERS

I t was the *Tikl 627 of Kahen the Second* when the Gesha occurred. Thus, the Age of Kings consummated in ashes.

Since then, eight years, equaling two tikls, have passed. The current was *Tikl the Third of the Gesha.*

Lakia's face had sweat and tears as she observed the broken Venka.

Affected by insanity and the plague, the lonely woman repeatedly drank from a leather canteen. Seeking solace, she swung herself rhythmically from back to forward. Kneeling on the bare ground, Venka warmed herself by a small bonfire in her pelts hut.

In a corner, the nine-year-old girl with light brown skin, hazel eyes, and wild black hair observed the dying sick woman, causing her to feel a deep affliction in her insides as she tightly squeezed her legs.

The most intense and devastating episode of desolation that Venka experienced left her in immense and unbearable pain. Her soul was in such turmoil that even Lakia could empathize with her.

She was Lakia's mother, though not by blood, a Molkan, an elvish of amber skin, yellow eyes, pointed ears, and blonde hair. The raw wound of her disgrace shattered her heart, even after two tikls.

Unable to bear her any longer, Lakia left the hut, bidding in silence farewell to the woman who had nurtured her.

With a heavy heart, Lakia raced across the prairie as fast as her bare feet would carry her until she came to a halt.

Her wet eyes looked at her surroundings.

Amidst the picturesque hills of pink grass, she focused on the circular and rustic city of Akiaba. Surrounded by watchtowers, the city stood as a tiny speck compared to the massive line of mountains known as the mystifying Karekall.

She recognized a taller hill on the other side with rocks, a forbidden area.

Rapid Lakia's breaths were coming out in quick succession. Across her face, sweat dripped, causing her black hair to become wet and staining parts of her misshapen, thin, waki fur attire, screamed as loud as her lungs permitted, and at that instant, a powerful gust of wind came to disturb the grasses with an invisible wave. Then, with silence, peace, and immobility, she knelt down, relaxed her body, and her heartbeat returned to normal.

An elderly Molkan man, who was limping, relied on a long wooden stick for support as he walked. His appearance was quite distinctive, with a lengthy white beard, bare feet, and clothing made of fur.

He approached the squatted girl—Uskam, the Sorcerer.

With tears in her eyes, Lakia watched him as his shadow enveloped her. "Did you give the Prairie Lily brew?" inquired with a lump in her throat. "Can it relieve her pain?"

"Aye," he replied with a nod.

"How long?"

"She will depart to the Gakia past the night."

Deep in her thoughts, she turned her sight towards the Karekall Mountains once again and spoke in a serious tone. "I can not think of myself without Mother Venka," she breathed with sorrow. "Tell me, sorcerer. Is there a reason everyone gets afflicted by the plague but me?"

The intricate question lashed at Uskam with surprise despite her age. He found a massive rock just a few steps away from him, took a seat, exhausted from his advanced age, and let out a sigh of relief. "Do you recall that lesson I taught with the Falte?"

"Aye, that circular game with black and white stones."

"As I taught you, everyone is in the right positions," nodded, moving his hand. "After Mother Venka passes, you will be in another position, your life stance."

"What is my life stance?"

"You can find your answer there."

Uskam used his stick as a pointer. He showed the rock conglomeration on the hill.

As she turned to see it, a rush of startled emotions flooded through her, a mixture of fear and a deep-seated suspicion welling up inside her. "You never allowed me to go there."

"Now it is the time."

In response to his request, Lakia provided helped him to stand up and then, with great patience, she guided his left arm towards its natural conglomeration.

Although it took them some time, they reached it.

Once Lakia reached the rocky surface, she explored the tall yet compact conglomeration. However, her attention attracted to a peculiar rapid heartbeat resonating from the entrance of a cavity that contained only a small chamber. As she explored the interior, her attention shifted to a peculiar sight—a tombstone, deformed in shape, with ancient scriptures meticulously carved into it.

She felt drawn, familiar, and strangely, it had some warmth. The myriad of emotions overwhelmed Lakia, leaving her numb with fear as she stood before the tombstone.

"She was your mother, your blood mother," Uskam revealed, approaching her with his distinctive limping. "It reads: *Here lies Princess Natahel of the Northern Territories, bearer of the Jewel, beloved daughter of King Vihen of Aranka, and cherished bride of Sir Cassandro Eskar of Casak. May the goddesses receive her soul.*"

Frightened, Lakia nodded, unable to express a word. Her hazel eyes directed on the tombstone.

"I could not believe the stances being placed, but it was all clear," continued. "Without a horse, a pregnant princess arrived alone from a distant realm. I was the only person she had met in Molke and pleaded for help."

"Why did she beg?"

"She was in pain and tired. There was no time to bring her to my hut. Thus, she delivered. I received you in the prairies, but she unfortunately passed away. I'm unsure if she truly saw you."

"She did not, and that is the sad part," Lakia said, glancing at the tombstone in sorrow. "She passed after I arrived."

"Do you speak with the dead?" Uskam, with a confused expression on his face, inquired.

"No, I have no words to express what I have." She turned to look at the sorcerer with tears. "But I can feel something inside. It is burning. It is light yet strong."

"You do not cease to amaze me!" he asserted, pulling his beard gently.

"I have a feeling there is more you wish to reveal. Have you forgotten?" she said with a fixed stare. "What is my life stance?"

"Aye, Lakia," he smiled with apprehension. "You were born as the Promise of the Jyistereerk, an empress entrusted with bringing balance to this ill world."

The girl, feeling a sense of tranquility, turned her gaze towards the majestic Karekall Mountains. She understood what dwelt beyond the formidable mountains and knew her purpose. Still, an essence of chilling mystery hid behind.

The night seemed endless under the glow of No Ta's crimson moon, but when the sun had just risen over the Karekall, Lakia sensed Mother Venka's spirit leave and nodded to recognize her transition to the Gakia, the afterlife revered in Molkan belief.

Uskam closed his eyes to acknowledge her passing.

"Mother. . .," she murmured, with sadness.

Indeed, she could not be by her side in her last moments, and it caused Lakia great distress and sadness. Despite her immunity, the sorcerer cautioned her against any contact with Venka.

Lakia and Uskam had stayed by the bonfire near the sorcerer's huts all night. remained by the bonfire, right beside the huts that were owned by the sorcerer. One of them with Venka's corpse inside.

Aided by his wooden stick, the sorcerer rose to his feet and then, with haste, reached for a nearby rod, which he carefully passed it through the flames in order to convert it into a torch. Limping, he approached and deliberately set fire to his two huts.

Horrified and startled, Lakia stood up from the ground. She did not believe he destroyed her home, leaving her to speculate on where they would find a new place to live.

Uskam made the choice to dispose of the torch and opted to drag a large hide bag of belongings with the left hand while with the right grabbed the stick. With a serious expression on his face, he gazed towards Lakia and spoke without pausing in his steps. "Let's meet trader Peken in Akiaba."

She followed him.

While walking along the long and quiet path to Akiaba, Lakia felt an overwhelming sense of deep sadness, accompanied by a rush of regret for all of his past actions, and an inexplicable void within his very soul.

She did not understand his insides. For some unknown reason, Uskam's once formidable magic weakened and eventually faded away, but she was aware of his past as a powerful sorcerer. He was now a regular, ill older man.

Lakia had not visited Akiaba, the rustic capital of the Molkan territory and the ancient settlement of the Kannestes Elvish Clan, for approximately ten months. It never appealed to her because, with every visit she paid, the conditions worsened.

She felt weak and unclean. Lakia had barely eaten some dry meat and Yalta tree fruits and could not go to any pond to clean herself or wash her fur clothes. The last two days were disrupting.

Near Akiaba, on the outskirts, she discovered all the ground covered in animal bones with some flesh, especially wakis, wasted and left to rot under the scorching sun as thousands of flies flew over. She struggled to walk barefoot among the bones without getting hurt. The hunters, driven by their greed and desire for destruction, had lost all respect for the fauna.

Lakia observed the watchtowers that used to have guards at the posts, now appeared empty, neglected, and abandoned.

While going by an improvised dirty street past the entrance, Lakia followed Uskam, who was dragging his bag covered in dust. Rubbish covered the entire area. In an instant, her heart raced as she observed the partially burned huts and abandoned corpses without proper funerals, sensing the darkness. Most people she saw were half-naked, stricken by plague, emaciated, and had empty eyes, making her uneasy.

"Do not mind them, Lakia," Uskam suggested as he advanced to a large, well-kept wooden hut.

As soon as they entered the hut, Lakia discovered amazed clothes, weapons, artifacts, and other items from every corner of Sankaris filling the inside. Despite its cleanliness, the place was in complete disarray, like a hoarder's territory.

Seated on a small chair amidst a cluster of wooden boxes and metallic chests was a middle-aged elf man. He wore a distinctive attire comprising elegant leather and green linen clothing, along with a feathered hat and a pair of well-crafted boots, foreign to the Molkan culture.

He had positioned an iron greatsword between his legs against the ground.

Lakia was so fascinated that she could not help but try to observe every single object in her surroundings.

Uskam opened his bag and carefully retrieved a pouch from within and tossed it towards the elf's feet, making sure it landed close to his blade. It made a metallic sound.

With seriousness, the elvish eyes shifted from the pouch to the elder. "Whatever you need is for free," nodded. "Coins are not of use when death is upon us."

Lakia had heard him. As she positioned herself beside Uskam, she knew without a doubt that he was right.

"Free or not, I need Lakia ready for a long journey," the sorcerer said, introducing her.

The unexpected request caused her to feel startled.

Peken observed to the girl with no gesture, but made a nod. "That Casarak child is best suited as a servant at a noble's house in Berrem!"

"Save your tongue and learn to address her properly!" Uskam demanded, distressed.

The trader kept looking at the girl with no apparent reaction. "What is she that you have required me the respect worthy of a royalty?"

The lack of replies caused an uncomfortable atmosphere, with the three sharing silent glances. Peken, at last, put his blade aside and walked towards a chest he opened. He searched for new but low-quality and inexpensive pieces of clothing.

Surprised, both Uskam and Lakia looked at the trader with interest.

"If my assumption is correct. She will have to go to Berrem either way," Peken murmured while choosing the fitting garments. "However, that realm possesses undesirable dangers for a girl her age. She will need to disguise herself as a boy."

"Why must you send me away?" Lakia inquired, troubled, but no one listened to her.

"Do whatever is necessary," Uskam replied.

Peken handpicked a few garments and compared them to Lakia's body, ensuring the perfect fit. Once satisfied, he put the clothes on her arms before leading her behind the elegant silk curtains. Previously, he had to give a concise explanation and patiently taught Lakia the proper way to wear each garment.

"I have known you since you were a lad, Peken," Uskam nodded and, tired, sat on the same chair where the trader previously was. "But you followed a calling and refused the ways of the Kannestes."

"Was it worth learning the ways of a clan already doomed long since Kasana's execution?"

Silence.

"As you can know, death is coming for us," Peken continued somberly. "Soon, the Kannestes will cease to exist."

Uskam comprehended and responded by tugging his white beard. "You have been there. Am I right?"

With a sudden tremor, the trader soon made his way towards a corner, where he poured wine from a canteen into a metallic cup. He drank it desperately, seeking relaxation, all under the watchful gaze of the elder. With fear in his eyes, he stared, still with the cup in his hand. "You do not know what the hell is beyond the Karekall!" replied with agitation. "You do not. . ."

"I know, Peken. The *Frelee Dee* has revealed me while in Salter," then pointed to Lakia, still changing behind the curtains. "Are you going to send her only in clothes?"

The trader assented and opened a wooden box to extract more items—a compass, a satchel, and maps—. Seemingly, he put his fears aside.

Lakia had gotten out, and she had a distinct appearance than before. Her outfit comprised a wool tan shirt, a brown vest, leather pants, and a hat that concealed her long black tied hair, giving her a completely unique look. It was hard to identify her as a girl, and she easily could pass as a boy.

"There she is!" Peken exclaimed with admiration.

"Go south. Keep the Karekall to your left," Uskam instructed Lakia in the middle of the prairie. "You will arrive at The Lowlands once you leave Molke. Keep going until you arrive at the Holy Mountains. After The Pass, Salter will be within your reach. There, request an audience with the High Archmage."

With her tearful hazel eyes, the girl nodded in agreement as the elder gave her directions.

"Have safe travels," he concluded.

The Sorcerer from the Elvish Clan of the Kannestes did not show any emotion as he swiftly turned his back, walked with his limping, and, with the help of the stick, Uskam began his return to the doomed city of Akiaba.

As Lakia watched him walk away, she held onto her leather satchel, making sure not to lose the items given to her earlier. Dressed as a boy, and with determination, she turned around to begin her journey south, and sobbed in disconsolation as gusts of wind moved the tall pink grasses going in her direction.

2

CASAKANS

The caliber of his new blade in the right hand amazed Alessandro. It was so reflective that flawlessly mirrored his tanned face.

A fine giefo sword.

He focused his dark, piercing eyes solely on his opponent, a formidable adversary named Marissa. Positioned in a combat-ready stance, the girl with dark skin, whose weapon was as expertly crafted as his, readied herself for the upcoming battle.

He also did the same and prepared himself for the upcoming fight.

The confrontation was, at first, visual. No one dared to give the first step.

As they assumed a battle posture and readied their lean bodies for the impending fight, she struggled for a moment before she could finally swing her sword at Alessandro. He stepped back, distancing himself to prevent any contact. Yet, the collision of the blades produced a forceful impact that was almost strong enough to make them bounce, causing them to grip tightly the hilts with both hands throughout the ensuing action.

As they were both students from the prestigious Academy, the two young combatants had engaged in multiple bogus sword duels before, just like this one.

With great agility, he dodged Marissa's sword, preventing it from contacting his right shoulder.

Alessandro attempted to knock her feet by squatting down entirely, but his aim was off as she leaped out of the way.

"Enough!"

A gray-haired black man in dark robes shouted and approached the youngsters.

The combatants stared at him, safeguarding their weapons.

"My apologies, father. I got carried by my excitement." Alessandro replied, in regret.

"As I do, uncle," she responded.

"It does not matter, lads. Please, return them."

"I am glad I no longer have to wear this tight suit!" Marissa shouted, irritated, unbuttoning the shirt by the neck as she wore a dark armored military uniform.

She made the way towards a grand wooden table. She approached an open leather case and gracefully placed back the sword.

But Alessandro remained impressed and examined every aspect of his weapon.

"Is everything all right, son?" Orssandro, the elder man, asked.

"I am still startled to see how it has no scratches. It is perfectly unblemished!" replied, returning it to the case beside the other blade.

"It results from an exceptional handmade job. And too expensive!"

"Expensive will be our nuptials here!" Marissa exclaimed with a chuckle extending both arms and dancing around to show the place where they were, a spacious ballroom found on the last floor of three in the Vykar Palace.

"It is worth every coin as long as you both can have a prosperous union!"

She gave a nod before unbuttoning her betrothed stiff shirt.

Dessidere, a tall young man dressed in fancy gray clothes, appeared and interrupted them. Orssandro Vykar noticed him with a disgusted gesture, excusing the young couple to approach him.

"My apologies, Sir Head," he said with a quiver and a soft voice. "We have received a pigeon with startling news."

"What is it?"

"Cassandro."

Orssandro became pale and looked anguished at the young pair, both sixteen years old, engaged in a game of pleasantries. "Is he... here?"

"No, sir. It was a stowaway that came in a merchant ship. He claims to know Cassandro and has a message for young Alessandro."

As soon as Marissa Taskar entered the forest, riding on her white stallion named Ghost, the enchanting view and delightful scent of purple orchids blooming on the trees captivated her. The breathtaking sunset at the edge of the lake left her in awe. She received the gentle breeze rubbing her face, and she could not help but notice the gradual shift from a warm breeze to a crisp one, presaging a chilly night.

At the dawn of the calm darkness, she appreciated the gleams that illuminated the captivating sight of Estolk, the capital city. Her wish to see the greenish No Nunn, the Moon of Life, in the sky was unfulfilled as she only saw the icy No Sak instead.

Dismounting her horse, an unpleasant yet familiar occurrence greeted her. The lake's waves caused dead fish to wash ashore, too decayed even for forest animals to eat. The fishermen faced a significant problem as they fought for survival. Shortage impacted some Estolk sectors.

A quick galloping rhythm made her turn around. She spotted excited the approach of her fiancé Alessandro on his black mare named Song, who stopped and dismounted.

She drew his attention to her attire, the light silk dress she wore in a vibrant red, which she paired with special boots meant for riding. However, as the night progressed, and the temperature dropped, she started rubbing her bare arms to keep warm. Anticipating that she would freeze, Alessandro took some thick waki furs from the mare's saddle and used them to cover her from the shoulders to her waist.

As a gratitude, she reacted by giving him a gentle kiss on his lips.

"How often have I told you to dress accordingly?" he nagged. "You will get a cold!"

"And how many times will you cease scolding me?" She replied with an alluring smile showing her charming teeth. "I am pleased with you by your concerns towards me."

She kissed him again.

He wrapped his arms around her, and both contemplated the lake. The couple embraced with passion, lost in their own bubble.

However, something concerned him, and he stopped startling her.

"My apologies, Marissa! I just recalled that Father has summoned me."

In a moment of irritation and despair, she distanced herself from him, lowered her head and clenched her fists, then showed her face with some tears barely surging from her brown eyes, looking exasperated at her man. "I have a fondness for my uncle. But do not be unreasonable!"

she exclaimed, denying with her head. "I did not object to his wishes when we went to the Academy, since we are together. . . But I want to be at your side without getting him involved!"

"I understand, but you shall know that he took me in when Mother was not around anymore, and I owe my life to him," he nodded. "I have no desire to tarnish the trust he has placed in me."

"You owe to him, aye. But heck that trust! We are engaged!"

"Shall I remind you that you also owe to him and obey his demands?"

Marissa's silence prevented a proper response.

"It is difficult. Right? Father has achieved the ways to be the most powerful in Casak after Mother," he nodded, taking her by the shoulders. "Times are not as before the Gesha. Reputation is important to him, and we do not have our complete resolve as we wish."

She roughly took his hands off her shoulders with tears drawing her black cheeks, not daring to see his eyes.

"Leave!" she yelled, startling him. "Do not let uncle wait long! Leave now!"

In frustration and anger, she took off the waki furs draped over her shoulders, intending to hurl them at him. However, she changed her mind and instead handed them back to him.

In a mix of sadness and admiration, Alessandro placed the furs back on the saddle, then mounted his mare, urging her into a swift gallop.

With a touch of sorrow in her gaze, Marissa observed her beloved depart through the forest, fading into the distance among the vibrant purple orchid trees.

She rested her hand on the left chest, feeling a strange and unsettling anticipation.

Deep in thought, the Head Orssandro found himself lost in contemplation, staring at his cluttered desk covered in papyruses containing official statements from the Assembly.

He knew it was time to take the last steps toward his coveted end.

In the chamber, a group of irradiated candles provided the illumination whose melting wax would either fall onto the furniture surface or onto the ground, depending on their location. Despite this, the chamber would also benefit from the additional radiance provided by the bleached icy moon No Sak whenever its light passed through the large window.

Because of its tropical climate, Casak was typically warm. However, the nights were chilly, especially after the occurrence of the Gesha, which compelled him to don a thick waki fur to keep warm.

Despite feeling tense, he attempted to relax his body on the large wooden armchair he was sitting in. He felt an apprehensive anxiety building up inside him and let out a sigh, hoping to find some inner peace. His gaze landed on an item placed in the right corner of the desk. The late King Vihen of Aranka presented a unique souvenir to Orssandro at an event held at the Equatorial Border. The large volume of aureate color, containing the secrets of the *Ykarte*, was an exquisite item that served as a reminder of their meeting during their younger years.

The volume was Orssandro's beloved treasure.

He held the position of a merely elected member of the Assembly, and he sent as an emissary from Casak to the king of Aranka.

Despite their shared desire for warmth and friendship, humans encountered diplomatic differences that proved challenging to resolve. However, peace prevailed.

Melancholy consumed him, and a profound sense of nostalgia flooded his thoughts. Nowadays, he missed the neighboring Kingdom of Aranka, now a desert that lies to the north of the border.

Despite this, the obliteration of the neighboring realm elevated him to be the most influential man in Casak against all odds, and thanked the Gesha in silence.

Startled by the sudden arrival of Alessandro, Orssandro promptly glared at the second armchair located opposite the desk. He observed the youth loosening his body on the furniture as the coldness infiltrating the window pleased him, yet covered in waki furs.

"Do you remember the balmy nights we had in the past, Father?"

"I do," replied, nodding as he stood from his seat with a faint grin. "I remember summer when everyone complained about sleeping in sweats."

Orssandro walked over to a small table next to a large bookcase filled with old and dirty books. He poured red wine from a dark glass bottle into two wooden cups and offered one to his foster son afterward. And took a sip from his drink and then leaned himself against the desk in order to be closer to him.

"Why do you want to see me this night?"

The Head, with a grave stare, took another sip before he could give a reply. "Tell me, son. What do you recollect from your childhood?"

Lowering his eyes, Alessandro toyed with his cup, using both hands, as he became lost in thoughts, with his fixed stare directed at the wine. Initially, he tried to remember while his father patiently waited for him. "I recall a woman who was absent the most, my mother, and there was a boy older than I, my brother Cassandro," sighed, looking at Orssandro. "I have vivid memories of the hardships we faced, one of which involved accompanying our mother to the tavern where she worked as a stewardess."

"What do you recall about Cassandro?"

"Not much, father. My memories are quite vague."

"I am sure your memories are stronger with Marissa."

"Indeed." Said nodding.

Letting out a heavy sigh, Orssandro made his way back to his comfortable armchair, carefully placing his cup on the desk before finally finding his voice and spoke. "The Gesha left us in a chaotic position, and my twin sister Tasarissa urgently went to look for you when she got the news of your mother's passing."

"I remember it was Marissa who came to my home."

"Aye, Marissa was concerned," gasped and continued. "You were eight years old then."

"But we were friends since four," pointed.

"Aye, and you found comfort in her. That is how you both became inseparable since then."

"Have you summoned me to discuss Marissa and me?" asked discomfortingly.

"I will go to the matter now," Orssandro replied with seriousness. "Your mother, as the Head before me, named your brother an emissary."

"Please continue, Father."

"Cassandro had indeed met with Princess Natahel of Aranka, who had already guided her people to safety from the plague that had afflicted their kingdom," nodded. "Upon her request for asylum, we generously granted her permission to settle on our island of Katalk."

"So?"

"Cassandro and the princess unexpectedly vanished with no explanation, after becoming entangled in forbidden passions." Orssandro took another sip of his drink. "No news about your brother was available, causing us to contemplate the possibility of his death. As of now, I am aware of the existence of a stowaway who has a message that is intended only for you."

Alessandro emptied all his wine and put his void cup on the desk with some agitation. "I will not get involved with someone who left when I was five!" he stood up and looked dubiously at his foster father. "I know it is not the fault of yours or his, neither mine, but sometimes it is best to let the water take its run."

"I could agree with you. But what if it concerns our realm?"

"As a Head. Could not you appoint someone more suitable than me?" he made a point by gesturing with his hands. "I am sure you can find somebody of great experience among our loyal members of the Assembly."

"The rascal will not talk to no one other than you."

"Do I have a choice?"

"No, you do not," he concluded.

3
SARAK

The gelid breeze collided against Alessandro's face during the early morning. He found himself on board a half-empty steam-propelled ferry. Leaning on the wooden railing, his dark eyes remained fixed towards his next destination. In the distance, he could perceive a shadow that seemed too far away, obscured by a light haze. By his side, he held the reins of his black mare, Song, keeping her close. He had almost completed his trip to the island of Katalk through The Strait.

He had the foresight to bring with him a reliable leather jacket and a stylish dark velvet hooded cloak, both of which would serve the purpose of protecting him from the cold morn air and ensuring his comfort until the sun's rays brought a more pleasant temperature.

In a swift motion, Alessandro turned his head to look behind him, where he caught sight of a group of merchants and their wagons, loaded with various goods that they were selling or planning to export. While he was observing, he noticed in the boat's rear an elderly pilot who expertly managed both steering the boat and depositing logs into the blazing furnace of the engine to maintain the paddlewheel's operation. Once again, he shifted his gaze to the horizon.

Song, feeling apprehensive, began tapping the wooden floor with one of her hoofs.

With one hand gripping the reins, Alessandro tenderly petted her head. "Easy, girl! I know you hate the water, but we are almost there," he whispered to soothe his mare.

Alessandro, who had departed the Vykar Palace slightly after midnight from Estolk, arrived on time for the ferry in Sostolk, which had already passed by during the sunrise. According to the orders given by Orssandro, he had no choice but to leave promptly to meet the stowaway at the Fortress.

Despite the testy encounter at the lake, he did not even get the chance to express farewells to his betrothed Marissa.

Soon he recognized a known place, yet different.

The Seaport of Sarak was crammed with a multitude of stationed ships, bustling merchants, and a diverse crowd of people from various ethnic backgrounds moving in disarray along the harbor at the back. From a vast number of wooden houses and stone buildings, the chimneys expelled thick black fumes into the air.

As the ferry made its way towards the harbor in calmness, a strong and unpleasant odor emanated from the polluted waters surrounding the vessels, forcing him to cover his nose.

Alessandro observed the dying palm trees that were once lush and thriving in the tropical climate, now forced to endure the harsh and cold conditions of the night.

Chaos seemed to have taken over the entire place. In the past, specifically eight years ago, Sarak was a picturesque fishing village known for its tranquility and prosperity. The significant impact of the Arankan plague and the Gesha soon overshadowed the few boats from the east, altering the place forever.

Alessandro observed how the pilot skillfully maneuvered the ferry, bringing it closer and closer to the small dock nestled between two massive ships.

Casakan sentinels had prevented non-Casakan people from accessing the boat as they heavily guarded the dock.

The pilot turned off the furnace a while back and then headed to the front to throw the ropes into a receiver for mooring.

Since Princess Natahel and her group arrived years ago, people of different ethnicities have been able to enter Katalk and even settle in with proper permits. Any attempt to enter the continent was against the laws of the Assembly, unless the person belonged to the Casakan race.

As soon as the doors opened, Alessandro wasted no time and mounted Song. He left, navigating through the passengers until he reached the dock. From there, he trusted and crossed the line of sentinels and the small crowd that eagerly awaited the ferry's arrival. His intention was to reach the narrowed and paved streets of Sarak as promptly as possible. When reminiscing about his childhood, he recalled the moment his adoptive father, accompanied by Marissa and Lady Tasarissa, took him to the city for the first time in a covered carriage. Although his memories were vague, there was a part of him that still kept some recollection of the city.

As he rode straight, he couldn't help but notice the dirtiness of the streets, in particular the left rubbish scattered on the sidewalks.

The people in the Breken Quarter were immigrants banished from a realm that lacked proper hygiene practices. The folks, who were tall and had enormous bellies, muscly, and escaped from a life of a strict military role to pursue a more peaceful existence. In the middle of the street, a group of women with their vast and swollen hands threw buckets of dirty and nauseating water, while a pair of men, using the same long axes they had previously used as weapons, cut wood.

As Alessandro rode, his gaze fixed ahead, the sight of the blood-splattered axes made him uneasy, thinking they may have wielded them in previous battles.

Although he had lost both of his natural parents and endured the challenges of the Gesha, as well as completing a rigorous military education at the Academy, he had never witnessed the cruelties of war, only hearing about them through books and word of mouth.

As he progressed further, he found himself at a particular canal where he would need to cross the bridge that would take him to the Fishermen's Square. On the left side, he came across the local cathedral, which was a stone church not overly large and had a simple design lacking artistic architecture.

As the sun set high in the sky, casting its warm glow over the plaza, the weather took a turn from cold to warm. Alessandro, feeling the change, removed his cloak and placed it on the saddle between his legs, yearning for even a fleeting moment of refreshing coolness in the atmosphere. As the temperature climbed, he noticed sweat building on his forehead.

Song and his rider galloped across the empty square, starting from the cathedral and reaching the opposite side. They arrived at an immense and sturdy stone structure known as the Fortress. The building, which comprised four levels, had an extensive security presence. Over fifty sentinels were on the rooftop and within each tier, surveilling the surroundings through the windows. Just before the thick wooden gate, the mare came to a halt.

Four guards in scarlet uniforms placed their hands on the hilts of their sheathed swords. Atop their horses, the guards' gazes fixated on the recent visitor with utmost discretion.

"I am Alessandro Eskar and Vykar!" shouted to the sentinels with authority. "I came in the name of the Head to see a prisoner!"

But only silence prevailed. The guards maintained their piercing stare, with an immense amount of distrust towards him.

"I have said that. . . !"

"We heard you!" interrupted.

Advancing towards Song on foot, a distinguished older man of higher rank, as noted by his chest adorned with a collection of emblems, surprised him with a nod.

"Please state your name and your position."

"I am Trasso, Guardian of the City."

Alessandro agreed, and reaching into his jacket, handed him a rolled papyrus.

The Guardian broke the Head's waxed seal and unfolded the document to read its contents. "So you came to see that prisoner. . .," Trasso sighed with a bit of disappointment.

"Is there any problem, sir?"

"A burden, I would say, master," nodded while rolling back the papyrus. "He is a Fennen, a filthy feline demanding to speak to the brother of Cassandro Eskar."

"Take me to him now."

"He arrived as a stowaway on board a Berremen merchant ship," Trasso guided Alessandro down the narrow and eroded stairs towards the dark underground below the Fortress, holding a burning torch in his hand to light the way. "That crap was hiding behind some provision boxes, but a crew member discovered him."

"Was locking him under here necessary?"

"Aye, master. In the past, these dungeons held dangerous criminals. I believed it was safe to keep him under."

"Safe for who?" he inquired with doubt.

"I intend to protect my soldiers from that animal!"

Both men arrived in a corridor. They kept walking through the darkness, only illuminated by the torch, while the rats ran into the walls' open cracks at their steps. They stopped at a metallic door the guardian unlocked with the giant key hanging by his neck. With a loud noise, he opened it.

"I truly doubt he attacked your soldiers for no reason." Alessandro warily asserted. "My father had met some Fennens, and they were courteous. Either he had a valid reason to defend himself or is that they fabricated an unjust lie to defame him."

Trasso, feeling insulted, appeared to not have paid attention, displaying his annoyance through his facial expression. He then grabbed a wooden rod that he discovered hanging on the wall, using it to produce a new torch, which he then handed over to his companion.

"Go ahead, master. It is the third cell to the right," said with a grave expression. "If you find it necessary to unlock and enter, you will locate keys nearby. However, I must caution you I will not assume any responsibility in the event of any occurrences before the Head."

Alessandro acknowledged with a nod and entered the hallway with caution, finding himself with empty cells at first.

Admitting his fear and distrust of Trasso, his training at the Academy equipped him with the ability to manage and overcome such emotions.

He encountered the referred cell. At first, the room seemed dark and empty, but the approaching torch revealed a figure with gleaming eyes. Despite his efforts, he could not get a clear view of him, so he had no choice but to throw the torch across the bars and onto the ground in order to get a better look at the prisoner.

The captive Fennen was a feline creature with a coat of light orange fur adorned with black stripes that covered his entire body. His eyes, which were of a shade of green, possessed vertical pupils, an inherent characteristic of his species. However, as Alessandro examined him, he could not help but notice that he was completely naked, bearing untreated wounds that were accompanied by dried blood. He had a few scars that were barely noticeable under his hair, and his hands and feet also chained him. With its body resting on the unforgiving ground, the feline remained silent and locked its eyes on the visitor.

"I am Alessandro Eskar, so to speak."

Although the Fennen had heard his words, there was no reply from him. At last, he could release his deep voice. "I was born in Finnerr, a slave worker in the Mines of Tiunnff for over two tikls. My given name is Corr," with no visible movement, he paused. "Just like me, your sibling was also a slave, and I made a solemn vow to deliver a message before his unfortunate death."

"I am here now. Tell me the message," demanded, a bit saddened by his brother's fate.

"Cassandro expressed his desire for you to take care of his child and his partner, Princess Natahel."

Alessandro was, without words, speechless.

He realized Orssandro would not approve of the news of a child being born from an Arankan royalty and a Casakan. A mixed royal newborn, a Casarak. He was unsure whether to tell his father.

"Where can I find them?"

"The expectant princess went all the way north to the land of the prairies."

"Is that all?"

"Aye. Done with my vow, you may leave so my soul can depart this body."

"No, no!"

Gently, grabbing the keys hanging nearby, Alessandro made his way to Corr after he unlocked the cell door. Once he had assessed the feline's weak conditions, he released him from his restraints, using the same key. He snatched a coconut shell from an adjacent bucket that was filled with water and offered to Corr to ease him his thirst.

"Why did you free me?"

"No one deserves to perish alone in a cell!" Alessandro exclaimed while encouraging him to stand on his feet. "I will not let you die!"

At exactly noon, a ruby pigeon made a delicate landing on the base of the window. It was awaiting the pair of hands that grabbed it and extracted the compact rolled paper attached to a foot. Upon reading it, Orssandro unfolded it and his eyes widened with surprise.

"Was it from Alessandro?" Marissa asked while relaxing on the chair behind the desk, though he was giving her the back.

He only nodded, but never showed his face. A long silence filled the room, leaving his niece in a state of complete suspense. However, he eventually turned his gaze towards her. The Head placed his hand on his cherished golden volume that rested on the desk. "I will confide a special quest to you. But no one has to know, not even him."

Startled, Marissa reacted by gently scratching the chair's wooden arms. "If it deems necessary," responded with hesitance.

"You shall go to Sostolk, where you will begin."

4

ARCHMAGE

As Alessandro stepped into the library of the sanctuary, he could not help but feel overwhelmed by its immense size, especially as he trailed behind the archmage, who wore a gritty brown robe and worn leather sandals, walking at a relaxed pace. The initial observation that caught his attention was the exceptionally high ceilings, veiled in darkness to where the extent of their height remained without end.

Against all logic, dozens of identical metallic giant golden medallions were mysteriously floating in mid-air. They were circles surrounding the Akareens, the eight-pointed stars representing the mystic symbol of the Mudiuhfaser's omnipotence in the world of magic.

As the two men made their way through the room, they passed by tens of wooden tables where a scarce small group of mages sat in complete silence. Completely absorbed in their forthcoming large volumes, they sat on benches that were arranged along the room. Dust often covered the books, the printed modern ones and the handwritten older ones.

The mages could engage in a diligent study of their texts, thanks to the illuminated candle holders placed on various surfaces and the strategically positioned lamps within the pristine white marble columns. These holders, meticulously maintained by a devoted young novice, ensured that the flames never extinguished with his nascent fire magic skills.

When they approached the last table, which was empty, Archmage Yasstro politely asked his visitor to wait momentarily while he ventured into a labyrinthine web of aisles that seemed to stretch endlessly. An unquantifiable number of towering wooden bookcases flanked these aisles, all overflowing with books of predominantly colossal proportions.

The magical men's profound silence and unwavering dedication, combined with the strange environment of tranquility and mysticism, impressed Alessandro while he was expecting something.

To take care of the Corr's wounds was a necessity, but Alessandro knew well that finding a medic or alchemist in Sarak who would assist a Fennen like him would be difficult. Fennens were a species that faced widespread rejection in most realms, primarily because of the ignorance prevalent among ordinary people. In need of help, he had no choice but to seek help from Archmage Yasstro, his former tutor, who coincidentally lived at the male mage's Sanctuary beside the Fortress.

Yasstro was kind to receive Corr, along with his fellows. As soon as the mages noticed his condition, they escorted him to the infirmary, where he received the proper attention.

Alessandro got surprised as the archmage returned, levitating a heavy volume of red leather cover and placing it on the furniture with a hint of satisfaction.

Yasstro clapped twice.

With a collective nod of affirmation, the mages exited the library at a leisurely pace, leaving their books open to mark the exact pages where they had halted their reading. The novice, too, followed them.

When they found themselves alone, the long bearded archmage gestured towards his former pupil, acknowledging him with a nod. "What you have told me is a delicate matter that only a small circle shall know."

"I am aware of that, tutor. I have only sent the news to my father, Orssandro."

The archmage, strangely, became startled and shut his eyes, revealing a solemn expression comprehending something only he knew. Yet, he disguised his disappointment with a smile, ensuring that his former pupil remained oblivious to his surprise.

With a touch of his magical hand, Yasstro opened the book and moved the sheets to the exact pages he needed.

The volume showed a large map with some manuscripts in Arankan. Using his elongated fingers, he traced along the rough fabric of the sheets.

The archmage assented for himself. "That land of prairies Corr is talking of is far north on the Continent of Ryza. Known as the region of the pink grass, Molke, an elvish territory of not well established borders with Berrem," then he glanced at Alessandro with his tired old eyes. "If my memory does not fail me, that is not even a realm, and two cities exist, but only one of them is inhabited while the other is dead."

"What happened there?"

"At the beginning of the King Kahen Tikls, there was a bloody civil conflict, the *Elvish War*. Today, Molke can not be a proper realm, and it will not flourish because of a strange curse."

"Do you think Princess Natahel and the child are in that inhabited city?" Alessandro was uncertain, but inquired. "I might need to travel there."

"Akiaba? Indeed, it is the only living place in Molke, but if you are contemplating a visit there, I suggest proper resources and people. It would be best if you did not go alone and unprepared." He nodded, opening his eyes wide. "Because of the vastness of the territory, it takes quite some time to travel, especially considering that the city is relatively close to the Karekall Mountains."

"Corr shall come with me, and I am sure he will be of help," Alessandro replied, adopting a thinking posture. "But I need an Arankan, a trustworthy one, loyal to the princess."

"You may trust and speak with Lady Fabehel so she can provide someone to accompany you on these lengthy travels."

"Who is she?"

Seated on the bench, the archmage placed his crossed arms on the table. "Fabehel used to be Princess Natahel's little sister, though not by blood. She was upset and disappointed when the princess left with Cassandro," he sighed and nodded. "But do not let her limitations and age deceive your eyes. She is brilliant, as you can not imagine. At a young age, she alone established and built a settlement with the people that came with the princess, the Arankan Quarter inside the walls of the former Head's vacation properties, and through my mediation, she achieved a long-lasting agreement with Trasso so they could live in peace."

"Shall we meet her?"

The second day in Sarak had already come, and it was well past noon when Alessandro realized how long he had been there. Following his encounter with the Fennen Corr at the Fortress, he spent most of the first day exploring the sanctuary and later slept in the same place.

After the research at the library, he departed from the sanctuary's gate, riding his beloved mare named Song and accompanied by his former tutor, the archmage, who was on a young mule.

With mistrust, Alessandro cast his gaze towards the Fortress next to the sanctuary. The sentinels, afraid, kept a watchful eye on them and had their hands on their swords handles. Upon sensing a potential threat following his disagreement with Trasso, he carried his sword in its black leather sheath. As Yasstro recognized his nervousness, he suggested they should continue walking across the Fishermen's Square, and later on, as he passed by the simplistic stone cathedral.

Both men went through the bridge over the canal opposite the harbor, the closest one to the island mountains.

They arrived at the street market on the outskirts of the Arankan Quarter.

The contrast between the rich diversity and plentiful resources of his hometown, Estolk, and the limited offerings of the local merchants startled Alessandro. Not only did they had scarcity of a wide range of goods, but the quality of their products was also lacking, leaving the general population with only the bare essentials. Yet, many people, both traders, and patrons, were fine with what they had. The produce was too green or too ripe. They also sold used clothes from the continent. The vendors distributed the limited meat from an old cow that had been butchered into many pieces.They were also offering rusted kitchen knives that needed sharpening.

Most of the people in place were Arankans, of white skin and red hair, but Casakans among them were also present, although in much smaller quantity.

Alessandro found most children, as the playful toddlers, from an unfamiliar ethnic group. Their skin color was not only unique, but their hair was also exceptional.

Yasstro noticed his astonishment while on his mule beside him. "They are Casaraks," assured. "Born from Arankans and Casakans."

"Were not the Casaraks prohibited?"

"Not after the Gesha. The Assembly suppressed the law and made an exception on Katalk under certain conditions."

"What conditions?"

"No Casarak shall go to the continent."

Just as both horses came to a halt, they cut the conversation off. It all took place right in front of the neighborhood's sturdy, imposing gates, which were enclosed by a tall stone wall. Dressed in brown leather uniforms and equipped with lances, a pair of Arankan sentinels were standing at the highest point guarding. However, as soon as the guards noticed the archmage, they issued an order to open the gate for both men. The distinct sound of horns announced the visitors. A picturesque and lively neighborhood revealed capturing their attention as people bustled around engaged with their daily tasks.

As outside, most were red–haired Arankans, with some Casakans present, especially women and Casarak children playing.

As they rode by the narrow paved streets with the indifference of the busy inhabitants, Alessandro restarted the conversation. "Why do Casakan women live here among the Arankans?"

"As King Vihen's emissary, Princess Natahel brought with her a large entourage of over a hundred northerners from the town of Byarte. However, she later requested exile because of the spreading plague. Most were married men and had children of their own," he replied. While taking the reins of his mule with one hand, he pointed to the neighborhood with the other. "In the aftermath of the Gesha, the male widows opted to unite with the fishermen's daughters as their brides."

With a certain sense of awe, the young companion gazed at the archmage before assuming a meditative posture and guiding Song on her way. "Based on my history lessons, I have realized that the Kingdom of Aranka was doomed even before the Gesha."

"Explain me," he requested, as accustomed when giving lessons to his former pupil.

"As you know, tutor. That realm had the plague and, ultimately, the Gesha. Do not you think a force of major nature or someone of great power caused its obliteration?"

Yasstro stared at him for a long in silence, showing only a light smile as his eyes recognized the answer. "I know what it caused."

His response startled Alessandro.

"How?" gasped.

"As I am acquainted with many secrets of the universe through my knowledge of the *Frelee Dee* in Salter as the high-ranking mages and sorcerers do," the archmage sighed before glancing ahead once more. "Among the received secrets with us, the cause of the Gesha is one of them. However, it is important to note that we are under a vow of silence, which strictly forbids any discussion about it."

Yasstro made a subtle gesture, pointing that they had finally reached their destination.

Other sentinels had already heard the horns beside the estate. A small wall that was white but in a state of decay surrounded it. They opened the gate.

The two men, accompanied by their equines, made their way into the following area.

After spotting a worker who was approaching to take care of Song and the mule, they dismounted.

They continued their course and across a magnificent garden filled with an abundance of vibrant red roses. Yasstro's fingers snapped with a soft smile, and a multitude of colored butterflies emerged from nowhere, creating a spectacle as they circled the blossoming flowers.

Alessandro walked behind the archmage along a narrow dirt path, and before long, they reached a spacious two-story house that had a rustic and attracting appearance. As soon as they entered, they discovered a spacious open area that was encircled by cloisters adorned with arched decorations. The place housed many closed rooms, each with small, sturdy doors.

A man, stout with a swollen face, appeared. He was an Arankan with a dagger holstered at his waistband. His attire comprised a dark blue shirt, leather pants, and worn-out boots. He made a request to wait before leaving with haste.

As he waited, Alessandro observed the many sentinels stationed on the roofs. By observing the quivers of arrows fastened to their backs, he noticed they were archers. He also had recollections of the other sentinels stationed at both gates, and at various locations within the quarter, armed with lances and swords.

It was strange that the quarter maintained its militia separate from the Fortress, especially when the Casakan Assembly did not grant permission.

The archmage's previous explanation about an agreement brought to mind the ongoing events between Trasso and the Arankans. But the concern rested in the fragility of that peace.

The man with the swollen face pushed a wooden chair with iron wheels. It startled the visitors. To their surprise, they were unaware of a wheelchair designed to transport a sixteen-year-old girl. A waist belt secured the girl to the wheelchair, guaranteeing her safety and preventing any undesirable falls.

Alessandro examined her. Her skin appeared softer and paler compared to most Arankans. Her long and tangled hair was a dark shade of red, her eyes were expressive and hazel, and wore a white dress paired with a dark fuchsia vest. However, he had no feet beneath her skirt.

Stepping forward with confidence, he bowed, prepared to introduce himself. "Allow me to introduce myself. My name is. . . "

"Spare me your saliva because I know who you are!" she interrupted with a hostile attitude. "Master Alessandro Eskar, I am unsure of the reason for your presence here, but if it were solely up to me, I would not grant you access to this quarter!"

"May we know the reason behind your upsetting?" Yasstro asked.

"I always welcome you, archmage, as I have known you as a wise and good man," then pointed to the youth. "But this one represents the twisted ways of the Head!"

"I genuinely assure you that my intentions are good and I came here with sincerity," Alessandro spoke smoothly, attempting to convince her.

In response, she delivered a resentful stare at him. "I do not care about your damn intentions and sincerity!" Fabehel replied, exasperated. "I would appreciate it if you would peacefully vacate my quarter, if you do not wish for my guards to escort you."

Alessandro understood it was hopeless to deal with Lady Fabehel and renounced the idea of asking her for a proper Arankan for his abrupt travel. "If you could kindly spare a moment to listen to me, I will then depart in peace as you wish," exhaled, uncertain. "I recently discovered the whereabouts of Princess Natahel and her child. They have been to Molke, which is in the northern region of Ryza."

As she grabbed the wheelchair's arms with strength, the girl opened her eyes wide, experienced a rapid palpitation in her chest, and trembled, finding herself unable to articulate a single word. She gazed at the archmage, hoping for an answer.

"Indeed, milady. Master Alessandro speaks the truth," Yasstro replied.

"With your permission, we depart in peace."

With this last word, Alessandro communicated to the archmage that it was time to leave.

Fabehel, unable to find words, watched as they departed, while the man with the swollen face remained behind the wheelchair, unaware of the ongoing conversation.

While the sentinels were sealing the dark gates of the Arankan Quarter, the watchful Arankan sentries from their positions atop the walls observed Alessandro as he rode away on his mare. The Archmage Yasstro kept a steady pace as he followed his former pupil towards the crawling street market.

Disappointment took over Alessandro as he scuffled with the idea that his foster father, Orssandro, or even the Assembly may have acted against the interests of the Arankans, leading him to blame himself. In the quarter, he had observed signs of misery and poverty, that even the market on the outskirts was in a sad condition as a significant sign of hardship. He heard a lot about the immigrants' suffering in Sarak, but it was the first time he could see it with his own eyes.

Lady Fabehel was right. The Head and the Assembly twisted the ways. As Alessandro was growing up, he encountered rumors and stories surrounding acts of deception perpetrated against the very ordinary people who had chosen them to represent them in government. Although he had no interest in politics, he found pleasure in entertaining with his friend Marissa in gullible games, creating a bubble of their own.

Despite the speculations, he respected Orssandro.

He stopped pondering and planned his travel to Ryza. Then, he spoke to the archmage. "I believe that only Corr and I will go," said in despair. "The hardest part is finding a vessel that accepts Fennen passengers."

Yasstro halted his mule.

Alessandro attempted to uncover Yasstro's motives, holding Song.

The archmage revealed his head by lowering his cowl, and pointed at the young man, drawing an odd smile on his face. "You will meet her!" nodded. "And Fabehel will be of significance to you."

"What are you talking about?" he replied, astounded.

"My esteemed pupil, you will have a great responsibility as the Borsen," he gave a head bow, then whispered. "You have my forgiveness."

Out of nowhere, a swift arrow pierced Yasstro's heart after the last word, and death embraced him.

His lifeless body fell onto the cold pavement.

The mule ran away as quick as it could.

Alessandro had to restrain a panicked and threatening Song, surprised and agitated.

With fear, the surrounding crowd made their way towards the Arankan Quarter, only to be met with disappointment as they found the gate shut. Despite the crowd's desperate pleas to be allowed entry, the Arankan sentinels, who were more preoccupied with the possibility of an imagined attack, ignored to their petitions.

Alessandro regained control of his mare.

From across the canals, he heard screams.

"Fire!" someone yelled.

A cloud of black smoke was ascending beside the Fishermen's Square.

The sanctuary library was burning.

5

LAIMET

After several days, Lakia arrived in Berrem's North-east on her tenth anniversary. Instead of commemorating her birthday, she found herself captivated by the enchanting surroundings as she journeyed from the Molkan pinkish prairies to the verdant valleys of The Lowlands.

Her fascination was even great when somewhere in the almost flat valley accompanied by the distant Karekall to the east, but before the hills to the south, she found an aligned formation of hundreds of pear trees in their splendor, glowing under the brilliant sun in a clear blue sky. Lakia approached one tree and smiled to discover fallen green pears on the grass. She grabbed some, squatted, put the fruit on a median rock, acquired a small dagger from within the satchel, and sliced the pears.

She put one piece in her mouth, tasting with surprise the sweetness. The pears were juicy and sugary, tastier than the sour fruit from the Molkan yalta tree.

Lakia turned around, glancing at bushes at a median distance, and smiled. "You can not hide forever!" she yelled, amusing. "Try this!"

She received no reply.

As the bushes rustled, a figure emerged from within. It was Peken, the elvish trader from Akiaba, dressed in a set of leather garments, a sharp blade secured in his sheath, and a medium-sized bag slung across his back. Lakia nodded and resumed to eat the sliced pears.

The elf's amazement and disappointment with himself grew as he approached the girl with an unbelievable stare.

"How could you know I was hiding there, lass?!"

"I sensed your presence, sir," she replied with her mouth full.

"Here behind the bushes?"

"No, I know you have followed me since Akiaba."

He shook his head in disbelief, showing astonishment.

Seated on the ground, he indulged in a few slices of pear. "Sorcerer Uskam has asked me to follow you until you reach your ultimate destination."

"I know," answered tranquil while grabbing another fruit to slice.

While Peken bit the last piece between the teeth, looked at her to make sure that her clothes disguised her as a boy, but his yellowish eyes noticed Lakia was barefoot and her feet had cuts and scratches as consequences of her journey in days. "I recall giving you nice moccasins back at my hut," pointed at her feet.

"They were not my liking. My feet were hurting, and I could not walk well," she said, making a disgusted gesture. "I will be all right. I never used shoes."

"Molke is of grasses and soft grounds, but in this realm and the others, they are different, and going barefoot will harm you more."

Standing up, the elf surveyed the valley, taking a moment to look around, spotting the east, towards the Karekall, while agreeing himself.

"What are you doing?"

"If my memory does not fail me, Carret Post is there. A craftsman should sell comfortable sandals you can use."

They left behind the valley of the pear-trees, Lakia and Peken arrived at a broken, ancient stone road that was positioned amidst small hills adorned with dense, resilient oak trees. The sight of the abandoned carts caught the elf's attention. Peken became suspicious as he walked along the empty road, which is crowded with farmers and their families during the day. He placed his hand on the hilt of his blade and the other one on his chest, dropping his bag, fearing that the place might hide creatures lurking in the bushes.

Lakia experienced intense pain as she traversed the road's rough and unforgiving surface and recalled the elf's comments regarding her feet. Even though Peken offered to carry her on his back, she turned down his help.

By coincidence, just ahead of them, they discovered an abandoned wagon filled with various wares and goods. Leaving his bag, Peken hastened towards it, generating a rapid and resonating rhythm with his rugged boots, as he eagerly searched into its contents. Lakia stopped and sat on the ground to rub her aching feet.

He inspected and came across a pair of leather sandals he gave to Lakia. With his help, she put them on and stood up, had a sense of relief as she walked. Although the sandals were bigger than her feet, they still were useful.

"I feel better. I prefer them to the moccasins," she said with gratitude.

"Let's keep going, lass," he suggested. "I do not think we should be outside in the dark."

Peken took his bag back and walked but stopped when he discovered Lakia standing, staring towards somewhere in the southeast.

"Is something wrong?" Peken asked, dazed.

"I feel darkness there. . . his soul is claiming for help. . ." she replied with a grave gesture.

The elf was in total silence, stunned. He again touched the chest. "What are you? A sorceress?"

"We must hurry!" Lakia walked and then hasted her steps, grabbing Peken's hand to go faster. He could not understand the reason for her urgency.

It did not take them long at all to arrive at their destination—the entrance to the garrison, Carret Post—. The gate was strangely open, and the watchtowers were empty. With caution in his every step, Peken released Lakia and unsheathed his blade. He motioned the girl to wait as he made his way to the location.

He found every building abandoned and neglected. The barracks with the fallen bunks beds, the archery with the destroyed targets by crows, the stables with floors covered in dry hay, the open command center with desks covered in papyrus, the blacksmith shops with cold furnaces, and others in a similar situation. Everything, along with tools, weapons, and unique items in their places or thrown on the ground, deserted, but no signs of any attack or conflict.

Peken kept touching his chest. He knew a wicked event forced everyone to leave the garrison and its surroundings.

With more questions than answers, Peken returned the blade to his sheath. When he went back outside, he discovered Lakia was staring at a wooden double-arrow sign placed in a road breakup. "We shall continue to The Midlands, lass," pointed to the south.

"No, the other way!" she demanded, gesturing with hazel eyes.

Peken noticed the arrow towards the southeast. "Laimet?"

"Aye, he is there asking for help!"

He grabbed his chest with a firm grip.

They glanced at themselves.

Peken, with a skeptical expression, placed his hands on his waist and shook his head in denial.

Just a few steps away from the walled town of Laimet, stood a burgh that was fortified and encompassed by a robust and towering wall. Atop the wall, the guards maintained a vigilant watch, their eyes fixed on the two visitors with caution, while determined they ensured that the wide gate remained securely closed. Even though they were only two visitors—Lakia and Peken—both found themselves harassed by dozens of sentinels who had their crossbows aimed at them.

The elf had noticed the inflated mistrust from the soldiers, dropped his bag, and lifted his arms as a sign of peace. "Hear me! We are only two travelers passing by!" yelled with hopes. "We must spend the night at an inn to continue our journey the next morning!"

For a while, he got no answer.

"That is not our business, and go away, you stinky pointy ears!" A soldier replied with disdain at the same time that some mocked amidst cackles.

Peken, feeling diminished and ashamed, did not know how to respond, shrugging his shoulders.

A bit offended, Lakia gave steps ahead and spoke with determination to the guards, lifting her head. "Let us enter because your lord is in grave danger and needs help!"

"Take your pet and go away, Casarak boy!" another sentinel answered, followed by a bothersome laugh. "No one enters, and no one leaves!"

Angered, Lakia stared at the sentries, feeling insulted by their behavior. Her emotions were boiling within her. Without warning, a sudden burst of wind emerged at this precise moment, causing the branches of the sturdy oak trees to sway forcefully and creating a constant rustling noise from the movement of their leaves. The sudden dust that emerged created a misty appearance that stretched across long distances.

The sudden rush of air that collided against their faces surprised the sentinels, leaving them perplexed and questioning the unexpected occurrence materialized out of nowhere.

Though amazed, Peken, with a steady gaze upon Lakia, had a clear understanding that the wind was coming from her.

She deliberately shifted her gaze towards the imposing gate, her hazel eyes fixed upon it, noting that a sturdy wooden beam securely locked it positioned behind it. At first, the doors emitted loud banging sounds, which caused fear among the guards. In a gradual manner, the gate started vibrating, initially at a slow pace but then rapidly, as if an invisible force were determined to open it. Eventually, this force proved to so strong that it broke the solid beam, causing the entrance to open halfway and exposing the petrified faces of the locals passing by the main street. In a display of cowardice, the sentries hastily ran away, leaving their posts unattended.

"A Korbeen!" a soldier in fear wailed while running.

Lakia had unleashed her hidden mystical strength for the first time, accompanied by the ongoing, robust wind.

"The goddesses have mercy!" Peken exclaimed, stunned, paralyzed, strangely unable to react.

With a solemn gesture and a determined gaze, Lakia walked and entered the burgh.

As the wind blew, all the residents could feel its effects while they watched the passing of a small but powerful figure, and the crowd, completely mesmerized, followed her.

A young captain riding a solid chestnut horse interrupted Lakia on her path. He had light olive skin and small eyes, but muscular. The official wore a clean green uniform that suited him well. His grip remained on the hilt of the sword. "Halt! State your purpose, boy!"

"Take me to your lord now!" she replied with absolute authority. "He needs my help!"

Usually, the officer would not have believed her, however, he had witnessed her using her mystical force to open the sturdy gate, and he also took the time to listen to her explanation.

The captain realized she was genuine.

He approached her with the horse and offered his hand. "I will take you with him now."

The captain, with a firm grip, pulled Lakia and positioned her on the saddle in front of him, then commanded the horse to gallop down a side street while the mesmerized crowd frantically ran to follow them.

And the wind calmed down.

In the cave's mouth, outside, Lakia stood there, determined, relentless in her resolve. Behind, the captain escorted her.

In the midst of the oak trees, a vast number of intrigued individuals, including children scattered among the branches, silently watched as the girl disguised as a boy awaited her moment, experiencing a mix of emotions and fears.

"How long has he been like that?" she asked, staring into the cave's darkness.

"Six months. The lord had hiked the Karekall, but we found him ill," the captain responded.

She nodded. "Let us enter."

"I have your back." The captain drew his sword.

As Lakia advanced further into the cave, she noticed how the daylight was disappearing around her. She did not need any light or torch since her senses guided her even in total darkness, feeling the tiny rocks under her feet as she took the first steps. Serene though cautious.

In contrast, she heard the captain's rapid breathing of fear yet accompanying her.

As they were in the complete absence of light, in pure blackness, the warmth of the environment turned creepily cold.

In a sudden halt, she pleaded to the captain to remain still.

Evilness in the air.

Horror was also present.

The sound of dragging chains.

A dreadful red light illuminated the cave.

Lakia experienced many startles as a shrieking and speedy grayish-horned demon, with its claws outstretched, tried to attack her. It was advantageous that the unmovable, large rocks restrained the demon by chains. Constantly moving his mouth of long, disarranged, sharp teeth, he stared at her in frustration with his blazing eyes.

The demon, even with his continuous screams and roars, remained unable to lay a hand on her. With his drawn sword, the captain behind observed the creature shivering in terror.

But Lakia, in total peace, only gazed at it.

Then she pointed her finger at the demon's head with a determined look.

"I order you to leave this body!" she yelled at him with commanding authority.

A burning Akareen star drew on the entity's forehead.

The creature fell, shrieked in pain, and his body changed. The cave returned to darkness as the red light disappeared.

The captain left the cave and rushed to his horse before the curious crowd. From the saddle's bag, he got a sizeable green banner with a golden castle representing the Lord-

ship of The Lowlands and hurried to cover the naked-
ness of a man he had just outed.

As he approached him, the multitude murmured in
astonishment.

A woman with long dark hair and elegant clothes
made her way among the people and ran to hug the man
covered with the banner, tearful with joy, kissing him
all over his face.

The crowd fell into silence as Lakia, clearly exhausted, emerged.

Then, the male looked at the girl with a light smile.
"I was condemned as this Lordship was! And she came
to liberate us!" The Lord of the House of Lai pro-
claimed. "I am forever in debt with the Promise of the
Jyistereerk!"

The lord kneeled to bow before her, followed by his
spouse and the captain. In the end, the people of Laimet
showed their reverence for the Promise.

Lakia, though calm, felt overwhelmed by their worship and surprised. She did not expect that her mystical
actions revealed her true identity as a Promise and as a
girl, even disguised. Her intentions were obvious—she
did not seek reverence or gratitude from others.

Because the lord, while as a demon, a Korbeen, could
see her soul.

And it revealed the purpose of the journey to Lakia.

The small red No Ta and the large blue-green No Nunn appeared with brief delay on the chilly night. Under them, Peken found himself seated in the same place next to his bag of belongings, just steps away from the gate where he endured the constant mocking of the sentinels during the day. His face appeared to be filled with discouragement, disappointment, and a perpetual tendency to gaze downwards.

Adopting a resigned posture, he placed his arms on the knees of his long, bent legs.

When he noticed the light brown scratched feet, with dirt under the nails, wearing the same sandals he had found in the wagon, his yellowish eyes moved and discovered Lakia standing and staring at him with her hands on the waist. From a considerable distance, he noticed that the captain, mounted on his horse, stationed near the gate, within the confines of the burgh, kept a visual watch over the young girl. "I heard the people, lass," said with dismay. "Everyone knows you are not a boy. . . and you are an empress. I now understand why Sorcerer Uskam demanded respect worthy of a royal to you."

"Is that why you are sad and deceived, sir?" she asked, denying with her head.

"From now, we part ways. You got yourself that good-looking captain to escort you on your journey towards Salter," said with a bit of jealousy. "I am just a coward like those sentinels!"

"No, sir. You may lie about everything you wish, but I know the truth. I can sense and feel your past."

Peken stared, stunned. She noticed in her a gesture of disapproval. "What truth?"

"A long time ago, you loved a gentle young lady of a pure heart. She was your childhood friend."

As tears streamed across his amber cheeks, the elf once again lowered his face. "She is gone! Venka. . .," he spoke as a knot almost choked his throat. "She was the reason for my living until. . . She fell for that hunter!"

"Aye, sir. But it was not the fault of hers or yours. Thus, you abandoned Molke and your future, heartbroken, and traveled half the world trying to look for yourself. Because you felt lost!"

Lakia kneeled and took Peken by his wet face with compassion and understanding, glancing at his eyes.

"You do still feel lost and diminished!" she said sweetly. "But I assure you are not lost if you stay with me!"

"What do you wish from me, this unworthy elf, lass? Why?"

"Come with me!" she stood up and pulled his hands, making him be on his feet. "Continue with me on my journey and help me build the Jyistereerk!"

Peken was stunned by her words and nodded as he cleaned his tears.

"You look small, lass! But you spoke the wiser words!"

"Let's go! The captain awaits us!"

"For what reason?"

"The lord has invited us to stay in his home! He offered chambers with beds to sleep in. And hot baths to get us cleansed!"

6

MANTID

Her face shined and sweated even though she tied her curly dark hair to give herself freshness as the scorching sun was on its zenith. Marissa kept polishing her long iron sword on the railing with an old piece of linen moistened with fish oil.

The remoteness of the blue Beyond Sea annoyed her. In her heart, she longed to return to the city of Estolk, to the gardens of the Vykar Palace, where she envisioned herself riding alongside her beloved horse, Ghost, while donning comfortable silk dresses adorned in vibrant and eye-catching tones.

Still in discomfort, she was inside a heavy and impenetrable armor instead.

On an official Casakan frigate called *The Seneschal*, Marissa Taskar embarked on a quest at her uncle Orssandro Vykar's request. This magnificent vessel boasted three majestic masts and an abundance of sails.

Marissa endured the inconveniences of the voyage.

Once she accepted the task from the Head, had to abandon the indulgent customs and learn the involved hardships. She ate dry meat, drank water, and avoided wine. She struggled to find privacy, could not clean herself for days, and slept next to her horse, Ghost.

And slept with the sword on her chest to defend herself from thieves among the crew.

However, the deprivations she faced did not hold as much significance to her as they should have, given that she carried a weightier burden than her circumstances—her guilt. She desired she had not separated from Alessandro the way they did, with no farewell and a quarrel, at the time that concern fell over Marissa.

It was a week ago when she stayed at the inn in Sostolk, awaiting the for *The Seneschal*. It was during that time she heard, from the mouths of the residents, the distressing news of the sanctuary library fire in Sarak and the tragic murder of Archmage Yasstro, who was Alessandro's former tutor. Once she had learned the events, she had a strong desire to give up on her mission to reunite with her fiancé at Katalk.

But she recalled the severe warning from Orssandro, and he did not care about the common blood uncle and niece had. Should Marissa, at any point, decide to abandon or fail the quest that was entrusted to her, it would be an act of high treason and the punishment for such action would be beheading.

As she polished her shining sword, her concerns persisted, yet they held no importance at this moment.

The weapon she held in her hands served as a memento, representing the reward she received for being recognized as the Academy's top student in Armory last year. She specialized in using mail-chain and plate armors, as well as swords and shields. It was uncommon for a girl to excel in these disciplines, which were chosen by lads.

In contrast, Alessandro specialized in fencing and sword techniques.

Even if it was unnecessary, she kept passing the linen piece along her sword, causing total resplendence on its surface.

Through the intense heat, she paused for a moment. Marissa reached down to her waist, where her canteen was hanging, and took a refreshing drink of water. She drank with a sense of relief as the water flowed from her mouth, down her throat.

Out of nowhere, a mature captain appeared, as he wore a distinctive black and green uniform adorned with various insignias.

At first, Marissa choked with the liquid, startled by his sudden presence, but recovered and gave an embarrassing smile.

"After tomorrow morning, we anchor in the Isle of Garterrem," he notified. "I believe you will get cleansed and rest."

"I appreciate the information, Captain Irsso," replied with a light bow. "Hopefully, the time will pass with haste for the Port of Sarrem afterward."

"If the weather allows us," the captain grinned, showing his yellow and unarranged teeth.

She nodded in agreement, rubbed her mouth to dry herself, and then fastened her canteen to her waist, clamping it onto the metallic belt.

Marissa noted that the sailors in uniform appeared to be young. The bigger kids handled heavy barrels, while the smaller ones did lighter chores. Their large numbers intrigued her. "Tell me, captain. How old are those kids?" pointed at them.

"The young rascals are of twelve years, the older sixteen," acknowledged.

"Did they come by their own will?"

"Only a few, milady," nodded. "Most of them had to choose from either the prison or to serve in our Navy."

"What crime did they commit?"

"They come from lower suburbs, and as you can see, they have no education and disregard for work," responded with arrogance. "They go to houses and markets to steal whatever they find, even a piece of bread."

An official called the captain. He had to excuse her and left with haste.

She was alone again, but dazzled. Marissa, who was used to a life of comfort as Lady Tasarissa's daughter, found it surprising to discover that *The Seneschal* crew resorted to forced labor because of their poverty and desperate need to survive, even if it was against the law.

The frigate experienced a sudden and brief shake, instilling fear in everyone, even though there were significant soft movements.

The vessel returned to its usual course. The sailors, including both inactive crew members and armed personnel, as well as the officials, gathered near the railing and searched the waters, but they could find nothing.

Marissa reacted by grabbing her devoted sword. She put her weapon in her sheath once the peace returned.

Despite the lack of any nearby land, she noticed a peculiar flock of black crows gliding across the sky over the middle of the sea.

"What do you think it was?" a boy asked a girl beside him.

"Perhaps a blind whale hit the ship!"

"I heard no sound!"

"Be quiet and focus in your labor!" she scolded and returned to scrub her floor section.

Once again, Marissa lay on the soft hay beside her beloved stallion Ghost, admiring his sturdy legs and observing the other horses that remained in the lower level of *The Seneschal*, where the stable was situated.

As she awaited her sleep that night, her thoughts flowed while seeing at the hanging oil lantern swung from the ceiling as its movement resulted from the waves rocking the ship.

With her hands resting on her chest, she could not help to fall asleep because of the discomfort from the plate armor she had been wearing for a week, though she had grown accustomed to it.

Since she learned about the crew's condition, opted to keep her sword in its sheath, expressing her willingness to not oppose anyone who might try to steal from her because of her compassion for the children.

Marissa discovered she was in the forest, surrounded by the majestic trees of the purple orchids, located right next to the serene lake of Estolk. At the moment of sunset, worn in her beloved red silk dress, turned to discover Alessandro.

He was smiling with these charming dark eyes, just standing.

"Please forgive me!" she pleaded, with a knot in her throat. "I will not quarrel with you again!"

He did not talk, only nodded.

He approached her and hugged, making her smile, and she cried with joy.

A violent convulsion interrupted Marissa's dream, discovering that tears ran on her face. To her surprise, she realized that Ghost, along with the other horses, let out terrified neighs and jumped, unable to escape. She tried to stand and met with an unexpected punch that propelled her into the sturdy wooden wall.

Marissa fought against relentless and brutal shakes as she found challenging to continue running. To keep herself, she grasped onto columns, walls, and various other fixed objects she encountered along the way.

A cacophony of terrified screams reverberated everywhere, and what followed were forceful shouting mandates, accompanied by the thunderous roar of a hundred cannons being discharged.

Despite the powerful spasms experienced by the vessel, Marissa attempted to ascend the two sub-levels using the stairs with bravery, even though she had to dodge falling objects from the outside, which she avoided using her armored arm.

Outside, she witnessed a giant reddish squid, much larger than the frigate, wrapping its tentacles around *The Seneschal*. The creature threw the three main masts earlier. Because of the monster's inclined elongated head to the left side, the ship tilted, yet it persisted in shaking as if it were being played by a child.

Marissa knew that the hostile behavior exhibited by the mollusk was unusual. A giant squid lived in the lower depths of the sea, known for its tranquility, and never ascended to the exterior.

The Seneschal cannons fired again but did not harm the monster.

The frigid glow of the moon No Sak let Marissa witness the growing chaos on the vessel. Stunned and with horror observed the members of the crew lying on the ripped floor. Most were injured or unconscious, causing panic among the young as others tried to hide on the boat.

Despite this, there were a few braves who attempted to use their swords to sever the invincible tentacles.

The tentacles tightened, making *The Seneschal* creak even louder, breaking and tilting the ship. This sudden movement made Marissa lose her balance and slide across the inclined deck until she grabbed onto a nearby railing, thus preventing herself from plunging into the sea.

Many youngsters fell into the water and drowned.

On the third occasion, they fired the cannons.

The squid experienced the pain, which triggered an immediate and furious reaction. Using its might, the creature broke the frigate into many fragments with agility, causing a massive explosion.

That night *The Seneschal* perished.

When Marissa's brown eyes opened, she realized that the sun had already risen, causing her annoyance as it bothered her. She took a moment to smell the fresh breeze and listened to the soothing sound of the waves crashing nearby.

As soon as she regained full consciousness, she recalled the previous night and took a seat on the sand to observe her surroundings.

Marissa looked around. The first observation that caught her attention was the fact that she had reached this unfamiliar beach using a piece of wood that once belonged to the broken ship. It kept her afloat, otherwise, the weight of her heavy armor would have dragged her into the depths of the sea, leading to her inevitable drowning.

Against all odds, she kept every single part of her armor, including the sword, which was surprising. But had lost her belongings and the pouch of coins.

As she sat there, realized that something else was missing, causing her to stand up with her heart beating faster than usual. "Ghost!" She screamed, searching everywhere with despair.

Marissa searched the beach for her beloved stallion, a gift from her uncle on her sixteenth birthday, but all she found was wreckage from *The Seneschal*, and the bodies of the crew washed ashore that devastated her. "So young and already killed!" exclaimed to herself.

At her feet came across the lifeless corpse of Captain Irsso. Even dead, his face revealed a terrified reaction, with his unsettling eyes wide open.

She did not believe there was anyone that remained alive from *The Seneschal*, but for a strange reason, either divine intervention or mysterious destiny, Marissa was the sole survivor.

The sadness invaded her when she realized she would not find Ghost because her stallion had drowned in the sea. She could feel it.

Marissa cried as she remembered her cherished times with her beloved horse, her unwavering companion, now gone forever. She moved back from the captain's body, attempting to wipe her face with her armored lower arm, but ended up getting dirtier with sand and creating cutting scratches on her skin.

She continued to retreat and discovered had reached the greenish bushes, concealed beneath the shade of different semitropical trees.

Marissa advanced into the forest with her hand on the sword hilt with restraint, watching, alert, constantly moving her brown eyes, and noticed that the forest was too quiet. No sound was present, not even the flap of a bird, and that was enough to make her suspicious.

Facing an unexplored dense forest. Marissa, calm, remembered the studies at the Academy. She needed to be relaxed and focused. Now she would take these lessons into practice. Made mental assumptions regarding her location while interning into the densest part.

Marissa believed she was near the Isle of Garterrem, but not this. Or else it would not be inhospitable. She believed she had arrived somewhere on the southern coasts of the Ryza Continent. Perhaps the place was Fenn itself, but the forest did not look like it. She did not discard the possibility of being further north from the isle and was already in Berrem.

If Alessandro was with her, she could know her exact location. He was excellent at interpreting cartographies, compasses, and sky orientations.

Startled by a hissing sound, Marissa drew her sword, looking around in fear but remaining alert. For the first time, she had to confront actual situations instead of mock simulations from her Academy.

She glanced between the trees and bushes with her eyes, heard no steps or other sounds, only the constant hissing.

Amidst the green foliage, blended, Marissa spotted an uncommon pointed head with two round black eyes that never looked away from her and came to a halt as the rhythm of the hisses increased with speed.

It was the sound of fear.

She moved her sword from one side to the other, observing how the creature's gaze followed the weapon and its front legs remained motionless. It hissed, paralyzed before her presence.

Marissa nodded, feeling relief, and returned her sword to its sheath, noticed the creature was a peaceful mantis of the same size as hers. Its pale green color was all over the body and the two front legs and four more in the rear revealed it was from a kind and docile species.

She had learned on different mantises through texts and she felt fortunate to have not come across the vicious red ones. She acknowledged many poachers smuggled nymphs from the docile species to be sold in Berrem for agricultural tasks and transportation.

In that instant, she understood that the location was the rarely visited Territory of Trunke, a realm of Mantids with aggressive and gentle mantises, and an old treaty forbade men and felines from settling there. It was the land between Berrem in the north and Fenn in the south.

"I do not intend to harm you," she said, showing both hands as a gesture of peace. "I only wish to go to Berrem. Perhaps you could tell me the way there."

The mantis maintained a stare at Marissa with no reaction. The hissing ceased, then it traversed through the woods, creating a narrow trail by clearing the bushes with its front legs' spines, enabling her to walk with ease.

But it was fast.

Weak and tired, she interrupted her way inside, requesting the disappeared mantis to stop as she had to run. Marissa wanted to quit, and sat on a fallen tree, panting and thirsty.

At the end the mantis came back and found her exhausted, amusingly turning its head to look at her with its big, round black eyes, wondering why she had stopped.

"I need water and food," said with a weak smile. "I require recovering myself first."

The mantis moved its long antennas, comprehending her, and she contemplated them with delight.

"By your charming antennas, you are a male!" she assured, remembering her biology lessons. "I will call you Brisel."

He hissed content.

7

SIEGE

E ight days had passed, eight days of mourning, eight days of no magic, and a week of funeral rites for the deceased Archmage Yasstro. No one could enter or exit the blemished sanctuary for seven days. Then, on the eighth day, the gate was open to everyone who wished to give their last respects to the departed.

In the presence of the burnt library, the mages placed the archmage's corpse on a pile of wood. They had cleaned the body, placed his hands on his chest, covered his eyes with flawless golden coins engraved with Akareen symbols, and dressed him in a new, brown gritty robe. The mages encircled the body of Yasstro in murmurs, mentioning some spell lifting their hands. The wood with the remains caught fire, producing a white smoke column.

Farther, a silent Alessandro observed the burning of his former tutor. As he recalled the spent moments together, he placed his hand on his chin, and then the memoirs disappeared to give place to many questions and confusions about the archmage's last words and assassination.

He turned and looked among the crowd of hundreds covering most of the cloisters and gardens. He had hoped that Orssandro, his foster father, and Yasstro's childhood friend, would attend the funerals. Still, to his disappointment, he was absent, and neither was Marissa, even though she was also his pupil.

It was not only strange, but also suspicious.

Among the silent multitude, Trasso was also present but disarmed by a mandate from the mages that no one shall not carry weapons during the rites. The Guardian of Sarak had a hard and cold appearance.

Brekens from their quarter had also come to present their respects. They knew Yasstro for being charitable to everyone, in particular the immigrants who arrived in Sarak.

Alessandro sensed a frightening presence that chilled his blood, making him turn left and discover a strange man amid the crowd. It was an elder. His appearance revealed he was Arankan in aspect, with white hair, blue eyes, and no beard, immaculate, and wore some strange black clothes.

Bothered, he glanced to his right and found, besides, immobile, the feline Corr witnessing the funeral clothed in some used gray jackets, pants, and worn-out black boots. The mages had gotten his garments from a charity.

He turned left again, and the elder of white hair had disappeared. The fear was also gone.

Wondering about his sanity returned to observe the burning pile. Recognized in the other extreme, far but near the circle of silent mages, Lady Fabehel also present to give the last farewell, along with the man with the swollen face of the name Tin behind her to help with the wheelchair.

Fabehel noticed Alessandro was staring at her, and he moved his eyes to the funeral pyre to avoid any visual contact.

The hours were long. The crowd of hundreds became tens to only a few as the fire consummated the pile.

Two of the mages approached the burnt remnants, with the help of their magic, separated the archmage's ashes from the charcoal, lifting them in the air, then deposited them into a small gold metallic box carved with the symbol of the Akareen. Later, in a special small ceremony, they would place the ashes of Yasstro in the crypts beneath the cathedral.

It was sunset, but the day was still up. The warm breeze was becoming a gelid gust.

After that, the mages left in a special procession to their quarters, taking the gold box religiously with them. Only

Alessandro and Corr stayed. Fabehel and Tin were also the last. All stared at themselves.

She made a manual request to her helper, and he brought Fabehel closer to Alessandro and Corr and smiled with kindness at the feline with a light head bow. "I am Fabehel of the Red Tides, mister."

"Corr of Finnerr, milady," replied with his deep voice, reacting with a complete bow to greet.

"I look ahead to meeting you. But for now, I require a private word with Master Alessandro."

The feline assented and excused himself to leave.

Alessandro witnessed her in distrust, Tin left at her request.

"What business do you have with me?" asked, resentful. "I thought you believed I represent the government's twisted ways."

"And I still believe so," replied with benevolence. "But I have known Archmage Yasstro for so long to tell me enough about his favorite tutor."

"Have you come to tell me that?" he inquired with bitterness, in disbelief.

"Actually. . . In goodwill, I am extending my help to ensure your safe escape from Sarak to the Isle of Garterrem."

Alessandro was in mistrust at what Fabehel had just said and reacted by taking his hand to his chin as a thinking posture to digest her words. It was hard to trust in someone who had been unfriendly to him eight days ago, just moments before Archmage Yasstro's assassination by an unclear stray arrow. And also suspicious. "Why do you wish to help?"

"Do you see that beacon?" she pointed to the tallest of two mountains at her right to show a wooden tower on top. "It will burn a red fire in less than five days. When that occurs, Trasso will order a siege in Sarak to his sentinels and persecute every non-Casakan to incarceration."

"I am a Casakan and son of the Head Orssandro. Do you know it?"

"Do not be naïve, master. I did not see the Head around here," she responded, denying with her head. "You can know very well that Archmage Yasstro was powerful, and Trasso dreaded him. The armies could not even blink at him, or he easily defeated them. The Head feared him too."

"I do not think that father was afraid of him," replied still roughly. "They were best friends once!"

"Aye! Best friends when Yasstro was not even a novice!" she exclaimed sharply.

Alessandro struggled to understand the surrounding circumstances. He recognized that Fabehel's words held a harsh truth, even if it was hard to acknowledge.

More than a former tutor, Yasstro was to Alessandro, the absent father he had never had and the close friend after Marissa. Despite his advanced age, the archmage enjoyed the youngster's company, and he helped him with the grief at his mother's loss.

He recalled the smile accompanying his long beard, giving a sense of safety and warmth.

Orssandro thought at first that having his childhood friend as Alessandro's tutor would help to mold his adoptive son in his ways for his future purposes. But soon disapproved of the archmage and the youngster's bonding and, using his political influences, sent Yasstro far to Katalk.

Despite the heartbreak, Alessandro resigned and had confidence in Orssandro's decision.

Alessandro, still with bitter feelings, nodded because Fabehel was right. With a sad gesture, he stared at her with a curiosity that awoke in him. "Tell me what else you know," requested with suspicions after reading her face. "I notice you have more to say."

Despite her fear, Fabehel nodded in agreement, acknowledging the importance of speaking the truth.

"Your faultless mistake was to send the Head a pigeon with the news of the princess' child. I can assure you it sped up things for worst."

Alessandro's heart sank, and his fists tightened with resentment and deceit. His teeth gnashed, and tears rolled down his cheeks as his blame fell on him because he thought that sending the pigeon killed Yasstro. His trust in Orssandro ended in deterioration.

"Do not let the damn guilt take over you!" Fabehel was sharp in her tongue. "As you know now, you can be in grave danger too, and you shall escape with Corr and me to Garterrem."

"Why?!" he yelled in cries.

Corr and Tin, who had become conversational friends, heard startled Alessandro's screams even though they were at far distances near the gardens but did not move from their places.

Fabehel, with humid hazel eyes, from her wheelchair she tried to reach his right hand in his emotional moment. She was trying to console him. He stopped his distress, staring at Fabehel.

His mouth trembled as he wanted to keep asking. "Tell me! Why?!"

"I apologize. I had to tell you . . ."

"No! Why?!" interrupted with insistence.

He knew the actual answer was in her insides, but wanted to hear it.

Fabehel left his hand with a scared look.

The clever Tin was about to draw his hidden dagger from his back, covered by his cloak, because he believed in his duty to defend Fabehel from Alessandro's supposed aggressiveness.

Corr stopped him, moving his head negatively, and, with a defiant stare from his feline green eyes, warned him not to go.

"The Head rejects the child," she murmured with hesitance. "The child is the Promise of the Jyistereerk and to him is a hindrance to his unrevealed plans."

He remembered a prediction Yasstro had mentioned before, involving Orssandro, and nodded in agreement. Alessandro became less agitated, pacing around Fabehel, breathing out, and sensing the chilly night as the large blue-green moon No Nunn emerged.

A novice used fire magic to light the lanterns around the sanctuary's exteriors.

Alessandro stopped his round stroll and crossed his arms before Fabehel with surprising confidence. "Let's find the child and to hell with that scoundrel!"

A lone, slender middle-aged woman in light sepia color attire showing the bareness of most of her pure black skin from her arms, the long earrings and the white pearl necklace gave her an attractive presence. Her vestment and jewels were part of her people's customs that she had to follow as Captain Governor of the Southern Isles by order of the previous Head.

She wandered around the main hall of the Casakan Castle in Estolk, enjoying ornaments and pieces hanging in the room as her hand passed from one chair to the other that were part of the Assembly's eleven seats of the long dark wooden table. Just behind the lofty Head's chair, at the beginning of the table, more than a hundred paintings were hanging on the white wall. All were former Heads' portraits.

Her eyes stopped in that specific canvas, the portrait of Lady Larissa Eskar, known by the byname of *The Doomed*. She remembered how she ascended from being an unknown waitress at a tavern to becoming an influential Head that elevated Casak to challenge a mighty realm, even stricken by the plague, as the Kingdom of Aranka. Still, she had a tragic end that no one dared to discuss.

Her attention to the portraits focused on the newly installed triangle banners hanging from the top of each of the six large windows that let the morning light enter, with the Casakan national emblem—an orchid of twelve petals representing the different Casakan regions.

Orssandro entered, disrupting her loneliness, visibly happy as he touched the woman's bare shoulders and kissed her cheeks. "Welcome, Lady Alyssa Taskar!" exclaimed with excitement. "How was the journey?"

"I am not that pleased, sir," she replied with a light smile and a head bow, but feeling uncomfortable. "As you can know, I dislike traveling long distances."

He made an understanding posture and took her hand. "I apologize for the urgency to convene the Assembly," nodded. "I considered it necessary to discuss a crisis happening these days."

"Katalk?"

Orssandro did not reply because of a sudden entrance of the remaining assemblers who made their presence by greeting the Head and themselves, besides some casual talk unrelated to government matters.

Last, Dessidere, in his assignment as the Monitor, in a gray suit and cloak, climbed the only step to reach the tribune by a corner near to the large table, then banged three times on the surface with a gavel.

Soon, all the members took their seats.

"In the Twenty-Second Day of the Second Month in the First Year of the *Tikl the Third of the Gesha!*" the Monitor clamored. "By the urgent summon of the Head Sir Orssandro Vykar from Southern Isles, I officially convene this Assembly!"

Later, the Monitor unrolled a blank papyrus, placing rocks in the corners that served as paperweights, wetted the tip of a long feather pen within an inkwell, and started writing the first lines of the affidavit.

Orssandro, at the beginning of the table, nodded to Dessidere to give thanks in silence, put both hands together on the surface before the expectant looks of the assemblers.

Every member had come to the gathering from every Casakan region and the Great Sanctuary of Casak and wore their distinctive outfits.

"Colleagues, I have summoned all of you because, as you can know, our dear Archmage Yasstro was assassinated, and the Arankans broke laws of the agreement that my antecessor, Lady Larissa Eskar, made," he paused as he cleared his throat. "Guardian Trasso of Sarak has advised me to start a siege to imprison every non-Casakan, and I have approved it."

All the assemblers glanced at themselves, staggered, then glared at Orssandro with disbelief, unable to answer.

"What is the basis for the siege?" Possertro Benke, a representative from Bestolk, asked, concerned. "Rumors came that a stray arrow killed the archmage. No proof it was them!"

"I second Sir Benke!" Archmage Missar from the Great Sanctuary intervened, exasperated, speaking from the last seat to the right. "It is truly dubious that the most powerful archmage of all Casak, almost invincible, gets easily murdered with the shot of an arrow."

Orssandro made a quick smile while toying with his fingers. "I am afraid that it goes beyond that," nodded, making an uncertain pause. "The Promise of the Jyistereerk, a child, is already in Ryza."

The assemblers murmured in astonishment.

"What is the relation with Archmage Yasstro murdering?!" Missar claimed with disagreement. "I believe the Promise is unrelated with Katalk!"

"You should know better!" he screamed angrily, slamming the table and scaring everyone. Even the Monitor stopped writing. "Yasstro knew perfectly that letting himself die had some obscure purpose favoring the Promise!"

The Head exhaled deeply to be calmer, while they could still perceive some fear in him. "I apologize for my behavior, colleagues. We are facing a crisis as a realm," Orssandro continued, trying to adjust himself.

"What do you suggest?" Ralyssa Vir, from the West Coast, asked, concerned.

"Mobilization," Orssandro proposed. "Let us prepare all armies and navies. Let us gather mages from all sanctuaries and cadets from academies. And let us deploy them along the Equatorial Border, around our coasts, and expel non-Casakans from Katalk."

The assemblers were in total silence.

"Are you certain these are the steps?" Alyssa Taskar, concerned, asked. "How do you know that the Promise endangers our realm?"

"The Promise is as omnipotent as the Mudiuhfaser was," Orssandro replied, glancing disgruntled at the Archmage Missar. "Is not that true, archmage?"

"We are uncertain, Sir Head," he responded with discomfort. "Mudiuhfaser was a man that went from mage to demigod, achieving total control to manipulate the planes of time and space. I do not believe a child, even the Promise, could have such ultimate powers as him."

"What if the child has the powers from birth and aims at another Gesha in our realm?" Benke inquired.

"I suggest the Assembly vote on the Head's proposal," Lady Ralyssa advised, uneasy.

Orssandro nodded and signaled Dessidere to coordinate the voting.

The Monitor banged the tribune's surface and requested to show the hands of all the assemblers.

In the end, nine voted for the mobilization, and only Alyssa Taskar and Archmage Missar were against the proposal.

Missar knew the real reason behind the mobilization.

Alessandro and Corr sought refuge from the chilly night by hiding behind the mare Song in the stables of the sanctuary, both of them wearing hooded cloaks to shield themselves from the cold. After the funeral rites of Yasstro, they recounted the decision to follow Fabehel's escape.

The darkness shrouded the inside of the location, while the outside offered a mesmerizing sight of a delicate silvery glow, a result of the icy moon No Sak, seen through the entrance. With a watchful gaze, Alessandro's dark eyes searched for a vehicle that would be capable of carrying them both away from their current location.

Armies from Pastak and Sostolk had arrived in Sarak earlier, and most had encamped covering the totality of the Fishermen's Square. The Guardian Trasso had ordered his sentinels to surround the sanctuary to await the launch of the siege.

Alessandro knew Trasso's intentions. Fabehel had already informed him.

He heard some approaching steps. He cautiously put his hand on the sword's hilt, taking a defensive posture but still hiding behind Song and requesting absolute silence from Corr.

It was a lad, a novice, in brown robes and sandals. The youngster approached Song to pet her. He glanced and nodded at the fugitives, grabbed the reins, and took the mare outside.

Alessandro proceeded to the exterior, followed by Corr.

Both climbed a cart with a large haystack and hid inside while the novice tied Song in the rear. Afterward, the lad approached the sitting coachman, an Arankan stout older man, who nodded and pulled the reins of his two Percheron horses, ordering them to advance.

The novice opened the doors with his beginner magic, and the cart exited toward the crowded square. As it was advancing across the boundaries toward the cathedral, the crowded militia launched sly stares against the coachman, even some interrupting their small activities only to look at him.

The older man kept driving his horses with unusual serenity and indifference. Alessandro and Corr were aware of the danger while hiding in the hay. Once the cart passed the cathedral, it went straight to the canal bridge. The place was empty and dark. Probably only the horses' steps and the repetitive sound of the wheels against the cobbled ground had their presence.

The vehicle arrived at the open space where the market used to be nine days ago, now empty streets since Yasstro's assassination.

As the cart approached the Arankan Quarter, the sentinels with torches on the top of the wall made a silent signal and unlocked the gate.

The horns sounded, and the coachman stopped his horses.

Alessandro uncovered his head slightly from within the hay to better observe the reason for the sudden stop. Again, the horns resounded, not by the Arankans but from the Casakan Armies.

Concerned, he glanced at the mountain.

The beacon had a red fire.

A swift and deep rumble of many horses approaching trembled the ground from afar.

"Out and go!" the coachman yelled as he jumped from his seat.

Alessandro exited from the stack by the rear, untying the mare and mounting on her without a saddle. As he heard the soldiers getting closer, concerned by the fate of the quarter drew his iron sword intending to defend it at a significant distance from the cart.

Corr had gotten out by the side, worrisome, witnessing Alessandro's behavior. The coachman removed the wooden plank that served as the surface of his seat and, from a space inside, along with other items, he got a blade and offered it to the feline. "We Fennen need no weapon!" he said, rejecting the coachman's offer.

The first mounted soldiers had arrived. They were not over ten at first. Wisely, Alessandro fought them, moving Song too often to avoid their attacks, but his sword clashed against their blades. In an intelligent move, he passed the weapon across a soldier's chest, killing him.

His innocence gone.

With the first slaying against his people, he had no time to feel remorse, but to keep fighting.

Still, they outnumbered him, and more were about to arrive.

Corr removed his boots and ran mightily with feet and hands. When he reached the confrontation, he pounced and let out a roar, attacking a soldier on horseback and leaving deep scratches on his face with his sharp nails. Then the feline proceeded to the closest one.

The Arankans archers joined to the sentinels on top of the wall and discharged arrows against the Casakans, and a pair fell.

"Forget and get inside!" the coachman screamed in vain to both fighters, noticing the proximity of more mounted soldiers.

The older man set his Percheron horses free. Then he signaled, moving both hands to the sentinels on the wall. One of them threw a torch to the ground, which he grabbed. From the space under his seat, he took a heavy ball the size of his hand, a powder bomb, and ignited it. "Run!" the coachman yelled.

Alessandro turned to notice that the coachman threw the bomb to the cart, evading some other blades, deviated his eyes to discover that dozens of more soldiers had arrived in a swift reaction, galloped towards Corr, who was on a frightened soldier trying to control his horse. With surprise, Alessandro took Corr's arm, placed him at his back on Song, and retreated towards the gate as the multitude of soldiers persecuted them.

The bomb exploded, and not only the cart caught fire but also a large area before the wall, and with it, the coachman also flew apart.

Song jumped across the fire with the two riders while the armies held. The mare galloped into the Arankan Quarter as the heavy doors closed. The archers kept shooting.

Behind the gate, a contingent of about twenty Arankan sentinels awaited, with drawn swords.

While riding fast across the streets, relieved, Alessandro noticed that the quarter was dark and all the buildings were empty. He believed they had evacuated the population in advance.

The mare passed the small white wall and slowed her steps across the garden of roses. Alessandro and Corr noticed someone keeping a torch, and they got closer to him.

He was Tin, directing to his right.

Song walked to the noted way, and the riders dismounted when they met Fabehel in her wheelchair, covered in blankets on her legs and wearing a brown hooded cloak on her tan linen dress, in front of a cave and with a concerned gesture.

She requested Alessandro to get closer as Tin reunited them with the torch. "You look miserable!" exclaimed, judging by his condition after his exchange with the soldiers.

"Your concerns are not of importance. We must haste now!"

"But I have grave news to give," nodded. "The Assembly had voted to mobilize Casak against the Promise."

He gasped, putting his hands on his waist and facing the sky, staring at the cold white moon. Alessandro got himself in a whirlwind of indecisions, distressed by the wellness of the Casakan people, and thought about Marissa. "I . . . must go back to Estolk," exclaimed in confusion. "I have to stop them!"

"You will get killed if you go!"

"I have to . . ."

"I forbid you!" she strangely interrupted in despair.

Alessandro noticed something in her plea as her hazel eyes had some tears, trying to understand her desperation to keep him with her. "It can wait," he agreed to her, pointing to the cave. "Shall we go?"

She assented, then directed her look to Tin with great sadness, requested his hand, and he offered it with heartache.

"I am forever in debt to you, Tin," she said, trembling. "It shatters my heart that you must go."

Tin could not speak as tears ran across his swollen face.

Alessandro and Corr witnessed the emotional moment but did not understand. For an instant, there was silence and sorrow in the air.

"Corr, please take my wheelchair across the cave," Fabehel asked the feline, deviating her eyes and wiping off her tears, then spoke to the youngster. "Master. May I mount your mare?"

Both agreed to her requests.

Alessandro gently lifted Fabehel from the chair as she, without explanation and for a brief instant, found some comfort in him when she placed her head on his chest. With care, he placed her on Song, marveling at her ability to ride horses despite her lack of feet. Even he offered to take the reins, but she kindly refused.

Tin approached Alessandro and gave him the torch. "Follow the way. You will not get lost," Tin explained. "After a long descent, you will arrive at a vessel, and people on board await you. I hope before morning, you are sailing in the Beyond Sea."

"Are you not coming with us?"

"Someone has to close the cave," he said, touching Alessandro's right shoulder. "I could not live past the night once those scoundrels arrive."

Alessandro understood with heartache and thanked him.

As the troops neared, Corr hurried him to depart, shouldering the wheelchair before entering the cave. Fabehel followed him with Song.

Alessandro nodded as a farewell as the last to set foot inside.

With the help of a puller, Tin moved the rounded stone door that closed the entrance to the cave.

Next, Tin swallowed saliva as he drew his dagger.

The Casakan soldiers had arrived at the roses' garden.

8
VAGRANTS

Marissa awoke to the sounds of small birds, and her brown eyes found the early sunlight peeking through the branches of the dense trees. She perceived the forest's brisk and humid aroma and the freshness of the natural pool beside her.

Last night she had fallen asleep and noticed her sword on the chest with both hands as a clear innate behavior of awareness.

That was her training that made her so wary of her environment.

The Academy had taught her well.

As she sat down, she noticed many live caterpillars on large leaves on her left, moved her head with a big smile, delighted.

They were almost one week together, yet the green mantis Brisel could not understand that humans had other habits from the Mantid. Marissa repeatedly tried to explain the feeding differences to him, but it was still useless.

In the days she had been in the uncharted Territory of Trunke, the Mantid realm had to eat raw fish from the many pools to her disliking or grab wild fruits on her way. She did not wish to start a fire to cook, let alone warm herself. While the nights were cold, the days were hot but unbearable once the afternoon arrived.

It was not worth attracting the red mantises.

Marissa was unsure regarding the proximity to Berrem. Still, with an effort from the geography conversations she remembered from Alessandro years ago, had been following the sun's position in the sky. While the sun was at her right during the morning, meaning east, she knew her way was north.

Brisel appeared from anyplace in the forest, startling Marissa, then looked amusingly at her. He pushed the leaves with the spine of his front leg, insisting on eating the caterpillars.

She smiled again and stood up, placing her sword in the sheath, revised that her armor was complete and in good condition, though dirty.

"This is not my kind of breakfast, but I thank you," she said with tenderness. "Hopefully, I will find wild cherries on the way."

Marissa kneeled and bent to drink the fresh water from the pool. Brisel watched every movement with innocent curiosity moving his long antennas. She stood up once done, drying her wet face.

"Let's go. Guide me to Berrem."

Brisel went inside among the trees and cut the bushes to make her way. For an odd reason, he knew where to go as he was guiding her to the north. He was still fast, and Marissa had to catch him at his speed.

In the first days after she met him, she found it complicated to go after him, but she caught up with him.

Sometimes, Brisel left in his way pieces of plants or wood that prompted Marissa to clear them with the help of her sword.

It took a long while before she could find something to eat, but she stopped when she saw an exquisite fig tree, grabbed fruits, enjoyed eating them, alleviated her morning hunger, and regained the needed energy.

Marissa was still consuming the figs when she noticed the disappearance of Brisel. She did not find him, but she recognized his hisses when she heard them.

He was afraid and tried to understand the reason for his dread.

The hisses stopped as a defense mechanism because Brisel did not want to be found.

Startled, Marissa heard a loud buzz from somewhere in the forest.

She kept her sword firmly, intending to safeguard herself.

A red mantis was near.

Marissa had found an orifice in a large old tree where she hid with her sword between her legs, ready to use it if needed. In silence, she blamed Brisel for his sudden disappearance and abandonment. She was frightened. She felt like a neglected orphan, alone, cold even on a warm day.

She recognized that the red mantis was on the roam as the buzzing sound moved nearer and farther.

She had read many biology books and learned many things about the Mantid species, but besides Brisel, never encountered them in person and ignored facts. She had combat training and experienced uncountable bogus fights with her classmates, but never a real confrontation. The Academy taught her practical lessons from skilled teachers who took part in the battlefield in the flesh, but learning from them was not the same as experiencing combat.

Marissa always had her sword and polished it too often. But never indeed used it.

The Seneschal shipwreck was only a tiny drop of her life's experience. When Marissa saw the dead crew, she lost her innocence.

She had her armor, yet her fear was still present.

The buzz got louder as a sign that the mantis was near. Not only it, but her brown eyes also widened even more when Marissa heard the continuous flapping of its wings.

It was a flying mantis, which made the situation even more dangerous.

Her cold sweat drew across her round face.

She could not hide within the tree forever. In the end, had no choice but to escape and confront it.

She used mental calculations to find the sun's position and ran north. She put her sword back into the sheath.

The buzz decreased until quietness and the flapping disappeared.

Marissa directly outed from the tree and raced as fast as possible. During her quick continuous run across the forest, she heard with terror the rapid approach of the buzz trying to reach her, but never looked back.

At this moment, the flying mantis was on her. She grabbed her sword's hilt, ready to draw.

Marissa fell into an unseen hole, resulting in scratches on her face and blows to her body. Astonished, she discovered herself in a mysterious opening beneath the ground, with no explanation for its presence. She climbed back up to the surface by clutching onto the emerging roots of the trees close by.

The silence suggested a supposed disappearance of the red mantis.

Covered in mud, she stood up and drew her sword, ready to defend herself. She retreated north, observing for the obstacles on the ground, especially another cavity, if any.

She did not like the total quietness. It was very suspicious. No birds were present, as well as not any other animals.

Still no sign of Brisel.

Marissa was alone, depending solely on her sword.

She turned back.

Nothing.

She turned again.

Nothing either.

She took the choice to give the first steps to continue her way.

A sudden loud buzzing and a scarlet streak caused Marissa to be pushed to the ground as the red mantis swiftly flapped its wings and tried to bite her head with its long mandibles. Its spines kept her by the shoulders. Scared, she pushed the creature with her left hand despite the great strength, and with exceptional effort, she passed the sword across its body with her right. To her surprise, even with the weapon impaled inside, the mantis still fought viciously with no signs of giving up.

"Die, insect!" she screamed desperately, keeping the frantic creature with both hands.

Marissa had her arms exhausted. Slowly the mandibles neared, almost to touch her face while its saliva fell in drops. She was sure that her death had arrived.

She fought. The creature had her completely immobilized, and she was feeling fatigued.

She closed her eyes and waited for the worse.

A clean and swift cut decapitated the red mantis's head by the neck. Its dead body was on Marissa. Astounded, with a scant breath, she opened her eyes, pushed the head-less creature aside, and stood up, distressed, looking at the slain mantis.

Next, she found a strong woman with long black hair, olive skin, and small almond eyes. She had a sword, a shield in her other arm, plate armor, and wore a helmet that uncovered most of her face. "When killing a red mantis, cut it by the neck!" said with disapproval. "Piercing in its body with your sword will still kill you!"

Marissa did not believe that a human was in the forest. "Why are you in Trunke?" asked, dazed, trying to regain her breath.

The woman looked dumbfounded at Marissa, then put her sword into her sheath. "You are in Berrem. In the Lordship of The Wilds," the woman replied. "These Mantids are threatening to invade other realms."

Marissa nodded, understanding her position, a bit em-barrassed of herself. "I. . . am truly grateful to you," she said, pulling her sword from the mantis's body. "I am Marissa Taskar, from Casak."

"My pleasure. I am Keleana of Estherleon."

Keleana arrived at an open grassland between the semi-tropical forest in the south towards Trunke and another similar in the north approaching inner The Wilds mount-ed on her palomino horse. During the brief trip, she heard the accounts from Marissa, seated in the back, regarding her encounter with Brisel and the week-long travel across the forest together until his disappearance. "The green mantises are the most loyal and docile you have ever known," Keleana replied while guiding her horse with the reins. "He knows your scent. He will use the antennas to follow you in the latter."

"Why? I am not his owner!"

"I am sure Brisel is an orphan. Since the Gesha, the green mantises, and other species became almost extinct, somewhat the red mantises changed to be voracious and vicious, rapidly multiplying," sighed, then continued responding. "Some of my mercenary mates have explored that forest, and there is a vast swarm at the heart of Trunke."

Marissa was speechless realizing the proximity to the red mantises in the forest, especially if the one she encountered was terrifying. She did not want to imagine how it would be alone against many. "Are you a mercenary?"

"Hired by the Gathering, they acknowledged the dangers from Trunke into Berrem," Keleana nodded. "But the lords spent their money on mercenaries rather than invest in their outdated armies."

"I noticed disagreement in your words."

"Aye, they decided it was best to shed the blood of vagrants than ship their countrymen to fight them."

"Yet you are here," Marissa emphasized.

She frowned and remained silent for a long time before responding. "I used to be a paladin, as a member of a guild of servants with unique abilities from around the world," replied softly. "We swore loyalty to King Vihen, then amid the hardships, we served his son, King Tahen."

Startled, Marissa discovered how Keleana discreetly cleaned the tears from her cheeks.

Quietness.

"We are almost there, Torret Post," Keleana pointed.

Marissa spotted a camp with mostly small tents as the riders on the palomino horse approached. There were sturdy buildings like a small sawmill, storage, a blacksmith workshop, and a stable for housing many horses. She also discovered how dozens of sawyers had placed hundreds of tall timber wood brought from the north forest on the ground, ready to build a fortification around the post.

Just arriving at the place, Keleana helped Marissa to descend from the equine, and then she dismounted. A lad took the horse away.

Both females walked among the tents towards the open center where twenty people in armors, most seated on stems, surrounded expectant a bonfire where a male cook roasted a wild boar with a boiling enormous cauldron of vegetable soup. Not too far, another bonfire had a median pot with warm beverages.

A mature woman in armor, whom Marissa speculated if she was Casakan by the color of her light brown skin, offered a metallic cup containing a caudel, a spicy mixture of milk, honey, and wine. She thanked her but could not stop guessing her origin.

Keleana noticed her curiosity. "She is a Casarak," revealed after a sip from her caudel, touching her torso with a fist. "I am a Berremark, daughter of a Berremen and an Arankan. Most are Casaraks and Berremarks," concluded, pointing to the vagrants in place.

"Keleana!" a loud voice screamed, making her turn.

A short toothless man with a long grizzled beard and rusted armor approached excitedly, extending both arms and broadening his clear blue eyes.

"Kekten!"

Both gave a powerful hug that noisily clashed their armors and spilled the woman's drink.

Marissa observed the incident with an astonished look.

"Long time not seeing y'all! How are the folks?" he inquired as an alcoholic smell emitted from his breath.

"Same old ones!" Keleana replied between laughs. "What news do you bring from the north?"

"Everyone is getting ready for the Carretem Festival, but the locals are, indeed, excited about the jousting tournament," he said, touching her shoulders. "Ya should take part!"

"If these damned insects do not irrupt into our way! I could be part of it," she nodded, patting his shoulders with affection. "Are the locals talking about the jousters?"

"Not, indeed. People are talking more regarding a small girl that liberated a lord from a demon." He widened his eyes to give a dramatic impression. "They say she is the Promise."

"The Promise!" Marissa exclaimed, astounded. "Where can I find the girl?"

Kekten adopted a much more severe gesture and stared at Marissa from head to toe, noticing that, despite being covered in mud, her armor was expensive, different from the ones the vagrants wore. He distrusted her. "Who are ya, lass?"

"Marissa Taskar. I had to save her butt from a red one," Keleana replied, minimizing the incident. "She tried to kill it by the body."

The man studied the engraved pommel of her sheathed sword, noticing a particular emblem. "The Academy in Estolk. Am I right?"

"Aye, sir," Marissa nodded. "I am here to accomplish a quest the Head has confided to me."

"I do not know what business brings you here, but ya do not mess with our affair here. Ya heard me?" requested with harshness.

"I will not, sir!" Marissa replied with anxiety.

"People in the Ri have said that the girl has arrived at Laimet, the seat of The Lowlands," he pointed north-east. "That is two weeks by horse stopping to rest at inns."

"When your green mantis returns to you," Keleana spoke. "You could get there in two days mounting on him, but my warning is that once the mantis runs will do straight, no curves, and if you do not stop him on time, you could fall to death on a cliff."

"Green mantises are the fastest creatures on the ground, but unpredictable indeed. That is why we prefer horses, even slower than them," Kekten assured.

"I do not mind. I will go with Brisel," Marissa concluded.

The sun descended into the west, but the daylight was still present. Marissa had cleaned herself and, with her recently polished armor, seated on an enormous chunk of wood between the grasses. She looked at the forest connected with the Mantid realm, hoping for Brisel's return.

She needed to accomplish that quest from her uncle Orssandro.

Marissa enjoyed her meal as she put the spoon into her mouth. The Casarak woman had saved her a boar plate with carrot and potato soup.

In the little time she had in Post Torret, she realized the strong bond between the vagrants. They were mature and experienced people, and no one was young. They had a life of nomads traveling from one realm to another, offering their services to whoever needed their swords. And refused to have a home to surrender to new ventures.

They had their glory during the Arankan Monarchy. King Vihen strongly supported the guilds, formed by different warriors of unique abilities and from many realms. He loved to observe them in quests that his kingdom confided in them.

King Vihen's younger tikls were the best times. The presence of guilds gave a colorful age filled with flourishing diversity.

But soon, the claws of the plague reached everywhere. Because of Aranka's anguish, the monarch turned his eye to alchemists and medics, and the guilds declined. The Gesha was the last nail in the coffin.

Marissa knew their history from the mouth of her teachers.

Almost finishing her meal, she noticed from afar an unusual figure. It was a walking elder in odd black clothes, white hair, and blue eyes, no beard, immaculate.

He inspired fear. Marissa's hands trembled, dropping her empty plate.

The man entered the dense forest.

Afterward, flocks of small birds flew from the trees, afraid.

A silhouette of a black dragon emerged with a vertical flight toward the sky, but the high darkness of the night from the late sunset made it impossible to keep track of it and became invisible.

Marissa stood up, astonished.

Dragons existed only in mythologies.

She believed that her mind was becoming insane.

Her heart was racing.

She heard the steps crunching the grass and, scared, turned around.

She almost drew her sword.

Brisel had returned to her as he stared at her amusingly, moving his antennas. His sudden reappearance made Marissa happy, and she impulsively reacted by hugging him by the neck.

Keleana was right. Her green mantis had followed her scent.

That windy next morning, Marissa was ready in the open grassland. The vagrants put together a special leather saddle with reins on Brisel. The green mantis was docile enough to let the people equip him properly. It took all night to make the mantis' seat.

At first, when Marissa mounted her mantis, she felt odd but realized that, except for minor differences, it was practically the same as guiding a horse. After that, she pulled his head with the reins. Brisel turned to see at her with hissing and moving antennas.

Kekten approached the mantis and moved him until his head was toward the north position. Then he spoke to Marissa. "Ya take care, lass!"

Next, Keleana approached and gave her a used helmet, somewhat dented. "I know that is not the same as your fancy armor, but it will protect your head in your journey," smiled. "Have safe travels!"

Marissa nodded gratefully, put her helmet on her head nervously, and tied the reins firmly around her hands. She exhaled, then kicked Brisel's body, pulling his head.

The mantis ran at an extraordinary speed, soon to disappear into the forest.

The group of vagrants applauded with joy. But two.

"What is her business with the Promise?" Kekten whispered with his hands on the waist. "Ya da know?"

"It grows in me certain suspicions as my guts tell me," Keleana replied with crossed arms. "That lass is the Casakan Head's niece, and I will find out once I am in Carretem."

9

YKARTE

The morning started off warm, but as the day progressed, the afternoon became cool. Dark, gray clouds filled the sky, hinting at an imminent downpour.

At the family estate, Vasso of fourteen years old eagerly helped his father to cut sorghum flowers and stored them inside his long palm basket that he carried with him. He wanted to finish his daily work before the rain, so they could sell their produce in the nearby town the next morning.

The father gazed at his son with pride and a smile.

Vasso hoped to finish the last batch of sorghum before leaving for dinner with his mother and his younger sisters.

As he heard a horse approaching, the father paused his knife on the stem of a flower. He turned his head and waited for the visitor to arrive at his own farm.

Vasso followed his example.

The town's constable appeared on his brown horse. He wore his military green and black uniform and greeted him with a somber gesture.

"What is the reason for such a visit?" the father inquired, startled, as he expected no one.

"It pains me. I am left with no other option but to obey the instructions given by the Head," he nodded in sorrow. "I am here to comply with the mobilization and take your son to the front lines."

Overwhelmed by surprise, the father let go of the knife he had been gripping.

Vasso remained unresponsive.

"I am truly sorry. Because of our bond in friendship, I have chosen not to take your daughters. However, I might come for you, too."

She hummed a tune to herself. The young black woman threw chunks of wood into the furnace hole and closed it with an iron door. Through her thick round glasses, searched for the overused kettle filled with water from a barrel near the door and put it on the stove to boil. She dried her wet hands with the white cloth tied to the skirt of her maroon dress.

Carlissa checked the level of castor oil in the two lanterns that illuminated the small, dark kitchen. Some nonperishable groceries remained in the pantry, but it was often empty, except for some mice running across the orifices. She revised each glass jar with herbal tea and chose the fresher one to put on a tray with four cups.

She sang her melody again. Her father always sang it every night. It was a song of love about a maid awaiting her lover's return from a battlefield—a piece filled with hope and joy.

She barely used the inn.

The Lake's Corner. In the past, it was a striving place where grilled fish was popular around Estolk. Her father was a skilled cook, a friendly innkeeper, and very pleasant. When the Gesha came, the misfortune arrived. Even though they tried other options, the inn could not keep its customers because of the unsuitability of the fish. Thus, it became desolate. It had irremediably to be closed.

Her father died of sadness. The inn was his life.

Carlissa, a herbalist connoisseur, enrolled at a local school to become an alchemist, wished to heal and assist medics through herbs.

Yet she was not currently studying but in the inn instead. The mobilization forced her school to close for the time being.

The inn remained closed, but a friend hired the place.

Someone banged on the rear door, and she responded with urgency.

She met a hooded man in a brown robe, all soaked as a heavy rainfall came down that afternoon and pulled him inside and closed the entrance. "Give me your clothes with haste!" she hurried, alarmed. "Do not let yourself catch a cold!"

"No need, Carlissa," he replied serenely.

To her astonishment, the man in robes snapped his fingers, and all the wet clothes became dry in a blink. He uncovered his head to show his enlarged brown face and gave a soft smile.

"You always amuse me, Archmage Missar!" exclaimed with a chuckle.

"Are they here?"

"Aye, sir. Waiting for you."

Glancing towards the narrow stone stairs next to the door, he nodded in acknowledgement, expressed gratitude to Carlissa, ascended the stairs, and produced light from his open hand to guide his path upward.

He arrived at an obscure room with only brief gleams from a pair of candles which, annoyed, with his magic increased the light with the same flames to illuminate the place entirely when he closed the door behind.

Archmage Missar found Ladies Alyssa and Tasarissa seated beside a round table. By the window covered in red curtains, on foot, in his gray clothes and cloak, Dessidere witnessed his entrance with his crossed arms.

Lady Tasarissa, a woman covered in light-blue silk veils and dress, showed wet eyes at the time that Alyssa touched the hand to console her.

The archmage noticed her. "What is the matter, milady?"

"Lord Orssandro refuses to tell her the fate of her daughter, Marissa," Alyssa replied. "Supposedly, she is on a confidential quest he handed to her."

"It is the same with Alessandro Eskar," Dessidere added. "His orders sent him to Sarak, but no one knows his whereabouts after the siege."

"That damned brother!" Tasarissa exclaimed hurtfully. "No one takes my daughter away!"

Alyssa tried to calm her.

The archmage pulled his chair without touching it and took a seat. On the table, he put his hands together and spoke. "The Head has gone too far. And the matter of the mobilization is a madness," sighed. "I have seen how the armies are taking my pupils away from the sanctuaries, but that nonsense is also separating families."

"Tell us, archmage. Is it true that the Promise is dangerous as the Head suggested?" Dessidere asked while some water leaks from the ceiling annoyed him.

"The Promise already made her first public move," revealed, surprising everyone. "The sanctuary from the Ri has informed that the child, a girl, liberated a lord from being a demon."

"And?" the drips still bothered him.

The archmage made a wave with his hand, and the leaks disappeared. "Do you think someone who liberates a man from an evil entity would be a menace to our realm?"

"I think the real menace is that scoundrel of Orssandro!" Tasarissa scoffed with exasperation.

"What do you suggest we should do to confront the Head and convince the Assembly the opposite?" Dessidere kept insisting. "After all, you were the one who summoned us here!"

"You are right, young man," nodded. "I am not suggesting but announcing that the elves are coming here."

"But they are dying!" he exclaimed in disbelief.

"Not the Molkans. I am talking about the ones from the West."

"Enough with stupidities!" Tasarissa slammed the table and stood up. "I will kill my brother with my hands!"

"Let us hear what else he has to say!" Alyssa suggested, agitated, pulling her by the arm.

The archmage kept his peace as he observed Lady Tasarissa return to her chair.

"Are you insane?" Dessidere inquired skeptically. "These elves have been in isolation since five hundred tikls! No one has found their land through the mist!"

"Not anymore!" the archmage smiled, startling everyone. "Archmage Yasstro sacrificed himself to summon them."

"How?" Alyssa asked.

"Once Yasstro knew the news of the Promise had reached the Head and that he had started his plans, he comprehended the necessity of bringing them. Using his magic, he deliberately shot an arrow at himself."

"After all, no one murdered him!" Dessidere shook his head.

"Why the elves?" Alyssa inquired again.

"The Sword of Kasana."

"What does it have to do with that damn sword after his death? I do not see the relation with the Promise and this mobilization!" Tasarissa said, irritated.

"The most powerful weapon of Sankaris that can bring either death or life all depends on who has it. It is somewhere in Casak, hidden," replied with a nod. "Archmage Yasstro somewhat notified the elves from the afterlife."

"I understand now," Dessidere nodded with a smile. "It all makes sense!"

"Care to explain?" Alyssa requested.

"Over five hundred tikls ago, a chunk of the mystical and precious metal fell on Sankaris from No Nunn. The monarchs of that time had a gathering and made the finest sword ever from it, and Salterans named it *Ykarte*." sat on a chair at the table. "The best black-smiths of that era forged the sword."

"Every king or queen tried the *Ykarte*, but the burden was too overwhelming for them," Archmage Missar continued with the story. "So, they had decided that the sword should go to the most deserving warrior in the world, and they organized a tournament with all the best warriors from every point of Sankaris."

"And a strong young tribal elf girl won. She had the mystical *Ykarte* in her hands," Dessidere said, tapping his finger on the table. "That was Kasana."

"She began bringing peace and prosperity to most of the Continent of Ryza. Wherever Kasana went, everywhere flourished. Kasana's accomplishments overjoyed the monarchs and people. Everyone spoke about how great the Molkan warrior was in bringing life."

"But in Molke, Kasana's brother, Renke, from the tribe of the Kannestes, courted a girl from the Tannes, a chief's daughter. The people from both tribes did not see their love with good eyes."

"Sadly," the archmage's face turned somber. "The Tannes murdered Renke."

"Kasana's thirst for vengeance consumed her, leading her to wield the mystical sword and execute her brother's murderers. The escalating rage resulted in a brutal civil war that engulfed all tribes in Molke, spreading into the ancient kingdoms of Berrem and involving humans, felines, and Brekens."

"*The Elvish War*."

"They devastated half of the continent when the conflict ended, and terrible epidemics surged."

"What happened afterward?" Alyssa asked with great curiosity. "What about Kasana and her sword?"

"The Tannes captured and handed Kasana over to the Kannestes. Shame was too much to bear that her own tribe executed her," Archmage Missar continued. "The Tannes seized the *Ykarte* with them, and they had decided that it should be placed in holy and incorrupt hands. They hid it till the time was right. They emigrated west, abandoning Molke and Ryza, and isolated themselves from the rest of Sankaris in an unreachable land in the mist."

"Please let me understand myself," Lady Alyssa Taskar uttered, insecure. "If I am not mistaken, the *Ykarte* is somewhere in Casak and . . . The Head wants it?"

"Precisely, milady," the archmage nodded. "That theatrical performance that the Head did to get votes for the mobilization was all to get the sword."

"And the Promise?"

"An immense obstacle he wants to avoid. He fears her. The elves intend to pass the *Ykarte* to the Promise."

"The goddesses save us if that sword falls in Orssandro's hands!" Tasarissa exclaimed, concerned.

"The Head knew the elves were approaching. That is why his last upsetting behavior at the Assembly and wanted to speed up his plans with a mobilization," Missar replied. "I am sure that a major war is coming."

Silence reigned the room with distress.

Carlissa knocked on the door and entered, smiling with lively eyes behind her round glasses, carrying a tray with cups of tea.

10

KNIGHT

The Black Forest of The Midlands was a dense place of broad, tall pines with large branches, where the sun's light barely arrived on the ground, a place of comfort for the owls to hoot in the night, and a home of black wolves always traveling around in packs. Small or big animals of land or air could roam free around the extensive forest that began from the end boundaries of The Lowlands until the very beginning of The Highlands in the south. But no beast dared to go near the Karekall in the east, as the mountain chain was always bald and strangely lifeless, only showing its bare, dry, tawny surface.

Two unusual visitors had set foot in the forest late evening where no one dared to enter. Lakia refused to keep her way on the road and asked to go by the woods instead. Peken had argued in disagreement with her choice but agreed to follow her.

Lakia pulled her chestnut horse by the reins, a gift from the captain. The equine carried a load of waki furs on the saddle and bags of provisions by the sides. Presents from the Lord of The Lowlands.

The lord's spouse tried to gift her a new linen gown to give Lakia a more feminine appearance. But she refused it, still intending to be disguised as a boy, as Peken suggested with insistence despite her revelation. She let someone else wash her clothes. However, she accepted new leather sandals to her size, made by the local shoemaker. Despite her persistent denial, a medic and an alchemist treated her feet.

Like Lakia, Peken had abundant meals, washed clothes, a hot bath, and a warm bed.

A crowd outside the lord's castle had to be contained as the people asked Lakia's magic for their sick relatives. Still, she could not offer them, as she did not understand her abilities yet.

She was not a mage, and she was not a healer either, but something else no one knew, not even herself.

On the fifth day in Laimet, Lakia decided it was time to depart.

During the nighttime, while most of the residents were fast asleep, Lakia embarked on her journey towards the southern region of the burgh alongside her faithful horse and Peken. This departure occurred when the frigid moon, No Sak, was at its highest point. They left behind a note with gratitude, but not farewell.

Peken proposed to continue their journey south across The Midlands, straight, hoping to arrive at the Holy Mountains, passing The Highlands, to reach Salter finally. But Lakia requested to deviate their journey southwest. She had heard about the Festival in Carretem and felt she had to go there. The elf did not agree with her option, believing she was only curious about the celebration.

But Lakia insisted. She desired to deviate from her original destination to keep building her Jyistereerk.

Peken did not understand her intentions nor the Jyistereerk, a strange word that sounded confusing to pronounce. "Are you happy?!" Peken grumbled, exasperated. "We are now lost! We keep going in circles!"

Annoyed, the elf threw his bag of belongings on the ground in a small clearing surrounded by trees as he noticed the late evening sun. He shook his head and looked around.

Lakia kept her laugh to herself, trying to look serious. "Do not concern, Peken," finally replied with a hopeful smile. "I am sure tomorrow morning you will know our way."

"Whatever!"

He closed his eyes and relaxed, inhaled deeply, feeling the freshness of the forest, then stared at the girl. "All right, lass. Please await here. I will get some wood for the bonfire."

She nodded and witnessed the elf interning into the darkness of the wood.

Lakia, alone, expected this precise moment. She had waited long for this evening.

Tranquil, she tied the reins of her chestnut horse to a nearby tree, approached a thick fallen branch on the grass, and sat on it. She took off her hat, letting her tangled black hair fall. She put her hand in the satchel, extracted a piece of dry meat, and pulled it with her teeth.

As the sunset was approaching, she sensed the freshness in the air.

She downed slightly to stare at the almost brownish grass while chewing her food.

Lakia felt the coldness of a sword's tip against the back of her neck. Rather than fear, she manifested calm and composure and swallowed the small meat piece she had in the mouth.

"Finish with your quest now!" Lakia spoke with authority but calm. "All you have to do is to push your sword firmly by the pommel, and you have executed me!"

Instead, she felt how the sword trembled, and the weapon fell on the grass. Afterward, heard some sobs.

Lakia rose from her seat in tranquility and turned around.

Marissa stood there with her face soaked in tears, crying uncontrollably as she shook her head again and again.

"If you feel you should follow orders, do it now," Lakia smiled.

"No! I can not!" Marissa replied, broken. "I beg your pardon!"

She fell to her knees.

Peken had returned earlier and, stunned, discovered Marissa pointing at Lakia's neck with her sword. Caught in panic, he let the wood he had gathered earlier fall. Paralyzed, he did not react to anything, only to witness through his yellow eyes.

Lakia approached Marissa and did her best to clean her face, showing a smile, and then rubbed her head with affection. "What to pardon you? For something he ordered you to do?" denied with her head.

"But my uncle. . .!"

"Be quiet, my friend," she touched her shoulders. "What occurred to you does not matter. Your stance is with me now!"

"But. . . What shall I do?"

"I would like to invite you to be part of the Jyistereerk," she nodded. "Be my knight."

Marissa replied in affirmation with a light smile that differed from her previous cry, humbled.

"What shall I call you?"

"Marissa Taskar."

"From now, you shall be Ser Marissa Taskar."

Lakia glanced to her left, extending her arm in the same direction. "Come here, little!"

Brisel approached the girl from his hiding behind the tree, amusingly stared at Lakia, moved his antennas, and bowed before her as a sign of utmost respect.

Peken, as an observant, realized that the girl was not only an empress trying to establish a sovereign.

He remembered the words of a sorceress and confirmed she was an exceptional type of divinity.

And comprehended that the ancient mythologies from a bygone world were not fantasies.

The chilly night had arrived, showing three of the four moons in the clean sky despite the tall pines that somewhat covered the celestial spectacle. Only the tiny rocky No Kra would be forever invisible to the eye, and no one would know its presence unless observed by a telescope. Marissa had seen that moon during her science classes at the Academy. She recalled her times while identifying No Nunn, followed by the red volcanic No Ta and the large gelid No Sak, from her position on the grass, recumbent, under a layer of waki fur, far from the bonfire where Lakia was asleep nearby.

Accompanied by the owls' hoots, she sighed in meditation in her new sudden stance. Right before sunset, she was determined to accomplish a quest that her uncle confided. This night she had become an empress' knight.

She reviewed her past hurdles.

Remorse because of a quarrel she had with her beloved Alessandro.

A shipwreck with a giant squid and a red mantis assault almost cost her life twice.

All the hindrances for a quest that had an unexpected culmination.

A pair of legs with leather pants and boots startled Marissa. She observed how the elf Peken sat beside her, offering a bowl with beef stew and potatoes in a wooden bowl. She also seated and accepted, gratefully, the meal he had cooked previously.

Marissa never saw an elf in her life. To her, Peken was someone new and did not avoid her fascination with his yellow eyes, amber skin, pointed ears, and blonde hair.

He noticed displeased by her curiosity. "Where do you come from?"

"Casak, Estolk," she replied after the first sip from her wooden spoon.

"I see," he nodded with no gesture. "Once in the Ri, I met a fine lady, Larissa Eskar."

"The late mother of my fiancé," Marissa nodded with a smile. "Alessandro Eskar."

She turned to see the dormant figure of Lakia under layers of waki furs.

"What is the matter?"

"The girl," pointed. "Is she the child that my uncle mentioned? The daughter of Cassandro Eskar?"

"How did you find us?" Peken asked with seriousness.

"It was Brisel. We were in Laimet looking for you, but the lord showed some sandals that Lakia used instead, and my mantis used his antennas to. . . smell?"

"Mantises detect scents by their antennas."

"Well, and we are here," she shrugged her shoulders.

From the elf, a tense silence surged. "Tell me, missy. You had the chance to kill her," Peken said with a grave voice. "Why did you not finish your task?"

Marissa got unsettled by his sharp question.

"Once my sword touched her. . . I felt a powerful and moving presence that reached my heart," Marissa nervously replied, with wet brown eyes. "I simply could not do that to her."

He nodded and stood up. "Your arrival caught me unprepared," said, in distrust. "But you have a warning. Lakia has named you a knight, but if I ever see you with any other intent to harm her, I will have no second thoughts about killing you." And Peken left.

Marissa held her stew bowl, gasping seriously as she watched the elf take his fur and lie flat next to Lakia.

The wolves howled from afar.

Early morning as the sun let its rays pierce the pine trees in the middle of a dense and white haze, the three journeyers had awoken and stood on their feet, keeping their furs on their bodies to protect them from the morn cold. Following the necessities of their bodies, Peken returned and packed everything to load on the chestnut horse.

Marissa found Brisel camouflaged by the trees, to feed him with leaves, but he refused by moving his head aside.

"He is not an animal, Ser Marissa," Lakia clarified, nearing them. "He is an intelligent creature that can survive by himself."

"Back in The Banks, where we rested for a while, I have seen farmers feeding their mantises."

"They had been raised and domesticated since nymphs," Peken intervened in the talks while pulling the horse. "Your mantis, in change, is a free-will creature."

Brisel bowed to the girl and then stared at her.

"Do you want to mount on you?" Lakia asked with a smile. "All right. I accept your request."

The ease of communication between the mantis and the girl surprised the elf and Marissa. Subsequently, the newly named knight tried to help Lakia mount the mantis, but a dubious Peken stopped her, and he put the girl in the saddle instead.

"Be careful, Lakia," Marissa advised, while giving her the reins. "Do not let him go at speed. I almost retched while going like lightning from The Wilds."

"He will not!" Lakia said, sure of Brisel.

"Are we still going southwest to Carretem?" Peken inquired.

"Aye, and we shall return to the road," Lakia replied.

The elf scratched his head without comprehension. "Is there a reason we shall now return to the road, lass? We entered this treacherous forest to avoid it. Then you desire to return."

"If you wish to help me with the Jyistereerk, you shall listen to my demands," said with authority but calmly. "My inside is telling me where to go!"

"Does your inside tell the reasons, at least?"

A small gust of chilly wind crashed against the journey-ers.

On Brisel's saddle, Lakia closed her eyes, showing an annoyance that scared Marissa. "When will you comprehend my reasons even after all you saw on the other side of the Karekall?!"

Peken's chin suddenly trembled, and he opened his yellow eyes widely. Only a brief memory of his experience in that dark place was enough to terrify him.

In disbelief, Marissa watched .

"If we have traveled by the roads, the bandits were already waiting for us!" Lakia replied, still with shut eyes. "My appearance at Laimet has attracted unwanted attention!"

The girl finally stared at him with the highest authority. "The animals here in the forests protect us as they feel my presence!" nodded, exasperated. "Are these reasons enough?!"

Lakia sighed and took off, leaving the startled knight and the panicked elf alone.

"Is that your nature, sir?" Marissa asked him with seriousness. "To distrust everyone?"

She ensured her sword was adequately within the sheath and departed.

In the end, he saw them moving away and tugged the horse to follow Lakia.

They still did not leave the Black Forest and reached the stone road between pines in a settled area by men far from the most uncharted wild woods. It took to them most of the morning to find their way. By noon, the day was warmer and clearer, contrasting the earlier freezing haze.

Marissa escorted Brisel as he carried Lakia on his back at a slow pace. By foot, Peken followed and pulled the horse.

The elf stared with suspicion at Marissa but yet silent. However, he was primarily concerned for himself. As a youngster, he had traveled most of the west and south of Ryza, but his travel turned dreadful after crossing the Breken Territory southeast of the Karekall. He dared not recall his travels, as he could not describe what he had experienced in that dark place.

He placed grabbed his chest.

Darkness would burden his soul if he reminisced.

He desired death.

"Tell me, Lakia," Marissa spoke during the walk. "How do you intend to build that Jyistereerk when you arrive in Salter?"

With fondness, the girl smiled and revealed her live hazel eyes as she held onto her satchel.

"This satchel and I were all my Jyistereerk when I started my journey," she nodded once. "Look at us now. It is bigger!"

Unsure, Marissa seemed to understand, yet hard to assimilate her words. In her walk, she glanced to her front, noticing the pass of a flock of sheep crossing afar from one side to the other, reminding her of a moment from her childhood. "I recall how Alessandro and I used to run after the sheep," she said with nostalgia. "We were eight, and we were inseparable till today."

"Is he your fiancé?" Lakia asked with severity in her expression.

"Aye, though we had a regretful quarrel," shook her head. "However, I am confident that the wedding will take place at the Vykar Palace."

They passed when the flock disappeared somewhere between the pine trees to turn right at a curve.

"You do not know how heartbroken you will be!" Lakia exclaimed in a sad tone.

Her answer startled Marissa. "What is the meaning of. . .?"

"Look!" Lakia interrupted, pointing ahead. "A wagon!"

They discovered a white and quaint wagon that made the journeyers stop. Marissa requested Brisel and Peken to wait as she placed her fingers on the sword hilt, keeping it in the sheath. She approached it with caution.

She heard sobs as she went ahead, wary, and gave a glance at the front box seat.

Marissa found a weeping adolescent plump girl in a colorful dress. Tears soaked her face. She discovered a body covered in cloth shrouds before the wagon on the road, unsettling her. Assessing her surroundings, she noted the absence of a horse. "What has occurred?"

"Leave her, or I will blast you with a rock!" a boyish voice demanded.

Marissa lifted her hands and kept them up as she turned to see him. She discovered a boy in shaded green leather shorts with suspenders. He had a Y-shaped wooden slingshot with a rock in his right hand, ready to throw. He had a deep look in his dark eyes, filled with fear and sadness.

The girl on the seat observed, stopping her cry.

"I do not wish to harm but to help," she said with calm.

"Help?" replied with skepticism. "As those bandits who pretended to be generous?"

"I can assure you of the help we will offer," Lakia approached prudent to him, then stopped, keeping a distance. "We are not bandits, but journeyers with a purpose."

"Who are you?" the boy asked, still ready to throw the rock.

"I am Lakia, and this is my knight, Ser Marissa Taskar."

Peken witnessed while inclining his body against the wagon with crossed arms. His presence also attracted the boy's attention.

"Why someone like you is traveling with a Casakan in shiny armor and an elf?"

"She is the Promise!" Marissa exclaimed, still maintaining her hands raised.

Lakia revealed her true self when she took off her hat, and the boy believed. Astounded, he let the rock fall and put his slingshot in his back pocket. He had heard about her from the news by word of mouth from The Lowlands.

Marissa could finally lower her arms and sighed, relieved.

"It explains your companions!"

"My condolences. Your father wished you to know he truly loved you and worked hard to provide the best for you both," Lakia declared earnestly. "He also asks for forgiveness to let your mother go."

Stunned, the boy nodded.

The girl wept again.

"I do not wish to know if you are a sorceress who speaks with the dead," he replied, giving some steps back, uneasy. "I am Juni of twelve. That is my sister Jumeni, of fourteen. As troubadours, my father and I intended to perform in Doimet and sell my sister's wooden crafts. But we encountered those bandits on the road that pretended to be kind and murdered our father to steal the horses."

Lakia approached Juni with a smile that scared him. Jumeni ceased to cry, astounded.

"Do not fear me, Juni. We will help you," assured. "We will give your father the burial he deserves and bring a pair of horses for your wagon."

"Horses?" Peken asked with skepticism, pointing to the equine beside him, still with crossed arms. "This horse and the mantis?"

Lakia stared, annoyed, at the sarcastic elf. "How many gold coins do we have, Peken?"

"What?" he replied, surprised. "A bag of coins, but still not enough! By good fortune, we could buy a pair of old, ill horses."

Lakia deviated her hazel eyes to her knight.

"Ser Marissa, please take the bag of coins and bring Brisel with you," Lakia mandated with authority. "Once you arrive at Doimet, look for a blacksmith and sell your armor."

"This armor?!" she shouted, alarmed.

"Only nobles and lords have expensive armors like yours," Peken clarified. "Traveling with that will attract unbidden people."

"You do not need armor to be a knight," Lakia replied. "Once you have sold your armor, go to the stables and buy two young, healthy horses."

Marissa got invaded by a sudden sadness as she looked at the plate armor on her body, made by the best blacksmiths in Estolk, and a gift from her mother for her sixteenth birthday. Complying with Lakia's demands, taking the bag of coins, and giving up her armor were tests for her given appointment as a knight just the last night.

Tests of sacrifice and loyalty.

Loyalty to an empress.

To the Jyistereerk.

She had the choice to turn back and leave, to return home to Casak.

But Marissa refused to deny her request, grabbed the coins that Peken offered, mounted on Brisel, and departed toward Doimet. Much later, ensuring she was far enough to be alone with only the mantis, she finally let out the cry she kept to herself.

Perhaps she had sacrificed her homeland, her family, and even her love, for an empire that only existed from the mouth of a mystic girl of great powers.

Lakia walked towards Jumeni, still in the wagon's seat box. She gently took her swollen hands and looked at her small eyes in her clueless face. "I know you are yet a small child despite your age," smiled. "Please, keep your heart pure and open!"

Juni and Peken observed with inquisitiveness Lakia's peculiar actions.

"Why she carries that name, elf?" the boy whispered with admiration. "I heard Lakia is a Molkan word that means *The Unfortunate*."

"She was unfortunate, lad," he replied with his crossed-arms posture.

II

DALEHEL

D estroying the tree, or its remnants, did not quite
satisfy Alessandro. He used his dented sword
to strike once and again the bare-standing, small un-
branched wood he had defaced without mercy. The sun
was cruel as the heat could forgive no one, not even him,
who sweated in abundance, and the rays burned his soft
tan skin turning into a brownish tone. He let his facial
hair grow until it became an airy black beard.

Half naked from the torso but wearing black leather pants and boots as he stood on the ground near the sand, a warm breeze blew from the sea not too far.

He did not care about the pain and tiredness of his hand. Even though it was tough, he kept swinging his sword at the wood. He had soreness in his back and arms.

After the *Siege of Katalk*, *The Seagull*, a median ship carrying diverse refugees from Sarak, had crossed the Beyond Sea in a week-long. In all that time, Fabehel never stopped to console and to look for the necessities of the displaced, even relying upon her wheelchair. At her request, Corr was always helpful at her side and also amused by the kids getting entertained around him.

Alessandro was the exception. He separated from the rest, as far as possible, by the ship's rear, submerged in the misery and in the burdensome guilt of the lost lives of three men—Archmage Yasstro, the young soldier he killed during the siege, and leaving Tin alone against a squad of soldiers.

At the harbor on Garterrem Isle, he departed with Song without bidding farewell. He only stopped to buy food and fill his canteen with water on the way, and went to look for an isolated place.

Upon arriving at the Garterrem Isle, loyal sentinels to Lord Pan Din transported the newly landed refugees in carts to the other side of the island across from the burgh of Dimmet. The construction of a small town, comprising only ten buildings, had begun by the island builders, but it was not sufficient for everyone. Lady Fabehel was determined to keep the locality growing.

Despite her encouragement for unity among the refugees, the Brekens established their own separate encampment of tents, following their cultural practices.

Arankans, few Casakans and Casaraks were the ones to occupy the new town, finding it with enough provisions and materials contributed by Lord Din.

In order to enable them to establish their own government, Fabehel organized a panel intending to grant them autonomy, thus freeing them from the need to rely on her any longer. The thought of facing the same destiny as the Arankan Quarter was something she was determined to evade.

Corr was at her side always. He had become her inadvertent ally.

Soon, Lady Fabehel received news from the continent of Ryza, delivered to her by Lord Din.

As a youngster who reached his seventeenth birthday on the Beyond Sea, Alessandro had never witnessed death firsthand.

Tragedy struck when he suffered the heartbreaking loss of his mother, Larissa Eskar, a highly respected figure as she served as the Head of Casak. The circumstances of her unfortunate death remained shrouded in mystery, as her lifeless body was found at the bottom of a cliff shortly after the Gesha took place. Neither had he met his natural father, nor had his mother ever told him about him.

According to Corr, his brother Cassandro fled to Ryza and died in Fenn.

Death was always around him, but he never faced it forthrightly until Sarak during the siege.

Alessandro halted to take a pause from striking the wood, left the forest area where he was to rest near the beach, sat on the sand, and drank some of the water from his leather canteen. He stared toward the Beyond Sea, felt the warm breeze, and perceived the strong sea smell. Grumbling in pain, he grabbed the handkerchief and opened it to discover the scarce and stale food. He took a piece of dry ham and pulled it with his teeth and hardly chewed the pieces. His lack of a good life did not matter to him.

He heard an approaching gallop and turned to glance to his right. He discovered a golden horse mounted by a certain red-haired girl.

He could observe well once the equine stood before him.

Fabehel drove the horse. She had a different and gorgeous look than her previous appearance in Katalk and at *The Seagull*. Her solid red hair radiated from the sun. She wore a clean white shirt and a brown leather vest. Her caramel mounting pants had their extremities tied with laces to cover the limbs of her nonexistent feet.

Alessandro observed someone appropriately strapped her legs to the saddle, although she had no problems in taking control of the reins and revealed her experience with horses.

Her cheeks had some glow, and her skin looked better than the dry whiteness shown in Katalk, but he was not sure if her blush was because of the climate or her indignation.

She grabbed a small hide sack and dashed it to the sand before him.

He gave a glimpse into the sack. It contained a chunk of goat cheese and fresh bread.

Still not done, she also roughly threw a water canteen.

He lifted his dark eyes to stare dazzled at Fabehel, yet showing tiredness.

"What a foolish way to waste yourself!" she said, bothered. "You have done nothing else than to be a coward!"

"You came and said your words, milady. Now, leave."

Astounded, Fabehel enraged herself and threw a dagger, puncturing the sand surface with an exact precision that scared Alessandro. "I might not have feet, but do not test my temper! Do not even try to make me an imbecile!"

He stood, upset to confront her near. "What the heck do you want from me?!" asked, furious and stubborn.

"Do what you came for! Look for your niece!" she replied, even infuriated.

Alessandro froze. He could not find the words to express what he had just heard. He kept gazing at her, immobile, not even a blink as a response.

Fabehel lowered her temper and exhaled deeply to relax when her hazel eyes observed him with understanding. Her anger left to feel empathy towards him.

"Aye, the Promise is a girl, your niece," she breathed. "Lord Pan Din has communicated to me she is located somewhere between The Lowlands and The Midlands. Right here in Berrem!"

"Let me look for Song. . . ," he requested.

"No, you shall recover your energy first. Eat and drink what I brought," she suggested, nodding. "Please, help me unstrap from the saddle and put me down. That company I will make for you."

He obeyed. Alessandro carefully untied her legs and carried her first by putting his hands on her waist while she put her arm around his neck, then put Fabehel on the sand to sit. He tied the reins of the golden horse to a nearby tree and returned to be at her side.

Showing kindness, he picked up the dagger from the sand and returned it to her. "If I may ask. What is the account of your feet?"

Fabehel lowered her face and opened the sack, silent. With the help of her dagger cut the food and put a piece of cheese between two slices of bread, and offered it to Alessandro.

Afterward, she did the same for herself. "I am from Byarte, in the then Northern Territories, where the red-haired people lived," sighed, before a bite of her food. "I was born with *Child's Paralysis*, and my parents did not want me."

Startled, Alessandro stopped staring at the sea to glare at Fabehel to his right and paused his chewing.

"Aye," she continued, noticing his attentiveness. "They abandoned me in the outsides of the Royal Estate, where I spent my first night, but early morning, Princess Natahel, in her usual stroll, found me and had me despite my twisted feet."

"You had feet, after all."

"But useless. My illness had made my feet viscous. I did not walk, but crawled on the ground instead."

"Please, continue," he suggested, restarting his meal.

"Princess Natahel, who I regarded as my eldest sister, had a habit of referring to me as *Little*. However, when I crawled instead of walking freely, she named me *Fabehel*, which is a feminine variation of Arankan *Fabe*, signifying a snail."

"Does not that name bother you, milady? She named you because of an illness."

"It bothered me. However, I learned it was not mockery but an affectionate naming," replied with a light smile. "Over time, I learned to love this name: *Fabehel of the Red Tides*, a surname I gained because of my rough character."

"I think your name relates to you very well."

"Anyway, I endured a life-altering experience at four when I got struck by a debilitating infection that came close to claim my life. In order to save my life from the infection, Sorceress Dalehel, who had extensive knowledge of medicine and healing, made the hard decision to amputate my feet." Fabehel paused, feeling a knot in her throat. "Even though it has been many years, I still vividly remember the pain that I went through."

Unable to find any words, Alessandro fell into silence, his mind consumed with thoughts of her, leaving him unable to react.

"In the months I was bedridden, Natahel never left my side," kept recounting regaining her composure. "It was her decision that I should no longer crawl on the ground and so she directed the blacksmiths in Byarte to fabricate a device for me to transport myself. They came up with a wheelchair."

"Are you able to move about with no restraints?"

"I love my freedom on a horse," smiled. "The horses are my feet that let me go wherever I wish!"

He gladly nodded and finished his meal. However, his face showed to be pensive. "Tell me, milady. Is that Sorceress Dalehel you mentioned, the same one from the books?"

"Aye, the same one," she replied, trying to understand his question. "Why do you ask?"

"Archmage Yasstro told me a particular story about her," he lifted his face to look toward the sky, reflective. "The sorceress had arrived in Aranka from her home in Salter. She had returned to the kingdom where she was born. But before King Vihen, she predicted the Promise. She was the first to announce it, and the Gesha did not occur yet."

"I can confirm she was the one because I heard her repeatedly talking about the Promise and her encounter with King Vihen."

"How old was the princess when she left with Cassandro?"

"She was of four tikls or sixteen years of age," nodded. "I was five, and she departed from Sarak. I was only a small child with the responsibility of the Arankans who survived the Gesha and had lost their families."

Alessandro observed how Fabehel ate her meal with trembling lips, noticing tears from her hazel eyes gazing toward the sea. At that moment, no one dared to speak a word. "Was not Sorceress Dalehel with you?"

She cleaned her tears, although her cheeks were still reddish, and with a sad smile, replied to his question. "Mother. . . Sorceress Dalehel had gone with Prince Dohan to Ryza to look for a cure to stop that never-ending plague and never saw her again."

"How did you manage alone with the Arankan Quarter?"

"Tin was always with me."

Alessandro, surprised, stood up, facing the sun with grief and guilt in his insides.

Fabehel noticed his reaction. "Despite the anger I felt towards your actions and your decision to isolate yourself, I understand," spoke with sympathy. "But it is best to honor those who died than grieve with guilt. I do not blame you and do not let yourself to consume by the deception of death."

He turned to look at her with high regard, nodding, amazed at her maturity and clever intelligence despite her being sixteen years old. "I have never met someone so remarkable as you!"

His words staggered her.

As Fabehel observed him, her heart beat rapidly, and by the second time, she felt safe with Alessandro. She first felt that way when he put her on Song during the siege. "Enough of words!" demanded. "Put me back on the horse."

Again, he obeyed her request. He lifted her from the sand, grabbed by her back and legs, and walked with her to the golden horse.

During their short walk, she placed her arm around his exposed neck once again, gripping firmly. The thought of separating from him was unbearable, and as she looked at his bearded face, strangely, she felt an unexpected urge to touch his lips. Despite this temptation, she controlled herself. She was not sure if he would react the same way.

She disapproved of her feelings going too fast. Not even two weeks had passed since she first met him.

She did not want to end his engagement with Marissa. She thought it would be unfair to harm both betrothed.

Fabehel was also terribly afraid of rejection because of her condition.

Alessandro put Fabehel on the saddle and strapped with care the legs while she was petting the horse's head. Next, he placed the reins on her hands with a smile that captivated her. "Have a safe return to Dimmet. Where shall I meet you?"

"Meet me at *The White Whale Inn*. I will arrange a room with a warm bath," responded at the time she touched his exposed shoulder with affection. "It is time for you to get cleansed and rested. Lord Pan Din wants us to go with him to the Festival in Carretem. Afterward, we will search for the Promise."

"I will be there, milady."

Fabehel assented, smiled back with vivid hazel eyes, and ordered her horse to gallop along the beach. However, a hint of insecurity seemed to distress her.

Immediately, Alessandro looked for his favorite black mare, Song, calling her with whistles.

A grimy Alessandro showed in sweats, with stripes of dirt on his white shirt, sand-covered black pants, and worn-out boots. He could not hide his surprise when he found an empty, neat, well-disposed tavern on the first floor of *The White Whale Inn*, but barely illuminated by candles on each of the dozen of tables.

Alessandro expected to find Fabehel in the place. Instead, he found Corr by such a discreet corner, with expensive clothes that someone provided him, relaxed with his feet on the next chair and toying with his brew mug on the table. The feline showed indifference to the visitor as he sipped his beverage.

Unsure, Alessandro approached Corr's table with a light smile. "Any news of Lady Fabehel?"

The feline interrupted his enjoyment of the brew, stared indignantly with the intimidating green eyes of vertical pupils, and spoke with his distinctive deep voice. "If Cassandro were alive, he would slap you for cowardice."

"You shall understand that I faced the difficulties surrounding death," he replied nervously.

"Your brother was my brother, even not by blood nor by race. He died in my arms with a vow to pass his message to you," Corr said, pointing to him. "Yet, I endured escaping from slavery, traveled as a stowaway, and imprisoned to give the word to you."

By the first time, Alessandro felt shame because he knew Corr was right.

"Do not be a wimp, lad!" Corr continued, emptied his mug, and threw a large key on the table. "Lady Fabehel already departed to Carretem and told me to give you a room upstairs, the last one in the aisle."

With no more words, he stood up, intending to exit the tavern hurried.

"Is that all, Corr?" Alessandro insisted. "Are not you glad to see me?"

The feline stopped right by the door.

"You stink!" groaned.

And he departed.

12

MAGES

By traversing a lengthy and arduous path composed of uneven stones, deliberately constructed to ascend the first of the Casakan Mountains, Orssandro arrived at the summit astride his powerful black stallion. Despite not being the tallest peak, the mountain offered a breathtaking and unparalleled scenery. As a Head, he wore the most attractive uniform that any official could have, his dark green uniform with black stripes on the shoulders covered with metallic medals and other emblems on both sides of his chest, his military battle clothes. He sensed the icy wind that passed across at a high altitude where the weather used to be warm in the past.

His daunting presence evidenced his notorious weight over Casak as a sovereign loved by many and hated by others.

He had successfully accomplished the mobilization he desired and cut off the entire realm.

Yet, he felt his grail was still incomplete. He needed that sword to meet his ambitions.

To his misfortune, a giant squid had destroyed *The Seneschal* as the news arrived from Garterrem. He believed Marissa had drowned in the waters, throwing away all hopes of a Promise planned assassination. Orssandro hid the news of his niece's death from Lady Tasarissa, her mother.

Orssandro was attentive. He knew that Archmage Yasstro's death was a way to call the enigmatic Elves of the West, and he did not like it. No one knew them as they had disappeared for five hundred tikls, and now they were coming to Tyza to recover that hidden sword to offer it to a Promise they had awaited after all that time.

His eyes gazed, sighing, at the emerald tropical panorama and identified the irradiated cities from afar despite the dense, dark afternoon. He studied them as he turned around with the help of his horse. To the southwest, he saw Estolk, the realm's largest one. To the northeast was the small fishing city of Ke Tok. And the Equatorial Post near the border to the north. He had ascended that mountain with a purpose for the three large burghs he could see.

The sound of gallops approached him and then silenced.

"Do you see them, Captain Trasso?" the Head asked, still sighting to the cities. "Do you realize what I am talking about?"

"I comprehend your intention now, Sir Head," Trasso, in his new captain uniform but with fewer insignias than he had in Sarak, replied with a nod from his dark equine.

"From here, you kill three birds at once," he said, turning to see his subordinate. "Each city has its sanctuary, with libraries. Archmage Yasstro hid the *Ykarte* in a library."

"What library do you believe is hiding the sword?"

"That is your duty!"

Trasso turned to his companion. A black man with a crooked presence was riding a gray horse. He wore dark robes with his face hidden beneath a cowl, revealing only his thick-lipped mouth. His chilling appearance seemed to attract some crows that overflew the mountain.

The birds distrusted Orssandro.

"How could we find the sword, Archmage Carrasso?"

"The mystical sword is invulnerable to fire. It will survive flames and heat when everything is in ashes. It will glow like the same sun," he replied, pensive and with a cavernous voice.

"I believe you have guessed my plan. That is why we bring you here," Orssandro said with disregard.

"Aye, Sir Head."

The dark magus dismounted his horse and gave some steps until he could see the first city of three, Estolk, from the same mountain. He then steadily walked ahead and stopped at the edge of a cliff. Lifting his hands, allowing his long sleeves to uncover his arms embedded in burnt scars, he focused on himself.

The sight of the enormous floating ball of fire that he had created brought terror into Orssandro and Trasso.

However, both officials had to keep calm, though they felt the heat on their faces and the brightness blinded their eyes. They had to control the horses as they were frightened, but not the lone gray horse that ran away.

Carrasso waved his hands but, keeping them up, divided the large ball into three smaller ones, yet more prominent.

He launched the first floating fireball. At an excessive speed and merciless, it pummeled against the Great Sanctuary's library in Estolk after traveling a long distance from the mountain over the tropical forest.

The archmage did the same to the smaller sanctuaries' libraries in Ke Tok and the Equatorial Post using the rest of the balls.

Carrasso's task brought satisfaction to Orssandro.

The three men awaited the fires to consummate the libraries, hoping to find the mystical sword.

"What if the sword does not appear in either of these libraries, Sir Head?" Captain Trasso asked. "We believed it hid in Sarak, but we found nothing."

"We keep doing the same with the remaining libraries," Orssandro replied, with his eyes fixated on Estolk. "We must haste before those elves invade our beaches."

"Do you think the elves are on the way here with their ships?"

"Nothing is certain. Neither do we know their weaponry, captain. Nobody has seen them in hundreds of tikls."

"Is not that terrifying?"

"It is," Orssandro nodded, still looking at Estolk. "I ordered the mobilization and placed inexperienced youths in the front lines to confront them. They will be our shields, so our armed people can effectively have time and learn."

Trasso heard him and could not believe it. The Head had used innocent kids as young as eight as human shields. The captain recalled doing many things in Katalk against the people, especially the immigrants, with no regrets, but he would not do something similar to children.

Since the Gesha, Casak mistreated the kids in particular those from poverty. Orssandro and the Assembly had imposed laws that affected them. After Lady Larissa Eskar's death, one of the first actions was enforcing obligatory military enrollments whenever the Assembly mandated.

The Head's words arose in Trasso's suspicions. A Casakan always defends and protects his people, but the man he had beside was the opposite.

He knew something was off in Orssandro.

He scowled at Carrasso, suspecting his involvement in the madness.

Carlissa left the inn's backside, stepping into the narrow alley and eluding the foul-smelling garbage. The noisy chaos attracted rats, then ran toward the street. She stopped by the corner and witnessed women, small children, and most elders running, panicked, with screams and cries towards her left.

Invaded by curiosity, she turned right to discover afar, some blocks of distance, the burning of the library's Great Sanctuary. Unfortunately, the fire had expanded to the adjacent houses, putting the cramped surrounding neighborhood at risk of disappearing.

The black smoke ascending to the sky gave a somber panorama, a sad event never seen in Estolk or felt since the Gesha.

In the opposite direction, Archmage Missar walked with serenity among the frightened multitude.

Carlissa observed him with amazingness and excitement through her thick, round glasses. She noticed he looked fixated on the sanctuary, especially in the burning library.

The archmage paused his walk and exposed his hands by lifting them from the robe's sleeves. In the air, he created invisible swirls.

Mysteriously, the dark clouds came too close to the city, and as Missar snapped with both hands, heavy rain fell to extinguish the fire.

Carlissa witnessed the magical act as if she were a little girl, with a big smile that showed her teeth. She did not care that the sudden and orchestrated rain soaked her in its totality. She noticed, however, that the water could fall everywhere except for the endangered Great Sanctuary and its burning library.

For a strange reason, Missar had let his sanctuary consummate into ashes, his own home, only saving the contiguous neighborhood.

The multitude stopped and observed in awe the dying flames.

Missar lowered his arms and turned his face to give Carlissa a tough look before rushing towards her.

His sudden attitude terrified her.

"You shall be inside!" he reprimanded harshly. "Do not expose yourself!"

"May I know the reason, Archmage Missar?" asked, unsure if she was trembling because of the rain or fear of his anger.

"No time for explanations! Go back inside!"

Ashamed and bothered, Carlissa obeyed him and returned to the inn.

13

KORBA

Alessandro remembered his exact clothes when he first arrived in Sarak—a good leather jacket and a dark velvet hooded cloak with black pants. Lord Pan Din bought him the same ones, but Fabehel selected them. He discovered the clothes on the bed, entering the room with fresh boots lying on the floor at the Dimmet inn.

Earlier, he had taken a hot bath and shaved the scanty beard he had let grow. He felt refreshed but futile. Once again, the intense midday sun made him perspire and feel drained, despite being accustomed to it.

He positioned both arms on the rail to contemplate the trajectory the boat drew on the bluish water from the rear, but maimed pieces of dead fish surged, floating, leaving a streak of red blood. Sharks had become vicious beings, biting everything in sight solely for pleasure.

The Gesha had altered the course of Sankaris' nature.

Alessandro turned around to observe the cabin on the second floor.

A gray-haired feline drove the helm with his furry hands to pilot *Little Fortune*, a slow-paced wooden steamboat equipped with a noisy iron furnace engine, a standard Fennen steam technology used for all kinds of transports in the realm. The vessel was a shared charter that departed from the Port of Pinn in Fenn to cross the Gulf of Triem, carrying passengers, livestock, and goods to Sarrem, stopping in Garterrem. It brought back items from Berrem during its travel.

In dark blue velvet clothes, Corr approached him with two metallic mugs containing water and offered one to his companion. Both drank the liquid with relief.

Alessandro comprehended the feline's insistence to board a vessel from his realm. Other realms' transports did not accept the Fennens easily and often mistreated them. However, because of an ancient treaty from the early Age of Kings, the felines could travel freely across Berrem.

He glanced at his surroundings to notice most felines and a few Berremens. He was the only Casakan on board.

Corr asked if Alessandro desired more water, and he nodded. The feline left, leaving him alone again.

When Alessandro returned to position his arms on the rail, he noticed the sudden blackness of the sea that took his breath away and impulsively receded with an unexplainable horror. He turned around to find himself alone. The boat had become empty and silent.

The hot weather had turned into a chilling cold one, with a freezing wind that burnt his face.

He was not sure if he was inside a dream or part of a hallucination.

An elder approached him. His appearance revealed he was Arankan in aspect, with white hair, blue eyes, and no beard, immaculate, and wore strange black clothes. The sensation of fear emanated from him as his stare was frightening, but he stopped and smiled.

A pleasant male voice emerged. "It is time for us to encounter Master Alessandro Eskar."

Alessandro did not reply promptly, discovering he had uncontrollable tremors in his hands, but he remembered him.

"You were at Archmage Yasstro's funerals!"

"Aye, I was there," nodded. "Because I was watching you."

"Who are you?!" Alessandro asked, agitated with distrust and fear, giving some steps back.

"For now, call me Korba," replied with a sinister grin. "And I am here to offer a proposition."

"What is it?"

"Abandon the search for the Promise and serve me. Take a seat to my right to reign my dominion," offered his white and soft hand. "In change, I will present you the gifts of the resurrection and immortality. You could bring back all your beloved, Yasstro, your mother, Cassandro, and all of you would live forever."

Alessandro heard him. He did not know who the elder was but realized he was someone of immense powers, perhaps a kind of mage or sorcerer, and sensed an aura of pure evilness in him. He studied the older man to notice his perfect physical appearance.

The elder was the nice-looking neat Arankan.

But his name and the fear of him suggested he was from somewhere else.

The offer was tempting, but Alessandro distrusted him.

"I shall not accept your proposal!" he replied, moving his head with shaking words.

"Let it be this way then," Korba said, grinning and nodding. "I assure you that refusing will bring the loss of your most beloved."

"Leave!" his request echoed.

Alessandro turned around when he felt a touch on his shoulder.

Corr, shaken by his sudden behavior, dropped the mugs, spilling the water on the floor.

He had recovered the sound of the steam engine and observed that the sea had returned to its color. The weather was warm again, and the passengers were on the boat.

Korba had disappeared as if nothing had ever happened.

"Are you all right, master?" Corr asked, still startled.

"My apologies," he said, with the fear inside. "I had an encounter with a wraith of nightmarish malevolence!"

Expressionless, Marissa walked on the stone road surrounded by pine trees during the warm afternoon. She had a pair of brown Sabino horses with white legs pulled by ropes tied around their necks.

After her errands in Doimet, she asked Brisel to go ahead. The mantis obeyed her and used his speed to reunite with Lakia and her group.

Marissa felt disappointment and sadness but did not expose them.

Alone in the road, as she wished.

As mandated by the empress, she sold her beloved fine armor to a well-known blacksmith. Afterward, she only had a wool robe on her body and assumed she could use some coins to buy proper clothes from an adjacent garment store.

She bought a simple dark red linen long shirt and pants and some used leather boots that she had previously traded with the merchant. Despite the emotional pain of leaving her armor behind, she felt lighter and fresh, relieved, recalling with nostalgia for her flimsy wardrobe back in Casak.

The only thing she kept to herself was her iron sword gifted by the Academy, carrying it against her left leg within the sheath kept by her belt around the waist.

She found a horse breeder in the marketplace after inquiring to the locals. Even with the bag of coins she received from Peken altogether with the money from her armor's sale, the amount was not enough to buy two young and healthy horses, as Lakia requested.

She had to bargain in the Estolk market like she used to with her mother, Tasarissa, but the breeder refused to lower the price. Things in Berrem differed from Casak. Finally, she could get the Sabino horses at the desired price. However, the horses were seven years old, not young as she needed, but strong and healthy enough to pull the wagon with no problems.

Marissa used the last three silver coins to buy food for everyone and placed it on the back of a horse in a large bag.

With some exhaustion but showing resilience, she kept walking at a slow pace. She had no interest in rushing.

She felt not only disappointed, but also miserable.

Her life changed in just two days. Marissa later swore loyalty as a knight to the Head's target.

Doubts filled her mind, confusion filled her heart.

After a failed intent to execute the Promise the previous night, Marissa was confident of her new loyalty. But her conviction fell apart after Lakia's request to sell her armor.

She had questions with no answers and was unsure about her choices.

Was Lakia an empress trying to build her Jyistereerk?

Or was she a delirious girl with an implausible chimera?

If so. How to explain the strange presence that touched her heart?

Marissa was pondering all these questions but was unsuccessful in finding answers. She did it while walking, not minding her environment.

She halted as her brown eyes widened when a feeling of trepidation invaded her body with a cold sweat that ran from her head through her face. Marissa saw how the pine trees became pure white, enlightened, while the sun's rays transmuted into blackness.

She believed it to be a kind of hallucination.

Her heart rapidly pummeled with terror, and with trembling hands, she tied the ropes to the nearest tree to secure the horses.

Afterwards, she unsheathed her sword, anticipating the worst, raising it high and gripping the hilt with caution. She sensed the threat but still had the perturbation on her insides.

It was confusing to see with the trees' luminous whiteness.

"I would listen and not point with a sword," a pleasant male voice said.

Marissa, startled, turned to her right. She discovered an elder who approached her. His appearance revealed he was Arankan in aspect, with white hair, blue eyes, and no beard, immaculate, and wore strange black clothes. The sensation of fear emanated from him as his stare was frightening, but he stopped and smiled.

She recalled him interning in the forest in The Wilds, the same place where she witnessed astounded the flight of a black dragon emerging. "Introduce yourself!" requested loudly.

"You may call me Korba, Ser Marissa Taskar," he replied with a sinister grin. "And I would like to propose."

"What is it?" Marissa asked, with distrust still pointing at him.

"If you serve my dominion, I will name you my commandant. You would guide all the armies on Sankaris, get legendary armor and mystical weapons no one has seen, and get the absolute glory that a hero wishes." nodded with a smile.

Stunned, Marissa lowered her sword but yet afraid, glancing at him, unsure to answer. "What shall I do for you?"

"Finish what your uncle ordered you to do," replied with another grin. "Execute the Promise."

She lowered her face and stared at the ground, apparently confused and terrified but tempted to accept his attractive proposal. Then her brown eyes looked at him with expressiveness.

"No!" Marissa yelled and impulsively ran with the sword against Korba. "I swore to protect the empress!"

But he evaded her by vanishing and reappearing from left to right, astonishing her while keeping her sword in attack position.

"Let it be this way then," Korba declared, grinning and nodding. "I assure you that refusing will bring dejected solitude."

Almost as soon, after an unexplainable white shining, everything returned to normalcy. The pine trees recovered their colors, and the sun's natural light passed between them.

Marissa discovered that the mysterious man named Korba had also faded away and sheathed her sword back. Her
fear was still in her insides but decreasing. Her hands still
trembled.

She nodded, grateful. All the doubts she had disappeared and affirmed her new loyalty towards Lakia and the
Jyistereerk.

Marissa smiled as she untied the Sabino horses. She
mounted one horse and ran as fast as possible, pulling the
other equine.

With confidence and determination but concern, she
hurried to reunite with Lakia.

To her empress.

Some farmers living nearby aided Peken in finding a small
spot by the road to dig a hole and place the murdered man's
corpse.

Juni and Jumeni quietly bid farewell to the afterlife as
the elf and the two farmers covered their father's remains.
While the boy showed no reaction, his sister sobbed with
a fixated look, trying in vain to be silent.

A woman, the farmer's spouse, read a passage from her
Sacred Book in a slow voice. She had a large volume covered in natural leather that looked old enough to have
passed from previous generations to others.

In her boyish clothes, Lakia sat on the ground between
two pine trees by the road and enjoyed the pear from her

satchel, a fruit she had picked up in The Lowlands. She sliced the fruit with the help of a short dagger.

With a somber gesture, Lakia directed her hazel eyes toward the funeral but did not dare to be part of the event. Sensing the soul of a deceased made her uncomfortable. She knew it was part of her yet unknown abilities, but she disliked being considered a *sorceress who spoke with the dead.*

When younger, she used to play in the ruins of the old city of Pakiaba, considered by the Molkans as a large cemetery. Lakia could hear the souls of all the deceased inhabitants, the Tannes, and knew tales of each one.

Once Lakia recognized the *Ykarte*, Kasana, and her destiny, along with the Tannes' ultimate departure, she ceased visiting Pakiaba.

She never said a word to Sorcerer Uskam. Till she saw her natural mother's tomb, she revealed to him her ability to speak with the dead.

Her power never bothered Lakia until Juni felt awkward when she talked about his deceased father.

A dagger's quick cut on her thumb while slicing the last piece of pear startled Lakia. She sucked the scant cut with a drop of blood to feel relief.

She looked back at the burial and found no one. The ground looked untouched.

Alarmed, she stood up and felt her rapid heart pulsating. Soon, Lakia sensed a chilling presence that invaded her body entirely with terror, touching her face with a cold sweat that ran across.

Lakia did not know where the fear came from, but knew who he was.

She was born an empress because of him and acknowledged it with dread.

Startled by a silent echo, she turned to her right and looked at the other side of the stone road. She observed how the forest was shifting darker. The pine trees were creepily turning into immobile, twisted, leafless wooden monstrosities.

The echo still called, hoping to attract her, silent murmurs only she understood. They were calling her by her name, not by the given Lakia, but by her mystical name, soon to be revealed in the coming time.

Lakia crossed the road steadily, passed along the gruesome trees, descended by an inclination covered in mud and dead leaves, and stopped after she found a conglomeration of giant rocks that reminded her of the similar one on the prairies of Molke containing the tomb of Princess Natahel. Differently, this one was a pure solid conglomeration.

There he was, outside, standing, expectant.

She discovered an elder. His appearance revealed he was Arankan in aspect, with white hair, red eyes, and no beard, immaculate, and wore strange black clothes. The sensation of fear emanated from him as his stare was frightening, and he smiled.

"You knew your origin by rocks like them," he stated, grinning and pointing to the conglomeration behind. "And with them, you shall know your life stance, empress."

"You are the reason for my life's stance!" Lakia's trembling lips suggested her fear, but she still spoke with authority and distrust.

"Call me Korba."

"What do you wish?!"

"Reign my dominion in my name, and I promise to concede power over every realm and continent in Sankaris," said with a dark grin. "And everyone will worship you."

"I do not seek to be worshiped but to establish a Jyistereerk! I came to bring back the balance you stole from Sankaris!"

"You were born with extraordinary powers and as an empress. Yet, you do not desire the glorification."

"You must not corrupt me!"

Lakia, disturbed, rejected the elder and created a mighty air current that moved the tall trees. A brilliant white aura materialized around her and slammed Korba, causing him to scream and crouch in pain.

Lakia was determined to put him down at once, even herself terrified.

Unexpectedly, the elder grew more prominent as his appearance shifted darker. His red eyes became abominably rounder, and his black skin into gruesome scales. He became bare, showing some repulsive hairy parts disappearing various clothes. His hands and his feet turned into grisly claws. A terrifying snout with sharp teeth appeared from his face, and long twisted horns emerged from his head. Last, he extended his long wings that violently flapped.

The aspect of a diabolical black dragon.

Despite her effort to attack him with her aura, Lakia noticed he was unaffected by his new hellish aspect.

Korba roared and released a red aura to counter Lakia.

She promptly shielded herself with an unseen field. The white aura almost disappeared, and Lakia grew weaker as she squatted.

The power of the red aura surged and almost ruptured the field.

The enraged Korba had his sights set on terminating the empress.

A small stone to the face distracted him, interrupting his aggression.

Juni ran towards Lakia, grabbing her to leave as far away as possible from the monster, disrupting the aura. He pulled her by the arm to sprint briskly within the forest.

Lakia was in a stupor, unable to react, trying to understand what had happened exactly, but as she hurried together with Juni, she noticed the slingshot in his other hand.

Meanwhile, Peken confronted the Korba alone by drawing his blade, but the dragon sensed something in him. Hastily, the elf opened his shirt to show him his long pulsating black scar across his chest, and the creature comprehended.

Korba decided not to fight him and speedily flew far away into the sky.

"Kill me!" Peken begged in despair, dragging his weapon to the ground. "Come back and kill me!"

14

JUNI

"Stop!"

Lakia yelled, prompting Juni to interrupt their forced rush. The boy detected in her a state of profound stupor. Her mind seemed absent as she widened her hazel eyes to discover the regular aspect of the forest with its pine trees showered by the sun's lights, not yet realizing she was already out from that nightmarish hallucination. Her trembling chin showed her terror, and she unconsciously avoided the look at her companion.

"Who was that dragon?" Juni asked, concerned for her.

"Ardek. . .," replied in murmurs, like hypnotized.

"The Ardek?!" he exclaimed, stunned.

To his horrible surprise, Juni noticed how she was getting pale and felt the coldness in her hand. He took a pinch of herbs from the pouch on his waist and passed by Lakia's nose to force her to smell the aroma. She fainted. Hastily, he grabbed and carried her toward a space surrounded by trees and placed her dormant body beside a dead, hollow wood.

He had learned herbalism thanks to the books his Arankan mother, Ashehel, left as a former alchemist. Though lacking experience, he knew enough to take care of his sister's needs and had these sleeping herbs to calm her when she could not control her combative tantrums.

Juni was always vigilant and afraid that the Korba would return. His small dark eyes always searched everywhere carefully, even the sky.

The boy took a seat beside Lakia and exhaled in disbelief. Just the day before, they were in their only home, the wagon, intending to reach Doimet. Two individuals, feigning kindness, killed his father this morning.

Then he met the Promise, the one mentioned by each mouth in every town.

As was customary in Berrem, following the funerals, he and his sister should offer their last respects to their father for seven days after his burial.

Instead, he was trying to protect the Promise from the dragon.

The Korba.

The one and only, Ardek.

Juni was five.

That night, he could not sleep when he discovered his father Kuni sitting at a table inside the small, hoarded wagon. He was reading under the light of a small candle, a large and thick volume.

His sister Jumeni was still asleep on the bed both siblings shared.

Kuni closed the book when he caught his son's approach, as if he had something to hide. But Juni saw the eight-pointed Akareen star engraved in gold on its dark red cover, attempting to understand the symbol.

He knew that his father, as a troubadour, memorized fragments from the volume to sing tales to the public. It was odd how he never showed the contents of the volume to anyone, not even his children. "What did you read, Father?"

However, expecting that Juni would someday follow his steps, Kuni shared what he had read with his only son. "About the lord who governs the dominion beyond the Karekall." He pointed his index finger upwards and widened his eyes to inspire fear. "There is nothing more sinister than himself!"

"Who is that lord?"

"His name is Ardek Korba," Kuni answered with a nod. "He is the Lord of the Netherworld. But he arose to build a reign on Sankaris."

"Why?"

"No one knows his real reason," sighed. "Someone summoned him, and he ascended with all his armies."

Under the small red No Ta, the only one present of the four moons on the nocturnal curtain covered by stars in a gathering of constellations everywhere. Motionless, Juni watched the bonfire intently. He had skewered a skinned rabbit onto a strong wooden stick and built a frame with fallen branches to cook it. Every so often, he would rotate the animal over the fire. However, his mind was still struggling to comprehend his new situation.

He looked over and stared at the sleeping empress lying on the grass and covered in leaves.

Juni recollected the earlier event.

While waiting for Ser Marissa to come back, the elf Peken requested a shovel to bury Kuni's body at a nearby farm. The kind farmer, after explaining the situation, not only agreed to loan his tools but also volunteered to help in the burial and offered his spouse to say the last rites.

Peken picked a location near the wagon to dig and the men placed the body in the hole with care. The farmer's wife read the holy text and comforted the siblings.

Juni witnessed everything along with Jumeni, who was tranquil despite her loud sobs.

Lakia preferred not to take part and waited on the other side of the road. No one understood the Promise's choice, but at that precise moment, it did not matter. She sat there and ate pear slices.

As the shovels completed burying the body, Ser Marissa's sudden arrival with the requested horses startled everyone, warning of the imminent danger for Lakia.

Peken glanced towards the road to discover Lakia's disappearance. She had vanished in an instant.

The elf, concerned, asked Juni to accompany him in his search. Marissa also desired to join them, but he, still distrusting her, ordered her to take the wagon with Jumeni and wait for a reunion in Doimet. She had to obey him, despite her insistence.

Frightened, the farmers promptly returned to their homes.

Marissa searched in vain for Brisel, cursed with irritation in frustration. She deducted the mantis had sensed the Korba's presence, and camouflaged himself somewhere afraid.

Both Juni and Peken interned into the forest. They kept running for so long in so vast territory, into unexplored areas, as they got away from the road. Unexpectedly, they found themselves lost, with no clue where to go.

The thought of Lakia being abducted by a bandit or vanishing because of evil magic terrified them.

The elf halted his run and caught Juni's attention because of a highly unusual phenomenon, more mystical than natural. He lifted his head, persuaded by a strange inner feeling, and saw flocks of hundreds of thousands of sparrows flying in one direction.

Juni almost jumped, agitated, as many dozens of brown rabbits hastened on the ground, noticing they were also going in the same direction as the birds.

Peken understood and restarted his run in the same direction as the animals, followed by Juni.

When they arrived at an inclination down, the birds and the rabbits dispersed and disappeared, realizing it was a manifestation of magic. They were unsure if the animals were authentic or a mystic illusion.

A demonic black dragon mainly impressed them, with terror, before the conglomeration of rocks at the bottom of the inclination, a Korba. The creature fought arduously with his red energy against Lakia to end her. She had conjured an imperceptible barrier for self-defense, hunched down, withstanding the force of the intimidating dragon and its flapping wings.

Despite being terrified and surprised, Juni noticed that Lakia's field was crumbling and on the verge of surrendering to a certain loss. He used his slingshot to launch a small rock at Korba's face. The boy caught the dragon's attention, and it turned its red eyes toward him, surprised.

He knew that a rock, although harmless, was a distraction to rescue the Promise.

Promptly, Juni ran to pull Lakia and escape across the forest. Luckily for them, Peken intervened to attract the monster's attention, avoiding a chase.

"How did you enter my field?" Lakia asked after she had awoken. And sat on the ground, interrupting Juni's solitude.

The boy got perturbed by her sudden question and stopped cooking the meat, putting it aside from the bonfire to avoid it burning. He spun around and contemplated Lakia's face, noticing dryness in her lips while she stared at him with immobile hazel eyes, expecting an answer.

He did not reply. Concerned, he grabbed a water-filled canteen he made with the rabbit's skin and gave some of the liquid into her mouth with care. She drank, relieved, feeling the freshness of the water. "Are you feeling in good health, missy?" Juni asked.

"I can not explain yet," replied, lowering her face and denying it. "These abilities emerged from me, but I made a mistake by confronting him despite knowing my limitations."

"Did you know who the Korba was?"

"Aye," looked at him. "I am truly grateful you have saved my life."

She responded by touching his cheek as a sign of gratitude.

Juni pushed her hand away, trying in vain to hide his cries and the abundant tears that surged from him.

Lakia did not seem surprised as she sensed his great sadness in him.

"I wish I could have saved my father's life!" Juni exclaimed between uncontrollable sobs. "I was an imbecile!"

The tears that fell from Juni's eyes deeply moved Lakia, and the empress responded with a comforting hug.

He finally let his locked desolation and guilt out.

The following morning was a cold one as a light rain fell. The scent of humidity, wet dirt, and leaves evoked the essence of the Black Forest. Two drenched youngsters walked southwest between the moist tall pine trees, questioning if the way to Carretem was correct.

Juni, at the front, in silence, gently pulled Lakia's hand, who followed him behind.

Their feet struggled to navigate the muddy, wet ground. While the boy had his feet covered with moccasins, Lakia went barefoot, removing her leather sandals.

They had been most of the morning advancing in the middle of the rain that had never stopped since the first moment of daylight, quivering of cold. Eating rabbits the night before was not enough to have their stomachs satisfied at all. The weather forced the small animals to seek refuge, leaving him unable to find anything to eat in the forest.

Juni halted and shielded Lakia from a sudden noise. He grabbed his slingshot and readied himself for a confrontation.

A toothless, short man with a grizzled beard and rusty armor mounted a pinto horse that was pulling a wooden cart filled with a jumbled mass of used items, made most of iron and giefo, along with two wooden crates and a big leather sack. The rider stopped when he found the youngsters in his way. "Who are ya? Tinklens?" his voice was very out of tune.

"We are no gnomes but two boys intending to arrive at Carretem!" Juni replied, offended, well aware of Lakia's disguise.

His head was spinning, and his clear blue eyes struggled to stay steady. "My apologies, lad!! I can not distinguish ya from a Tinklen! Indeed, I, Kekten of The Rose, had come after vanquishing this cart from a game of cards."

He pointed to his winnings, but his body twirled while on the horse.

"Could you be kind in allowing us to go aboard the cart? Someone will recompense you."

"Nah! We, indeed, vagrants serve people as ya!" he spun, trying hard to keep himself on the equine. "Go ahead if ya do not mind to be onboard a week. . . to . . . Carretem. . ."

To the surprise of both youngsters, the heavily armored body of Kekten fell unconscious against the muddy ground before the horse's indifference.

Juni approached him and detected an intense stench he could not stand, but checked his throat to detect his vital signs. "What a reek!" complained. "He drank too much wine!"

"Do not judge him, Juni," Lakia suggested, observing from behind, with compassion, sensing the man. "He once served my grandfather and lost everything."

The boy, still crouched to attend to the collapsed Kekten, glanced at Lakia and asked.

"Who was your grandfather, missy?"

"King Vihen of Aranka."

By noon, the rain stopped, and the weather warmed.

Among the things in the cart, Juni stumbled upon a used and scratched waki fur, which he used to protect Lakia and keep her warm. He did not find another one for himself, and he did not care.

They also found some sacks of food, various fresh fruits, and dry meat. Despite Juni's insistence, Lakia only took the usual pear she found in a large sack.

In spite of the weight of his rusted armor, they successfully placed an unconscious Kekten inside his cart. Both of them had dirty and humid clothes.

Juni sat on the driver's box and took the reins to guide the pinto horse, determined to continue traveling to Carretem. Lakia was at his side, covered in furs and eating her slices. With caution, he made sure the wheels did not get stuck in any muddy holes as they advanced. Lakia placed the slices she cut into Juni's mouth.

The warm temperature made Lakia uncover her body and abandon the furs that early afternoon.

Juni kept driving, but as he spotted a strange inclined place between pine trees where no human had been before, he pulled the reins to hold the horse.

"What is occurring?" Lakia asked with fixated and scared hazel eyes. "Ardek?!"

"Silence, missy. . .," Juni took his slingshot and readied for something. "I mistakenly drove ourselves to these woods. . . They belong to the black wolves."

She exhaled, relieved, and recognized something. "I heard falling water. . . What is it?"

"I hear, too. Must be a cascade, but even it is wolf territory."

"I do not mind! I wish to take a bathe and cleanse my clothes!"

Lakia got off the cart and ran towards the loud stream.

Juni sighed and rolled his eyes, unable to stop her. He looked back inside the cart and found Kekten still unconscious.

In his sleep, his vagrant's body had moved. He extended his legs and arms over sacks, crates, and even the old iron and giefo armor and weapons he had taken. His awkward position made him roll his eyes again.

Concerned by Lakia, Juni bounced from the cart in her direction.

After some instants, he found the river. It was small but of quick water. He found her footprints and followed them along with the current.

He stopped. But his eyes widened, paralyzed.

Lakia was engaged in conversation with a pack of black wolves. With a light smile, she remained calm.

Juni saw a large one, the leader. She was petting and whispering to him.

Once she finished muttering, she stood up, and the wolves cast a wary look at him before fading into the woods. Lakia expressed disapproval and glanced at Juni. "Why did you follow me? Do not be concerned!"

"I. . .," he could only point to the wolves that had just left with a trembling finger, impacted.

"They give us permission to be in their territory as it deems necessary, Juni," she declared, irritated. "And they inquired me about the Gesha."

"Do you. . . speak with animals?"

"Aye, return and await, if you would! I need to bathe and prefer to be by myself!"

Juni nodded, ashamed, and then turned around to go back to the cart.

Juni used the dry meat and vegetables he found in the sacks, added them to a cauldron with water, and cooked over the bonfire to make a stew. He added healing herbs from his pouch and stirred the soup with a large spoon until it boiled.

He turned to his left to observe the man with a long grizzled beard and blue eyes seated on the ground, half awake and half-conscious, still reeking of wine.

The boy pondered whether he ever removed his dirty and rusted armor. Merely by glancing at him, he felt discomfort.

But he had another concern. The evening was already dark, and No Sak's moon surged from the horizon as the weather became chillier. Still, Lakia had not returned.

"Were not ya two?" Kekten asked with dizziness and confusion. "Indeed, I recall two boys!"

"Aye, she. . . he went on some errands," Juni replied hesitantly. "I believe he soon will come."

"I appreciate your generosity in taking care of me," massaged his forehead, annoyed by a discomfort. "With these roads full of bandits, indeed, I was lucky enough to find ya."

"Do you have a headache?"

The vagrant nodded as he still rubbed his head.

Juni stopped moving the stew, extracted some rosemary leaves from his pouch, and placed them in his mouth. He then sat beside him.

"Tell me, sir. Are you a vagrant?"

"Aye," he took a metallic mug with water the boy offered and gave a relieving sip. "At your service!"

"Some tongues have said you have served King Vihen, as far as I heard. You have things only the rich and the nobles can have. Yet you look like a pauper."

Kekten drank plenty of water the second time he took the mug to the mouth. "In the finest times, I was part of a guild, one of the best, and we had Kaiden of Estherleon, our legendary leader, at the service of King Vihen." He sighed and looked at the boy with tired eyes. "We were a group of people with unique abilities and skills, but we were a family and raised Keleana, the leader's daughter, after her mother had departed."

"That Keleana, the paladin and champion?" Juni widened his eyes in admiration.

"Indeed, the same one."

"What had occurred later? Was it the Gesha?"

"Many guilds fell under the plague, and King Vihen turned his attention to the medics. Indeed, we were forced to leave Tyza to Ryza to survive, to look for fresh adventures, but with no king," a sign of sorrow showed on his face. "Our leader succumbed. Keleana took his place, but no guild afterward, and we had no more specific abilities anymore. . . we simply became people with no home, in vagrants, always at the service of the people. Indeed, the Gesha came soon after, and it bewildered us."

"You will have a family again!"

Lakia, in her clean, boyish clothes, had come back and spoken to the vagrant with a smile, catching the attention of both. With affection, she approached Kekten and gently caressed his cheek, leaving him impressed.

"That headache! It is gone!" Kekten let show his clear blue eyes entirely. "Who are ya, boy?!"

"It does not matter. I am not a healer but I still can do little things," kept smiling. "Promise me you will no longer depend on the wine for your sorrows!"

Juni witnessed her stunned. He still believed she was a sorceress.

Kekten had gone to sleep again, on the ground and covered by the furs Lakia wore earlier.

Only Juni and Lakia finished eating their stews. He found a bear pelt that sheltered them both from the cold under the white No Sak. They had not spoken for a while since her encounter with the vagrant. The bonfire's flames wavered in front of their faces.

No Sak made a giant presence in the night sky, and not too far, the brown-green No Nunn in a smaller appearance.

Owls hooted. And wolves howled.

At last, Lakia talked. "Did you ever cleanse yourself?" had looked at his still dirty aspect, although it was slight than before. "Did you bathe?"

"I only washed my shirt and cleaned my face and hands down in the river, missy," Juni replied with no reaction. "I wished to do it with haste to be at the cart and respect your solitude, as you requested."

"I appreciate it," smiled. "I am sure some lady will find you very considerate when you grow up."

"I might have found that lady, but I am unsure if she was real or a dream." Sighed, glancing at the gelid moon. "I am still searching for her."

"Care to tell me about it?"

"I was seven. I was picking the small branches my father needed. And a lady of mature age, Casakan, or Casarak, approached me from the woods," he nodded with a remembrance expression. "At first, I thought she was a sorceress, or even worse, a witch, but I noticed her pure white clothes and looked sad. But she gave me a smile even her eyes revealed sorrow."

"Did she say something?"

"—Before I go, I wished to see you one last time—," he gasped emotionally. "These were her words. . ."

Juni turned and, surprised, discovered Lakia in silence and with tears along her cheeks.

"Do you know. . . ?"

"Aye, I know, but I choose to save my words. Long time will pass before you find her. . ."

Lakia left her bowl on the ground and receded to lie and sleep nearby.

Her sudden reaction was unusual to him.

"A match for a copper!" a barefoot, dirty, small girl offered to sell her matches from a worn-out small wooden box as she tried to wake the sleeping travelers. "Please buy these novelties and help me with a piece of bread tonight!"

She was on the verge of stepping on the smoldering bonfire on this chilly morning.

Juni was the first to get up. He realized she was extremely muddy and her torn clothes were almost black. He witnessed her dirty blonde hair, so filthy that they could not see its actual color. Feeling sorry, he rose and took a copper coin from his second pouch, intending to give it to her. He took his first steps.

"Do not approach her!" Lakia, awoken and seated, begged Juni with fear. "Do not move!"

He stopped listening to her request.

Kekten, who had also just awakened, was trying to figure out what occurred.

"A match for a copper!" the dirty girl insisted.

"What is wrong?" Juni glanced at Lakia.

He turned again to look at the girl again.

She had vanished.

"She is not what you think she is," Lakia clarified, alarmed. "Terrible things will happen at Carretem!"

15

ENCOUNTERS

A fter a ten-day journey from the Port of Sarrem, they finally arrived at the Kings' Bridge. The main entrance to Berrem's second largest city was the ancient overpass, commissioned by the monarchs of old. The burgh of Carretem was in constant danger of floods from the once mighty Donerr River, which was crossed by the solid structure. Pot Dam in the east caused Donerr Creek to become a lengthy waterway. Accompanied by his mare Song, Alessandro spotted the over twenty long columns that connected The Midlands with Carretem in The Banks, stretching down to the creek before crossing the bridge.

Corr rode alongside Alessandro on a gold stallion he purchased upon arriving in Sarrem, which he named Thunder. Lord Pan Din had previously provided enough coins for him and his companion to sustain the journey into Carretem. Fennens rarely depended on animals, like horses or mantises, for transportation or loading. Despite this, Corr was adamant about not delaying the journey and they both galloped promptly to make it to the Festival on time.

Visitors from other towns, along with nobles, merchants, farmers, and jousting participants, crossed the bridge. The impoverished ones, slow journeyers, casual traders, artisans, vagrants, beggars, and even some bandits descended to cross the creek and ascend to the city, knowing that the sentinels would forbid their entrance by the bridge.

Alessandro glanced ahead and requested Song to advance, followed by Corr and his new stallion. Both encountered several people, mostly Berremens. Some were from other realms, mounted on their horses, pulling carts or wagons, but especially farmers who had loaded their merchandise on donkeys, mules, or domesticated green mantises.

Fabehel had previously sent a pigeon days ago for Alessandro. It had a message announcing a unique audience with Lord Pan Din and some members of the Berrem's Gathering of Lords and had some instructions to arrive at the Jarrdine Villa on the peripheries. While keeping the piece of compact paper between his fingers, Alessandro spotted the frigid formality in her words, opposite to the warm and revealing conversation he had at the beach. He suspected something, and her unexpected absence at *The White Whale Inn* in Dimmet was odd.

At the gates of Carretem, Corr pointed to his left, and both riders continued their way across the crowded Musician Garden.

The wagon pulled by the two Sabino horses went along the Donerr Creek as a part of an extensive line of visitants, the less privileged that had to enter Carretem from under the King's Bridge and ascend a hill. While emotionless, Peken had the reins controlling the equines. Marissa, at his left, looked amazed at the overpass' colossal columns gazing with her brown eyes upwards to distinguish the end of them, the bridge, barely noticing the moving multitude on it.

In the nine days since the confrontation with the Korba, Peken barely had said no word, and Marissa was concerned about Lakia. She turned to see her back inside the wagon to notice Juni's sister still busy with her handwork.

Since her brother's disappearance that day, Jumeni, strangely, entered her father's wagon and worked nonstop on a piece of wood all week. She was so gripped in her labor, making a figure with her chisels, she only stopped to eat or when the body's necessities demanded her. She looked nothing like the weeping girl at the funeral.

Marissa was also glad to have Brisel back two days after the incident. He followed her scent to walk beside the wagon to her left. She could not blame the mantis for his nature to camouflage and disappear in the most dangerous situations. She also recalled that Brisel was a free-will creature different from the domesticated mantises she observed among the disadvantaged farmers in the moving crowd, especially with loads in their backs.

Oddly enough, Brisel could not pick up Lakia's scent.

The vanishing empress was a mystery Peken did not speak about, silent for more than a week.

But the elf finally talked to his companion after all these days. "I am sure Lakia and the boy Juni are already in Carretem." Peken did not show any reaction or emotion. His face showed a hard semblance while guiding the horses by the reins, with a fixated stare.

"What happened there?" Marissa asked, crossing her arms.

"I choose not to speak about it, as it is a matter of profound intimacy."

She reacted with a mocking gesture and showed her tongue. Marissa found the elf's manners miserable and irritating.

Peken did not see her response and kept driving the horses.

The distrustful Berremen sentinels, adorned in golden and scarlet uniforms, allowed the Casakan and the Fennen to enter the alluring Jarrdine Villa by invitation of the Gathering of Lords.

While riding Thunder, Corr discovered the extensive gardens that were reserved for the wealthy. It had a variety of multicolored flowers and different trees and bushes. They enjoyed the company of small birds, like hummingbirds, pigeons, and peacocks. Girls of all ages, from young to grown, worked as gardeners, and sweat drenched their faces.

"So much entitlement and harmony!" Corr said to his companion with indignation. "But Berrem has no interest in doing the same with Fenn!"

His declaration startled Alessandro while on Song.

"What is the relation between Berrem and Fenn?"

"Berremens and Brekens interfered in our affairs and created a never-ending civil war," responded in his deep voice. "They handle the exploitation and slavery by tikls."

"Why?"

"The giefo, the source of Berrem's wealth."

Giefo. Alessandro recalled very well weapons made of that precious metal back in Casak, especially during his training at the Academy. Only the wealthy had them. Orssandro, inclusive as an influential Head, had his small collection of giefo weapons.

He revised his Academy lessons mentally. Corr had truth in his words.

The giefo held the reputation of being the most valuable metal in all of Sankaris. However, extracting it was complex and resulted in the loss of thousands of lives of enslaved individuals in the Tiunff Mines, managed by Fenn, Berrem, and the Brek Nation through a deceptive treaty that favored only two realms, while excluding Fenn itself.

Deceived by the treaty, the last kingdom in the world had become weaker over time, afflicted by a series of seditions and corruptions at all levels, falling into a spiraling civil war where the Fennens fought unsuccessfully for new kinds of government.

Such prized metal was so rigid that only well-trained and specialized blacksmiths could fabricate weapons from their settlements on the border with Trunk. To make one sole small giefo dagger was a labor of over two months for the same price as a basic house in a country town, to mention one of the many examples.

Berrem had significantly benefited from the extraction of giefo, using it to sell either raw or fabricated into different weapons, giving the realm a wealth never seen since the end of the monarchies. A metal belonging to Fenn but discreetly appropriated by Berrem and at the cost of thousands of lives.

The giefo situation with Brek remained unknown because of its isolationist nature.

"Master. . ." Corr disrupted his thoughts.

Both riders stopped their horses. The feline pointed toward a garden with abundant roses.

Alessandro discovered Fabehel, and his heart suddenly pounded rapidly. She was calm and had an elegant purple dress that, once again, made her look gorgeous. She enjoyed the red roses at her front, smelling some and cutting the best ones with a tiny knife to put them on her lap.

She seemed to be alone, as no one was with her to help with the wheelchair.

"Go ahead, Corr," whispered to his companion. "I will meet you in the villa."

The feline nodded and commanded Thunder to advance.

Once Alessandro saw him disappear among the gardens, he dismounted Song and slowly advanced towards Fabehel, where he stopped beside. She did not flinch at his presence as she continued cutting her roses.

"Welcome to Carretem, master," said without interrupting her activity as her hazel eyes fixating on the flowers. "I am glad you had safe travels from Sarrem."

He noticed some indifference in her, not the usual self he had met before. "I expected to meet you personally at Dimmet," Alessandro replied with crossed arms. "But I found Corr instead."

"My apologies if I was not there," Fabehel continued, placing roses on her lap. "Lord Pan Din requested me to accompany, and I could not refuse him after he has done plenty for my people and the Promise."

"We could have gone altogether, milady. Corr and I could have done a more comfortable journey for you."

She placed the last rose on the lap but never deviated her sight from the flowers, avoiding at all costs to look at Alessandro, immobile.

"Lord Pan Din has asked me for marriage."

Alessandro did not understand why he shook, but spoke with trembling lips. "Do you love him?"

Fabehel turned to see him directly in his dark eyes with no gesture.

"What manners are these to ask such a daring question?!"

"I apologize, milady. It was not. . ." he acknowledged, embarrassed by his question.

"I will answer anyway because I do not want bad tattles of me!" interrupted with signs of irritation. "The lord asked me to be his wife because he thinks it would be convenient for both of us. He believes Berrem should equally embrace the mixture of races in these uncertain and new times. And as his wife, I would be in a greater position to help communities of displaced Arankans."

For a moment, Alessandro did not speak. Unexplainably, he felt fear.

"Have you accepted his offer?"

"I have not answered him yet. But I might accept it."

"Do you think it is worth to unite in marriage with him only for political advantages?" claimed in total disagreement. "Perhaps I have known you a little time, but I am sure this is not what you wish."

"Do you have a problem with my choice?!" responded, angered. "Do I have to remind your engagement with Marissa Taskar?! Heed in your business!"

He looked away and shook his head. With no more words, he mounted Song and left.

She watched his departure with tears that ran down her cheeks. Her heart was hurting for him. Her right hand had some blood as she discreetly clenched it against the thorns of a rose.

Fabehel concluded it was wisest to avert emotional attachments. She thought life was too unfair to be with him, so she chose a different path.

She blamed her heart.

Corr witnessed Alessandro's arrival at the ostentatious residence, allowing a lad to take Song to the stables after his dismount. The feline noticed in him a somber face and speculated that something had happened with Fabehel, but he did not dare to ask.

Alessandro joined his expectant companion.

A mature man of bronze skin and small eyes in elegant leather clothes approached them and introduced himself as the butler. He requested to be followed inside.

Entering, both visitants noticed the excessive luxury of the villa.

The inner golden marquees decorated the corners of the tall ceilings covered with realistic ancient paintings telling the Berremen monarchs' bygone glories. Despite the place's opulence, every spotless room they passed was unfurnished.

As Alessandro and Corr followed the servant, they heard their own steps on the shining white marble floors, where dozens of small crouched girls around scrubbed restlessly.

Loud male voices followed by clamorous laughs filled every corner of the building.

The visitors found themselves in the largest room, the only one equipped with a large, dark wooden table and many armchair-equipped chairs. However, only three men were in their seats and they fell silent in surprise upon seeing the guests.

The butler excused himself and left.

An overweight man in elegant, dark silk and leather clothes scratched his beard with his swollen hand as he nodded and smiled excitedly. His covered fingers with precious rings petted his tiny cinnamon dog on his lap afterward. He was in the middle of two men.

"This is a great pleasure to see you again, Corr," he said with a light nod.

"As is mine, lord," the feline bowed with reluctance.

The stout nobleman directed his small eyes toward an immobile Alessandro and studied him from top to bottom.

"Master Alessandro Eskar!" he exclaimed with a wretched grin. "Let me introduce myself as Pan Din, Lord of the Garterrem Isle."

"Is that the Promise's uncle?!" a skinnier man in green clothes seated to the right asked, widening his eyes.

"Sure he is!"

The scrawny man left his chair and approached to see him, then knelt and bowed, startling Alessandro.

"I, Tom Lai, Lord of The Lowlands, forever in debt with the Promise, offer my infinite services to you!" stood up and continued with expressive eyes. "The Promise and her

Jyistereerk will be my highest priorities. And I assure you that all my lordship is with the empress!"

Alessandro was so shaken that he could not speak nor react. As Corr also showed surprise.

"All of Berrem, by word of mouth, voiced the intent of devotion from nobles and commoners for equal toward the Promise," the elderly man of scarlet clothes to the left said. "I think our realm is ready to embrace an empress. This is something never seen since the end of the monarchies."

"That is why I am providing my wealth to you," Lord Pan Din clarified. "I am more than pleased to sponsor the future of an empire you are part of."

Alessandro, frightened, took a few steps back, wanting to leave, shaking his head in disbelief. However, Corr advised him to stay and speak with the lords.

"Master Eskar, Corr. Please be seated and serve this exquisite wine," Lord Tom Lai suggested and returned to his chair.

Nervous, Alessandro sat, and Corr did the same beside him. They were before the lords on the opposite side of the table. He observed dozens of copper cups, most empty, along with filled jars.

Alessandro served his wine and drank a few sips to relax. The feline kindly refused to drink.

"Before we continue with the matter, I have some grave news from Casak," Lord Pan Din said. "Orssandro has started a mobilization for war."

"War against what? The Promise?" Alessandro finally spoke. "I knew about the mobilization and Orssandro's madness, but I do not know his real purpose."

"I would be concerned, master. I got word from the sanctuary in the Ri that a total war would occur when the enigmatic Elves from the West invade your realm."

"Why?" he asked, disconcerted. "What is their intention?"

"No one knows, but I believe they are the latest consequences from the Gesha."

"Has the Promise attracted them?" Corr inquired.

"No, I assume the Korbas spread the evilness in Casak, and I am sure Orssandro had something with them." He nodded pensively, surprising everyone. "One has tempted me while on the way to Sarrem."

"It was them," the elderly lord affirmed, moving his cane between his legs as a sign of uneasiness. "I always knew the Korbas would eventually invade this part of the Karekall."

"We need to find the Promise with haste," Lord Pan Din suggested. "But I am certain she is on the way to Carretem or here already."

"The Promise's name is Lakia, and she is with a Molkan elf," Lord Tom Lai revealed. "While in Laimet, my servants overheard her wishing to come to Carretem despite the elf's opposition, who insisted on taking her to Salter. And she travels disguised as a boy."

"My best hope is that we can finally encounter her this night," Lord Pan Din assured. "Everyone goes to the Festival's Feast at the Ambassador's Square, even the thieves looking to loot from the crowd."

Lord Tom Lai stood up and paid attention to the mistreated Alessandro's sheath with his blemished sword.

"May I know what has occurred with your sword, master?"

"I had... A personal incident that dented my sword," he said, ashamed.

"I will gift you my sword," the lord smiled. "No one shall go unprepared for this night."

16

TROUBADOR

Kekten halted his horse at the Ladder Barrio in Carretem's north and whistled, then looked back at his cart. Juni and Lakia surfaced to stand up and leaned on the cart's edge. They spotted impressed the tiny houses on inclined narrow streets with few pedestrians. From their place, both kids admired the greatness of the picturesque burgh, a mixture of solid primeval buildings, thousands of small dwellings, beautified parks, and squares in between.

Kekten, the vagrant, looked for a sidewalk corner where he could wedge a large rock under one of the cart's wheels. He was cautious about an accident and did not want to let the cart go downhill on its own. Juni secured it and then helped the disguised Lakia descend. "It was a pleasure spending time with ya, but if ya need something later, come look for me at the Lance Square, lads," he suggested. "Indeed, we all vagrants encamp there for the jousting."

"We appreciate your attention, sir," Juni thanked with a bow. "Where shall we look for our companions?"

Lakia redirected her attention to another spot that grabbed her eye.

"Ya might go to the Ambassador's Square to the west this night. Indeed, the Gathering of Lords will officially inaugurate the Festival, followed by a feast. Everyone will be there, but I warn ya of a big crowd."

Lakia nodded and apprehensively led Juni towards a fountain, where they stopped captivated by the shimmering water columns rising in the sunlight.

Kekten smiled, seeing the two kids' delight from afar, removed the rock, mounted his horse with some effort because of his short stature, and left for his final destination.

The empress' hazel eyes sparkled before the fountain's aquatic dance. She contemplated the swan sculpture at the center and the many white pigeons roaming around.

Although with admiration, it was not the first time for Juni to see a fountain, and he did not understand Lakia's overstated excitement. "Do you know it is a fountain?"

"I know, Juni," she replied, but she never removed her sight. "Sorcerer Uskam told me about fountains in big cities. Life in Molke is simpler, where only the Karekall has the breathtaking view every day, and the only big city with structures is a giant lone cemetery."

Juni could not respond as he gazed at Lakia's back. She turned to him, trying to accommodate her hat head to assure her disguise was unalterable, but he noticed in her eyes some tears.

"Are you all right, missy?"

She wiped away her tears and gave a nod.

"Let's go to find that Ambassador's Square!"

Lakia looked captivated by the long ascending stair toward an embellished building with red domes and enormous gates. She saw many young people seated across the hundreds of steps, either playing a musical instrument or reading large volumes. She knew the place was a locally distinguished university because of the references given by the locals.

A man playing his mandolin on the first steps captivated her. Even though she could not understand him as he sang in another language, she cherished the verses' harmony and flow.

Juni approached her, minding more on the surrounding wide, paved streets. "The way to the square is still far, missy."

"Tell me, Juni. Do you sing?" Lakia asked, still staring at the singer. "Were not you a troubadour?"

The boy did not reply, but his face showed a light gesture of sadness.

Lakia turned to see him with touching hazel eyes and a modest smile. "Please, sing something for me," requested kindly.

A feeling of nervousness invaded him. Pensive, he stared towards the ground, where his father's image formed into his dark eyes, before glancing at Lakia and to nod.

Juni approached the singer and requested to borrow his mandolin. He ran his right hand over the instrument, feeling its eight strings and testing it with a bone pick.

He directed his gaze towards Lakia and saw that she was patiently waiting. He climbed a pair of stairs, closed his eyes, then exhaled.

Juni let his hands go alone to start an alluring melody across the mandolin's strings, creating a perfect tune. He then stopped. "Ladies and gents!" shouted, causing many casual people to stop curious, then pointed at Lakia dramatically. "And especially thou, missy!" He played the mandolin again and stopped. "From the remote lands of Molke, the Promise and the elf traveled for long into The Lowlands in a journey towards Salter," told the story with manual dramatic effects. "But they arrived in the city of Laimet and received grave news of their ill lord."

Excited, Lakia noticed a growing crowd of people behind her as Juni attracted them.

"The Promise requested to be taken to the afflicted lord and found him inside a cave!" Juni played the mandolin once again and stopped to start a verse. "The Promise met a chained demon,"—"and she ordered him to leave."

—"But he wished her execution!"—"She ordered again to leave!"

He continued the tale with music. "Leave! Abandon this body! I demand you! The Promise ordered and pointed at him!" Juni stopped the mandolin with an open hand on the strings and lowered his head, then lifted his face to look at a smiling Lakia with heart-warming eyes and whispered. "Demon ran because of the Promise's enchantment, and the lord returned to be himself. The Promise had won her first battle. And that is the end."

Soon, the crowd exploded into cheers and applauses, followed by unexpected coins, most copper and bronze, thrown to his feet.

Unnoticed by her disguise as a boy, Lakia nodded as a sign of appreciation.

Juni greeted and thanked the people gathered before him, but steadily left, vacating the street.

Catching a quick glimpse, he saw his father's wagon in the distance, Peken leaning on it with a serious expression and Marissa nearby. Both of them saw the young troubadour's performance.

Juni gestured to his unique spectator, prompting her to head towards the wagon. He returned the mandolin to its owner and reunited with the elf, leaving Lakia behind in the way. He did not care that some beggars recollected the coins anxiously from the ground for themselves.

"You were too dramatic, lad." Peken shook his head. "I was not even there when that event occurred, and you shall revise the accurate accounts."

"I do not mind, elf!" he exclaimed, agitated. "Is Jumeni inside?"

"She is in there," he replied, pointing to the wagon on his back with his thumb. "Since the funeral and that unfortunate encounter with the Korba, she has been working in some piece of wood without end."

Concerned, Juni pushed the tied chestnut horse and entered the wagon by the rear. After he made his way among the hoarded tiny space, he discovered his elder sister was so busy that she did not flinch at her brother's presence.

All the floor around had wood chips, and the chisels on the dusty table mixed with pieces of food and a wooden cup with water, but she, seated on a small stool, with the help of an easel, was painting her handwork in a combination of gold and black.

"What are you doing, sister?"

Jumeni stopped her brush, twitched her round face, and looked at him with an intense stare that petrified him, then returned to continue painting.

Concerned, Juni understood his sister had somewhat changed and exited the same way where he entered.

Peken was still leaning on the wagon when Juni returned to the street. But found Lakia reunited with Marissa and could hear their conversation. Brisel only looked at them with his charming eyes.

"We meet again," Marissa said, exasperated. "And now you must depart again?!"

"I shall do one last thing, Ser Marissa," Lakia responded with seriousness. "All of you must go to the Feast and be vigilant. But when the time is right, I will find you again."

"You and your inside, lass!" Peken exclaimed with disagreement. "Nothing can stop you!"

"Aye, the time for the Jyistereerk is near, sir," replied, sure of herself but tranquil. "My stance will not have the same shape after this moment."

"Shall we be vigilant because of the Korba?" Juni asked, approaching them.

Lakia smiled.

"Do you have a cloak to loan me?" she inquired, avoiding his query.

The boy nodded and apprehensively entered the wagon.

While awaiting him, Lakia's hazel eyes gazed at Marissa, startling her.

"As my knight, I have a mandate for you," said with authority but a sweet attitude. "You must joust in the empress' name."

Juni returned with a raspy brown cloak he placed on Lakia's back. Belonging to him, it was slightly oversized as it reached her feet in sandals. Right away, he secured the cloak's laces around her neck.

"Why do you wish me to joust when you have sent me to sell an armor I no longer possess? Only this precious sword is all I have!" she reacted, pointing to her weapon attached to her waist.

"Juni will help you get a proper armor," responded. "And Jumeni has something she made especially for you that has my blessing."

"How is that possible?!" Marissa protested, unsure. "You took me away an armor, and now you will give me one again!"

"Please trust me entirely because it is crucial for the Jyistereerk," her last words silenced Marissa.

Discreetly, Lakia took off her hat and concealed her head with the hood. With a silent nod, she moved away from the wagon and headed towards Peace's Square through the bustling street, determined.

The group of four observed her unrushed departure with some melancholy.

"Let her be!" Peken exclaimed, inexpressive, but his yellow eyes showed sadness, yet with crossed arms. "She meant her ascension as an empress."

"What the future has in store for all of us?" Marissa inquired, with humid brown eyes petting a gloomy Brisel.

Juni could not look away as Lakia's small figure vanished into the sea of locals, travelers, and farmers with horses or mantises, whether on carts or on foot. A mass of mainly Berremens mixed with Arankans and a few Fennens. After plenty of time, the empress vanished entirely into the crowd.

Senses of guilt and affliction invaded Juni. He shook his head and ran to look for her among the people. As he searched every small space between the persons or animals, he fell in despair, believing he had failed in his pursuit. Memories flooded his mind from the past week, starting with Lakia's first encounter after his father's passing and ending with their journey alongside Kekten.

He also sought between the park's trees and benches in vain.

His eyes wetted, and he was about to cease on his purpose when a light wind crashed on his face. He sensed her and turned to glance to the left.

Juni found her.

Lakia stood under a cherry blossom tree of white flowers. She was immobile and covered by the cloak's hood and with boyish clothes. The wind, her wind, made the loosened flower's tiny petals descend on her like a snowfall. Her hazel eyes stared at him inexpressively.

Juni rushed and halted when he had her before him. His breath was fast that he could barely speak. "Please! Forgive me! I should not have called you a sorcerer!" gasped, with a regretful and sad face. "You are more than that!"

Lakia did not react in an instant, then showed a light smile. Surprising him, she moved closer, stood on tiptoes, and kissed his right cheek. Done with her gesture, she took a pair of steps back and nodded. "I know, and I thank you," she acknowledged with serenity.

"Wherever you go, please take me!" begged with anguish. "I will take care of you!"

"Not, Juni," gave a smile. "This is something I shall do by myself. But I assure you will have an important stance with me in the Jyistereerk."

"How?"

"It does not matter now. Until then, farewell."

Before Juni's stunned stare left him with an open mouth, under a new rain of white petals blown by the wind, Lakia turned around and walked again to disappear into the crowd.

17

ANTEBELLUM

O rssandro knew this was the night.

He had his open golden volume on his grimy desk surrounded by cluttered papyruses.

The bloodstained No Ta coincidentally contrasted the light from the pale icy moon of No Sak through the large window, expecting a war—a sign he foresaw.

On his chair, he gazed at a page from the aureate volume the late King Vihen gifted him, and since he read the first pages a long ago, he realized it was a book of premonitions. It was not Arankan, but indeed stolen from Salter. He concluded of its origin from the text in the ancient mystical language that only the wiser could translate, different from the current spoken in that realm.

Orssandro had explored multiple sanctuaries to research the ancient mystical language, but his discoveries were few and he only decoded part of the volume. He had to figure out the unknown text he could not translate.

He passed his dark fingers across one specific page from header to footer. It was an illustration, a bright radiance wrapping a silhouette of a noticeable kid. The page's bottom, with stylized golden fonts, included the words *Nehel Jyistereerk Mudiuhfaser*.

"The Promise," Orssandro whispered to himself. "That must be her name."

Also, a particular word was present in most of the book, naming different symbols—*Ykarte*—. It identified the radiance, but as he turned the pages back, he discovered that it also pointed out to a palace, to an unidentified person, to a shining, but the most to a weapon. He stopped at a page where it illustrated a black-skinned man lifting a mystical *Ykarte* sword. The text called him *Torsen*, as it was the translated designation for Head.

He believed the book predicted the Sword of Kasana in the hands of Orssandro.

He nodded and realized why King Vihen gifted this specific book. He knew it since the first time he contemplated the illustration.

"They are here, Sir Head."

Captain Trasso interrupted his solitude with his sudden presence.

Orssandro nodded, closed the aureate volume, and stood from his seat. From a nearby chair grabbed a waki fur and covered himself with it. In haste, he departed from his room, with his subordinate close behind.

Both men walked with urgency by the Vykar Palace's furnished corridors, passed by a hall, and exited to a balcony.

Outside, on the immense grounds surrounding the residence, legions of thousands of Casakan soldiers, young and mature, both genders, awaited in their respective formations. Each one equipped with a large metallic shield covering their bodies. They held long lances and had short iron swords into their sheaths strapped to the waist and upper legs. They gathered themselves into perfect squadrons.

To the left, brigades of archers and cadets from different academies and mages to the right. The rear position had cavalry battalions positioned before a hundred cannons that could launch explosive powdered balls.

They pinned a thousand long rods with blazing torches among the troops into the ground, giving a spectral luminescence that seemed in harmony with the small red moon of No Ta eclipsing the icy white No Sak at that precise moment.

"We could gather and train almost a million adults," Trasso claimed. "This is the greatest army Casak had in all its history."

Orssandro observed impressed his militia at the time that he positioned his hands on the metallic railing. He felt immense power and nodded, knowing that similar armies were in other Casakan cities.

He deliberately deployed inexperienced children and young recruits on the front lines, recognizing the sacrifices they were going to endure.

As rarely seen, he emitted a light smile as his intense dark eyes studied every part of the army.

The Head was pleased.

The unit's captain, Vasso, used his spyglass to observe with awe the astronomic phenomenon, the passing of the bloody moon NoTa at the front of the bleached cold largest No Sak. He was a boy still fascinated with his inner world, to escape from his shattered childhood dreams.

The Head sentinels recruited and separated Vasso from his family weeks ago through a constable.

His eyes gazed ahead to the extensive marsh's silhouettes, knowing the beach was behind. His superiors had told him the Promise's fearsome armies would arrive from that direction, and he was always wary of it.

He glanced down while descending the ladder into the trench with his spyglass.

Vasso's superiors chose him to lead the squad despite his brief training. His position entitled him to new and proper equipment, including a well-crafted iron short sword.

His people had not have the same luck.

Vasso had to lead a squad of fifty unprepared children. The sentinels handed helmets that were bigger than their heads, chests made of rusted plates that were too heavy for them, and they had to carry their swords by hand because they did not have sheaths.

His fascination turned into sorrow as he walked alongside the deep trench, checking on each of the innocent subordinates, avoiding the powder and ball bomb piles, a few crates of stale food, and a pair of barrels with dirty water. The entrenched little soldiers rested on muddy ground, attempting to catch some sleep in the dark and cold. The presence of the powder forbade them from starting any fire.

With sadness, Vasso knew children were the first to fight.

It was no sacrifice.

But manslaughter of innocents.

He heard sobs and turned his head. He noticed a barely eight-year-old girl squatted, silently crying, and approached her.

"I want my mama!" she begged with her barely visible face in tears as her oversized helmet covered her eyes.

In compassion, Vasso sat at her side, feeling her fear, and hugged her by the shoulders. He felt her naked arms cold as she only had an adult dirty, ragged shirt with no sleeves covering her body. She had put her chest and sword aside. The captain removed his cloak and, with it, wrapped around her, hoping she would warm soon.

Vasso recalled his infancy at his parent's farm, remembered the times preceding the Gesha when day and night were always balmy, and he could enjoy his swims with his sisters at a nearby pond. This had changed. Warm days in Casak were shorter, and nights unusually colder.

He did not even recognize his realm as a tropical land.

As the young captain felt how the girl fell asleep on his chest, he let a tear run across his dark cheek. He had fear and the burden of fifty children on his shoulders.

Dazzled, he heard a perfect melody that startled him and stood, awaking the girl, drawing his sword. As he listened to the music, mesmerized, wary and afraid. He followed the tune and discovered that it came from the other side, opposite from the marsh, towards the tropical forest.

The girl, who also received the music, was afraid. She took his hand, but he ordered her to stay down and wait.

Vasso went to the ladder at the other extreme and cautiously climbed it. As he ascended at a prudent pace, holding his sword dumbfounded, he found an unexpected presence.

It was a young adult girl. She was a beautiful elf with long blonde hair, golden skin, perfect pointy ears, and yellow eyes. She sat on the grass, legs crossed, wearing a shimmering silver dress, playing magical music on her panpipes harmonica.

The soldier boy approached her, stunned and stopped to mere steps of distance with his weapon, terrified. Noticing his presence, the elf girl stopped playing as her yellowish eyes directed at him and emitted a light smile.

"Do not be afraid, child," spoke with sweetness. "We do not have the desire to battle you."

The words left the young captain in disbelief, causing him to take a long time to respond. "If you did not come to battle us. Why the Promise sent you here then?"

"The Promise did not send us as we do not know her yet," sighed, still smiling. "However, as our Divine Empress, we have a mission to accomplish in her name."

"What mission?" he asked, still distrustful.

The captain caught his children's squad gathered behind him, with swords at hand. The small girl had notified all of them about the elf's presence and witnessed their conversation.

"Let my sisters and myself take you somewhere safe, where you may feel the peace you deserve," nodded. "We do not force you, but ask you to come with us in free will."

Vasso checked the forest to ensure they were not ready for an ambush.

"How do I know it is not a trap?" Vasso asked with doubt.

The elf girl stood, putting her harmonica inside her pouch, then clapped twice.

From the bushes, dozens of young elvish girls and women with identical silvery dresses but barefoot appeared and stood immobile to show themselves. They also had similar golden pouches.

"Let me introduce myself as Akartaki, Overseer of the Comforting Wind Sisterhood, and they are my sisters," responded. "We are to offer aid."

"I am Vasso, and those are my soldiers. They force us to fight against our will," he introduced himself with trembling lips. "If you came to aid, please do it. End our suffering with death!"

The sisters looked fixedly at the innocents' squad and, one by one, reached each child and took their hands affectionately. The youngsters, fascinated and moved, dropped their weapons and equipment against the muddy ground and followed the sisters inside the forest.

In the end, Akartaki made her way over to Vasso, the last one still standing. She removed his helmet and caressed his cheek with warmth. "We will end with your suffering. But with life!"

The Head established the Casakan army at the Estos Grasslands between two rivers following the forest surrounding Estolk and its lake, north, near the road to Sostolk, driven by his presentiments. The area saw the establishment of a massive encampment.

He had also received a ruby pigeon from a newly built beacon on the mountains, notifying the elves' sudden and mysterious arrival. Orssandro guessed they had landed on any of the coasts, but by the accounts from the watchers, no one, neither ship nor person, had arrived at the beaches. However, they were already in Casak and well inside the territory.

They were like ghosts that appeared from nowhere.

He was confused.

The Head examined the maps, analyzing the enemy's positions on a dark wooden desk in the main tent, sitting on a folding chair under castor oil lamps that lit up the interior adorned with tapestries and carpets. He put his hands together as a sign of a thinking posture.

The tall young man Dessidere in grayish clothes entered but awaited when he noticed the Head's profound meditation.

Orssandro discovered his presence and asked him to get closer to his desk, inviting him to sit on the chair across. "You should attend your assignments at the palace, Dessidere," Orssandro said with a cold semblance. "What is important that you had to come here?"

"Lady Tasarissa had requested me to get answers, Sir Head."

"My sister can be obstinate!" acknowledged. "My guess is about my niece, Marissa Taskar."

"You are certain," he replied, moving his head and crossing his long legs.

"I believe it is time to tell you," Orssandro said with a fixated glare. "It is unfortunate that Marissa ended up on *The Seneschal* during her special mission to Ryza."

Right after the news, Dessidere was in sudden distress. He did not understand if the feeling he experienced was anger, surprise, or both. "Mission for what?!" asked, upset.

"I wanted her to execute the Promise," Orssandro replied with calm. "I have to look for the best interests of Casak."

Dessidere's inner turmoil reached a boiling point. In an instant, he could not control his intense outrage.

"All for that damn sword . . . !" stunned, he silenced and control himself, wondering if the Head had heard him.

Orssandro caught every word. He made no gesture, but his eyes widened. At that moment, he discovered where his long-time monitor and aide's loyalty was.

Both gave a suspenseful stare exchange.

"Sir Head," Captain Trasso interrupted the tense moment with his abrupt presence. "Two elvish riders wish to meet you."

Orssandro got up and made his way to Dessidere, giving him two pats on the shoulder with a nod, and then headed over to his subordinate. "Send in sentinels and tell them to behead him," whispered in Trasso's ear with discretion.

The captain accepted his request, glanced at the young man, and left the tent with the Head, leaving him alone.

Dessidere heard his whisper from his seat, and panic surged over his body. He swiftly rose and used his dagger to tear open one side of the tent, creating an opening through which he fled.

Dessidere easily evaded the sentinels with no issues, as Captain Trasso had not given them any orders yet, but he was terrified for his own safety. He reached his blood bay horse and mount him. He did not waste time galloping at high speed traversing the extensive encampment similar to a small town.

He noticed soldiers either in their small tents or outside, trying to pass the time with chats or games of cards. They had to be constantly vigilant, getting no sleep.

The young man galloped south across the grassland under the imposing spectacle of No Ta, recently separated from No Sak in the night sky. The wind against his face caused by the speed was bitter.

He was conscious of his mistake in mentioning the sword to Orssandro. Saving his life was crucial, but delivering the heartbroken news to Lady Tasarissa was even more vital.

Approaching the lake next to Estolk, Dessidere pulled the horse's reins amidst a forest of purple orchid trees. Once inside the woods, he searched everywhere.

He found Lady Tasarissa staring towards the city, past the lake in a dark silk dress with waki furs on her shoulders, and though she sensed his arrival, she never turned to see him. Despite the cold weather, she seemed not to care enough about the rotten dead fish under her boots, nor the rancid smell that emanated from them. Her white stallion, identical to Marissa's Ghost, was beside her as her sole company.

He dismounted his horse and cautiously approached her, stopping at a short distance. He sighed in fear, unable to speak because of her fierce and raspy nature.

"This used to be Marissa's favorite place as well Alessandro's," spoke with a strange serenity, noticing the scarce lights from Estolk. "Both were inseparable, and I felt blessed by the goddesses that my daughter had found solace in him after my husband's passing. I mistakenly believed they already had an established future together."

"Madam, what is the significance?" Dessidere asked, unsure.

"We live in uncertain times, and so do they, too."

Confused, he tried to understand her words. "I have something important to say!"

Lady Tasarissa eventually looked his way, tears glistered in her aged brown eyes, and her curiosity sparked. "Please, speak."

"The Head sent Lady Marissa to execute the Promise," he said, gasping with nervousness. "But she perished in *The Seneschal*!"

The mature ebony woman listened to him and reacted with a light smile. "I know, and she is alive," asserted.

"How can you know?!"

"A vagrant contacted Archmage Missar through the sphere. Marissa is with life," she said, sure of her daughter. "I do not know her whereabouts, but she is somewhere in Berrem."

"Did she execute the Promise?"

"No, as far as I know, she did not follow her uncle's orders. I heard the Promise is still alive according to the locals' accounts." Her face showed some distress. "However, we are concerned about her safety. That vagrant used to do paid missions for Orssandro in Ryza, now their contract ties are severed, but the vagrant still believes my daughter will accomplish her mission to murder the Promise."

"I am pleased to hear your daughter is alive," he replied with apprehension. "But I have another concern to tell."

"That is why I have sent you to my twin brother, to know more, young man," she said, touching his shoulder, reminding him of Orssandro's last gesture at the tent. "Speak and do not be afraid!"

Ashamed, Dessidere forced himself to speak with a downcast face. "I have committed a grave fault, madam. Confronting the Head, I have slipped and mentioned the sword."

Lady Tasarissa, with fixated eyes, observed him with understanding and nodded, expecting more.

"Because of my imprudent words, I heard the Head ordering Captain Trasso to cut off my head, and I might have put all of you in danger," he continued.

The ebony woman did not react by some instants, only silence and stare. She was more reflective and tranquil. Without hesitation, she reached to her white stallion, took something from a pouch on the saddle, and went back to Dessidere. "Take it and save yourself," she placed a bag of coins in his hand. "Go to Sostolk and take a clandestine boat to Berrem, search and care for my daughter. Protect her, as you always have done since you were children."

"What of all of you?!" he asked, stunned.

"That is something we will deal with that scoundrel of my brother!" Tasarissa cried, enraged. "Missar! Alyssa! Myself! Even if he wishes to behead all of us, we will fight to get Casak back to our people! Do not be a fool and leave with haste!"

"But. . ."

"Do not waste time and leave now!"

Dessidere assented with apprehension and mounted his blood bay horse. Once seated on the saddle, he gave one last glance to Lady Tasarissa with a pinch of sadness and a sensation of guilt as quick nostalgic memories came to his mind. He shouted to the equine, pulled the reins to gallop briskly, and disappeared among the orchid trees.

"Sir Head, the riders have been waiting for a long time," Captain Trasso reported from his horse.

Orssandro, on his strong black colt, gazed with great curiosity at the pair of riders waiting in the middle of the grassland under the white moon, No Sak while No Ta was disappearing on the horizon. The strange riders were elves, but they were alone, standing too away from interacting with the people, yet the long distance and the nocturnal darkness did not impede the Head from studying them.

Both mounted white horses. Judging by his complex aureate uniform and authority posture, the one in the front seemed to be a prominent official. His companion in the rear had simpler clothes and kept a small lantern in his right hand to illuminate enough of their own space.

The riders had otherworldly weapons. They had scimitars instead of straight swords, made of an unknown metal but not iron nor giefo, not sheathed but placed on their belts like fetching magnets.

The elf of the higher authority had a long slender pole carrying a triangle flag of gold with white edges and had no symbols. It moved along with the light icy wind harmoniously with the grasses' dance.

At the Head's request, Trasso brought a pole bearing the two Casakan flags—one had a sword on a black diagonal and green background, and the smaller one had the twelve petals orchid—which he snatched from the expectant troops behind. Orssandro seized the banners, hoping for a more amicable dialogue with the elves.

Alarmed by the sudden presence of the flying crows, Trasso looked up.

Inside the troops, a group of archers prepared to shoot, but Orssandro intervened, riding with hastiness towards his soldiers. "Halt!" he ordered, irritated, unconsciously waving his flags. "Whoever lifts or shoots a weapon without my order will be executed by my hand!"

The archers returned the arrows to their quivers.

As Orssandro reunited with Trasso, he noticed the unhurried approach of an ominous figure in dark robes on his gray bony horse and stopped to his left.

"I am pleased you joined us, Archmage Carrasso."

The magus only showed a sinister grin with his visibly thick lips as the cowl covered half face.

The Head turned to Trasso, who had a torch in his hand.

"Shall we go ahead, captain?"

The official nodded.

Orssandro advanced, and his two men followed on horses, steadily among the tall greenish grasses affected by the chilly wind, with the persistent presence of the tremendous icy round moon on them, and stopped to a few steps from the elves.

The elvish official studied with seriousness the Head with the reins in one hand and the flag in the other. He looked curious and uneasy.

"I am Orssandro Vykar, Head of Casak," he introduced himself with harshness, then pointed to his companions. "With me are Captain Trasso of Sarak and Archmage Carrasso."

The elf heard him, and his yellowish eyes examined them. "I am Commandant Kartak from Kasnasga," replied with an appealing accent. "And behind me, First Official Partak accompanies me."

"What is your business in my motherland, commandant?" the Head replied with annoyance but keeping calm. "All you disappear for five hundred tikls, and suddenly you come back to invade my realm! You did not even care about the Kingdom of Aranka during its crises and its obliteration by the Gesha!"

"Do not pretend your apparent innocence, Head!" Kartak answered adamantly. "We realize the reason behind this hostility is a sword."

"A sword you will not get!" Orssandro screamed, furious. "I order you to leave my land!"

Trasso placed the hand on his sword's hilt, ready to draw it, same as the First Official Partak with his scimitar, but carefully kept the lantern he held in the other hand.

Carrasso put his hands together, intending to create any magic.

Kartak did not show any impatience or irritation. He was tranquil, but his face manifested a solid coldness that could hide any emotions.

"We intend to bestow the sword to the Divine Empress, and as our Promise, she will know what to do with her hallowed wisdom," the commandant talked with his familiar harmonic voice. "It can not be in the wrong hands. Otherwise, Sankaris would suffer a similar cataclysm as the one caused by Kasana. Or even worse than the Gesha."

"Nonsense! All are tales from invented myths to fright children!"

"As the frightened children you had recruited and sent to die?" Kartak said, moving his right eyebrow in a kind of casual twitch he had. "We do not intend to occupy Casak, but take back what is not yours."

"We will fight for that sword," Orssandro warned blatantly. "I will use all my resources to expel you and take it away from the Promise!"

"Dare you to shed the blood of your people for a sword?"

"Someone has to replace that void the Arankans left. I will not throw away my chance to become the master of all Tyza!" he denied with the head. "If you desire war, I swear you will have it."

"Let it be this way," Kartak concluded.

With no more words to exchange, Kasnasgans and Casakans galloped in opposite directions.

The chilly wind blew stronger, flattening the grassland's wholeness as a prelude to war.

Archmage Missar, wearing waki furs to ward off the cold, walked through the tombstones as No Sak faded on the horizon. He searched for specific graves with the help of a light he produced with his hand at a cemetery on the outskirts of Estolk.

Carlissa followed the mage behind, perplexed and afraid, tripping almost over the place, keeping the thick round glasses she wore from falling, blaming and cursing herself for her clumsiness.

Since the sanctuary fire she witnessed, Missar grew from being friendly to being jealously overprotective. She thought he had feelings for her, but was worried about the possibility. He was her father's close friend, and she could only see Missar as a relative. Annoyed and concerned, she demanded a direct explanation of his impulsive behavior.

Missar promised to explain everything at the cemetery, which was too strange.

She had known him since her childhood. She trusted him.

The magus stopped, and Carlissa did the same. He was before two tombstones, but he neared his light to one of them and asked her to read the inscription.

"Aye, that is Passar Bistror, my father," nodded, puzzled. "How does it relate to the explanation I asked for?"

"Now this one, Carlissa," he illuminated the adjacent tombstone.

"Carlissa Bistror. . .," as she read the engraved name, her tearful eyes widened and gave some steps back, gasped for air, and her ebony face became pale from the impression. "What is the meaning of it?! Why is my name there?!"

Archmage Missar closed his hand to extinguish the light and approached the girl to take her by the shoulders.

He whispered meaningful words in her ear, intensifying her shaken state.

"This is not possible!" screamed in panic. "No!"

18

FEAST

Despite the cold weather, a large crowd gathered, unaffected by bitterness. The starred clear night sky was quite perfect for the event, embellished by the blue-green moon of No Nunn. Thousands of locals and visitors gathered in Ambassador's Square, Carretem's largest plaza. The Feast marked the beginning of the Festival, hosting various art and sports exhibits throughout the week.

The bygone monarchs had established the Carretem Festival to bring all of Berrem together in a time when it anciently separated into nine different small kingdoms. It only occurred once every tikl.

The eager populace stood in front of a large stage, safeguarded by dozens of sentinels in gold and scarlet uniforms holding their respective attentive black dogs by chains and collars, constantly watchful to avoid anyone getting near. Amidst the crowd, hundreds of other guards searched with their lances for any thief or bandit to be arrested and placed in the nearby dungeons.

The sentinels had taken custody of the delinquents who had attempted misdeeds.

"A match for a copper!" a barefoot, dirty, small girl offered to sell her matches from a worn-out small wooden box as she tried to make way amid the compacted crowd. "Please buy these novelties and help me with a piece of bread tonight!"

The people's indifference towards the grimy girl was immensely resilient. Yet, she insisted on continuing her search for a buyer.

At the northeast corner of Ambassador's Square stood the inn, which had three floors. From the rooftop, a specific group witnessed with avoidance of the massive multitude. Peken knew the inn's proprietor and got permission for the rooftop.

Besides the elf, Marissa and Juni observed the people's arrival.

The only person missing was Jumeni, who stayed in her wagon to finish her unrevealed handcraft, with Brisel and Lakia's chestnut horse nearby, stationed outside the Ladder Barrio.

"We are all here, but I do not know why lass sent us here!" Peken grumbled, crossing his arms with a fixated stare at the stage. "All I see is a jumbled multitude!"

"Be silent, elf!" Marissa scolded him, annoyed. "And take vigil!"

She shook her head, feeling the cold engraved pommel of her iron sword with her delicate fingers, and touched Juni's shoulder with empathy, seated on the rooftop's edge.

The boy had told her about the week-long travel with the empress to Carretem with the help of an old vagrant following the battle against the Korba, revealing Peken's confrontation before the black dragon. She sensed his sadness. She knew Lakia and Juni had created a strong bonding in the last few days, especially since the boy lost his father clinging to her. Marissa discovered that Lakia's strange departure had left him with a concern he could not describe.

"They are coming!" Juni shouted.

Over a hundred candles were lit by a dozen lamplighters around the stage. After finishing, they carried on working with the pole lamps around the square.

When the stage was fully lit, a diverse ensemble of twenty musicians stepped forward, showcasing an array of unique instruments—accordions, mandolins, violins, and suspended cymbals. They all wore attractive dark green lederhosen and positioned themselves on the right side.

The musicians reminded Juni of his suit with suspenders while performing as a troubadour, and he wore it until recently. He opted for a more casual and subtle attire for the Feast.

Stewards arrived to carry and arrange chairs, forming a six-line on the stage, before leaving. The three current members of the Gathering of the Lords appeared one by one. The stout Pan Din petted his tiny cinnamon dog as usual.

The multitude fell silent and directed their attention to the lords emerging.

The scrawny Tom Lai followed, and the older lord with his cane, Kong Rim. Lord Rim, affected by his old age, attempted to sit on the first chair to the right, but Lord Lai intervened, assisting him and sitting next to him.

Pan Din, insulted, removed and tossed the fourth chair under the stage, all while holding his beloved dog.

The stewards lifted Fabehel with her wheelchair ascending the small stairs, then pushed her onto the stage where the fourth chair used to be. Pan Din made sure his servants took good care of her new wheelchair with wooden wheels covered by iron planks, and cushioned leather. The Lord had previously commanded the blacksmiths to construct it.

To convince her to marry him, Lord Din got her an expensive peachy dark blue dress that exposed her shoulders. He sat at her side.

The sight of an Arankan girl sitting on a peculiar chair, with limb-like feet, left many perplexed.

Corr's presence took the crowd by surprise. The opening ceremony featured a Fennen for the first time, alongside Berrem's highest lords.

As Alessandro took his seat beside Corr, clad in his usual dark clothes and brandishing a new sheathed sword from Lord Lai, the people could not help but murmur with suspicion. Not everyone approved of the sudden inclusion of a feline and a Casakan.

"He is here!" Marissa shouted, emotional, making Juni turn his head and notice her wet brown eyes and with a big smile. "My fiancé is here!"

She desired to leave the inn's rooftop to reunite with him, but Peken stopped her.

"I understand your feelings, Ser Marissa," the elf murmured with a strange warmth. "But as you mentioned, we shall be vigilant for whatever is first. The Promise's mandate comes first."

She nodded, looking at his yellowish eyes. "You are right this time, sir. I shall await and take vigil." Her smiling face turned sorrowful but hopeful as her two companions returned to watch the development on the stage.

An intense sound of cymbals announced Lord Pan Din's initial speech as he walked to the front, with sentinels ensuring the crowd stayed at a considerable distance from him. He looked down at people with a snobbish attitude. "Ladies and gents! Welcome to the Carretem Festival!" The lord's small eyes noticed an uneasy crowd, their faces showing more questions than excitement. "Tonight's opening is quite exceptional!"

A brief loud music started as the lord extended his hand to greet. The musicians fell silent to allow him to speak.

"As we prepare for great times to come! This festival will have much to talk about!"

Lord Pan Din observed the tense silence of the crowd, which still questioned the foreigners' presence at the Festival's opening. The tradition dictated that only distinguished Berremens could be on the stage during the Gathering of the Lords.

To the multitude, outsiders on the stage had one of two meanings—invaders or carriers of top news. Yet, they were expecting somebody other than them.

"Bring us the Promise!" A man from the public shouted.

"We want the Promise to speak!" A woman yelled.

Frightened, Pan Din gave some steps back as his flustered cinnamon dog barked.

"We do not want damned outsiders but the Promise!" another male shouted.

The crowd demanded her presence, a petition no one on the stage could satisfy with their requests. A general loud clamor began from the thousands in the square.

The sentinels had to pull back their guardian dogs as they growled at the people.

"Shall I intervene?" Alessandro whispered to Corr.

"Do not, master," the feline suggested. "Even if it is about the Promise, your niece, I believe it is a matter only the lords must resolve."

Fabehel gripped her wheelchair's arms, terrified. The people made her feel not only uncomfortable but also overwhelmed. Among the crowd were a few Arankans, and she recognized them as settlers of the new Garterrem Isle colony.

"I did not expect that request," Peken expressed from the inn's rooftop to his two companions.

"Is that the reason Lakia asked us to take vigil?" Marissa replied.

"I am uncertain."

The unruly crowd threw bottles and rocks against the stage, hitting some sentinels and their dogs, demanding the Promise's presence. Lord Pan Din stepped back, paralyzed and unable to do anything. His tiny cinnamon dog in his hand did not cease to bark, scared.

"Enough!"

The elder Kong Rim yelled, hitting the floor with his cane, standing. His shout had caused a mystifying reverberation that resounded across the square, reaching his purpose to silence and appease the multitude. Even the ferocious black dogs were well-behaved.

Alessandro observed the older man of trembling hands recalling the past with Archmage Yasstro as he did something similar. He wondered if the lord was a kind of mage or sorcerer because his abrupt action was definitively a magic skill. But he knew it would not be strange for the lord not to practice his abilities anymore, since old mages usually had their powers vanished.

It impressed Fabehel. Despite her close relationship with Yasstro and being raised under Sorceress Dalehel, her eyes had witnessed a few mystical deeds.

"Let us not delay more, and let us begin!" the elder raised his voice in a normal tone. "Food and music, please!"

Amazed and hesitating, Pan Din returned to his seat.

Lord Lai helped Lord Rim again to return to his chair.

Hundreds of young men appeared with wood planks and trestles to assemble an impressive, colossal table around the square. In the same way, the stewards placed a table on the stage for the lords and the three guests.

Following, many groups of servants and cooks from all Carretem's inns brought exquisite food to the square's table, and instantly the crowd formed into distinct lines to get their food distributed under the sentinels' watch. They distributed the rations in affordable metal plates that were supposed to be returned, although many were stolen.

Youngsters stationed carts pulled by horses containing many barrels at the square's center. They opened them and poured wine into mugs for the excited and apprehensive people. Some did not want to eat but to drink only, and many were getting easily inebriated.

The multitude took advantage of a feast paid by the Gathering of the Lords. The most unfortunate, like beggars or the homeless, were also present to eat some food, but saved parts of their ration to satisfy their constant hunger in the following days.

As the distribution of food and drinks started orderly, slowly, the crowd unfolded to become tumultuous as many danced under the music, drunkards began making their misconducts, and many were abusing the food by getting more than a ration pushing away the less fortunate ones who could get nothing.

No one, the lords or sentinels, cared about their disorderly conduct as long as they were not affected.

"I dislike how the lords treat the people," Alessandro whispered to Corr and shook his head with disapprobation. "It is like throwing bones to the dogs!"

"Do you comprehend my disgust for the Berremens?" Corr responded with discretion. "I have learned to despise them during my slavery."

Despite the loud music, Fabehel's hazel eyes widened as she heard fragments of their conversation. She silently nodded in agreement with the feline's assertion.

Alessandro noticed the three lords submerged in a futile discussion about the length of distinct pleasures they had. "Yet you are here among the Berremens, Corr."

"I am not here because of them, master," replied with his deep voice. "Do not you recall I came with you because of your brother Cassandro and to search for his daughter, the Promise?"

The stewards intervened and served extravagant delicacies, expensive versions of the common food. Roasted piglet, a pile of small chickens prepared with aromatic herbs, a skinned goat cooked by steam, all dishes accompanied by vegetables, corn, rice, fresh fruit, and potatoes. They poured the wine into metallic cups. The lords ate aloud and drank with lavishness, in particular Lord Din.

Fabehel saw the lords' uneducated manners and had no appetite except a pair of grapes to moist her dry mouth.

"Everyone is eating or drinking, but we have yet to vigil!" Peken whined from the rooftop.

Annoyed, Juni grabbed a small bag from his pouch and threw it at the surprised elf.

"Eat berries and be quiet!"

Marissa glanced at Peken with disapproval.

Corr refused to eat anything from the lords as a sign of his dissent with them, although he did not show his unconformity, and no one knew except his two close companions.

Alessandro ate just a few chicken pieces and drank some sips of wine. He tapped his fingers on the table to the rhythm of the music, enjoying most of it. But when he looked at the dancing crowd, he turned his dark eyes towards Fabehel, noticing her awkwardness.

She was trying in vain to ignore the lords' constant slabber. Pan Din was at her side.

As he observed her, Alessandro knew he should let Fabehel alone decide on the marriage with Lord Din. However, something inside told him not to surrender his feelings, and he wanted to be closer to her. He looked at the dancing crowd and devised a plan.

Alessandro stood and gave steps at the back of Corr, disturbing him, and stopped behind Fabehel's wheelchair. At a slow pace, his mouth approached her right ear and whispered, unsettling her.

"Shall we dance?"

Fabehel widened her eyes, rolled them up, and shook her head in disbelief, unable to react. Her heart started pounding, and she struggled to breathe. "Are you mocking me, master?!" she protested, gasping. "Are you damn blind to see that I can not dance?!"

But he did not care about her stark words. Alessandro pulled back and rotated the wheelchair to be in front of her.

She felt a strong connection staring into his eyes. Only looking at him understood the honesty of his heart as a youth that had fallen in love. He was just a young man captivated by her.

So he also captivated her.

Deep in her heart, she knew she desired to be with him, and despite the argument, she truly wanted to dance.

"Shall we dance?" he pleaded again, offering his hand. "May I have your trust?"

She nodded, permitting him.

Alessandro took the wheelchair and asked the stewards to assist her in getting down. With caution, they brought her down the stairs, and once on the ground, he moved her.

The amazed lords interrupted their gibberish to notice the young couple descending toward the square along with the stewards. Lord Pan Din was stunned when his intended fiancée openly agreed to dance despite her limitations.

Fabehel and Alessandro found a space between the sentinels and the stage, listening to soft music. They never stopped looking at their eyes.

"I will guide you," Alessandro asserted with confidence. "Please take my hands."

"Aye," she nodded, mesmerized by him.

With the music as their guide, he gently shifted her from side to side, along with the wheelchair. She had an indescribable feeling of safety as she gazed into his dark eyes, not wanting the moment to end.

Alessandro made sure she was comfortable with the way he danced with her.

Fabehel did not matter about others looking at her. Her happiness emerged because she could dance for the first time, thanks to the man she truly cherished, regardless of the short time she knew him.

She was not a simple person for smiles, but the occasion made her an exception.

He could not stop realizing her beauty and noticed how she finally gave her heart to him.

Alessandro halted the wheelchair with both hands, leaning down to bring his face close to hers. Their gaze was unbroken.

She did not stop smiling as she felt an intense impulse. With a slight slant, she moved forward, and her red lips approached to seal his.

Ultimately, with closed eyes, Fabehel and Alessandro tasted the love through a long kiss both yearned.

Pan Din stood and watched the young couple kiss amazed, but Lord Kong Rim got his attention by tapping his foot with the cane.

"You were curious why Lady Fabehel never responded to your marriage proposal," the elder smiled. "There is your answer!"

On the inn's rooftop, Marissa, heartbroken, watched as her fiancé kissed another girl. Her tears traced lines of despair on her cheeks, in a silence loaded with hopelessness.

Peken noticed her deception but did not intervene in her misfortune. His main concern was the sudden palpitations that made him touch his chest, leaving him to question if it was a disturbing premonition.

"A match for a copper!" the barefoot small girl kept trying to sell her matches that no one bought. "Please buy these novelties!"

Surrounded by a disorderly mob, the child ventured through the chaos, enduring constant dancing and drunken misbehavior. She often had to nudge people to make her way through the cramped spaces, but all she wanted was to reach the center of the square.

Overwhelmed with despair, the girl gave up on the matches and left her worn-out box on the cold stone floor, subjecting it to mocking kicks from people. The matches spread over the ground, becoming useless as countless feet stepped on them.

Despite the crowd, she struggled to walk, but remained determined to reach the wine barrels on separate carts. She hurried restlessly.

A drunk woman trying to dance shoved the girl against the ground.

Her small mouth bled profusely, and continuous drops fell, creating a red pool on the floor.

The girl did not cry or complain. Despite the brutal wound, she behaved as an immutable doll.

A man with an alcoholic smell approached and pointed to the lying girl with loud cackles.

She gazed at him with a fearsome attitude, causing the man to slip and fall.

The child's appearance grew darker as she outgrew her clothes and they tore. Her eyes turned red and larger, her skin transformed into disgusting black scales, exposing repulsive hairy patches. Her hands became menacing claws. A chilling snout with sharp teeth emerged from her face, and short horns emanated from her head.

As she underwent a transformation, she became a wingless black dragoness and wasted no time in grabbing the mocking drunk and tossing him across the square.

In a state of panic and confusion, the crowd scattered in all directions, desperately trying to find safety, but the demonic creature persisted in seizing and throwing individuals to their inevitable deaths. The dragoness let out a merciless roar while also slayed many with her tail.

The terrified people knocked Fabehel and her wheelchair to the ground, cutting off the intimate moment as they invaded the sentinels' territory, and she struggled to free herself with horror. She received scratches on her right shoulder and arm.

Alessandro, also thrown to the ground, regained his feet. Indecisive, he unsheathed his sword, torn between fighting the dragoness or aiding her fallen partner amidst the chaos.

"Do not concern about me!" Fabehel yelled, crawling herself free from the wheelchair. "Save the people from that monster!"

The musicians ran from the stage, terrified. The only sounds at the square were the roar of a furious creature and hysteric screams.

The three lords stood up, petrified.

Lord Kong tried to conjure a specific magic action. His weakness prevented him from doing so as the recent magical reverberation drained his energy.

The sentinels tried in vain to fight the dragoness. Some perished in combat, others fled in fear.

The ruthless tail crushed the fierce black dogs.

Alessandro did not know how to kill the monster as he ran towards her, with the creature still violently tossing people from side to side. The Academy taught him sword fighting for military enemies, but not for a mythical monster that was believed to be non-existent. Luckily for him, the dragoness was facing the other way and did not notice him.

He was hesitant and paralyzed. His mind went blank.

"Pierce under the long neck!" a male voice shouted.

Alessandro turned to discover Peken on his right with a drawn blade.

Marissa stood next to the elf, casting a resentful glance at Alessandro before shifting her gaze to the creature holding her iron sword. Her fiancé was less important than the creature at that moment.

To his surprise, he found his betrothed in Berrem. "Anything else, elf?" Alessandro inquired, fixated on his aim.

"We shall move around with haste to distract and kill her," Peken responded, signaling at Marissa. "This Korba is smaller than the one I met last week."

"But still huge," he replied.

"I have seen bigger ones," the elf assented and signaled. "Please, both of you distract her, and I will try to stab the heart with my blade."

Alessandro and Marissa nodded, and both began a familiar maneuver they had learned at the Academy with their classmates. She made signs with her hand to suggest a strategy. He agreed.

By then, most of the crowd had abandoned the square, and the dragoness searched for more to take. The dozens of dead bodies under her feet were still not enough for her. But the creature easily got distracted by two armed youngsters running around with avoidance that she could not grab them.

Marissa yelled and moved briskly, getting the dragoness' attention, but as the creature threatened with a menacing approach, Alessandro shouted to attract her, making the same movements.

Both fighters, with constant motions around, made her feel confused and undecided about her next attack.

In a moment of still, Peken ran fast with a scream and jumped to a high altitude, natural for an elf, and pierced the blade into the dragoness' chest with the strength of both hands.

The creature cried in pain and plummeted against the ground, producing a resounding wave across the square before Peken's vanquishing gaze. The dragoness was vanquished and slain.

Stunned, Alessandro approached the elf, observing the monster's dead body before returning his sword to the sheath.

"Korbas are shapeshifters," Peken replied with seriousness, pulling his blade back from the dead dragoness and cleaning the blood with his handkerchief. "You never know when one of them is among us, which is the worst."

Marissa joined them, amazed.

"I am glad you are well and in Berrem," Alessandro told her. "I . . ."

"Spare your words!" she interrupted him with outrage. "I do not deal with deceivers!"

She sheathed her iron sword and headed back to the inn, stepping over the bodies.

Peken made a nod of gratitude and left to follow her.

Alessandro understood her disappointment and realized Marissa saw the kiss at the dance. He did not regret his actions, but pitied her. He remembered and, with concern, turned his head to witness Fabehel being helped by Corr to get back in her wheelchair.

Fabehel nodded, glaring at Alessandro to let him know she was unhurt but with minor scratches.

He breathed, relieved.

Pan Din noticed with seriousness the invisible communication in the fresh couple. Filled with concern and shock, the two lords approached him, leaving him unable to react, and they began discussing whether to proceed with the Festival.

Tens of dead bodies, including the dragoness, lay on most of the Ambassador's Square.

The tragic event became known as the ominous *Feast of the Dragoness*.

19

JOUSTING

Marissa recalled Lakia's anticipations staring at herself through a full-length mirror she had previously requested to Juni, placed by a corner inside her tent, to study her naturally shiny face with thick lips, assuring it was unblemished and gorgeous. She tolerated any sacrifices she had faced in the last weeks, but she still had a bit of vanity inherited from her mother as the upper-class girl she used to be. She would not forgive the lack of a mirror before her first and grand performance as a knight in an official jousting tournament.

Tying her spiraling curly black hair so that she would not have difficulties placing her helm on her head, Marissa remembered Lakia's requests to vigil during the feast and to take part in the jousting.

Lakia predicted the tragic night, and she requested Marissa to be part of the jousting because, as she pointed out, it was crucial for the Jyistereerk, though the ways were unknown.

The empress knew a jousting tournament would take place despite the dire event.

The *Feast of the Dragoness* would cause the cancellation of the whole Festival. But the lords, unsure of the celebration's fate, summoned Bin Kam, Lord of the Lake and Chair of the Gathering, to resolve the predicament.

Lord Kam insisted on going forward with the Festival, despite the mourning days in the general population. He cited historical events from hundreds of tikls ago when even heartless massacres occurred at the hands of brutal monarchs, yet the Festival kept going at the time that women grieved their husbands. "A Korba will not take away our festival!" Lord Kam exclaimed to the Gathering while mandating the festival's officials to continue. "We must mourn the murdered, aye. But we shall keep Berrem united!"

His words were final. By law, no one could refute a Chair's mandate.

Marissa, three days later, found herself before a mirror, adjusting the gridded guard over her shoulder on a rusted plate armor borrowed from Kekten, and nodded. At the Academy, she also specialized in equestrian martial arts. She held bogus jousting tournaments with her classmates and used a quintain to practice on Lakia's chestnut horse.

Peken considered that the horse's strong body constitution made him fit for the jousting, and Marissa herself named it Twist.

Marissa took her beloved iron sword that was previously cleaned with fish oil and kept it the sharpest possible with a small grinding stone she always carried. Marissa studied the gleaming pommel with the engraved Academy emblem, feeling it with the tip of her delicate fingers. Memories of her scholar times came to her, but they filled most with closeness to Alessandro. Recalling the happier times with him made her cry in private as her heart sank for a moment.

She did not expect to find him in such a togetherness with another girl.

"Are you ready, ser?" Juni asked, following his appearance into the tent.

"Aye," she turned, startled, cleaning her tears, placing the sword into her sheath. "Is Twist prepared?"

"My sister Jumeni has something to gift you," the boy asseverated and pulled the entrance's curtain.

The silent girl entered with a piece covered by a ragged cloth and stared at the knight with her small eyes. Her gaze revealed a desire to communicate something to the knight, even though she remained silent.

"Is that. . .?" Marissa pointed to the object, nervous.

Jumeni nodded with no gesture.

Marissa pulled the cloth and discovered a beautiful, small curved rectangular shield. It had carvings and great detail in the painting.. It displayed the eight-pointed Akareen star in gold on a black background. At the star's center, two engraved letters. "I do not know the meaning of the N, but I do with the J," she said with wonder. "It stands for Jyistereerk!"

Juni revised the shield rear and shook with disapproval.

"You may not use it, ser. This is a pinewood shield, and you must use a birch wood one."

"I do not mind!" she burst out with confidence. "If Lakia said it has her blessing, I shall use it!"

"But. . .," he stammered.

"Do not you comprehend, lad?" she widened her brown eyes. "I will carry this empress' emblem with proud!"

Marissa wore her mail gauntlets, tied them by the wrists, approached Jumeni, and took the shield. She nodded as a sign of appreciation and left the tent.

Juni stared at his immobile sister, unable to understand how she could make such a detailed shield with engraved initials. Although she was skilled in woodworking, her condition only allowed her to do a few things. Her inability to speak was one of them, and neither she could not read or write.

Mysteriously, Jumeni had engraved two initials in mystical letters only seen in Salter.

Juni was sure that Lakia influenced his sister.

Although Alessandro had already witnessed six previous combats, he was not fond of them, and now he was going to see the seventh one. Besides the fight, the distressing presence of any Korba among the cramped individuals in the venue also caused his mental strain, all while enduring the scorching heat of the sun. Peken revealed him a valuable lesson about the dangers of having shapeshifters among the multitude during the dreadful encounter with the dragoness at the Ambassador's Square.

Instead of focusing on the jousting, he constantly glanced around with his eyes, never fully concentrated, and his hand always rested on the hilt of his sword, which annoyed Corr, seated beside him. A tough group of twelve sentinels watched over them safely at the second level, behind the Royal Box.

"Your uneasiness bothers me, master," the feline declared with exasperation.

"I can not avoid my distress of another monster near us, Corr," whispered, still searching for suspicious activity.

The arena's heralds resounded through their long trumpets, announcing the beginning of the next confrontation.

Alessandro discovered two female knights on the field galloping to the wooden line's opposite extremes.

On a grey horse, a skinny girl was readying, accepting her shield with the crest of The Shore from a squire.

A sturdy young woman mounted a strong white stallion from the other side, letting her squire install the coronel on the lance tip.

For a moment, Alessandro got distracted from his anxiety and heard a spontaneous conversation from Lord Pan Din, right in front, on a fancy chair, to Fabehel.

Since ancient times, the Gathering has taken the place of the Berrem monarchs in the Royal Box.

"Women from The Banks are tall and robust," Pan Din spoke to the left while petting his tiny dog on the lap. "I believe it is easy to predict the victor."

"Do you wish to make a bet?" Lord Kam, a stout, bearded man, advised with a grin of yellow teeth. "Ten golds to the bony one!"

In silence and cautiously, Fabehel glanced tensely at Alessandro from her wheelchair, taking advantage of the distracted lords in their deliberation over their bets.

For the lords, especially Pan Din, the dance and her kiss with Alessandro were rebellious moments. And they thought that Fabehel's inability to decide to marry Lord Din was also a juvenile mishap.

Unluckily, the lords had their ways of thinking and minimizing much younger people than them. Alessandro appealed to the lords to cancel the Festival. He warned of more Korbas. The lords listened to him but waited for Bin Kam's choice. However, the Chair belittled him, giving a futile long speech about Berremen's traditions. Even glad to meet Alessandro as the Promise's uncle, Lord Kam considered him an inexperienced and mindless youngster with lots to learn.

Only Lakia's freed man, Lord Tom Lai, gave the proper respect.

If Kam's long declaration was insufficient, he ordered the hundreds of sentinels to knock on every door in Carretem and the outskirts to force the people to make their presence in the jousting tournament conditioned to severe unjust punishments.

The terrified people applauded and pretended to enjoy the fights because the sentinels around enforced them.

The Knight-Marshal faced the lords and opened a papyrus to read the combatants' names. Once done, left. The sergeants positioned at different points of the field were ready to witness the combat's outcome and prepared with their white triangle flags.

The female knights had small crested shields and long wooden lances equipped with coronels pointing beside and over the line, showing their readiness. Their horses neighed as if they envisioned a clash soon to happen. The strong woman nodded and covered her face with the helm's visor. The scrawny girl signaled her preparedness with a sign.

The sergeants lowered their flags.

The knights on their horses went underway in immense haste.

The robust woman had no difficulties pointing her lance at her opponent. Still, in change, the skinny girl struggled to carry her weapon, quivering toward her adversary.

No clash occurred. As predicted by Lord Din, the stout woman had won with no mercy by placing the coronel directly against her rival's neck, throwing the girl from the horse upside down, striking her head on the ground, and leaving her unconscious. None of the lances struck any shield. The culmination was accurately unpleasant and quick.

The attendees at the venue had no choice but to applaud for the winner. Sentinels coerced them.

In a sudden outburst of excitement, Lord Din scared Fabehel by touching her hand. She turned to Alessandro with a look that begged him to take her away.

Alessandro grabbed upset the armchairs to the lord's attitude, wishing to help her, and in an instant, he did not care about being constrained under the strong watch from the guards. He wanted to stand up and confront the lord. But Corr, by his feline solid instincts, stopped him and shook his head.

In that instant, Alessandro witnessed the Fennen and realized his purpose extended beyond delivering a message about the Promise's existence—he had also come to care for Cassandro's younger brother. Corr treated him as an older sibling more than a new friend.

Many runners drew close to the fallen knight to help her stand and walk out of the field, confused and beaten, touching her neck with clear pain and coughing to recover her breath. Other runners cleaned the ground for the next confrontation.

The heralds resounded the trumpets, once again announcing the eighth combat.

The Knight-Marshal approached the lords and the public again with the open papyrus and read aloud. "Lords of the Gathering! Ladies and Gents! We have an oddity in this jousting with two outsiders!" paused as his face drew disbelief. "To my left, we have Ser Marissa Taskar, Knight of the Empress!"

Stunned, the lords, along with Alessandro and Corr, stood up from their seats. Fabehel was equally amazed. Everyone, nobles and commoners, glanced at themselves. All they were wondering why the upcoming knight represented an empress.

"Is she fighting in the Promise's name?!" an agitated Lord Rim whispered to Lord Lai.

"I have hopes to re-encounter her!" he replied with a smile, shaking with excitement.

Tom Lai's eyes searched for the Promise in every direction with apprehension.

"Is she mad?!" Alessandro exclaimed to Corr, livid. "She did not tell me she was with the Promise!"

"Calm down, master! Let's wait to see what events await us," the feline suggested, placing his hand on his shoulder.

Everyone eagerly wanted to know the knight who had not shown up yet, thinking she had failed to come forward.

Her entrance evoked gasps and oohs from everyone.

Ser Marissa trotted the chestnut Twist. A protective chamfron covered the horse on his face and a white used caparison on his body that Peken could get them loaned. Her pinewood shield, crested with the Akareen star, the symbol of the Jyistereerk, shined with brilliance, and she held it with pride, smiling despite the rusted armor that gave the public much to discuss.

A few dared to say, mistakenly, that the knight was a sorceress or enchantress.

Juni had her dented helm under his arm, and Peken carried the lance supported on his shoulder. They followed her behind.

"How can she fight for the empress showing poorly?!" Lord Bin Kam complained.

"And to my right!" the Knight-Marshal continued. "Keleana of Estherleon, Servant of Aranka!"

The spectators did not wait long to see a strong black-haired woman on her palomino horse covered in a new golden caparison. Her armor, though old, was well-preserved. She had her shield with the crest of the obliterated Kingdom of Aranka, the golden castle of the three towers.

The people murmured, questioning how a Berremark woman held a shield representing a nonexistent realm. But many recognized her because she, as many others that accompanied her, was a well-known vagrant traveling to do good deeds in different realms.

Marissa recognized her as a familiar face on the other side. She was the one who saved her life from a vicious red mantis. She smiled and nodded to greet her, alleviated.

But Keleana did not respond. She showed a cold semblance, and her eyes were resentful.

Kekten was her squire and accompanied her by carrying the lance. When he discovered Juni beside Marissa's horse, he was strangely disappointed and regretful for loaning the armor Marissa wore.

"I will say something in front of all here!" Keleana pointed at her adversary and yelled with a steady and loud voice, "The Head sent the Casakan in front of me to murder the Promise!"

The spectators expressed surprise and disapproval, and some threw rocks and stones at Marissa, which frightened Twist. Despite this, both she and the horse remained unharmed. The knight had to control the equine to keep him still.

Alessandro wanted to intervene to defend her, but once more, Corr stopped him. Fabehel discreetly discovered his intention, and her heart pounded again.

"Aye! My uncle has sent me to murder the Promise!" Marissa responded with sorrow. "What do you gain from that accusation?"

"I do not seek personal gains but to take revenge in the name of King Vihen's granddaughter, the empress you claim to represent!" Keleana responded with tremendous distrust. "Where is the Promise that I have not seen her anywhere?"

"She is not here now," Marissa answered tremblingly. "That is why I fight in her name."

"Or is that you have already murdered her?" assumed with a twitch. "In what river did you abandon her body?"

With some tears of rage clenching her teeth, Marissa requested the helm to cover her head, then asked for the lance. Once she had all, she got readied for the combat.

Both Peken and Juni did not hide their concerns about her accusations. The elf wanted to defend her, but something on his inside stopped him for a reason only he knew.

Keleana also prepared herself, descended the helm's visor to cover her face, and grabbed her lance to point it at her opponent with determination from her exact place.

On an unconscious impulse, Pan Din wanted to summon the sentinels to stop the combat and arrest Marissa, believing in the vagrant's words, but Lord Kam ordered him to be quiet and not to take any action.

"Let the combat begin. Once done, we will take measures," Bin Kam whispered to Pan Din.

Fabehel turned her face back to see Alessandro. She noticed him with a fixated look towards Marissa, and his expression showed strain and fear while Corr kept him by the shoulder. She suddenly felt helpless, strapped to her wheelchair, wishing to leave. It was one of those moments of despair when she wanted to do something but was unable because of her condition and desired to run and escape, far from Berrem and everyone trying to get her emotionally involved.

She did not wish to marry an awful lord and love a confused man. She had regrets about her choices.

Knight-Marshal made a nod. The sergeants took their places, ready for the confrontation.

Silence.

Suspense.

Tension.

From nowhere, sudden and continuous mighty gusts of dry wind appeared, lifting most of the dust from the ground, surprising everyone in the venue, and the crested flags installed in the surrounding poles waved violently. The spectators had to clean their eyes, affected by the dirt.

Both knights and sergeants had to wait until the wind speed decrease and the dusty clouds dissipate. They could not start the combat until the view was clear.

Peken and Juni, from afar, stared at themselves. They knew the meaning of the gusts with nervousness.

Although her visor covered the half-face, Marissa's lips drew a small smile, understanding and sensing the abrupt phenomenon.

As expected, the dust descended, and the Knight-Marshal approved the combat.

The sergeant's flags lowered, and the horses galloped with recklessness. The equines wildly neighed.

Since the knights had prior jousting experience, they knew how to hold their long lances against opponents.

Keleana, as a forty-year-old woman, had taken part in many tournaments in different festivals or events between Aranka and Berrem, but was not always a winner. However, Keleana had won many awards and recognitions in the past, and King Vihen had even awarded her a medal when she was only eighteen years old. She was an outsider but a great jouster who used to be one of Aranka's best paladins.

Marissa had practiced bogus jousting combats at the Academy and took part in some Casakan towns to amuse the population in charitable events but had never been in an official competition. She was one of the best students in all of Estolk and too experienced, despite being sixteen years old.

Boisterously, the lance broke after hitting the shield, and the knight fell from the horse with her back against the ground.

Juni tried to run, alarmed, but Peken had to grab him to stop his intention.

Alessandro's face turned pale, and he became frozen.

The silence reigned in the venue. Only the soft wind made a whispering sound.

The spectators widened their eyes, stunned.

Keleana dismounted her palomino horse, threw her shield, and drew her sword to bash repeatedly against her adversary on the ground.

Scared and surprised, Marissa protected herself with an undamaged pinewood shield before the blade's constant strikings. The crested softwood shield had some mystical field that shielded her efficiently.

Made by Jumeni, but a gift from the empress herself.

"Die you damn scoundrel!" the vagrant kept bashing against Marissa with fury, but, amazed, could not do her some harm. "Die!"

Still on the ground, Marissa could only cover herself under the unblemished shield, resisting the constant attacks with effort, afraid and unable to counterattack.

"Enough!" Kekten intervened, stopping Keleana's arm. "Do not ya see that, indeed, the Promise is with this knight?!"

The vagrant woman stared distrusted at the short man, then returned to glare at Marissa, pulling herself away from him. "Tell me, savage! Where is the Promise?" she demanded, pointing at her adversary's face with the sword tip.

"Here I am! Alive!"

Everyone witnessed a small walking figure covered with a gritty brown cloak and sandals. She walked with calm and entered the venue, passed past the sentinels, and approached to stop at mere steps from Keleana. Afterward, she uncovered her head, showing herself with severity and authority in her hazel eyes.

Lakia left Keleana in disbelief, yet she sensed an unexplainable presence within her.

Kekten identified her by her face and discovered she had disguised herself as a boy on the trip to Carretem with Juni, pleasantly surprised to have known her with nods.

"I am the Promise you demanded to see! And I request you to take that blade away from my knight!" Lakia mandated. "What she has done or intended against me is all forgiven!"

"Are you forgiving her and making her your knight, even being sent to execute you?!" Keleana exclaimed resentfully. "She deserves only death!"

"Then you shall kill me first," Juni intervened, positioning between the sword's tip and Marissa. "I am her accomplice."

The vagrant noticed Kekten supported the boy in agreeing with the empress' request.

To the lords' surprise, Alessandro descended to the field, followed by Corr. Hurriedly went to cover Marissa beside Juni and verbally confronted Keleana with his hand on the sheathed sword's handle.

Lakia smiled lightly when her uncle passed by her, feeling a strong bonding with him for the first time.

"If the Promise mandates you take away this blade, then you shall respect her wish!" Alessandro demanded with rigor. "Now, you have greater authority over you!"

Keleana stared at him, nodded gravely, and withdrew her sword. With a glance at Lakia, she bowed down entirely before her, showing total submission by kneeling with both legs.

"Your Majesty, I beg your forgiveness!" she said with understanding and regret. "I have served King Vihen and King Tahen, and now I shall show my utmost devotion to you!"

"Except that she is not a queen, vagrant!" Peken approached and revealed. "She is more than an empress! She is the Divine Empress!"

Everyone in the venue observed with awe and admiration at Lakia. She had that strange and mighty presence no one could understand.

First, Kekten kneeled following Keleana's example.

Marissa, Corr, and Juni bowed too.

Peken observed around, stunned, and also did the same.

Tom Lai, with tears, knelt and helped Lord Rim to do equally. A hesitant Pan Din also made his reverence, even the arrogant Bin Kam, although dubious.

A relieved and pleased Fabehel placed both hands together to signify gratitude for the goddesses. Her tears ran, knowing the girl was Princess Natahel's daughter.

The entire multitude and the sentinels also bowed to show devotion to the Promise.

Lakia knew this precise moment would happen much earlier, but the people's reaction astounded her. She felt overwhelmed, not wishing reverence for her, but she knew it was part of her unique stance.

At the end, Alessandro knelt and offered the utmost respects, promising loyalty and obedience to his niece, the empress.

20
BLOOD

"This is simply unacceptable!" Lord Kam slammed against the table in a mixed mood between fear and anger. "We must not let our realm vanish!"

His sudden desperate behavior startled the three lords.

Lai and Rim responded with widened eyes from their seats.

Pan Din was standing and nervous by a corner with a cup of wine. It was strange to see him without his dog, and his anxiety made it hard for him to speak.

The *Feast of the Dragoness* and the empress' exposure were enough drastic events to cancel the festival indefinitely, leaving the Gathering in a weaker position over Berrem, as it had never been since the monarchies' end.

Despite Lord Kam's efforts, Berrem had interrupted the Festival for the first time in a thousand tikls.

"Do I have to remind you that the Gathering exists to fill the void the monarchs left hundreds of tikls ago?" the elder Kong Rim replied calmly. "We call ourselves *lord* when chosen by our predecessors and sometimes by our people, but we do not possess royal blood in our veins."

"We are in uncertain times, Lord Kam," Tom Lai said. "The Promise. . ."

"Divine Empress!" Rim interrupted, hitting his cane against the floor, correcting him.

"Right. The Divine Empress came to resolve our world's dire crisis, and I think it is important now."

"Berrem will not vanish, but everything will differ from now," Lord Rim continued. "Berrem will have a monarch now. That changes."

"But what about us?!" Kam asked desperately, showing a bunch of papyruses in his hands and throwing them to the table. "I know we have committed to her from early, but I did not expect such damn eventualities! What will happen to the Gathering?!"

"Some lords have resigned to the Gathering, but can replace them. Even with an empress, Berrem can not exist without a Gathering," Lord Lai answered tranquilly. "The only difference is that we will work under the Divine Empress' name."

"What if we offer Berrem as her empire's capital?"

The two seated lords and Kam turned to see the anxious standing lord drinking the wine from his cup with an insecure look.

Lord Din had suggested it and noticed that everyone wanted to hear more. "Let's open that palace in the Ri and offer it to the Divine Empress so that she can establish her capital in Berrem," explained, stammering. "That way, we do not lose our control over Berrem."

"I do like the plan!" Kam pointed.

"That haunting palace that has been closed for almost four hundred tikls?" Tom Lai inquired in disbelief. "No one dared to enter since the last king closed its doors!"

"We will reopen it again!" Bin Kam exclaimed with excitement.

Alessandro saw Lakia leave in a luxurious chariot, protected by the sentinels as the lords commanded.

Marissa, as her knight, rode on the chestnut horse. She neglected to remove her worn armor or clean up after the combat and followed the chariot once she saw how the guards took Lakia, cautious and distrustful. Peken's trust in her succeeded during the combat.

The elf allowed Keleana and Kekten, along with Juni and Jumeni, to join him in the wagon.

As usual, Brisel had disappeared since the *Feast of the Dragoness*. Juni assumed he had camouflaged again. This time, he would take longer to show himself.

Alessandro's encounter with the empress was sudden, as he saw her for only a moment and when expressed his allegiance to her.

Fabehel, as expected, had left separately with the Gathering. Uneasy of her safety, Alessandro asked Corr to look after her.

Alessandro found himself alone, either by misfortune or fate, in the afternoon sun. He stood indecisive in the center of an empty jousting field.

All he did was watch as Song wandered through the deserted knights' tents, whistled, mounted her, and rode off towards the Pot Dam.

Between the pine trees on the road back to Carretem, he observed relieved people returning home without being monitored by sentinels. Most of them were locals, and a few outsiders who planned to return home.

Strangely, they were together, singing as if they were whole.

Songs of hope.

The Promise had brought back the long-lost solace since the Gesha.

And a renewed pride since the end of the monarchies.

In a rush, Alessandro departed from them and proceeded along his own path until he reached the outskirts of the town, where he stopped and stumbled upon a small tavern. Dismounted and tied his black mare in a post, and entered.

He found a small place with barely five wooden circular tables.

Only two drinking customers were present, glaring suspiciously at his expensive black clothes.

As he approached the counter, he noticed the owner placing a golden-painted tinfoil Akareen star on a shelf between two lotus-adorned clay vases.

Alessandro inquired about the star.

"We now have an empress!" the innkeeper smiled. "What can I serve you?"

"A mug of ale, please."

He paid two coppers for the drink, gave some sips, and stared fixedly at the shelf. He chose the counter over a table.

Alessandro had been planning and traveling since he heard the news from Corr to meet Cassandro's daughter, overthinking countless ways to communicate and see her. Despite taking Marissa's side and defending her against the vagrant, his only choice was to bow down to his niece.

Instead of following her to where she was, Alessandro was at a tavern, just drinking, indecisive.

Insecurity.

He asked himself a question.

"Why my cowardice always grabs me?" shook his head.

He noticed his empty mug and requested another ale.

Images of Fabehel occupied his mind, reminding him of the kiss he shared with her, longing to experience it again and feel her soul. He also remembered his brief moments with her back in Katalk and on the beach at Garterrem, desiring to be at her side.

Yet he was still at the counter, swallowing his ale across his inner throat, emptying his second mug. "One more!" he requested apprehensively.

"Is Master Alessandro Eskar here?!"

Alessandro, startled and afraid, cautiously touched the sword pommel and kept the weapon in its sheath as he turned to look at the entrance. He saw a high-ranking Berremen official who had just entered.

In awe, the taverner and the two customers observed.

"Aye, it is me," he nodded. "What is your concern with me?"

"You were urgently summoned, master," the official replied with a salutation to the chest that surprised him. "We need you at the Jarrdine Villa."

"Tell the Gathering I refuse their request," he said, recalling his sour meeting with Lord Bin Kam.

"It is not the Gathering, master. It is the Divine Empress."

Alessandro's surprise led him to release the pommel and grab the counter.

When Alessandro reached the villa, he encountered many people outside the estate's gates. He also recognized a large vagrant encampment that had moved from inside Carretem. Sentinels monitored them from different points.

All they wished was to be near or see the empress.

Alessandro swore never to return to the Jarrdine Villa. After the awful meeting with the Gathering following the *Feast of the Dragoness* and the subsequent nights before the jousting tournament, he refused to stay at the extravagant palace. Later the same day, he and Corr witnessed the locals' grieving parades transporting their deceased to the cemeteries along the streets while looking for a place to sleep, something never to forget—the dragoness' victims.

But he was at the villa again.

Once on the estate and across the gardens, he could find no one who had traveled with Lakia. Same with Corr or Fabehel.

He dismounted Song and entered the building, afraid to confront the Gathering, as they disgusted him.

Relieved, Alessandro saw none of the lords. Still, the official who escorted him from the tavern across Carretem guided him to the chambers of the intricate villa on the second floor, which only special guests and visitors occupied. Upon ascending the stairs, he noticed on his left were some rooms. To the right, only large interior doors in gold signaled the entrance of one chamber.

Sentinels were around in great numbers from the outside gates, across the gardens, and inside the villa towards the chamber.

Some guards opened the door, letting Alessandro enter. The official who accompanied him requested to remain in the antechamber, informing him that the empress did not finish her bath yet, and he had to wait alone.

Alessandro was nervous, and he recognized it himself. He desired not to take a seat in any of the furniture, mostly cushioned chairs, and preferred to wander but could not avoid his glances at the door to the main chamber, anxious and, by a moment, wished to leave the villa.

He could not understand what was wrong with him. Lakia was his niece, his brother's daughter, still he could not see her any other way than an empress.

Trying to relax, Alessandro admired the surroundings of the antechamber by studying the murals. Looking at every aspect of the paintings on the walls, he realized it told the story of ancient mythology. It illustrated a battle in the sky between wingless and unarmed people and the black dragons. Seemingly, they were the Korbas fighting the enchantresses and mages. The battle was being watched by illustrious monarchs painted on the room corners. He then lifted his eyes to gaze at the ceiling, where a powerful silhouette of a man with open arms came from between the clouds.

With a look at that silhouette on the ceiling, Alessandro recalled Yasstro's teachings. According to his former and deceased tutor, he was the omnipotent Mudiuhfaser, the known and the unknown from the past and future. He was the presumed originator of all the mysticism over Sankaris, although that hypothesis lacked credibility thanks to many academics.

Indeed, he never understood Yasstro's lessons at all. "Mysticism is always full of confusions and contradictions," he chanted. "While general physics is straight, mysticism will always be twisted." Recalling these words, Alessandro's eyes went from the ceiling to the chamber's doors, where an Akareen star decorated its top frame.

From the chamber, a loud noise startled Alessandro. He observed how the door opened in two, and immediately, four strong mature women exited carrying a heavy metallic bathtub with haste across the antechamber until they disappeared after the second door, followed by two younger ones carrying buckets of used water. Subsequently, a dozen small orphan girls showed up with soap, towels, rags, dirty clothes, and other unidentifiable things in their hands.

Then, an elderly Casarak woman emerged in her graceful maid attire and spoke to him. "The Divine Empress is ready to receive you, master," she said with reverence and left the room.

He nodded in gratitude.

Alessandro glanced at the chamber and swallowed his saliva. He gave steps inside.

Initially, he came across cushioned chairs to the left next to a vanity with an oval mirror. The gold and red had harmony with the villa's interior color palette. To his right, he found a poster bed that had already set up with clean sheets. The sun was still high for the afternoon and illuminated plenty through the six large windows.

He gave the last step and stopped.

He found her just before him, and her appearance had changed entirely from the one in the jousting field. She was only wearing a white sleeping gown, her long wavy, combed black hair fell over her back, and she seemed not to care about the coldness of the white marble floor she touched with her barefoot feet. She stared and enjoyed the view of the gardens from one window.

The last king had died when Alessandro was still small, but he heard from people such as his mother or Orssandro that it was required to make reverence when greeting a monarch. He did the same and knelt.

"Your blood and mine run as one in our veins," Lakia turned to show a cleaner face and look at him with mesmerizing hazel eyes, offering a light smile. "This is the second time you bow before me when you shall not."

Startled, he stood up, offering a rigid posture. "My apologies, your majesty," replied, with uneasiness. "Have you summoned me?"

She laughed a bit.

"Address me by my name! I am Lakia. Please be informal with me and speak freely. After all, you are my uncle!"

"Well, I do not know how to address you, Lakia," he stammered. "You are my niece, but also an empress. I think it is a kind of complicated."

"I did not choose to be an empress," she replied, as her face became serious. "However, I was born to be one, and I am aware of my responsibility towards Sankaris. This is my binding stance."

"If I may ask, where is Princess Natahel? Why is she not with you?" he asked out of curiosity. "All I heard was news from you and an elf traveling together."

Lakia showed sadness.

"She passed right after giving me birth. I never could meet her. A good Molkan woman who had lost her baby raised me as her own, but she also departed to the Gakia before my journey to Berrem."

Alessandro, as usual in him, crossed his arms pensively, touching his chin. "What do you know about your father? My brother Cassandro."

"I never met him either, and he did not have the time to acknowledge me," kept answering, wishing to sob. "I can not speak about him, but you should ask your friend, Corr."

Suspicions grew by the tone of her reply, and Alessandro realized the Fennen did not tell exactly what happened with him. "My apologies, Lakia. I did not intend to bring sorrow on you."

"It is all right," she cleaned her scarce tears. "It is more important that I finally met you. After all, in the past, future, and parallel times, we have been, and will be, together in the building and governing of the Jyistereerk."

Her response startled and puzzled him. Though not easily understandable, the profound wisdom of a ten-year-old amazed him. He witnessed her enlightening nature once at the jousting field and again at this moment.

And he could not comprehend the powerful presence in her. "Did you summon me because you desired to meet me?"

"Aye, but there is a greater purpose," Lakia said, signaling with a nod to someone behind him.

Alessandro turned to encounter Marissa with surprise, who approached the girl beside him with a severe and cold gesture.

He noticed her already cleansed and wore leather clothes more proper for a man than a female. Although she dressed the same way at the Academy for combat practices between classmates, he typically knew her for her colorful fancy silk dresses since childhood.

"Ser Marissa, Master Alessandro," Lakia addressed them with formality. "I have a crucial request to ask."

"What is it?" Marissa inquired.

"I need only both of you to accompany me to Salter," she replied with an affirmative nod. "My stance will have to wait until I have my rightful ascension ceremony."

Alessandro and Marissa glanced at themselves, stunned.

"Another journey?! How many more weeks?!" Marissa asked, agitated.

"Now that my presence is public and the Korbas are menacing this side of the Karekall, we must travel with haste, and that is why I am only taking you two," the empress clarified. "I wish to take Brisel and another mantis since they are quick."

"I would not recommend it!"

"I have made my mind, Ser Marissa," the girl silenced her with authority and changed the topic. "I believe you both have something to discuss. And if you excuse me, I wish to take a rest."

In compliance with her orders, Marissa bowed and departed.

Alessandro, unsure, imitated her actions and proceeded towards the antechamber, leaving Lakia alone.

As Marissa closed the empress' chamber doors behind, she took a quick glance at Alessandro, who returned her gaze. Despite being heartbroken and having her soul sickened by disappointment, she had stayed strong ever since the *Feast of the Dragoness*, not just for her own sake but for the sake of everyone, in particular Lakia. Despite her uncertainty in recognizing him, she found solace because his dark eyes were a clear sign he was still the same Alessandro who had been by her side since, even through their engagement and time spent at the Academy.

Alessandro found himself in a state of complete silence, completely surprised by the unexpected re-encounter with Marissa.

"May I know why you have kissed Lady Fabehel?" she inquired with restraint. "Are you exploiting the opportunities presented by influential women?"

"It is not an advantage. Believe me, I have done all efforts not to listen to my feelings, but there is this candor inside I have never had before and only with her," replied with a soft nod, finally opening to someone who trusted plenty. "Marissa, I never intended to hurt you."

Marissa comprehended and rubbed her cheeks to clean the tears. "The way you defended me siding with Lakia at the jousting. Was it love for me?"

He looked at the white marble floor as a reaction, and many thoughts came to his mind. After an instant, he glared at her with warmth. "Being close to Fabehel made me realize many things," he gasped to find the right words and exhaled. "You and I were too little. You had lost a father, and I grew up without one, and we frequented too often as your uncle worked closely with my mother. We liked the same games, the same diversions, and the same books. Even most of the time, you accompanied me during Archmage Yasstro's lessons."

"Aye," she agreed. "We had a lot in common that even Mother and Uncle suggested we get married."

"At the lake with all the orchids, our favorite place, you asked me for marriage."

"With great joy, I mounted Ghost and galloped all the way to the palace to share the incredible news of your acceptance," a smile stretched across the face as memories flooded her mind. "My uncle threw a grand celebration!"

"Marissa, I was still too young to comprehend the meaning of my feelings," he shook his head. "The love I have for you is like that of an older brother to his younger sister."

Marissa, letting tears wet her face, nodded, understanding him. "Are you sure she is the one for you? I have heard not good things about her," she said, widening her eyes. "I inquire out of concern. . . as your younger sister."

"I appreciate it," smiled. "I would not wish to lose you."

Marissa stepped closer, observed his eyes, and offered her hand.

"I officially end our engagement!"

Both made a handshake.

"What shall we do now?"

"Lakia is what matters. She is our empress now."

21

LAKIA

Inside the confines of her small villa room, Fabehel of the Red Tides found solace and comfort. Though well improvised to have the luxury with the best furniture and decorated by orders of Lord Pan Din, she felt distressed. The more she got from the lord, the more obligated she was toward him.

While she had no desire to enter marriage with him, she knew she needed to provide a reply. After she committed to establish her refugees on the isle, the lord assisted by building a town and giving provisions. She owed him.

Yet, Lord Din did not consider her mature enough to make a choice of her own. Under this premise, he would want to take her as a wife with or without consent.

She deeply regretted the agreement she had made with Lord Din.

Breaking out was her only chance to escape from him and reunite with her people at the settlement in Garterrem.

She wished Tin could be alive to help her while admiring the morning sky through her only window, imagining he was somewhere among the clouds. But she recalled with fast sadness that her only companion, watcher, advisor and her paternal figure, was no longer at her side. The Casakan soldiers had previously murdered him during the *Siege of Katalk* in a sacrifice to let everyone escape.

Fabehel then thought of fleeing alone, moving her wheelchair independently if she could, or even asking help from any servant to steal a horse and gallop far away.

Her room was at the beginning of the maids' chambers at the ground level so that she could move by the villa and the surrounding gardens. Her inability to ascend the stairs to the second floor would not let to have a more proper chamber. However, she did not have the guts to escape. Not because she was in a wheelchair or Tin was not with her anymore, but because her heart still told her that her kiss was not juvenile mischief, and she did not want to disappear without seeing Alessandro. She wished to be with him at least once more.

Despite this, she thought Alessandro should still be engaged to Marissa. It was unjust to shatter her dreams of marriage.

Fabehel turned, startled by the approaching sound, and instinctively placed her hand on her leg where she hid her dagger beneath her scarlet dress as a precaution.

The steps ceased, and silence prevailed.

Her hazel eyes observed the dark wooden door, expecting the worst.

She slightly lifted her skirt, ready to take the dagger still hidden.

A double knock scared her.

"Who are you?" Fabehel asked with a shaking voice.

A small figure appeared.

Lakia came.

Fabehel was in disbelief. She let go of the dagger and grabbed the armchairs.

She did not expect to meet the empress in her room. The last and only time Fabehel had seen her was at the jousting field defending Ser Marissa, but afterward, despite both staying at the Jarrdine Villa, she never saw her again.

Lakia had reappeared with boyish clothes and, as usual, still wore sandals, all new. Unlike last time, she had a perfectly combed black braid.

Though small, her presence was indescribably enormous.

"May I help you with something?" Fabehel inquired nervously.

"I am about to begin my journey to Salter, but you were not there with the others for my departure," replied with calmness. "I came to bring you outside."

Her answer left her speechless. "Do you ever know that this is the first time you have met me?"

"Aye," nodded. "But I have known you for so long."

"How?"

"My mother has revealed to me all about you."

"My apologies, but I do not comprehend you," Fabehel said, shaking her head. "As far as the words have told to me, you never met your mother."

"Aye, you are correct. But my mother, Princess Natahel, the one you have called sister, even after her departure, I sensed her."

"And she. . . told you about me?" she asked, skeptical. "What has she told you?"

"You were her *Little Snail*. She always missed you, even in far realms."

Fabehel could not hold back her tears and covered her face with both hands. Finally, she released all her locked emotions and resentments, granting the liberation she deserved after all these years.

Understanding and with serenity, Lakia approached her to touch her shoulder in consolation.

Fabehel kept sobbing, holding onto her tightly and crying with her face pressed against the girl's chest.

Moved but with a light smile because her purpose was done, Lakia caressed her red hair.

Eventually, Fabehel calmed down after a while, and the empress gave her a white handkerchief to clean her face.

"My apologies. . .," she cleared her throat. "I am not an easy person to weep as I have done now."

"That is all right, Lady Fabehel!" said energetically. "Let me take you outside so you can give me farewells!"

Lakia went behind the wheelchair and pushed her toward the door.

"I shall not let an empress push me!" she demanded. "Please let me summon a servant."

The girl stopped and spoke.

"I might be an empress, but I am the greatest servant, and no one will stop me from serving my people."

Fabehel's eyes widened, confirming her unique wisdom.

"I. . .," replied, unable to find the right words.

"Do not concern yourself about Lord Pan Din now that you have found me. And please do not close yourself to Master Alessandro."

Lakia pushed the wheelchair, surprising Fabehel as they left the room.

Marissa hoped her scent would lure Brisel out of hiding, as she planted her sword on the ground and the knight knelt expectantly to the south.

Still, she could not help but feel despair. Six days had already passed from the *Feast of the Dragoness*, and no signs of him.

Her eyes seemed to catch some hopeful excitement when a mantis appeared from between the garden's bushes and stood up with a smile, but a disappointment took over when she saw Peken behind it.

The elf guided the mantis, and both approached the area. It was not Brisel, but a different one, and unusual. It had no antennas, and the color was brownish but still close to green.

Marissa shook her head with disapproval. She understood Peken had gotten it from a market in Carretem.

The mantis stopped and hissed, showing paralysis as its round eyes observed, afraid of the more than a dozen waiting persons outside the villa under the searing sun of Sankaris approaching noon. Peken took something from his pouch and gave it to the mantis's mouth to help it relax. The elf then deviated his yellowish eyes to look at Marissa, noticing her curiosity. "I got this mantis from a farmer who urgently needed to return to The Banks. He offered me a good price for it."

"But look at this mantis!" complained with a bit of compassion. "Someone mangled its antennas!"

"Once a nymph is born or sold to a farmer, the antennas are mangled," replied with severity. "Remember that in Berrem, they domesticate mantises and put them to use in farming."

Alessandro overheard Peken while talking to Corr and joined him and Marissa. "What is the purpose of having the antennas mangled?"

"The antennas help them follow scents and hide by camouflage, master. Without them, they are only simply defenseless animals."

"I have told you that Brisel is special! And smart!" Marissa exclaimed.

"I might have something that will bring him back," Peken said, searching his pouch to extract a small package covered with linen. "The domesticated mantises eat mostly leaves, but free-will ones follow their favorite scents. . . and special food."

Marissa took the package and slowly opened it to discover a handful of live crickets and caterpillars. She comprehended the purpose and nodded, then went back to her sword. She squatted down, placed the insects on the ground with the linen piece, and awaited Brisel, gazing towards the south once more.

Alessandro observed the enthusiastic Marissa.

The elf kept the bought mantis with a rope around its neck. "Even if we have this mantis you would mount, it needs a guide. If Brisel does not come, there is no way you and Lakia could arrive at Salter in one day."

"I would have to take her on my mare, Song. But the journey would take days." Alessandro adopted a thinking posture. "Where shall we go?"

"From that sword Ser Marissa placed," Peken replied, pointing. "All the way south until Seled Post, then east through *The Pass,* a route between the Holy Mountains and Cayderr Range, considered by many as the natural entrance to Salter."

Lakia was more comfortable staying by the stables on a haystack and observing Alessandro talk with Peken among a small crowd, rather than being attended by servants in a luxurious chamber, despite being the empress. She disliked all the attention.

Juni pleasantly surprised Lakia by offering her three pears, which were her favorite fruit, since she arrived in Berrem. With gratitude, she placed them in the satchel Peken had given her in Akiaba. They exchanged no words, only smiles and stares, and he sat at her side.

Lakia continued to watch Alessandro, and her eyes fell upon a peculiar sword in his sheath. She realized it was the same one that belonged to Lord Tom Lai, which she remembered from her stay in Laimet. She then deviated her eyes to find at her right Jumeni, seated on a bunch of logs beside the stable's entrance, noticing her concentration on carving some small wooden piece with the help of a small knife.

A sudden whisper startled Juni as Lakia spoke into his ear. At first, he was stunned by the unexpected request, but in the end, he agreed. She also whispered to Jumeni after leaving the haystack.

The silent girl stopped her activity, and her eyes widened. She never looked at Lakia but nodded and, as if nothing happened, returned to work in her wooden sculpture.

Afterward, Lakia discovered the Gathering standing by the corner on the other side of the stable.

They were watchful, wishing for something from the empress.

She approached them.

"Divine Empress!" Lord Bin Kam exclaimed, with a bow that bothered her. "We will await you at the Dri after your missive in Salter."

Lakia distrusted the lords. She knew they were corrupted, specifically sensing darkness in one, although it was unclear who was, and foresaw a grim future for the Gathering. She knew the reason for their motives, yet she asked. "What do you intend to do with me?"

They looked nervous.

"Berrem is ready to embrace you as our empress, and we will help you establish the Jyistereerk at the Ri, offering the ancient palace that once belonged to monarchs as your home," Lord Kam spoke with excessive reverence.

As the empress glared at each lord, tried again to identify the one with a shadowed soul and also observed their impatience for an answer. "The true monarchs have expressed their desire for me to occupy that throne, but there is one condition." Her response left the Gathering confused. She searched everywhere until she found Keleana and Kekten far among the bushes, waved them as a request to join her.

At first, the two vagrants looked at themselves skeptically but approached the girl under the lords' amazed look.

"I wish the vagrants to be the Imperial Guard," she mandated with authority, surprising everyone. "Keleana of Estherleon shall be my marshal and Kekten of The Rose shall be my admiral."

Keleana and Kekten, stunned, responded by kneeling before her as a gesture of gratitude.

The Gathering, impacted, could not speak or react. Lord Tom Lai barely nodded, representing the other lords with a smile, followed by Rim's silent approval.

"Marshal Keleana, Admiral Kekten, please stand and hear me!"

The two vagrants obeyed her and, recalling old times in Aranka, saluted her with an open hand on their chests, placing them on the hearts with a pinch of nostalgia—the *Arankan Soul Salute.*

"Gather all the vagrants and meet me at Seled Post after my ascension. Take them away from The Wilds and let the sentinels deal with the menace in Trunk!"

"But...!" Lord Pan Din almost protested.

"In all fairness, the sentinels should defend their realm! Not displaced outsiders that once were heroes!" the empress interrupted with noted authority and wisdom. "The vagrants deserve a family, and I am giving one!"

Except for Marissa and Jumeni, everyone witnessed Lakia's demands with the Gathering.

Fabehel noticed and saw a chance when Lord Din got distracted by the Gathering and the empress' request. She gestured to Corr, the closer one, to call Alessandro.

The feline's whisper to Alessandro compelled him to turn and approach Fabehel.

"May I help you with something, milady?" he said, wondering at her intention.

"I wished to say something, master," responded with apparent coldness. "I do not approve of such a daring embrace without my permission!"

He was silent for an instant. "Do you mean that... kiss?" his answer came with a scratch on his head.

Fabehel's cheeks blushed, and her eyes descended. Removing it from the dress' sleeve, she presented him a white handkerchief.

"Please take it as a memento of mine!" although she still spoke with harshness, her eyes showed warmth. "I beg for your safety in this journey and bring it back to me."

Alessandro took the handkerchief. "While I'm gone, please take care of Song. If that mantis appears."

Marissa screamed with excitement, making everyone turn their heads.

Brisel had appeared.

"After all, I will take care of your mare," Fabehel assured.

22

KORBEEN

The scorching sun dominated Estos Grassland, with no wind to stir the tall grasses. In the middle of the daylight, a battle was about to begin, menacing the harmony of the rich panorama as a flock of white herons departed the nearby Gustolk Lagoon.

Orssandro studied across the grassland with the aid of a spyglass. With severity, he noticed the thousands of elves gathered at the opposite end, mounted on their horses, and saw that only the front line, behind Commandant Kartak, held golden flags.

The Head saw the peculiar formation from the Kasnasgos, known as the Elves of the West, as a clever tactic. All elvish soldiers were on white horses, only white and no other color or breed, with scimitars and no shields or other weapons, no archers, no mages, no ballistas, not even catapults.

An army, possessing everything the elves lacked, waited behind the Head. Despite this, he knew the Casakans would face an unfamiliar force, yet he did not understand how the Kasnasgos arrived at Casak without being noticed, like ghosts, and deep within the realm instead of a coastal landing.

Returning the spyglass to his black horse's saddle pouch, Orssandro called Captain Trasso to his side. He revised the plan with his subordinate and requested to take positions.

Trasso, bearing only the flag of the orchid, galloped among the troops to get ready and instructed his officials.

Orssandro veered right and pleaded with the ominous Carrasso on his skeletal steed to withhold his magic and use it only as a last resort. The dark archmage nodded in agreement.

Trasso returned from his duty and spoke.

"Are we going to be the first, Sir Head?"

"In this battle, aye," he replied with solid determination. "They are the ones who invaded our realm."

"I bet it will be an easy battle," Trasso grinned. "We have a significant advantage over them!"

"I would not be that sure, captain," he said, glaring at his opponents. "They are an otherworldly army!"

From afar, Kartak's yellow eyes witnessed the attack formation from the Casakans. He summoned the First Official Partak by lifting his right hand and did a sign of language communication only the Kasnasgos could understand. His subordinate approached. "Are our men ready for a preventive stance?"

"They are, commandant," he replied, showing un-easiness. "Are we going to use our scimitars?"

"We will confront them, aye," Kartak answered, still glaring at his opponents. "But not to deprive their lives as they only follow the Head's orders."

"What if they try to deprive ours?"

The commandant looked to see Partak with annoy-ance.

"We shall not oppose the Divine Empress' nature!"

"Why the Divine Empress?! You talk about her like we knew her, but we do not!"

"We do, brother," Kartak returned to glance at the windless grassland. "Overseer Akartaki and her sisters have spoken with the goddesses and revealed the true empress' nature."

"What is her nature, then?"

"A Nehel among us," Kartak replied with his casual twitch of lifting his eyebrow, then deviated from the subject. "Get ready, my brother, that Casakans are coming now!"

At Orssandro's sign, Trasso lifted the fist, upholding the beginning of an offensive. As planned, the thousands in the Casakan cavalry, led by the Head, dashed on the horses as they drew their swords, determined to give the first blow against the opponents. Behind, soldiers with tall shields and long lances ran, followed by mages on horses.

The Kasnasgos responded altogether with a swift galloping, lifting their scimitars.

Carrasso and his mages invoked their powers to create different weapons they wished with natural elements. The dark archmage had made a fire sword. Because they did not use magic yet, but opted for melee tactics on their own terms.

With sign language, Commandant Kartak ordered all his men to begin a skill. They waved their scimitars into the air with great harmony and perfection, as if they were dancing while galloping on their horses.

The Casakans, while approaching the enemy, did not avoid their amazingness before the Kasnasgos' unusual actions. There were even those who mockingly laughed, thinking the elves were performing a war ceremony.

The elves created some invisible field around themselves that was, in a brief instant, visible. It surprised the opponents.

The two forces clashed.

Wisely, the Kasnasgos only placed the scimitars back on their legs and went around the adversaries with no fear or hate.

The Casakans, by all means, tried to attack them, but whatever weapon they used, any intent, was useless. The swords bounced against their fields, and the arrows and lances deviated.

Affected by the impotence to cause them any harm, the mages, especially Carrasso, abandoned their melee weapons and used their magic, but still futile.

The elves only kept moving around with their horses, observing how their opponents attacked them, but warmth and respect for the enemy showed in their yellowish eyes. They had no intention of claiming any life.

In despair, Orssandro approached with madness, repeatedly bashing Kartak with his sword.

The commandant observed surprised the Head's insane behavior as he felt protected under his invisible field, unharmed, understanding that it was an ominous sign of something about to happen.

The elf had seen that kind of delusion before, during the *Wars in the West*, and he knew the answer.

Alarmed, Kartak lifted his hand, trying to communicate with signs to his cavalry. However, it was a vain effort since everyone was busy evading or moving around the opponents. Yet, he still had a crazed Orssandro striking him, afraid that losing his concentration would weak the field.

The Head's insanity was not his fault.

Kartak's eyes looked up with fear, predicting a somber presage.

The shadow filled the sun.

A curtain of blackness covered the totality of the skies.

Everything on the land disappeared from any sight or light.

Darkness, total darkness.

Screams and gasps.

Silence.

The darkness shattered into countless flying black dragons. Korbas descended and ruthlessly assaulted each warrior without discrimination. The dreadful creatures had the power to penetrate the elves' invisible fields.

Casakans and Kasnasgos changed their objectives to protect themselves, but the large number of aggressive giant dragons outnumbered and overpowered them.

The fierce beasts seized their prey using their snouts and claws, breaking them like fragile figurines.

Like many experienced Kasnasgos that had fought the Korbas in the past, Kartak used his scimitar and fought them well. Knowing their weak points, he executed them by piercing his weapon under their necks.

It was fortunate that these dragons, although towering at the height of three men each, could be dealt with proper training. The veterans had seen bigger ones than them and harder to kill.

After slaying two dragons, the unscathed Kartak observed with terror how the inexperienced recruits had fallen under the Korbas' claws and teeth, and Casakans were not the exception.

Bit by bit, the grassland changed into a field blanketed with corpses.

With a quick look, the commandant spotted Trasso battling two creatures, swinging his blade up to strike them. In the end, his arm got torn from his body while holding the weapon by the clamp of a dragon's snout, causing him to fall from the horse and scream in agony. Accidentally hiding in the tall grass spared his life from the Korbas' rage.

Kartak looked to his right and saw Orssandro engaged in a fight on foot, trying to stab a Korba that was avoiding him. Another fierce creature arrived behind him, preparing its sharp tail.

"Turn around, Head!" Kartak screamed.

Orssandro turned to see the commandant with a clueless look.

At that instant, the demonic dragon's tail crossed the Head's body from back to chest and left him abandoned on the ground.

With courage and fury, Kartak urged his horse to gallop faster, leapt from the saddle, landed on the monster, stabbed its neck with his scimitar, killed it, and ran towards the other dragon.

The commandant arrived late.

With widened eyes in panic, a young Casakan soldier used his long lance to execute the Korba with fear, kept his weapon against the dead creature's body, and observed Kartak in surprise.

The elf, concerned, checked on Orssandro.

Although unconscious and severely wounded, the Head was still alive. His breath was weak and bled.

"Leave it and come to help me, lad!" Kartak yelled at the young soldier. "Come with haste!"

The soldier nodded. Trembling ran towards the elf, where he crouched and helped to lift the wounded Orssandro, took him to the commandant's white horse, and sat him on the saddle.

Kartak asked the soldier to get a horse while he mounted behind Orssandro.

The confrontation with winged demonic Korbas continued, growing fiercer by the moment.

The soldier found a lone gray equine. He mounted and followed Kartak as both went extremely briskly between dragons and soldiers still involved in their unequal fights.

Most elves and men fell lifeless on the grassland than Korbas.

Commandant Kartak pulled the reins while keeping the bleeding Orssandro by his chest, safety against his body, and stopped his horse. He searched around in the middle of brutal chaos and asked the young soldier beside him, agitated. "Is there a safe place to take refuge?!"

"There!" the lad pointed east. "There is an old abandoned palace by the Gustolk Lagoon!"

The horses ran as fast as possible, evading any Korba they encountered. Kartak could not have his scimitar when he had Orssandro with him and risking lives from any dragon.

They escaped the bloody battlefield and enter the lagoon's low levels surrounded by tall green grasses. They soon discovered a three-level stone palace with a ghostly appearance.

Carefully, Kartak laid Orssandro on the cold floor in a dark corner of a deserted palace room.

The young soldier came with some dry hay he spotted on the way and made a small bonfire with the purpose of warming, at least to try, the shivering Head.

In the firelight, the elf saw the seriousness of his injury in the middle of his chest, observing the blood growing darker and thicker.

Orssandro opened his eyes, trembling from the inner cold, laying, gasping, and trying to breathe, but he knew his fast wheezing was a sign of his end's proximity as a human being. He glanced to discover Kartak at his side and noticed sorrow on his face. "I will become one. Right?" he said in a weak whisper.

"Forgive me, Sir Head," Kartak replied with profound sadness. "I tried to save your life."

"Is he going to die?" concerned, the young soldier asked naively.

"I am afraid it is worse," the elf shook his head. "He is becoming a Korbeen."

"An undead demon," the Head answered, serene. "What is your name, lad?"

"I am Diesso of Kokork, sir. Lancer from the thirty-fourth squadron."

Orssandro displayed a rare smile, as the young soldier reminded him of Alessandro and made him long for his company.

He let tears fall as sudden regrets took over him. He wished for forgiveness from Alessandro, his sister Tasarissa, his niece Marissa, and especially Casak for his grave mistakes. But he understood it was too late to right his wrong deeds.

Exhausted, Orssandro removed one of his many medals splattered with dark red blood, a specific one, and placed it on Diesso's hand.

The young lancer observed the special medal, engraved with the symbol of a twelve leaves orchid, and looked perplexed at the Head.

"Go to Estolk and meet Missar at *The Lake's Corner*," he mandated, choking. "Tell him to take my place. . . Lead the Assembly. . . And give him this medal as proof."

"Will do, sir!"

Orssandro turned to Kartak.

"Make sure the Divine Empress has the sword."

"Aye, sir!"

"Now leave!" he mandated wheezy.

The Commandant Kartak nodded in agreement. He placed his hand on Orssandro's head and said some quick prayers in an intelligible language, then stood up and pulled Disso by the arm, startling him.

Orssandro Vykar closed his eyes, and his inner being disappeared, becoming something else.

"Are we leaving him here?!" Disso exclaimed while being dragged outside.

"He is almost a Korbeen now!" Kartak replied with severity. "Let's leave this place before the Korbas come here!"

Understanding the seriousness of the situation, Diesso ran and followed the elf.

The riders mounted their horses and, with dread, they observed the skies becoming clouded with dark-shadowed flocks of flying Korbas as birds heading towards the desolated palace, gliding effortlessly through the air. The demonic dragons had won the uneven battle, leaving hundreds of thousands dead on the grassland.

Casak and the Kasnasgos suffered a defeat.

While many could escape, others were not fortunate. They had fallen dead or wounded.

Or, even worse, transformed into Korbeens.

The Korbas had in their claws their crafted undead from the battle, and they were going for the last one and the most important. . . the Korbeen of Orssandro.

The defeated would remember the *Assault at the Estos Grasslands* as infamy.

The worst Casakan defeat in all its history.

An elvish shame.

And a somber beginning to a new uncertainty in the realm.

Amid the darkness, Archmage Missar climbed the stone steps while someone banged loudly on the doors. But he used his magic to light the place with a small fireball floating on his hand.

As it illuminated the inn's empty basement, which used to be a cold food storage, the fire revealed the tense faces of Lady Tasarissa and Alyssa, covering Carlissa by their backs. Both women wielded their daggers with concern and fear while the young of round glasses behind trembled.

Missar made a sign with his unoccupied hand and awaited by stopping himself in the last two steps before the doors secured by a beam. As a caution, the mage was determined to use the same fireball as a weapon to defend themselves.

Someone banged on the doors again, louder than last time.

"Who is it?!" Missar shouted with distrust.

"It is Lancer Diesso of Kokork!" he replied loud. "I bring news from Orssandro Vykar!"

Surprised, Missar turned to look at the women, who nodded, giving permission but still held daggers.

Shortly after, the mage removed the heavy beam from the doors and cautiously opened them.

Bothered by the sunlight covering his face with the hand, he found puzzled the young lancer accompanied by Kartak and Partak behind. He assumed they were prominent officials judging by their blood-stained uniforms. But the two elves disconcerted him.

"What is the news, lad?"

"The Head has fallen in battle, sir," responded with trembling lips, extending his hand to show the medal. "This is a proof of his last wish to transfer powers and take control of Casak as new Head."

Missar's face turned pale, overwhelmed by disbelief. He did not react for a while, but his eyes turned to look at Kartak.

"As a witness, I swear the veracity of Lancer Diesso," Kartak intervened with seriousness. "I tried to save him in vain."

"I must look for Missar," the young soldier said while searching the basement visually. "I have been told I could find him in this inn."

The archmage, still impressed, inhaled deeply and then exhaled to control himself.

"It is me, lad," replied with certain insecurity.

"We shall be at your mandates, Sir Head!" the lancer bowed as a sign of respect.

The elves stood still.

Archmage Missar, with shaking hands, turned around to see the women in the basement's bottom, finding Lady Tasarissa fainted and unconscious as Alyssa and Carlissa tried to revive her. Shortly after, he glanced at the alley and the subsequent street, discovering bodies on the ground because of the Korbas' assault on Estolk, resulting in casualties and destruction.

"Sir Head," Kartak spoke. "We may have failed in battle, but I assure you, the Kasnasgos are here to help Casak defend your people altogether."

"It is. . . getting out of hands," Missar murmured with widened eyes at the commandant.

"We shall also search for the *Ykarte* sword to bestow it to the Divine Empress."

"I know where the Sword of Kasana is!" the archmage exclaimed, startled.

23
PASS

As the early morning sun rose over the snowy Holy Mountains, Alessandro sat on a rock, holding his sword downward, captivated by the sky spectacle. Throughout the night, he remained awake to watch over the sleeping empress.

With thoughts of Fabehel, he tucked the white handkerchief under his sleeve.

As the day became clear, he noticed Lakia and Marissa resting on the ground, covered with abundant waki furs, beside an extinguished bonfire.

Not far, in the same valley but by nearby trees, two mantises slept standing. Brisel was one of them.

They had arrived in the northern The Plains, at the geographical corner with The Highlands and the mountains. As he remembered his geography lessons, the Holy Mountains were half the wall, the northern side, while in the south, the Cayderr Range completed the natural wall surrounding the mystical realm of Salter.

He recalled his unusual journey. From the Jarrdine Villa in Carretem, his tamed mantis followed Brisel with Lakia and Marissa on him. Alessandro's stomach could not handle the mantis' extreme speed, so he had to halt and vomit, forcing him to cut short the travel.

Marissa avoided retching while traveling with untamed Brisel. She had mastered self-control while going at high speeds.

Lakia, in change, was unaffected. She showed to find pleasure in the velocity.

They resumed the journey once Alessandro looked better with Marissa's advice for overcoming the effects. Although they reached Seled Post this morning, waited for daylight because of the dangers of traveling at night, especially with the Korbas in Berrem.

Alessandro did not forget the disturbing experience at the *Feast of the Dragoness*.

He did not sleep and refused Marissa's offer to take turns. He was not comfortable.

And he had a strange feeling that something had happened.

Lakia surprised Alessandro by finding her on foot right in front of him, as he did not see her wake up. He noticed her with great sadness on her face and humid hazel eyes. "What happened?"

"A nightmare," replied with sobs. "I dreamt a battle where elves and men fell under the Korbas. . . It was in a grassland. . . somewhere far from here."

He got struck by her declaration. He glared at her. Knowing her unique abilities, he comprehended that something terrible had occurred in Casak. However, he remained calm and focused on his assignment to bring her to Salter.

His sudden reaction was to clean the tears running down her cheeks, showing a light smile. "What is more important now is Salter."

She nodded, then sat beside him on the same rock. She took a pear and a knife from her satchel and cut into slices, giving some to Alessandro when she ate a few. "Tell me. Was my father like you?"

"What is the meaning of your inquiry?"

"Sorcerer Uskam has told me that my mother was of pale skin but black hair, so tell me. Was my father like you?"

Alessandro sighed. He understood that, despite being an empress of might skills, she was only a girl with innocent curiosity. Yet, to him, it was beyond comprehension how she knew many things, such as Cassandro's bleak fate. "Contrary to my tan skin, he was dark. I want to believe that my brother got my mother's traits while I got from my blood father's," acknowledged, noticing a thirst for more answers in her eyes. "Casakans are diverse, and our realm is of tropical climate, at least before the Gesha. The southernmost area is where the darker ones originated, like the Southern Isles, where Marissa's mother comes from, as my mother was also from somewhere near before she emigrated to Estolk."

"What can you tell me about your father?"

"Mother did not wish to talk much about him. But once she told me he was a trader from a small town near Kokork in the Casakan North, where tan-skinned people live," sighed again. "However, shortly before leaving, my brother Cassandro revealed me that bandits had killed our father on his journey to the mountains."

"And that is why your mother had to work at a tavern."

"How do you know?" he expressed surprise.

"She has told me," Lakia replied, pointing at the sleeping knight. "Ser Marissa still strongly holds onto her attachment to you, despite her consensus about your true feelings."

Alessandro felt puzzled. Lakia had passed from being a regular girl searching for answers to an empress with unique wisdom.

"So. . . What shall I do?"

"It is not your fault, but do not be dull either. Love and mysticism have the same essence. Both may be twisted and irrational, but with a common purpose," assured. "In your stance, you have a heart's purpose."

Alessandro and Lakia got distracted by the sudden yawning of an awakened Marissa, who stretched her arms after sitting.

"Am I missing something here?" she asked them, clueless, with bright brown eyes pushing away her furs.

Judging by the sun's position towards the west, it was the beginning of the evening. Alessandro knew they were near. He had spent most of the time mounted on the brown mantis, following Lakia and Marissa on Brisel, and could finally adapt to the speed while traveling south along the Holy Mountains to his left.

He recommended a quick stop at Seled Post to rest, grab a light meal, and then continue across *The Pass* into Salter.

Lakia enjoyed the fast travel, holding Brisel's neck between the legs of her knight. The chilly wind crashed pleasantly against her face. However, her initial excitement faded as boredom set in, and she longed to reach her destination.

Marissa had the responsibility of keeping the empress firmly against her body to avoid any accidental fall that would be fatal. She had to control Brisel with the help of the reins.

For an instant, Alessandro could not avoid his concern for Casak. If Lakia's dream was true, he believed that the Korbas had spread beyond the Karekall and across the Beyond Sea. He knew Sankaris was in a grave position.

He did not have the guts to tell it to Marissa. A hissing removed him from his meditations when he felt the brown mantis run faster than usual, almost reaching Brisel and his passengers. Surprised, he turned to look back while grabbing the mantis' reins.

Scared and stunned, Alessandro discovered a giant flying black dragon behind, trying to catch the travelers at speed.

"Darn Korba!" he yelled, drawing his sword.

Marissa's attention got caught, finding Alessandro and his mantis beside and not behind. She looked back and unsheathed her blade, holding Lakia with excessive strength in a desire to protect her with her life.

The empress discovered and sensed the dragon's presence but did not see it as the knight's body blocked her visually.

The winged Korba proved its speed by surpassing the two mantises and reaching the brown one. Alessandro swung his sword, desperately attempting to contact the creature. Without warning, the dragon was directly above him, ready to snatch him with the claws.

Lakia sensed the danger to her uncle and closed her eyes, using her aura to generate a powerful wind in the opposite direction. This wind, although slowing the mantises, pushed the creature far away.

Alessandro battled against the wind created by Lakia but was relieved when it pushed the Korba away, ensuring everyone's safety.

He smiled at Marissa, but noticed her wearing a serious expression and her eyes widening.

The Korba regained its velocity and could evade the wind. The flying creature prepared to attack with its sharp tail this time.

Marissa pulled the reins to go faster. She could finally devise Seled Post on the horizon.

Brisel hissed in panic.

Fear had also invaded Lakia, and unable to use her aura. Recalling her past confrontation against Ardek Korba made her hesitant about her abilities.

"No!" Marissa yelled, alarmed.

The dragon stung, slaughtering the brown mantis.

Alessandro's body violently landed upon launch, resulting in a repeated oscillation across the green grass, tearing his clothes, and eventually coming to a stop in the vast valley. The sword given by Lord Tom Lai vanished near a cliff in the vicinity.

Next, the Korba landed before Alessandro and roared, giving a dreadful look with red eyes.

Marissa slowed down Brisel, jumped off, and instructed her mantis to take Lakia to safety. She ran to Alessandro, troubled, wielding her sword, even knowing she was too far to save his life.

Regardless of the pain, scratches, and bruises, Alessandro rose, with blood dripping from his forehead, grabbing the white handkerchief defiantly, ready to confront the massive creature using just his bare hands. "I will not let you touch the Divine Empress, you scourge!" he screamed furious, pushing the handkerchief under the sleeve. His heart, however, raced.

The dragon leapt, poised to end him without mercy.

Without warning, two gargantuan arrows penetrated the creature's head and chest.

The dragon fell heavily before Alessandro, shaking the ground.

Marissa was stunned and stopped in her race, gasping for air. She turned around and saw the Berremen sentinels on the outskirts of Seled Post who had shot their ballistas. She dropped her sword and fell to her knees.

Lakia, surrounded by the sentinels, clung to Brisel's neck and sobbed.

Alessandro shook his head with relief. He exhaled and looked at the dragon's head, noticing its eyes changing from red to black as its body became lifeless. "You will not touch the Divine Empress, you pest!" he murmured.

Alessandro switched out his clothes with a sentinel's, who had a similar size. They were not the fancier black ones he was used to, but mostly peasant attires made of leather. He did not care about his attire as long as he had something on his body. As he placed his arms through the sleeves of a wool shirt and buttoned it, he made gestures of pain because of his sore body. Some bruises were visible, and a small patch was on his forehead.

Marissa bit her bottom lip as she empathetically observed him feeling his soreness.

An amazed Berremen official was beside her.

A weak fire under the chimney illuminated most of the garrison tower's interior.

The new morning appeared as the moon No Sak hid in the day's curtain. The first sunlight drew across the tall window, stamping a momentary mark on the stone floor.

"Were you able to get a mantis, sergeant?" Marissa inquired.

"I am truly sorry, ser. All we can offer are horses," the official shook his head. "In these high and cold places, mantises do not survive easily."

"We will not go in mantises nor horses!" Alessandro replied while getting a bite of a dumpling filled with ground lamb meat. And spoke with a full mouth, making his words almost unintelligible. "We shall go to *The Pass* by foot!"

The garrison's cooks had previously placed trays of regional dumplings with jars of sweet amber tea on the solid wooden table for the travelers, especially for the empress.

"What is the reason for your recommendation?" Marissa, in disagreement, inquired. "It is two days to arrive at Salter when we should be there already!"

Alessandro served a cup of tea and drank plenty to help swallow the dumpling in his throat, apprehensive in answering her.

"I believe our speed attracted the Korba, Marissa," he replied, signaling his index finger upwards. "The flying dragon spotted us while coming here."

"Do you suggest that going mounted on any animal could attract them?"

"Indeed," he nodded. "We shall travel by foot to avoid any attention."

Lakia awoke on a bench near the chimney, rubbing her eyes and yawning.

Marissa poured tea into a clean cup and offered it to the empress.

Alessandro glanced at the official's sword and pointed it with indiscretion.

"May I have your blade, sergeant?"

At Alessandro's request, a dozen sentinels escorted the empress on Brisel to the boundaries of *The Pass*.

The three journeyers, two on loaned horses, stopped to admire the tremendous natural corridor between mountains. The Holy Mountains and Cayderr Range glanced at themselves as white giants struggling to offer a stunning panorama.

"Here is where Berrem ends," the sergeant affirmed with a smoke of icy breath. "My men and I may not enter."

"So, this is Salter," Alessandro nodded, noticing the adverse ascending corridor. "We are too close, yet too far."

Except for the sentinels, the travelers also wore white waki furs to protect them from the gelid environment at a very high altitude.

Marissa, accustomed to her realm's warm climate, and despite her thick clothes, she could taste the frigid environment to her bones. The intense chilly nights in Casak were nothing compared to the surprise of an icy noon before *The Pass*.

"The few who dared to enter perished," the sergeant revealed. "There is a reason only mages and sorcerers can reach."

Lakia, dismounting Brisel, glared at the official when she noticed Alessandro and Marissa with worrisome looks.

"Are you sure you want to keep going?" Marissa urged the empress. "It sounds treacherous!"

"Do you recall that conversation we had, Ser Marissa?" Lakia replied with authority and discomfort. "I began my journey with this satchel and intend to take it to Salter!"

"But. . . "

"Look at us now!" she interrupted. "I said that the Jyistereerk started with my satchel. Our growth has resulted in me being entrusted with Berrem. Despite everything I said and did, you doubted me countless times, and your loyalty almost vanished."

Everyone silently witnessed the empress' words and noticed how Marissa shuddered.

Alessandro made a surprising gesture.

"I apologize, Divine Empress." Marissa dismounted the horse and knelt before her in total submission. "Please, remove me as your knight if you suggest I do not deserve the title."

"I do not seek to banish you but your comprehension!" Lakia clarified as she compassionately touched her cheek, her eyes denoted affection. "I am an empress, aye. But alone, I can not take the reins of an empire. That is why I have chosen you and Alessandro to give me the required guidance. Together with me, you both shall be the Pillars of the Jyistereerk."

Marissa found herself moved.

Alessandro reacted by dismounting his horse at the time that all the sentinels made a unique reverence towards the empress and her two chosen companions.

Later, once the three journeyers left for Salter, the sergeant sent Brisel back to Carretem at Marissa's request, but with a message to the Gathering of the Lords.

The empress' appointment of Alessandro and Marissa as the empire's Pillars circulated throughout Seled Post. The devoted locals and sentinels voted to change the name of *The Pass*. They sent those voting results in that message.

The Gathering of the Lords received the message from Brisel and news from other mouths. Afraid of imminent implications from the empress, they willingly approved and ordered all cartographers to change maps.

As a result, they changed the name to *The Empress' Pass*.

24
METAMORPHOSIS

T he freezing sensation penetrated their bare faces
as they constantly ascended along the corridor
between the gelid mountains. The frigid environment
menaced rough lives. More than walking, it was seemingly like climbing steps made of irregular and slippery natural rocks. They endured the icy day, going
with haste as desired, but the harsh conditions and the
awareness of potential perils slowed them.

Gasping for air and carrying Lakia at his back, Alessandro stopped momentarily. The furs and all the clothes were not enough to protect him from the weather, but ascending with a girl behind helped to keep his body warm as he observed Marissa going ahead.

Lakia wished to sleep on Alessandro's back, shivering. She widened her eyes, trying in vain to be alert to her surroundings. "Please, put me down!" Her discomfort in wearing boots derived from her preference for going barefoot or with sandals.

Listening to her request, Alessandro obeyed and put Lakia on a nearby broad stone where she sat. Then he grabbed a water canteen from his pouch and offered it to her.

She refused to drink, asking him to do it first, noticing his fatigue.

Alessandro nodded and poured the water into his mouth with relief, feeling bits of ice from the frigid environment.

Marissa descended back, concerned. "What has occurred?"

"I. . . just needed to stop," Alessandro replied, trying to recover his breath. He studied the surroundings and observed the corridor until his eyes could not see far from the mountainous horizon. He sighed, worrisome. "Archmage Yasstro has told me many marvels about Salter. But all I see is this damn cold and mountains!"

"I remember his books, Alessandro," Marissa recalled with a light smile, shaking. "He used to show us illustrations of silver towers in Salter at that library."

"The Book of Wonders," he chuckled a bit. "It looked more like a fairy tale than an actual place!"

Marissa observed the empress fixated on a group of white ruminant wakis feeding on scarce grass in a ravine near the Cayderr Range. "Are you all right, Lakia?"

"I see them, and I recall. . .," Lakia replied with some sadness, signaling at them with a discreet gesture. "When I was very little, Mother Venka used to take me to see the waki herds during the summer seasons. . . They were abundant, vivid, as Molke was. . ." Eventually, she fell into a dormant state, struggling to stay awake.

Marissa prevented Lakia from falling by grabbing her and lifted her unconscious body in her arms.

"Let me stay, Saki!" Lakia exclaimed, delusional with immobile eyes. "I want to feed the waki!"

Alessandro, concerned and suspicious, touched Lakia's forehead. "She has a high fever!" After searching, he found a small space surrounded by a few bare trees nearby and proposed going to that location.

Marissa rushed after him, holding Lakia in her arms, until they arrived at the mentioned site. Hoping to warm her up, she sat on the cold ground and covered the girl with her thick furs.

Alessandro placed his canteen on Lakia's lips and started pouring water into her mouth.

"I am hot, Saki! Let's go to the pond with the kapakis!" she kept saying, still delusional, with closed eyes.

"What is the meaning of it, Alessandro?" Marissa inquired, alarmed, assuring that furs wrapped Lakia's body together with hers. She had doubts about their chances of surviving the harsh cold.

"I believe she is speaking with Molkan words," his lips trembled as his weakness invaded him.

Marissa gave the reason to the sergeant, remembering his words. The few that dared to enter *The Pass* had perished. "Have we failed?" She had a heartbroken look, begging quietly that Alessandro could resolve a hopeless complication while gripping the dormant empress inside her clothes.

Alessandro lifted his head and his body fell straight to the ground. He gazed at the clear blue sky, soon to become night, drawing the face of Fabehel in his mind when he felt the handkerchief under his sleeve with his fingers. "Please, forgive me, Lady Fabehel!" murmured faintly. He realized Marissa was unconscious, cradling Lakia, and returned to observe the sky.

The last sight before darkness consumed him was a flock of Korbas, far away, circling as if they were expecting something.

Blackness.

"Wake up, Nehel!" a whisper summoned. "Open your eyes and follow the wind!"

Lakia let her hazel eyes show and noticed the darkness surrounding her. However, she could see Marissa, who had wrapped her arms around her. Surprised, she comprehended the knight's desire to protect her from the cold. She tried in vain to wake Marissa by poking her cheek. Lakia had to exit from her arms that held her with force, and once she was finally free, strangely, she felt a warmth in the environment, as opposed to the frigid condition. Feeling hot and sweaty, she abandoned her thick furs.

"Follow the wind, Nehel. . .," the whisper still called to her.

She knew it was not a hallucination or a dream.

As she walked without difficulties, her feet felt like floating.

As her boots contacted something, she stopped and bent down to see what it was. To her delight, she discovered Alessandro unconscious on the ground. His hand grasped a handkerchief. A smile spread across her face, and she stood up and continued with her steps.

From nowhere, a gust crashed into her head. Lakia knew the wind was hers, but someone else controlled it.

Still, she followed it, walked, walked, and walked. . . through the darkness.

She found it. Far, a cave where a fire danced inside.

The wind stopped.

Lakia kept going and reached the cave.

With no fear and with confidence, she entered.

She found a small ascending way before her to a natural half wall, covering some bonfire that illuminated most of the cave. The girl walked to the other side and found an enormous cauldron on a large fire inside a hollow.

Lakia studied around the ground. There were some small stools, empty and filled bottles with unknown substances, dirty bowls with dry leftovers, and also, she discovered some clean animal bones. She looked ahead and found a wooden cot with a leather cover and waki furs.

She heard dragging steps behind from a powerful presence and slowly turned.

Lakia discovered an ancient woman with a severely degraded and deformed face. She noticed her blank eyes as evidence of a profound blindness.

"Nehel. . .," the grotesque lady mentioned with a harsh voice opening her toothless mouth. "My Promise. . ."

The girl recognized her with a large hunchback with dirty and dark rags of what were once fine clothes. She had a fetid, pungent smell.

"I know you, madam," Lakia nodded with seriousness, immutable. "You were great among people!"

The sightless lady extended her trembling and bony hand to touch the empress' face, studied it with her fingers, and felt her hair. "I have waited for long, my Promise."

"Tell me. How did you lose your sight?" asked at the time that compassionately held her hands.

The lady did not remember as she twitched her head several times, but vaguely recalled and spoke after a while.

"I had traveled with Prince Dohan. . . to seek a cure for Aranka. . . and a demon touched me. . .," responded slowly.

Lakia adopted a thinking posture and recalled the lessons from Sorcerer Uskam.

"Can you know your name?"

"Name. . . I do not recall," the lady replied, twitching her head again.

"You are Sorceress Dalehel," she said with a light smile. "You were the mother of my mother!"

"Sorceress no more. Witch now. . .," she clarified with another twitch.

A sense of sorrow washed over Lakia as she empathized with the older lady. She pulled and guided her onto a stool she found near the cauldron.

Both took a seat on the stools.

Lakia observed to the witch, and her eyes almost got tearful. She recalled Uskam's words.

Sorcerer Uskam once taught her that four different people existed in Sankaris' world of magic, but no one was born with magic. One aspiring student had to learn the basics and nature of magic, and later, the abilities grew stronger or weaker, depending on the person's age, intelligence, or personality traits. Like him, the sorcerers and sorceresses learned the magic through one guardian, teacher, or tutor. The sanctuaries formed directly to the mages, enchanters, and enchantresses. Although uncommon, brotherhoods and sisterhoods in elvish communities also learned and protected the magic through nature and the goddesses' blessings, and they were the third type.

The fourth type was the worse. If evil entities like demons or Korbas tainted peoples with magic, they would become into warlocks or witches.

Lakia also knew through Uskam that groups of warlocks and witches named Aquelarres existed in the darkest places east of the Karekall and heard frightening stories about them.

However, looking at the elder Dalehel, the girl did not think she was a witch, but more like an ill poor woman.

"Are you my princess?" she inquired, confused, twitching her head. "Please, be nice with Fabe. . ."

With surprise, Lakia grasped the confusion and hastily rose to hug her.

"I am not my mother, madam!" she exclaimed, moved.

"It is you, Natahel?" the witch insisted, feeling Lakia's arms on her head.

Lakia's sudden reaction was to step back, frightened and staring at the witch, shaking. "No! Do not request it!"

The girl sensed hidden deep inside the witch's body, the real Dalehel as a faint voice, making a particular desire.

Lakia started sobbing, not wishing to do it when the lady twitched her head continuously. Despite her reluctance, she understood the necessity to fulfill her duty and grant Dalehel the freedom and peace she deserved after enduring tikls of hellish suffering.

The empress knew she had to put an end to the suffering, even if she despised the thought.

Lakia closed her eyes and hugged the witch again.

Between sobs and a strong wind that appeared, Lakia kept the lady in her arms.

She felt how her breath stopped.

The witch's body became softer until it dissolved.

Then, nothing was in Lakia's arms.

As she opened her wet eyes, only a tiny pile of ashes was on the stool.

The witch, and so the legendary Sorcerer Dalehel, had died.

One of the lasts from the bygone world.

Lakia turned to notice how the cauldron vanished, emptying the hollow.

And the fire quenched, bringing darkness to the cave.

The hollow became a gate, letting enter an abundance of light. Lakia, at first, covered her eyes partially as the luminescence hurt her pupils. Still, she discovered it was an exit to a prosperous valley of vivid green with colorful flowers, plenty of butterflies, and leafy pear trees distributed along the place. All accompanied by a clear and beautiful blue sky.

Paradise.

Exiting the cave through the gate, the girl felt altered, yet unchanged. But her eyes descended to notice that the uncomfortable boots had disappeared, but her bare feet pleasantly stepped on the rich grass instead.

Surprised, she also wore a pure silky white tunic with long sleeves, giving a unique type of brilliance.

She stumbled upon a pond nearby where swans were dancing, and she hurriedly made her way to it. By the edge, she kneeled and slowly inched towards the pristine water. The mirror reflected her face and eyes, but she had tied back her short, curly hair. She looked immaculate and perfect, even with the natural imperfections on her face.

She lifted her eyes to find an older bald man in azure robes under a pear tree, leaning on the trunk with hidden hands under the long sleeves. She sensed in him peace and wisdom.

He was expecting her.

The transformed girl stood up and walked to approach the elder, showing seriousness.

He widened his blue eyes, but did not show an expression on his wrinkled, hairless face. He nodded, and at last, gave a light smile. "*Nehel Jyistereerk Mudihufaser,*" the man named her with a sweet voice. "*Nehel Jyistereerk Friyterkfer.*"

"Aye, I am," she agreed, also nodding. "And who are you?"

"I am known as Selee since my naming as High Archmage of Salter," he made a respectful reverence.

"Why am I here? Am I dead?"

Selee chuckled. "You are not, Divine Empress. What you see around is the consequence of Sorceress Dalehel's liberation. You made it possible and just exited your cocoon, transforming into your true nature."

"How is that possible? I did not want to do what she wished!" She shouted as her tearful eyes glanced at her trembling hands. "I knew I had to do it because she was suffering! But I have committed an atrocity against my life's principles!"

"Do not fear!" the archmage smiled again. "Her already tainted blood was because of an attack from a Korba while traveling with Prince Dohan, but she did not become a Korbeen because her herbalism knowledge allowed her to create a potion to save her, but with a terrible curse of a corrupted blood always incurable." Selee paused for a moment. "In the end, her body and mind were dead, but trapped in an afflicted limbo when she should have died plenty. So no, you did not murder her."

The empress heard him, and his soft voice gave her relief. However, she was still confused and had many questions.

"What occurred to me? And what is the relation with the sorceress?" she inquired, showing herself. "I look different from I was before!"

The High Archmage touched her shoulder and suggested sitting on the grass under the same tree, anticipating a significant explanation, sighed and started. "After the incident, I forbade Sorceress Dalehel to enter Salter again, as I knew of her poisoned blood and overseeing her transformation into a witch. So, learning about the close perils with the Korbas and, as my brothers and sisters insisted on a petition, I allowed her to become a gatekeeper to Salter. She accepted and watched over *The Pass* so no one could enter our realm."

She comprehended the reason travelers did not arrive at Salter easily.

"At first, she only used her abilities to push away anyone who dared to enter Salter," he continued with his sweet voice. "Still, as she was becoming corrupt and especially after the Gesha, she killed the last travelers." He shook in disapproval. "We needed a new gatekeeper."

His silence said everything, and it startled the empress.

"Am I that gatekeeper?!"

"Aye, we could say so. As an empress, you are opening Salter to the world again for good. . . and for bad."

"But. . . I do not comprehend at all!"

"Did you think you were an ordinary girl?" chuckled. "Please come with me."

She stood up and followed him.

Both walked among the pear trees in silence.

The girl observed, stunned, at the valley's great richness, as if it was from a children's tale or a perfect dream. She noticed the colorful presence of all kinds of animals and the flowers. She stopped at a dwarf tree heavily surrounded by butterflies, and even a few landed on her white tunic.

Selee showed her a branch containing a hanging cocoon among the invading butterflies.

"Look at your circumstances, Divine Empress," the High Archmage spoke with a certain solemnity. "You arrived as the first and only one born with magic. Your mother was an Arankan king's daughter. Your father was a Casakan Head's son, and his brother is already with you. You were raised under an elvish mother who fed you with her milk and an elvish sorcerer who got you ready for your stance. Do not you think that these are coincidences?"

She adopted a thinking posture, yet she did not comprehend him.

"Divine Empress. Do not you recall that magic is perfect but imperfect in opposition to the world's natural laws?"

"Aye, Sorcerer Uskam taught me it."

"You were a small girl that had to live the hardships on Sankaris, and supposedly, you should have waited for your metamorphosis until you were of four tikls," nodded, pointing at the empress. "But knowing the perils that Sankaris has to face, Sorceress Dalehel kept suffering and waited long for you so that she could speed up your metamorphosis into your true nature before her death. She was the only one who could give you that needed metamorphosis!"

"Metamorphosis into what?"

Selee snapped his finger and showed with his hand how the cocoon was slowly opening, and a white butterfly emerged, extending its wings.

"As this butterfly, you were a caterpillar, unprepared because even you did not know who you were. You liberated a lord from a Korba, aye. But you were not yet ready to confront Ardek Korba, which was your mistake," he asserted. "You were like the caterpillar trying to fly even before entering the cocoon."

"Who am I?"

"Lakia is dormant now. You had a rebirth from that cave as the Nehel, the divine jewel, in the same way as the butterfly. . .," Selee sighed, failing to hide his excitement with a smile. "You are a demigoddess, a divinity among all peoples."

25
WALLS

Alessandro woke up gasping for breath, drenched in cold sweat, sensing the moisture around his neck. A sharp pain pierced his dark eyes, triggering a headache that brought back memories of hangovers from nights spent with classmates or soldiers at Vykar Palace. He sat down and realized, to his alarm, that he was in a different place.

He examined his surroundings and discovered he was in a spacious room adorned with white and silver walls and a tall, curved ceiling. It had some strange, simple furniture with similarities to the shapes of the tree, yet it looked comfortable and aesthetically good to the eye. He did not understand where the soft illumination came from, since no oil lamps or candles were present, but he guessed these came from magic.

He was on a bed with comfortable white silk cushions and sheets and turned to his right to find Marissa asleep on another similar bed beside him. He massaged his neck to ease the pain and turned his head to find a small round table holding a bowl filled with fresh fruits.

Alarmed, Alessandro remembered the flock of Korbas before his fainting and stood up, disturbed, trying to draw his sword, but he felt his hand grasping only air. He found out somebody disarmed him as Marissa, too.

Concerned and trying to look for answers, he awoke Marissa.

As she opened her eyes and discovered herself in a different location, she stood up with apprehension. "Where is Lakia?!" yelled, still feeling the sensation of the dormant empress in her arms. "What place is it?!"

"I am uncertain, but I am sure someone brought us here," he replied, moving his eyes to look around with distrust. "Not all dungeons are dark and miserable places."

"This is not a dungeon, but a place only those with wealth can have! Are you damn dull?!" she reprimanded him in disbelief, but still unclear about the room she was in. "Where is Lakia?!"

"Lakia is no more, my fellows."

Alessandro and Marissa looked towards the source of the sweet male voice and found Selee in his azure robes.

They were unsure if he had entered by the entrance or emerged as a ghost.

"What have you done to the empress?!" she screamed, clenching her fists, determined to give an unforgettable beating to the archmage, but Alessandro pushed her away.

"Please, Marissa! Let's see what he has to say."

Selee reacted with a smile, immutable to her reaction, and nodded.

"I would react the same way, so it is understandable."

"Tell us who you are and what has occurred to the empress!" Alessandro demanded, while keeping Marissa behind.

"I can assure you the Divine Empress is well," Selee replied, extending his hand towards the fruit bowl. "Please eat to regain your energy, and I will explain everything."

Although with unconformity, they listened to him and grabbed fruits. Alessandro took a ripe peach, feeling a unique sweetness with the first bite. In change, Marissa only threw some red grapes to the mouth with distrust.

"I am Selee, High Archmage of Salter, and I apologize for the way we had to bring you here. We knew about your coming and the perils you were enduring."

He impressed Alessandro. Although he had heard about Selee countless times, this was their first meeting. "If I am right, you knew Archmage Yasstro," Alessandro asserted, toying with his half-bitten peach. "My late tutor always spoke about you."

Marissa heard them and comprehended, gaining the trust. She took more grapes and sat on her bed, throwing more into her mouth.

"Archmage Yasstro was determined to make you a fine sorcerer, Master Alessandro," Selee smiled. "But magic was never for you!"

"Why do you say Lakia is no more? Where is she?" Marissa inquired with curiosity.

"She had to face a transformation to become the empress she should be. The Lakia you had known is no more. She is now Empress Nehel and getting ready for her ascension."

"May we see her?" she requested as her anxiety slowly overcame again.

"You may, Ser Marissa. A maid awaits you outside to take you to her," Selee replied, pointing to the exit. "But you, Master Alessandro, shall accompany me, as I have an urgent and meaningful matter with you."

Alessandro deviated, startled, his eyes from the finished peach's seed to Selee.

Alessandro could not avoid his astonishment at finding hanging plants exiting the chamber and being mesmerized by a crystalline pool below where many children swam, enjoying aquatic games. The great diversity of races captured his attention in an instant. Every child seemed to come from every corner of Sankaris, even some he had never seen.

He noticed Arankans, Berremens, Brekens, Casakans, Elves, and Fennens. Berremarks and Casaraks were not the exceptions. Also, other races he only learned from the Academy books, like the small Tinklens. Inclusive, some that were unknown to him.

The children showed the most uncorrupted happiness as they dived and raced in the water. Their laughs had the purest innocence, and they lived their moments in an environment that was in perfect harmony.

Near the pool, some maids, also from different races, had already installed a table that contained large plates of fruits and vegetables, and some infants grabbed them with excitement to eat with enjoyment.

Alessandro observed them, recalling the miserable children's condition in Casak, often mistreated by the Head and the Assembly, and bits of sorrow and shame invaded his interior. It was a contrasting difference.

Selee discovered his curiosity, noticing how he leaned on the baluster with his open mouth of amazingness. "Before your eyes are the anticipation and future of the Jyistereerk, master."

Alessandro turned to see the archmage awed.

"Is it what the empress is trying to build?"

Selee only responded with a smile and a nod. "Please, do not stop and follow me."

Both men walked by a covered aisle of hanging plants beside the pool and descended some ramp of broken tiles floor.

Despite the abundant luminescence similar to the sun, Alessandro could not detect any sky or ceiling, only a shining and hard-to-see end of heights.

They crossed by a gate to leave the bright pool to enter a semi-dark place with hundreds of columns, where dozens of men and women in robes and heads covered by hoods walked in different directions. They seemed to pray as they had their hands together under their long sleeves.

The place reminded him of the sanctuary's library in Sarak, where he last met Yasstro before his death. It was almost identical—tall columns with no end in sight and oil lamps. The exception was the lack of tables and books.

"We just left the Citadel of Salter and we are now at the Great Sanctuary," Selee notified. "It would have been two days by horse."

Stunned, Alessandro stopped to look at the archmage with disbelief, who interrupted his steps. "How?"

"Salter does not know the laws of physics, as here is the land of magic," he asserted. "It is something you never dared to understand during your lessons with Archmage Yasstro."

"Not that I wish or not, archmage! My poor knowledge did not allow me to understand, but confusion instead."

Selee again requested him to continue in their trajectory.

It did not take long when they crossed a similar gate to find themselves in another entirely different place.

Alessandro had heard about it uncountable times from Yasstro, but he never expected to see it personally. His eyes widened, and he could not close his mouth.

The legendary walls.

"The *Frelee Dee*," Selee named it. "Blessed under one hundred and twenty stars and built by Mudihufaser himself as a gift to the magic of Sankaris. More than walls, it is a maze that can reveal the past and the future of the one who walks inside."

The colossal two white walls he had before strongly overwhelmed Alessandro, inviting him to enter the maze. The structure's magnitude and energy full of magic left him speechless. These were under a strange nocturnal sky full of stars. "What. . . is the purpose of bringing me here?" Alessandro asked, trembling and impressed. "I know only a few fortunate have seen it!"

Determined, Selee gave his first steps on the bright, wide floor between the walls, grabbing Alessandro's arm to enter together.

At that instant, the walls changed shape and form, and the maze's way transformed into another different one, giving a feeling of fear and surprise and, simultaneously, wonder.

As both moved forward, mystical fire scripture appeared on the walls in the Salteran language.

"Drelee, Trihen, Lonehen, Arssen, Brenerr, Askaj, Uskam, Kaiden, Dalehel, Yasstro. . . and myself are some of the few that have seen the *Frelee Dee*," Selee replied with a soft but severe tone. "All of them were great mages, enchanters, enchantresses, sorcerers, sorceresses. . . The most influential ones on Sankaris."

"I am not a mage!" Alessandro exclaimed, frightened. "I. . . do not even know who I am!"

"I brought you for a greater reason, and you shall pay attention!" Selee reprimanded, halting in his walk. "Salter has its days counted. . ."

"What is the meaning of it?"

"The predictions spelled from my mouth are the same ones written in these walls, master." he nodded. "I assure you that Salter will not last long. Korbas have already broken into our magic and are eyeing our realm."

"But the empress will liberate us."

"You are mistaken, master," Selee smiled again. "Empress Nehel was born to bring balance to Sankaris, aye, but it is not the same as liberate."

"Please explain."

The archmage suggested his companion to resume walking. As they created the steps, more fire scriptures appeared on the walls. "Do you notice how this maze created a path without apparent end? The more complex the maze, the more difficult are the times to come." He pointed to the walls. "Divine Empress Nehel will bring a balance on Sankaris, but a balance of two opposites that will always be in conflict."

"Did not she come to save Sankaris?"

"No, but along with the balance, she will open the way to new generations and launch a movement . . . the *Deken Karsaker*," he nodded. "The Reclamation War."

"Wait!" he interrupted him. "You just mentioned that the empress did not come to save!"

"I have said she is not the savior, but will launch a movement!" he reprimanded again. "I suggest you listen carefully to my words!"

"My apologies. . ."

"The *Deken Karsaker* will last twenty tikls. It is a war of eighty years, and as every time approaches, times will be the worse," he pointed at Alessandro decisively. "Master, you will bear the burden of the Jyistereerk carrier and the man of all battles who will survive generations and tragedies. You will win and lose encounters. . . You will be the Borsen."

Alessandro recalled Yasstro's with heartache. "Archmage Yasstro's last words. . .," he mentioned with sorrow. "What is the meaning of Borsen?"

"This is something you must discover yourself." Selee smiled and continued walking. "There are things not allowed to reveal."

"Tell me, archmage," again Alessandro stopped him with annoyance, pulling his sleeve. "What was the purpose of showing me the *Free Dee*? To tell me about the complications? To reveal the empress' stance? To be named in something I must yet to discover?"

Selee only responded with his frequent smile. That bothered Alessandro.

"I recall Archmage Yasstro teaching me that only the ones who showed greatness over Sankaris were the ones who deserved to be at the *Frelee Dee*," Alessandro continued, beating his chest tearfully. "I am not great, nor virtuous but just an orphan boy who had the misfortune of losing both parents and a sibling, who had to live through hard and uncertain times under the influence of a few who drove me to many guilts, doubts, and disarrays! While I have yet to discover others that truly cherish me when all I do is walk away like a damn coward!"

"Are you finished with your words, master?" Selee asked, tranquil, attentive.

"I am not done!" he cleaned his tears and grasped Fabehel's white handkerchief, signaling to the walls. "This. . . thing. . . I do not know what you call that! Fate! Destiny! Whatever you call it! I did not choose! I did not choose to be under the care of the Head Orssandro! I did not choose to learn weaponry at the Academy! Much less, I did not choose to be at an empress' side!" he gasped for air to continue. "I would rather go back in time and live in that house beside the tavern, where Mother used to work, and spend time with my brother! That way, I could choose my fate. . ."

"Do you realize the *Frelee Dee* made you speak your words? This is your past!" Selee asserted. "May I now speak for myself?"

"Aye. . .," he acceded, startled, still wiping his eyes, relieved from his emotional burden.

"I am an Arankan, as you have noticed, master," Selee began softly but with seriousness in his face. "My parents in poverty sold me to an old sorcerer who needed someone to cook, clean, and care for him, but over time, he taught me magic, which I learned immediately. But soon, he passed, and a foreman from a nearby sawmill took me in to work there for food and bed as payments." The archmage nodded with an unusual, sad gesture. "I got mistreated, and as a boy with a bad temper, I used my uncontrolled fire magic to burn the sawmill, murdering the workers inside. . . most of them had families, but it did not matter to me."

The silence reigned as Alessandro widened his eyes, stunned.

"What had occurred later, archmage?"

"Sadly, the news of my crimes reached the king's ears, and he ordered to imprison me in the deepest dungeons under the palace's underground, where I have faced the worst tortures you can not imagine. It was unspeakable that even with all my magical skills, I can not forget." His own words moved him. "A mage from Salter made a deal with the king and liberated me. He brought me here, but they forever banished me from the kingdom. And the mage allowed me to redeem my misdeeds by learning at a sanctuary here but accompanied with a curse."

"I. . . am at no words. . ." Alessandro was almost speechless. "May I know your curse?"

"No words needed, master," Selee replied with a new smile. "Because of my past, I have the curse of immortality. As you guessed, I am much older than you can imagine."

"However, you do not appear overly aged."

"As you see, most who had a harrowing past achieved more remarkable things and experienced undesirable burdens. It does not matter how short or long the life was," he touched the master's shoulder. "Is it not our fault when we can not control our destinies, but we shall accept our conditions and paths because that is how the circumstances have presented to us. This is what *Frelee Dee* is teaching us! And showing us the past and the future!"

"I apologize for my sudden emotions. I realize your purpose in bringing me here," Alessandro nodded understandingly. "What shall we do now?"

"We shall be at the empress' side always," suggested with a smile. "She may be mighty as a goddess, but imperfect as a human."

"Do you suggest she is a demigoddess?!" he inquired, stunned.

"Aye, you said so," nodded. "And even myself, I can not explain her nature."

26

ASCENCION

When Selee mentioned a maid awaiting outside, Marissa never thought she would wait to ride on a white camel. One of these animals only found in places like Breken Nation and east of the Karekall. She had learned about the camel through her Academy lessons but never saw one. However, she was on one of them and in Salter.

She was not taking the reins of the camel but being pulled by the maid.

A young girl in white robes, a headdress covering the brown skin, and long wavy hair with a mixture of black and blond colors, a Casarak, was ahead on her albino camel.

Marissa confirmed the veracity of Yasstro's words, the Citadel of Salter, always mentioned in the Book of Wonders. She acknowledged this by discovering the many silver towers colossally tall, always pointing to the nocturnal sky.

The night was clear and full of stars. As the book mentioned, the Salteran nights were always eternal, and a never-ending magical light illuminated the cities.

With awe, Marissa discovered pleasant weather. It was not cold or hot, but tempered and windless. The streets were bright and moderately crowded, with people of all ages and colorful clothes, and they walked in all directions but in order and harmony. She noticed some people outside their homes with their small tables. Each one had a different produce or food. She initially thought they were vendors, but gave them for free, allegedly.

Indeed, they were bartering. No coin was involved.

As she turned her eyes ahead, she discovered a massive circular building covered by a silver dome enough to occupy the polis' most area. Tall sentinels with lances in silver armor strongly guarded around the structure.

The maid stopped before the curved and closed giant gate.

Marissa's camel knelt first by the front legs, forcing her to grab by the saddle to avoid a fall, and then it continued with the back legs to lie down. Once on the surface, she could dismount and step on the stone ground. Later she approached the sentinel, noticing her reflection on the mirrored silver armor, seeing it was two times her height, but slender. It looked like a statue, perfectly immobile, wondering if someone was inside. She felt minimized and intimidated by it.

"If you think that one is a man, you are mistaken," the maid told her, pointing to all the sentinels. "All of them are creatures made by magic, invisible, but visible only by their armors."

Marissa's eyes widened as she kept admiring the magical sentinel.

"Do not delay!" the maid insisted. "It is yet time before the ceremony."

She listened and followed her to climb the stairs as the silvering gates opened by half, only slightly enough to let them enter.

They turned left to walk around a circular corridor with several doors.

"More silver! Why do they not change colors?!" Marissa whined to herself, rolling her eyes, bored with the silvering environment.

The maid stopped at an entrance and opened it, pushing it with her hand, allowing her companion to pass.

When Marissa entered, she did not avoid her surprise and admiration.

The spacious windowless chamber was all-white, and more than a dozen maids were present, mainly working on small chores. As usual, the soft lighting came from somewhere unknown—a product of Salteran magic.

At the center, Marissa found a floating strange white throne of circular shapes where two maids in white, a Berremen, and a Casakan, were standing on both sides.

Seated on the throne, the empress had her legs crossed beneath her flowing white tunic. Placed gently on her knees, her hands remained still. Her closed eyes showed she was sleeping or meditating.

Marissa was in awe to discover she was overly different from the girl she knew as Lakia. Her appearance denoted a powerful presence never felt before, and she realized the empress's limitless essence.

Insecure, the knight knelt before her under the maids' impassivity.

Nehel opened her hazel eyes with some initial blinking and emitted a light smile. "Ser Marissa! I am delighted to meet you again, alive and well!" she exclaimed, offering her hands. "Come here! You shall not offer me reverence!"

The empress' knight stood up and approached her, moved, relieved to find her in good condition after the awful experience at *The Pass*. She took the hands, but she was still unsure if the girl was the same one.

"Even though my name, Lakia, is no longer with me, I am still the same one you have known!" she assured, sensing her.

"How shall I call you, Divine Empress?"

"Call me Nehel! It is my duty and desire to be known that way!"

The maturity did not go unnoticed by Marissa. Without realizing it, tears welled up in her brown eyes, as she

experienced a profound feeling of calmness while join-
ing her hands together.

Once more, her presence has moved Marissa.

Marissa recalled their initial encounter as she held her
sword against Nehel's neck. She was then Lakia.

"I wish you could be with me longer, my knight,"
her smile disappeared. "But I must be ready for the
ceremony."

"Will I meet you?" Marissa inquired, feeling a strong
attachment, strangely, not wishing to separate from her.

"Aye, you will," she replied, separating the hands.
"Do not be concerned for me and go to the corridor.
Someone is waiting for you."

Marissa assented and stood up, leaving the chamber.

The empress again took her original posture and
closed her eyes.

With a burst of energy, Marissa rushed over to Alessandro and gave him a surprising hug, breaking down in
tears on his shoulder.

Once her sobs had subsided, she gazed at him with the
same fondness she had always held for him, disregard-
ing the fact that Alessandro had chosen another girl
over her. However, she soon remembered Fabehel and
hastily distanced herself from him, feeling ashamed.
"My apologies!" her lips were trembling. "I. . . just saw
Lakia. . . Nehel. . . I do not know what she is!"

Alessandro did not react to her sudden manners. Instead, he returned her blade, which she accepted with a big smile. He had back his Seled Post sergeant's sword. "She is not what you think she is. . .," he replied while placing her hand on her blade's hilt. "She is a demigoddess. . . and Peken knew it all the time along."

Marissa gasped in surprise.

"What matters now is to tell the grave news from Casak."

"What had occurred?"

"A Korba invasion. . . Our Casakans fought them alongside the Elves of the West. They lost the battle at the Estos Grassland."

"Is Mother fine? What about my uncle?"

He shook his head and swallowed saliva before an answer. "I believe Lady Tasarissa is safe at the Vykar Palace. . . But Father. . . Orssandro. . . fell victim to the Korbas. . ."

"I shall go back to Casak with haste!"

Alessandro grabbed her arm, forbidding her sudden departure. "Let them resolve their situation! Do not let your mindless impulse to behave that way!"

"But. . . !"

"Our stance is with the Divine Empress and the Jyistereerk!"

"Indeed, Ser Marissa," Selee approached and affirmed with his characteristic smile. "Once you accepted your duty as a knight, you belong to the Jyistereerk now."

Marissa stared at the archmage, noticing a familiar treatment towards Alessandro as he spoke. His behavior was like Yasstro's.

"I must be ready for the ascension ceremony."

A pair of maids carried a long, dusty wooden chest and placed it at the archmage's feet. He used his magic to open it.

The uncovering of a wooden staff with an attached blue sphere awakened the curiosity of both Alessandro and Marissa. The rod had a rustic appearance, revealing its elvish origin.

"This is one of the most powerful weapons on Sankaris. The Sorcerer's Staff," Selee explained, pointing at it with his hand. "For two thousand tikls, this staff belonged to the sorcerers from the Clan of the Kannestes. It passed from mentor to disciple by generations as mystical leaders."

"Why do you have it?" Alessandro inquired, clueless. "I have read about it at the Academy, but do not quite understand why it is in Salter."

"When the Gesha had recently occurred, Sorcerer Uskam summoned me, and I went to his request," nodded, glancing at both youngsters. "Once I was at Molke, he introduced me to the infant Lakia and told her story with her natural mother. He suggested me take her to Salter to be under the maids' care and my tutelage. But I refused."

"Why did you refuse her?" Alessandro asked.

"I knew she was the empress, the Promise of the Jyistereerk, and with the Gesha obliterating the Kingdom of Aranka, I could not risk putting Salter in danger," another smile accompanied his response. "But Sorcerer Uskam suggested taking his staff instead since no one deserved to have it anymore. . . and his disciple departed to other realms. . ."

"Peken!" Marissa interrupted, realizing who the disciple was.

"He mentioned Molke was in a grave position of having both the staff and the empress. If I do not take the empress, the staff should be with me then."

An older maid summoned Selee with signs.

"It is time to initiate her ascension," he announced, nodding to the maid. "Let's not delay anymore!"

The same older maid, Akhimeni, guided Alessandro and Marissa to a balcony at a high level and requested to wait. Selee had previously informed that both would be simply spectators during the ascension.

Both youngsters observed with admiration and wonder. They were under the colossal silver dome.

The shine was too bright to make everything perfectly visible, almost hurting their eyes.

They studied the silvering place. A long, clean aisle crossed by the exact half of the circular site from the entrance to the semi-spherical throne placed on a large, rounded platform eight steps up, at the other extreme under the symbol of a floating Akareen star in contrasting gold. Except for the aisle, they covered the entire floor with engravings of another star, this one in silver.

"This is bigger than the Vykar Palace and the gardens!" Marissa exclaimed, impressed.

"It is, in reality, a temple, though it has no given name." Alessandro did not stop examining. "If my memory does not fail, in Yasstro's words, it is a ceremonial site to ascend those humans who finally reached a divine state."

"Mudihufaser was one of them," she recalled with a warm stare at him.

"Aye, he became part of the one hundred twenty stars. He first discovered the divinity's secrets and shared it with only a very few," nodded. "He was the first."

"How do you explain with La... Nehel?"

"I believe you and I are not the only ones puzzled," he glanced at Marissa. "Even Archmage Selee cannot explain Nehel's divinity. She was born as a demigoddess and with magic!"

A resonant and continuous sound of metallic beats quieted them.

The tall and hollow mirroring silver sentinels made their presence. They were half a hundred when they slowly walked and hit their lances against the floor, creating a rhythmic sound to follow their steps until they took their stances by the edges of the circular place. And silence returned afterward.

"The sentinels are the first to enter and to announce, to safeguard the integrity of the ascender," Alessandro whispered to Marissa in her ear, recalling his lessons with Yasstro.

Next, a crowd of maids of all ages and races appeared in white clothes with no order, but soon arranged themselves in the spaces between the sentinels, where they stood firmly and immobile, leaving the aisle free.

"Five hundred maids, representing the five hundred realms that existed, exist and will exist in Sankaris from its existence to the end."

A crowd of multiracial mages, enchantresses, sorcerers, and sorceresses in colorful clothes entered and positioned themselves by the sides of the aisle. Each one had their typical staves from their realms of origin. They had formed two lines from the entrance until the first step of the throne platform.

"Who are they? Mages?" Marissa inquired, curious.

"The most prominent mystical men and women on Sankaris," Alessandro whispered again. "One hundred twenty of them, representing the divinities visible in the stars."

"Will Nehel's ascension increase it to one hundred twenty-one?"

"I did the same inquiry about the Mudihufaser to Archmage Yasstro," he chuckled. "It does not work that way in the world of magic. No matter how many divinities, the number will always be one hundred twenty."

"It has no sense!"

With their rhythmic beats, the mechanical sentinels hit the floor again, setting the pace for the slow march.

In a magnificent display, three maids dressed in elegant white attire emerged from the entrance, carefully holding various items in their hands. While the first two carried small golden chests, the last one had an object of significant length hidden beneath a beautifully crafted mantle made of silk-white fabric. With each step carefully taken, they slowly made their way towards the throne.

Subsequently, Selee followed them, carrying the Sorcerer's Staff wearing his usual azure robes.

At last, Nehel appeared in her white tunic, barefoot, with a fixated look ahead, inexpressive, following the rhythmic music while giving the steps.

As the empress walked by the aisle, the mystical people inclined their heads as signs of reverence and respect.

Alessandro placed both hands on the balcony's rail, and his heart sped up. He discovered her differently than the Lakia he knew briefly, sensing an immense power that emanated from her. He could not believe that she was his niece, the daughter of his brother Cassandro, yet a divinity.

Moved, Marissa felt a heartache.

The two maids with the chests climbed the stairs and positioned at the throne's left side, the last and Selee on the right.

Nehel carefully sat on the semi-spherical throne, which floated slightly from the floor, only enough to let her feet be in the air, avoiding any contact with the surface.

The hollow sentinels silenced.

The five hundred maids knelt to salute.

Selee stood before the empress and shouted.

"*Nehel Jyistereerk Mudihufaser! Nehel Jyistereerk Friyterkfer!*" the archmage lifted both arms with the staff in one hand. "*Laki Lakia Myken Hikis!*"

"*Nehel Hikis!*" everyone responded harmonically.

Selee signaled one maid, and she approached the empress. She carefully knelt, put the small chest on the surface, and opened it. She extracted a pair of golden sandals and carefully placed them on Nehel's feet.

"With thy sandals, please accept the powers to travel every realm on Sankaris!" Selee invited with the raised staff and loudly, devoted.

The second maid opened her chest to get a white cloak and covered the empress' back and part of the throne, tying the lace around her neck with great care.

"With thy cloak, please accept the powers of kindness on everyone!"

Nehel still was inexpressive.

The last maid uncovered a long golden rod with an Akareen star at the high end. And she placed it in her hands.

The Nehel symbol, the Jyistereerk symbol, and the Mudihufaser symbol.

"With thy rod, please accept the powers of authority over friends and foes!"

The High Archmage turned around to make sure everyone could see him, and then he made a gesture before striking his staff against the floor, prompting all the mystical people to follow him.

They repetitively beat their staves eight times rhythmically, resulting in a resounding noise that obliged Alessandro and Marissa to shield their ears.

In just a moment, they felt a powerful vibrating tremor from underground.

Then, silence and peace.

Nehel kept herself immobile, immutable, with fixated eyes.

"I can not comprehend what is occurring here!" Marissa expressed her fear while grabbing Alessandro's arm firmly.

"I believe all was channeling to the empress," he responded, startled.

Selee lifted the staff and kept it with both hands, gazing at everyone with authority.

"Nehel Jyistereerk!" the archmage yelled.

"Nehel Hikis!" all the multitude answered except the silvering sentinels.

"Divine Jewel!"

"Nehel Hikis!"

"Divine Empress of Sankaris!"

"Nehel Hikis!"

"Queen of Aranka!"

"Nehel Hikis!"

"Mystical Leader of the Kannestes!"

"Nehel Hikis!"

"High Sorceress of Salter!"

"Nehel Hikis!"

Selee turned around again to face the empress.

This time, her hazel eyes looked at him.

The archmage knelt, placed the Sorcerer's Staff at her feet on the floor, and spoke submissively. "Divine Empress, as for now, I resign to Salter to be at the service of the Jyistereerk," he nodded with an expectant bow. "With you here, my leadership is no longer needed."

"I gratefully accept your wisdom and experience, archmage," Nehel replied with a light smile. "Your first task is to form a council of the most prominent to govern Salter before you travel with me."

From their position on the balcony, the two youngsters could witness the entire events.

"Just like that, half west of the Karekall and Aranka are now under Empress Nehel!" Alessandro whispered, impressed. "The Jyistereerk, that mystical empire, is expanding at an incredible pace and becoming even more powerful."

"And her Jyistereerk began with a satchel!" Marissa murmured with widened eyes.

27
HEAD

The *Assault at the Estos Grassland* was the most disgraced, unforgettable, and saddest battle ever for Casak in all its history.

An elves' dishonor who was wrongly overconfident in their mystical and apparent impeccable armies despite their past successful experiences against the dragons.

The flying Korbas had killed, maimed, and taken victims during the battle, ravaging Casakan cities and towns with no disregard for compassion.

Men and women mourned their spouses or descendants. If they had found their bodies, they have been fortunate enough to bury them and know their locations under their tombstones. The most unfortunate could not find them either alive or dead, missing. They indeed became demons.

Into Korbeens, at the Korbas' service against their will.

Yet, even if their bodies were absent, they mourned their spouses, sons, or daughters. Either way, they also were dead. A Korbeen was only a body that was easy to manipulate, a soulless entity.

Following the Casakan traditions, Archmage Missar used his magic to set fire to a gigantic pile of wood at the center of the Vykar Palace grounds to mourn the Head Orssandro, and promptly, the smoke elevated towards a sky colored in red as the sunset began.

It did not matter how wrong or right Orssandro was in the past, how evil or good he was. A Head was a servant to the whole people of Casak, a Head of State, a Head of Assembly.

"My brother should be there!" Lady Tasarissa ground her teeth with tears that drew alongside her dark cheeks, shaking her head, staring at the funeral pyre without a body. "These damned Korbas have no shame!"

Lady Alyssa Taskar touched her shoulder as a sympathy to her sister-in-law, but despite the formalities and forgiveness, she would never accept Orssandro's done deeds. She attended the funeral for the people she cared about, not for him, despite his faultless demonic corruption.

Captain Trasso, with most of his body covered in blood-stained bandages. Without a right arm and lots of pain, even though herbalists and medics made it possible to give him relief. Observing the pyre, he cried because of the unbearable agony and profound sadness. His respected Head was gone, and he wanted to give his last respects, standing firmly despite his weak condition. Indeed, Trasso disapproved of many things from Orssandro but still admired him.

Archmage Missar touched the hanging orchid's medal the young lancer Diesso placed in his hands that infamous day, feeling the heavy responsibility of being the new Head of Casak. This devastated realm went from a crisis to a catastrophe. His eyes observed the fire consuming the wood as his mind raced to thousands of solutions to help lift his motherland.

Recently, he communicated with High Archmage Selee through the spherical portals. He knew about Empress Nehel's ascension and Salter's transfer of powers to her. He later gave the news to Commandant Kartak.

But while the empress' news was of joy for many, grief and sorrow existed at Casak. Yet, her ascension gave hope.

The elves were keeping some distance away from the funeral but were present to give respects to the one who was their opponent. In silence, Kartak and Partak were at the front of a selected group of soldiers.

Akartaki and her sisters were also present.

Behind Missar and Tasarissa were the surviving and latest members of the Assembly—the newly joined lancer

Diesso of Kokork, Ralyssa Vir, Possertro, and Orssus—. Including Alyssa, seven left from eleven.

At last, way too behind, between trees, almost hiding, Carlissa witnessed the funeral under a brown cloak's hood. Her eyes behind the round glasses gave bizarre sparks in her scowl.

Only Carrasso was strangely absent.

The burden of a chaotic realm overwhelmed Archmage Missar as he sat at the beginning of the table as the new Head.

A cold and anguished morning. The day after the funeral.

He observed an unharmed long table in a hall at the Casakan Castle that showed most of the damage caused by the Korbas. An unknown fire burnt most of the former Heads' portraits. Broken windows and pieces of glass still littered the floors. Ripped triangle banners erased any evidence of the orchid emblems. Unknown perpetrators destroyed the ornaments. The time was not enough to do the cleaning, but delicate enough to be cautious about the possibility of more assaults.

He noticed the table's distance with fixated eyes, wishing to resolve the complications that even his magic could not do. It was more complicated than bringing fire or water from nowhere.

The last days were strenuous and sleepless. His first task with the Assembly was to reorganize and form a new army with the elves to defend Casak, and he had to pass an exhaustive revision of every Casakan that dared to join the surviving troops, even in their elderly years.

He had great relief to find the unharmed Casakan Army in different ports. The Korbas did not find the powder deposits in the harbors, but Missar instructed to leave them intact since they were supposed to be used as a last resort.

And he had the painful task of consoling the families of the fallen.

As a Head, his magic was useless.

The Assembly suddenly disturbed Missar.

Some members had to lift chairs that were thrown. Others took handkerchiefs to clean them before taking a seat.

Lady Tasarissa and Alyssa Taskar sat on either side of him.

"What the heck of upheaval we are in!" Possertro exclaimed in disgust, glancing at everyone. "That scourge of Orssandro Vykar had no shame in putting us in an awkward stance!"

Tasarissa clenched her teeth in a mixture of sadness, anger, and embarrassment. "Let us not blame him for his involuntary madness!"

"Enough!" Missar tried to keep the peace. "I believe it is not time for recriminations but to look for ways to lift our fallen realm."

But Possertro slammed the table with both hands and violently stood up, throwing his chair, scaring most of the presents, although the archmage showed immutability.

"We were one of the finest realms on Sankaris while Lady Larissa Eskar was in charge!" screamed. "Only for that idiotic Orssandro to become Head and ruin everything! We no longer have the prestige, the dignity, the respect, and we have lost the children to guarantee our future!"

In his outrage, a quiet assembly observed how Possertro Benke let his emotions and tears out, surprising everyone.

"Why do the goddesses punish us in that humiliating way?!" he continued among sobs.

"Despite the fall, everyone in Ryza knows how the Casakans fought with bravery," Commandant Kartak intervened, startling the assemblers. He had coincidentally entered the hall at Missar's previous request and confronted him with empathy. "Casak may have lost a battle, but your realm is not dead nor weak. It is growing stronger and renowned around Sankaris."

Possertro glared at him in apparent distrust, but nodded in comprehension.

Kartak placed back the chair and kindly sat him. "Our sisters have your children in safety," he addressed the Assembly. "They are doing activities they should be—playing games, laughing, learning new things, being healed—and not forced into labor or war."

"Do you plan to keep our children far from their families, commandant?" Missar inquired with curiosity.

"To protect the children is one of the greatest commandments in Kasnasga, but yours do not belong to us. If you request, we may return them to their families."

"I vote for our children to stay with the elves until peace is restored," Ralyssa Vir suggested. "The return of the Korbas is uncertain, and I do not want the innocent to suffer while searching for their lost loved ones."

The Assembly voted in favor of Ralyssa's proposal unanimously.

"Next matter. . . " Missar murmured, tired, apprehensive about ending the session.

"Tell us something, archmage. . . Head?" Alyssa suggested, unsure.

"Call by my name. . ."

"We know you have ways to communicate with the Ri or Salter, and you might have news from the Promise. What could you tell us?"

Missar exhaled and joined his hands together before offering a reply. "The Promise has ascended. She is now the Divine Empress Nehel and has taken over four realms, Aranka inclusive," he emitted a light smile as rarely shown in him. "The Jyistereerk is becoming a reality under her reign and her two appointed, the Casakans Master Alessandro Eskar and Ser Marissa Taskar."

"Not a threat?" Assembler Orssus inquired.

"She was never a threat. She will be our most important ally against the Korbas."

"I propose then to offer Casak to the Divine Empress!" Possertro stood again. "Heard from mouths that she is also too Casakan as Lady Larissa's granddaughter!"

"I second him!" the young new assembler, Lancer Diesso, supported his proposal.

One by one, they stood as a sign of approval.

Missar placed both hands on the table once again. "It would honor me to offer our realm to the empress and be part of the Jyistereerk."

"Long life to the Divine Empress!" Diesso shouted with a fist to the air up. "Long life to Master Eskar and Ser Marissa!"

Kartak nodded as his eyebrow twitched.

Followed by Kartak, Archmage Missar, entered the chamber that once belonged to Orssandro Vykar. To his dislike, he observed the spacious, wooden solid desk covered by cluttered papyruses and other items. A bit annoyed, exhausted, and apprehensive about taking a rest from his constant activities, he passed his hand over the desk to use his magic.

Papyruses and items came to life and flew to arrange themselves in bookcases and shelves, and a cloud of dust lifted from the desk.

The elf fanned the dust with his hand. He almost felt the need to sneeze.

The aureate large volume slid to the desk's center, and to the archmage's snap, it opened to a specific page. It illustrated a black-skinned man lifting a mystical *Ykarte* sword. The Salteran text called him *Torsen*, as it was the translated designation for Head. "Salter owns this book of premonitions based on the *Frelee Dee*. However, during King Vihen's reign, someone stole it and gave it to the

Head," Missar explained to Kartak's curiosity. "Orssandro Vykar always believed he would have the sword, the *Ykarte*, and based his obsession on this page."

"Archmage Yasstro warned us before his departure to the Gakia through Akartaki," the elf nodded. "The Sword of Kasana is such a delicate relic that it changed the fate of Sankaris. It can not be in the wrong hands."

"Your assessment is correct, commandant," the archmage asserted. "Yasstro received the *Ykarte* from enigmatic travelers and hid it in his sanctuary's library. That is why Orssandro was obsessed with burning mystical libraries to find it. And our archmage had to use his special abilities to camouflage it."

"You have told me you possess the *Ykarte*." He twitched his eyebrow, satisfied with the explanation. "Where is the relic?"

"The Ykarte is coming right now," Missar smiled mischievously despite his bagged eyes.

They heard ascending steps. At first, the sounds were vague, but slowly became loud as they approached the chamber.

Commandant Kartak readied himself to see the relic.

Carlissa entered with shyness by the door. She gave a glimpse through her thick glasses, fearful. Her brown, gritty cloak that wrapped her customary maroon dress covered her.

Her hands were empty.

The elf was deeply disappointed.

"Indeed, the Head had the *Ykarte* in his hands," the archmage pointed to the book. "She has been with me most of the time."

"But. . . Where is it?" Kartak inquired, confused and startled, glancing at the standing girl. "The lass is here with nothing with her!"

"Do not be mistaken, commandant. *She* is the *Ykarte*!"

The one-armed Trasso glared at the Beyond Sea from a cliff on his black horse. The herbalists at Estolk could finally reduce the pain he had been suffering from his wound through unique and expensive herbage, yet it bothered him. He could breathe with relief the fresh breeze that afternoon as he awaited him, relaxing his discomfort and enjoying a moment of relief and peace.

He did not understand the extent of the damage caused by the *Assault at the Estos Grassland*. In days since losing his arm, he had learned to drive his horse, taking the reins with his left hand and planning to relearn the basics of combat without a right hand.

His life had changed drastically. Yet, despite his age and incomplete body, he was determined to keep his military career that had started as a mere soldier in Sarak until he became the City's Guardian and later captain of the Casakan Army.

A flying flock of black crows in the sky startled him, but he knew the meeting was close.

On his skeletal gray horse, the chilling, crooked man under the gritty dark robe's cowl approached Trasso and stopped beside him.

"I hope you are pleased with your recent deed," Trasso glanced at him with anger, discreetly yet immobile on his equine. "You have taken away Lord Orssandro, and I have lost an important part of my body!"

"I had promised rewards, but sacrifices had to be made for greater purposes," Carrasso spoke through his thick lips. "Sacrifices and patience are crucial for the plan."

Trasso stared at him with tremendous distrust. He felt a revolving disgust in his entrails.

"Tell me. I have never seen a black mage in many years, but something tells me you are more than it," he spoke, harsh. "What are you?"

"A warlock, captain," his answer came with a grin of yellow and disordered teeth. "Ardek Korba has blessed me with the unique gift of the invocation!"

The morbid gesture did not surprise but impressed the captain.

"I have suspected it was you who summoned them. Was it necessary?"

"Both the Kingdom of Aranka and *The Seneschal* required it."

Trasso was appalled and speechless.

"I am going north and disappear for a while," Carrasso grinned again with a nod. "I've completed my tasks for now, but I will be back when the empress comes of age."

The warlock mandated his horse and instantly galloped inland instead of the cliff and the Beyond Sea as the flock of crows followed him.

The captain observed him descend until he disappeared into the marshes, and the birds over him dispersed completely.

28
CONVEYANCE

As Alessandro approached the giant wooden platform in the valley, he did not believe his eyes. He wondered how people assembled the massive structure made from thousands of timber lumbers or how many trees they had to cut down and guessed hundreds, enough to have cleared a good part of a forest.

But what forest? He recalled his geography lessons and knew Salter was primarily a place of valleys and plains from

The Pass to the Karekall. He knew the far east lands were arid, though not well known.

And how could they transport a structure as large as a frigate, similar to the ones he saw at the Port of Sostolk belonging to the Casakan Navy, to the Ri?

"We could make a whole town from it!" he exclaimed with widened eyes to Marissa beside him.

"This is the intention, master," Selee joined them smoothly and smiled. "I built this palanquin, but when its purpose is done, it will construct a town."

"How?"

"Await and see."

Marissa listened to both men with admiration. And she turned to study her surroundings.

While they remained at Salter, the sky displayed a starred eternal night.

She noticed mountains on the horizon, the Holy Mountains and the Cayderr Range, and recognized them. *The Empress' Pass*, which was renamed by the Gathering in Berrem, was within sight. But something seemed altered from the last time.

The fresh wind arrived like a breeze and moved the valley's tall emerald grasses, announcing an empress.

Nehel dismounted her camel and walked to Alessandro.

He noticed her in her pure white tunics as she approached, stopped, and took his hands. He observed some concern on her face. "What troubles you?"

"When we reach Seled Post, please do not worry, uncle," she responded with expressive hazel eyes. "You are more blessed than you realize."

Alessandro did not understand her, but nodded. He was still overwhelmed to see his niece transformed into a powerful empress.

"I know you are conflicted about me," Nehel revealed with a smile. "But I assure you, I am the same girl you have met at the villa. I am still your niece!" The empress asked him to kneel so she could reach his cheek with a kiss, which caught him off guard.

On the horizon, a vast group of maids in white appeared, following their empress in a slow march, as Nehel turned around. They all walked together through the valley towards the platform.

Alessandro, Marissa, and Selee observed them aiding Nehel in climbing the palanquin.

The maids followed with no effort. Seemingly, they used their abilities to float, but yet their hands and bare feet touched the lumber. They assisted the empress to ascend the ladder to the high wooden throne exactly at the center, a tiny dot compared with the colossal structure, a tower with enough height to be visible to everyone. Afterward, they held hands along the edges of the platform, creating a chain that faced outward.

"I comprehend your emotions, master," Selee approached Alessandro, finding him glaring at the event, visibly moved to the event. "It is difficult to deal with many emotions and encounters at once."

Alessandro prevented him from seeing his face by cleaning his eyes and moving to the side, as he noticed the archmage beside him. "What are you? A medic of the head?

Are you trying to use your magic on me?" he muttered with exasperation.

Selee chuckled. "At this moment I am only a man, an ancient man talking from experience," he nodded. "While many lads your age are courting lasses, still learning about the life and taking their first responsibilities to become men. Unique circumstances forced you to perform certain duties proper for more mature males."

"Aye, archmage," he downed his head. "If only Cassandro were alive and could take my place. Lakia, Nehel. . . whatever her name is, deserves a father and not an uncle."

"Does she have a strong resemblance to her father?"

"Every time I see her, I can recall his face. . . And that hurts. . . I thought I had not forgiven him by leaving me as I tried to erase him from my head. . ."

"Master, you may not forgive him and erase him as many times as you wish, but he still ties your heart."

At last, Alessandro turned to see the archmage and gave a dubious smile.

The chain of five hundred maids took their hands and lifted their faces toward the nocturnal sky and, by their gestures, seemed to make silent prayers.

"All those maids have offered their complete lives to the empress, as mystical sisters, and that is what they did during the ascension," Selee whispered to explain.

"What are they? Messengers? Servants?" Marissa inquired with curiosity.

"They are a sisterhood to assist Nehel," Alessandro replied. "Similar to all these brotherhoods and sisterhoods that existed en Molke long time ago, to be precise in the times of Kasana."

"Be quiet!" the archmage mandated.

A strong rumble felt from inside the grounds, followed by a persistent vibration.

Alessandro and Marissa witnessed, stunned, besides of a pleased Selee, how the platform slowly levitated with perfect balance, as the empress showed complete peace from the top of the high throne. The platform stood in the air for a long time before it moved forward at a great pace.

The spectators heard rhythmic and harmonic metallic steps coming and turned their eyes left.

The mechanical silvering void, mystic slender sentinels, followed the platform in two precise lines. They were thousands carrying their lances.

"What are they?" Marissa asked, perplexed. "I have seen them in the Citadel."

"They are Artensens. They live because arcane magic is inside them," Selee explained. "An ancient invention from the early mages, but no one is certain of their true origin."

"Why are they following the palanquin?" Alessandro inquired.

"They are abandoning Salter to be the empress' guard."

"All of them?"

"Aye, it is pointless to stay in a realm that is already doomed."

Marissa was concerned as she observed the Artensen sentinels depart when the platform visually vanished. "Are we to follow them? Or are we to fly even?"

"We will mount them," Selee chuckled and pointed to three two-horn stags that mysteriously had appeared. The animals were ready with their own saddles. "These fine creatures are proper to go down into Berrem."

The conveyance through *The Empress' Pass* was unique as it descended, maintaining a perfect equilibrium that neither the maids nor the empress were affected. Wherever it went, the platform was in a perfectly horizontal position, floating in the air.

The Artensens had no problem in the descent, their impeccable mechanical movements allowed them to walk in any kind of terrain.

Alessandro, Marissa, and Selee were the sole strugglers in their descent. Although they were on stags, the riders faced discomfort because of constant movement hurting their backsides and the risk of falling in treacherous soils made them hold on to their horns.

Mainly Alessandro, as Marissa, noticed with surprise how the Salteran night was gradually transforming into a day sky at every step they were going down. He also discovered, surprised how the pass showed a different aspect than the previous gelid one they had encountered and suffered during their climbing. He felt a more template temperature and found a rich place with greenish grass and colorful flowers.

"What had happened here? I can recall we were going through bitter cold and slippery lands, but I find a bliss instead!"

"Many things had changed since the empress' metamorphosis," Selee replied.

"Are you saying she made all this?!"

"Aye, though it was not her fault."

"But not that!" Marissa shouted, pointing to the sky.

Alessandro dismounted the stag and drew his sword in distrust, resolved to fight. He has seen the flock of flying Korbas in the sky going in circles and recalled that time when he first saw them before his eyes closed to his unconsciousness. The long distance and the sun's brilliance did not allow him to observe well to determine their sizes and kind.

The floating palanquin came to an abrupt stop, but the maids and Nehel did not lose their balance and remained motionless.

Marissa also dismounted and drew her beloved sword.

The Artensens, along with the platform, stopped and turned right. Their metallic helmet-shaped heads lifted to observe the dragons. They held their lances with one hand in an upward direction.

In an instant, the dozen Korbas ceased their circular pattern and descended, aiming for the empress in a high-speed attack.

Although useless, Alessandro and Marissa ran terrified toward the platform.

The sentinels, imbued with magic, hurled their spears and killed all the dragons mid-flight, causing them to fall to their demise. All but one.

The surviving Korba was smaller than the others that died, and a lance could only pierce its wing. He spiralled down and vanished into a cluster of small trees.

Marissa stopped running and breathed a sigh of relief as she saw Nehel on her throne, radiating an incredible sense of peace and perseverance. As she turned, she noticed Alessandro making a desperate run towards the trees with the sergeant's sword in hand. She followed him.

With caution, Alessandro entered a small patch of greenish and leafy trees, sensing an unfamiliar darkness. He walked with caution, feeling his heart beating with a fast rhythm as fear suddenly overtook him and cold sweat ran down his face, searching for the wounded monster determined to kill him.

After a long time, he arrived at a space where the sun made presence through its light. He found the creature there.

The black dragon was slightly larger than any human and used its wings to regain balance on his feet. He had long horns and screeched constantly with an ominous sound enough to produce multiple goosebumps.

From a safe distance behind a bush, Alessandro watched his injured wing heal as the small Korba only showed his deformed back by a moment. With determination, he rose and wielded the sword, ready to chase and execute him from behind.

Alessandro began with his run and aimed the sword at him.

The creature turned and showed his face.

Horror pounded Alessandro, and he dropped his weapon in surprise. Falling to his knees, he widened his eyes in consternation.

"Uncle!" Marissa yelled with dread. She had recently arrived to discover the creature.

The monster observed the two witnesses with his red eyes as his saliva oozed from his fangs filled mouth and twisted horns from his head. He had a recognizable face, clearly unmistakable.

He had the same semblance as Orssandro Vykar.

He was an undead Korba.

He was the same Head transformed into a demon.

A Korbeen.

Not recognizing both youngsters, the monster flew high into the sky, healed, screeching.

"He is not the same Orssandro we knew," Alessandro clarified with quivering words to Marissa from his knelt position. "It was his body, but Orssandro is indeed dead!"

Marissa only stared at the sky with tears that ran along her cheeks.

Following the encounter with the Korbas, the Artensens resumed their journey down *The Empress' Pass* with no further incidents.

Alessandro and Marissa drove their stags with somber and static gestures in complete silence.

Selee trailed behind them with a serious demeanor, unlike his usual smiling self. Alessandro briefly recounted the unfortunate encounter with Orssandro's Korbeen.

Marissa's eyes were still humid.

Alessandro directed his attention towards the conveyance, trying to forget about the awful experience. He identified *The Empress' Pass'* opening as the platform crossed the narrow exit between the Holy Mountains and the Cayderr Range, and instructed his stag to halt.

Following his lead, Marissa and Selee stood beside him.

"What is the matter, master?" Selee inquired.

With a nod, Alessandro pointed to Seled Post visible from a far distance.

A massive crowd of hundreds of thousands gathered on the outskirts, waiting anxiously. As soon as they caught sight of the enormous palanquin and saw the empress seated regally on her elevated throne, they erupted into a chorus of merry cheers.

It was a triumphal return to Berrem.

The Promise had returned.

Empress Nehel had made her way back to reclaim the balance on Sankaris.

29
GREATSWORD

Corr did not bother to light the chamber, preferring to let the No Sak's moonlight stream in through the windows while he held a metallic mug. Having spent a majority of its life enslaved in the dim Mines of Tiunnff, the feline felt comfortable in the shadows of the night.

The Fennen had his feet in a relaxed position on a chair. Corr awaited someone, as he chose not to take part in the festive celebrations honoring the newly ascended empress. He longed for silence, but his sensitive ears picked up the continuous commotion caused by turbulent drunks in the distance, despite the curfew imposed by the local sentinels to avoid attracting any Korba.

Corr observed a door being opened, revealing the silhouette of a man with a torch. He knew him. "Welcome back, master," his deep voice greeted before taking another sip of his brew.

Alessandro put his torch in a holder on a nearby wall and approached the table where the feline was. With an irritating sound, he dragged a chair across the floor and sat down with a serious expression, gasping for air.

Corr noticed him exhausted, dowdy.

"What are you drinking?" Alessandro pointed to the feline's mug.

"Honey brew with mint. It is refreshing."

"Pour me one."

Corr nodded, placing his mug on the table, then grabbed the nearby jar and poured the brew into one of the four metallic cups on a circular tray, handing it to Alessandro.

He drank from his cup with desperation and let out a relieved sigh.

Then, Alessandro slammed the table, showing a pair of fingers to him. "Tell me two things that you have not told me, Corr!" exclaimed in exasperation. "Where is Lady Fabehel?"

With its green eyes and vertical pupils, the Fennen observed him with fixation and immutability. He had been expecting that question for a while. Instead of providing an answer, he retrieved a small papyrus from his dark blue attire and presented it to him across the table.

"What the heck is this?!"

"Lady Fabehel had requested me to give it to you before her departure."

Alessandro declined the papyrus, but Corr placed it on the table.

"You tell me!"

"From quite some time ago, Lady Fabehel had sought me help, which I refused initially since I dislike involvement in private affairs. She did not wish to marry Lord Pan Din, and she had a conflict at heart because of you," he sighed and drank again from his mug. "She inquired about the Arankans living in Fenn and provided her recommendations for where she would go."

"What followed?"

"I assisted her in getting your mare ready, master. Song," he emphasized. "I made sure she had enough provisions for her journey, and I gave a letter of recommendation so one of my acquaintances could receive her."

Alessandro was in disbelief, then looked at the papyrus on the table.

"What is the second thing you wished to inquire?"

"What is the truth about Cassandro? I know you are hiding something from me."

Corr emptied his mug, stood up, and went towards the door. But before leaving, he stopped and replied, with his back unturned.

"Lady Larissa never approved of Cassandro's relationship with Princess Natahel. As she failed to stop him in

Katalk, she hired a vagrant who ultimately captured and sold him as a slave in the Mines of Tiunnff."

The feline departed the chamber after his words resonated with Alessandro. Trembling, he turned to see the papyrus and unrolled it, discovering a letter written by Fabehel.

Master Alessandro,

It pains me. I have to warn about my abrupt choice, especially when my heart is telling me many times to be near you, and even our exceptional empress had suggested to follow my feelings and embrace the love. But I do not deserve thy love because of my uncertainties, and my people have been always my priority since my five years old.

The Gesha pushed all of us to leave behind our beloved motherland recently ravaged, putting me in a unique situation. Princess Natahel's abandonment forced me to rely on my dear Tin, while I had to learn the ways of the ruling and sacrifice the pleasures of the children.

To benefit my people, I accepted Lord Pan Din's marriage proposal to keep supporting the colony on Garterrem Isle. Even my soul and body had yet to be given.

We have met. I initially despised you, but being with you learned to love. You are the only person who has given me a sense of security and shown me kindness, despite my inability to walk, run, or dance like we did on that tragic night. I thank you for stealing a kiss from me, my very first kiss, and believe me, there were many times which I wanted to kiss you overly.

Once again, I must prioritize my people over myself. I expected grave consequences for the refugees if I denied Lord Pan Din and chose my people first. And I desired to look for other Arankans in Fenn. He comprehended my reasons for kindly declining him, and he even pledged to continue funding the Garterrem town. Unfortunately, I had to sacrifice you.

Please, accept my apologies for stealing Song. I acknowledge the mare's importance to you, but she is also a reflection of who you are and I want to remember that forever. Forgive me for not loving you the way you desired. I will understand if you decide to return to Marissa at some point. Do not look nor wait for me, move on, and assist as much as possible you can to the empress, your niece, as she will need you dearly. Lakia and you remind me of Tin and me.

Even though I may sound and write like a mature woman, I'm still a sixteen-year-old girl experiencing emotions.

With regards, Fabehel of the Red Tides.

From his wagon, Juni surveyed visually the gates, shielded by thick waki furs. The frigid moon of No Sak lit up the scene as the smaller red No Ta emerged from the horizon. While trying to get warmth, he saw how the newly appointed Imperial Guard kept a strong watch over the garrison and its surroundings.

Vigilant sentinels had giant ballistas on the thick walls, ready for any possible Korba threat.

Earlier, the mystical Artensens seized the garrison while the empress entered on foot along with her Court of Maids. The metallic guards soon abandoned it to safeguard the immense platform in the valley on the outskirts.

The local sentinels pushed the crowd away after the celebrations, and Juni saw it happen. The curfew enforced a rule that only the military could be out late at night.

From his clothes, Juni grabbed a pear and glanced again at the garrison. In the afternoon, he could see Nehel from afar to avoid the cramped multitude, the same Lakia with whom he had developed a close friendship during their journey to Carretem alongside the vagrant Kekten. He hoped to have a direct meeting with her to confirm if she was the same person, afraid.

Juni was unsure of the empress's sleeping quarters, but assumed she had the prestigious chamber for high-ranking officials. He had been to Seled Post before. He knew the garrison well from his previous visits to this place as a troubadour with his father.

All he needed to do was enter on his own, ensuring he stayed out of sight.

Juni took off the furs and put on a raspy brown cloak, the same attire Lakia wore when she vanished at Carretem until her reappearance during the jousting tournament. Juni leaped off from the wagon, ignored the cold puddles that filled the irregular holes in the ground, and dashed towards the gate, where vagrants on duty wielded their swords without drawing them wary of a shapeshifter Korba.

"What purpose brings you, lad?" a male vagrant in rusted armor inquired in distrust.

"It is true what they say about the mantises?" Juni pretended to ask with insistence. "Is it true the red ones eat heads?"

"Bug off!" the guard demanded, annoyed. "We do not have time for childish nonsenses and carry out with the curfew!"

Other vagrants joined to oppose Juni, requesting him to leave from the gate.

The boy pretended to be hurt and ran with fabricated loud tantrums that disconcerted the guards. Instead of going back to his wagon, he took the path towards the garrison's walls.

The vagrant wished to follow Juni, but his comrade stopped him by the shoulder.

"Let the whiner go!"

They soon returned to their duties.

By exploiting the darkness of night, Juni located a small fissure in the wall where he hid and cease his act. He climbed, placing hands and feet in the crevices until he reached the end. He noticed a space between the giant ballistas where he stood, wary of the Berremen sentinels that may discover him.

He crouched and swiftly sprinted through the ballistas, avoiding the sentinels, until he reached a fortified tower with illuminated torch-lit spiraling stairs. At the bottom, he stumbled upon a spacious dining room only for the military and went inside.

But someone petrified Juni.

The boy's presence attracted a male scrubber constantly relying on a mop and a bucket of dirty water to wipe the sturdy stone floor, and he glared at him with his twisted and deformed eyes. "What are you doing here, fool?!" the grumpy man complained. "This is mine! Your place is in the stables!"

Juni nodded, startled and ran exiting to the exterior court.

He stopped and discovered his intended aim, a balcony. The chamber remained illuminated, showing that the empress had not yet gone to sleep.

By studying the balcony's surroundings, Juni uncovered a wall hidden beneath a dense vine. His gaze darted around, cautious of the sentinels' watch from above.

Crouching low, he sprinted hastily across the court, making himself visible only under No Sak's bleach light, and then quietly slipped into the vine to hide. Once again, he wasted no time in climbing towards the desired destination.

He hesitated at the edge, fearing the guards or vagrants would notice him, determined leaped onto the stone balustrades. In an instant, he discovered his inability to fully reach it, forcing him to depend on the railing to avoid slipping, but his grip slowly loosened to a sure fall.

Juni looked down to acknowledge the mortal hardness of the stone ground as his body hanged. He glanced at the chamber, convinced that he had failed to succeed, and was ready to die or, in the worst-case scenario, to cripple himself.

While trying to hold on, he noticed the empress exit and give him a stern look with her hands placed on her waist.

She shook in disapproval. "Do you know you could have entered by the door?" she scolded him.

"Please! Help me!" Juni gasped and begged desperately as he was still slipping.

Nehel took his hands from the railing, but she did not pull him. Instead, she used her power to float him, slightly lifting him, until he landed beside her. Even in safety, she still held his hands out of affection.

She looked at him with captivating hazel eyes and emitted a smile.

Juni forgot about his frightening incident to notice her changed. He found her dressed in pure white attire with her hair beautifully tied up, revealing her flawless girlish face, in contrast to her past boyish appearance while disguised.

Her appearance mesmerized him. She truly resembled an empress.

Juni got no words.

"I. . . I. . ., " he stammered, unable to say anything. Still, he reached into his clothing and pulled out a pear, offering it to her.

She smiled again, excited, and impulsively hugged him.

Despite being startled, he still embraced her, but with some hesitation.

She separated from him, snatched the pear, and cheerful hurried into the chamber.

"Lakia!"

"Come, Juni!" she invited from inside.

Upon hearing her, the boy obediently followed her and got into a chamber filled with a vast assortment of presents. When he found her, she had taken a seat beside a circular table that had a peculiar arrangement—a large bowl filled with a selection of fresh fruits, including pears. However, Nehel preferred to slice and savor the one from Juni.

She looked serious and pointed with her short knife at Juni. "My name is Nehel now," she clarified, putting the slices in her mouth. "But I am still the same despite my change!"

"Uh?" Juni nodded, aghast, and noticed her busy with the fruit and studied the hoarded chamber. He knew that upon entering Seled Post, the crowd had presented her with many gifts, and she graciously accepted them with the help of the maids. In a state of fascination, he scrutinized a diverse selection of gifts, ranging from opulent gold cups and bags bursting with coins to giefo weapons that the wealthy provided, as well as humble sacks of rice and modest dishes provided by impoverished farmers. He stopped when he found a large circular board, a checkered game on the ground leaning against a hefty sack of Breken coffee, and opened a small pouch beside that contained white and black stones. It looked familiar. His father had told him about it, but did not remember at all.

"This is a Falte," Nehel explained, standing beside him. "The Molkans used to play it to learn about stances in life. And that is how Sorcerer Uskam taught me about my stance as an empress."

He stared at her while he tried to find the right words in his mind.

"Father told me that in the old world, three kinds of monarchs existed during the begone times," he recalled crouched, touching the board with the tip of his fingers and adopted a more serious gesture. "The Benevolent, the Hatred and the Blands."

"Why do you tell me it?" she inquired, perplexed, though she sensed something from him.

He stood and fixated his gaze on her eyes.

"What kind of monarch are you, missy?" he extended his hands to show her sudden wealth through spread gifts over the chamber, only forgiving the bed with silk sheets. "When I have met you and even I knew you were an empress, you were yourself even disguised. An unfortunate born with a stance of being an empress apprehensive to establish the Jyistereerk. You were Lakia and not Nehel! A simple girl with a satchel who enjoyed pears!"

Nehel smiled, serene, with brilliance in her eyes.

"Lakia is still my given name and I will carry it always as my elvish mother gifted me, but Nehel is my regnal name and this is how I shall carry the Jyistereerk," with affection and sensing his inner, touched his cheek. "Aye, I got these presents from the people who entrusted to me, but I assure you, none of them are for me. They belong to my sovereign and all its people."

"A monarch should unite the people and avoid all distinctions, yet you are accepting such gifts from everyone when you shall side the less fortunate! Do not allow the corruption to take you!"

"My intentions are always good, so, I suppose, I am the Benevolent one," Nehel assured, avoiding the subject. "There is no need to be troubled, Juni."

Juni closed his eyes and nodded, drawing a smile. "I apologize, missy." Although the empress' slight changes still caused him discomfort, but he remained silent about it and chose not to keep with the conversation. "I shall now make my way back to my wagon."

"You will not!" she chuckled. "I have already requested some of my vagrants to look after your wagon, and my maid, Akhimeni, is on her way to take you to your new quarters."

"How you did it?" he inquired, stunned.

"Did you forget who am I?!" in a sarcastic tone she scolded with hands, again, on her waist.

Nehel woke up from a terrifying dream and sat on her bed, gasping for breath. As she observed her cluttered chamber, she noticed with astonishment the candles, which had previously emitted a dull light, were now shining with an intensified and rare luminosity.

Affected by fear, she experienced a sense of terror as someone invaded her space. Despite her desire to let out a piercing scream and call her guards, she inexplicably felt a sense of powerlessness.

She discovered a young woman, most likely a maid, who had silver hair and wore in white garments. This graceful Casakan woman was eating grapes from the fruit bowl with disdain, all while examining the gifts that surrounded her.

Except that she was not a maid.

"Have you come to take me?" afraid but firm Nehel inquired from her bed.

The woman turned to see the empress with her live red eyes, still chewing the grapes. "I wish to take you, but your transmuted aura does not let me," the woman replied in a very recognizable, sweet male voice. "Besides, I came for another reason."

"You will fail, Ardek Korba!" she claimed as her fear slightly wore out. "How many more worlds are you going to keep condemning?!"

"Do not you get, empress?" the disguised Korba grinned. "The evilness of your world summoned us!"

"Who summoned you?!" Nehel left the bed to get near the Korba but keeping a wary distance.

"The blood of Kasana. . ."

She closed her eyes and downed her face.

He was right.

"Aye, her thirst for revenge tainted her blood, and when it seeped into the earth, it summoned you here."

"Thus, at the moment of her execution, the *Ykarte* gave you life, too."

With a commanding presence, Nehel lifted her face and opened her hazel eyes. "In the precise instant when the *Ykarte* beheaded Kasana, it conceived me as a living essence, because in death, it claimed life."

With a grin, Ardek Korba tossed grapes into his mouth while still appearing like a charming woman. "I am the reason for your existence. Eh?" Said with an insulting tone.

"It is the truth," she affirmed with confidence. "Kasana's tainted blood summoned you, and the *Ykarte* deemed it necessary for me to be conceived in order to confront and put an end to your advancement."

"Empress, is that why you attacked me during our first encounter in the Black Forest?"

"Aye, and I was wrong to go forward with overconfidence. I know it now. And I shall await for the right time to confront you. . ."

"Spare your words and listen to me, empress!" the Korba demanded with certain annoyance while standing up, interrupting her. "I will give you another opportunity to serve me as I proposed already. Or we will keep trying to get your blood tainted to serve us!"

"Even with your threats, you will not corrupt me as you have done with others, and as you tempted me with all this abundance!" Nehel claimed with uneasiness, showing the gifts with both hands, but firm. "I will bring back the balance you have disrupted to this world! It is my stance!"

"As you wish," Ardek Korba nodded. "I have proposed and warned you, and others will face the consequences of your choice."

With a mesmerizing disguise as a breathtaking woman, the creature emerged onto the balcony, transforming into a gigantic black dragon, and without hesitation, set off towards the red No Ta while the chilling No Sak melted away into the horizon.

The terror returned to Nehel once again.

With a sigh and a swift pace, the empress exited the chamber and encountered two vagrants guarding the door, who greeted her with a firm salute as she entered the torch-lit aisle. Korba's presence went completely unnoticed by them, showing their lack of alertness. "Could one of you point to Juni's quarters?"

"This one, Divine Empress," one of them signaled the next door to the right.

The empress expressed gratitude and proceeded to her intended destination. She crossed the threshold into the private quarters, quietly shutting the door behind her. In her search, she stumbled upon three adjacent quarters, which were open and each had a military bed, but no soldier occupied any of them that night.

Juni, completely exhausted, was sound asleep underneath a pile of warm bear furs on the last bed by the window, still dressed in his regular attire. As he snored, his head found a resting place on the lumpy, feather-filled mattress.

The opulent and hoarded chamber where Nehel slept in did not persuade her indifference towards the current place or the bed. All she wanted was to feel safe and at peace. Seeking comfort, she snuggled up to Juni in bed, gripping his hand tightly, and hoping to sleep.

Juni woke up, feeling her trembling hand, barely seeing her, still lethargic. "Are you all right, missy?"

"It is just. . . a nightmare I had. . ." she lied, but her face showed sadness and fear.

"Take my arm, if you wish. . ." he suggested, falling asleep again.

In a tender gesture, Nehel clung onto his arm and closed her eyes.

She could not sleep, but remembrances came to her mind.

She had a deep yearning for her mother, Venka.

She had the desire to go with her as she used after her nightmares, to sleep and hold her close for solace in the hut they called home.

She yearned for her younger times in Molke.

She longed to be a regular girl, not an empress, for the first time.

To be Lakia again.

Corr awakened Alessandro at sunrise.

The feline discovered him in the same place he had left last night after revealing the news. He discovered him lying and sleeping on the table with the empty brew cup. In his hand, he still held Fabehel's small papyrus.

Despite his reluctance, he had to wake him.

Alessandro slowly opened his eyes, revealing a clear redness from sleep deprivation and overindulgence. He tried to sit properly on the chair to fix his posture but ended up rubbing his sore neck and glaring at Corr with resentment. "What the heck do you want?!" he yelled.

"I know significant burdens are on you, master. But should not be reasons to be always consuming fermented drinks, especially at that your young age. You must consider having a healthier life."

"Is that why you came to tell me that baloney?"

"The Divine Empress had mandated me to bring you to the forge."

"For what? Is she there?"

"Aye, she awaits you."

Pushing the chair loudly, Alessandro left the place, leaving the papyrus behind, and made his way to the court. Walking speedily, he removed the white handkerchief from his sleeve and threw it down.

Corr eagerly retrieved it and tucked it into one of his fancy jacket's pockets.

The freezing exterior weather caught the attention of both as the sun came up from the east.

Alessandro wore the same peasant clothes borrowed from a sentinel days ago, feeling the cold on his skin, but he did not mind.

The garrison's tower was just a short distance away from the forge. They arrived in no time.

Upon entering, they discovered three vigorous men forging their tools on anvils while a blazing furnace illuminated the scene. The blacksmiths perspired heavily, with smearing carbon blackness on their faces.

Alessandro scanned the area, but at first, there was no empress in sight. However, he soon noticed an unfamiliar modest child approaching, wearing a wool tan shirt, brown vest, leather pants, and sandals. He recognized Nehel as she got closer.

Temporarily, she had set aside her white robes.

The constant cacophony of the mallets against the anvils bothered her as she tried to speak. She turned and screamed. "Take a breath and have something to eat, lads!" Nehel mandated.

The blacksmiths paused, put down their tools, acknowledged with bows, and headed to the court.

"Why have you summoned me?" Exhausted and rubbing his neck, Alessandro inquired.

Nehel called someone from a corner.

Jumeni appeared with a leather apron that reached to her feet, and black spots covered her face. She got closer with a greatsword on her hands and presented it to him.

Alessandro, feeling overwhelmed, examined the weapon and found pleasure in his hands. A distinct Akareen star adorned the pommel, while the furnace's fire reflected a unique silver metal. The blade was lengthy and remarkably sharp. Despite its iron composition, he found it lightweight as he moved it with one hand. He noticed a word carved in Salteran scripture—*Borsen*—on the grip.

"Back in the villa, I requested Jumeni to fabricate a special sword only you may use," Nehel explained. "With my blessings it is light when using with one hand, and heavy with both hands. This is my gift to you, uncle."

"Why me?" he asked with widened dark eyes, still observing astounded his blade. He tested it with a hand first and confirmed its mystical heaviness while handling it with both hands.

"Because you have lost swords of your own," she replied with a sign of tenderness for him. "I wished for you to possess something that is uniquely yours."

Waving his weapon in the air, Alessandro could not contain his excitement.

"How Jumeni made the blade, Divine Empress?" it puzzled Corr to see such exquisite blade with great precision and detail only made in just days.

"While she may not talk and her mind may remain childlike, her skill at crafting unique artifacts is extraordinary," replied with a modest smile, pointing at Jumeni. "She will be my artificer, and I will be her enchantress."

"Is that what you both did with the shield Ser Marissa held in the jousting?" the feline inquired, curious.

"Corr, it doesn't matter if they did it," Alessandro responded kindly, paused waving his weapon and shifted his gaze to the empress. "Why did you decide to gift it to me?"

Nehel lowered her face, showing sadness as she shut her eyes.

"You constantly distance yourself because you are always in torment," she pleaded. "If you are going to distance yourself from me, the least you can do is accept a meaningful gift from your niece."

Alessandro, overwhelmed with astonishment and emotion, let go of his new greatsword and knelt down to hug his niece, realizing the consequences of his mistakes with sudden remorse.

30

PLAINS

P eken remained by the large pound surrounded by vast pastures as he roasted the fish he had caught earlier, using a wooden stick from the scarce trees nearby. Enjoying the aroma of his cooked meal, he took small bites but accidentally burned his tongue and lips. In a hurry, he reached for his canteen next to his median bag with belongings to relieve his mouth with grape juice. "Darn hot!" He resumed to eat, contented.

The midday was clear and pleasant, an unreal day.

The elf believed it was best for him and everyone else to go back to Molke, so he embarked on a solo journey. He thought he had fulfilled his duty from Sorcerer Uskam to escort Lakia, although not all the way to Salter as intended. He accompanied Juni and Jumeni on their wagon, followed by Brisel. Once they were close to Seled Post and ensured their safe arrival, he bid them farewell and parted ways.

Despite the plague and the smell of death, the idea of going back to his Molke's hut in Akiaba brought him happiness. He, too, got infected and had the choice between dying or becoming a Korbeen, both paths leading to the same outcome.

However, he placed his hand on his chest as an indescribable premonition.

The sudden departure of the ducks from the pond grabbed his attention, leaving him curious about the reason for their fright.

His face turned left, and a sword's cold tip grazed his cheek. Despite being paralyzed, he moved his yellowish eyes and saw someone he recognized. "It had to be you!" he exclaimed with unconformity. "Ser Marissa Taskar."

She sighed and sheathed her sword. "What are you eating, elf?"

Marissa snatched the stick with half bitten fish and tested fragments of it with delight.

"How did you find me?" he whined, stood up and discovered the mantis behind her. "Ah! That Brisel!"

"Aye! He followed your scent," she replied with food in her mouth.

Peken observed her donning a brand new iron armor. Although not elaborate or ostentatious, it was a simple and well-crafted design, with a distinctive and engraved small Akareen star on her left chest, symbolizing the empress and the Jyistereerk. "Ser, I see you have your new armor," he acknowledged, nodding and somewhat proud, with his arms crossed. "You are now a true Empress Lakia's Knight."

"I am afraid, sir, that is not the right response. It is Empress Nehel," Marissa threw the stick with the remains of the fish, bothered. "Now that I recall. Why did you hide us Lakia's true nature?"

"To which aspect of nature are you referring?"

"She is a demigoddess! You knew it and never told us! You may have abandoned Sorcerer Uskam and his lessons, but you had to tell us!"

Peken sat beside his bag and spoke with his eyes fixated to the ground. "Before heading to the Kingdom of Aranka, Sorceress Dalehel had a meeting with Uskam and me. She visited us in Akiaba."

Marissa seated on the ground after unfastening her belt with the sheath, eager to listen to him. "Please, Peken. Continue."

"She had extraordinary abilities that even surpassed to those of Uskam," he nodded with expressive yellow eyes. "As we were talking in the hut, she saw Venka carrying water to her home, and pointed her out. She foresaw she would raise a divinity."

"So you knew that Nehel, or Lakia, was the divinity?" insisted apprehensively.

"Did someone let you know that mysticism is always twisted?"

"Many times! Yasstro!" rolled her eyes up. "Tell me!"

"Very well. When Venka, my childhood friend and my cherished with whom I intended to have a future, was forbidden by Uskam to see me, she gave up on me and went with a prominent hunter. . ."

"Wait! Why did Uskam forbade her from seeing you?" interrupted.

"You should know better that all mystic men and women have a life of abstinence. Thus, I committed too, but that did not mean I agreed with the rule. Following Venka's elopement with the hunter, I left Uskam's tutoring, heartbroken, and embarked on a journey for several years. Uskam's hope for my return to Molke to continue lessons was in vain because I did not wish anymore. He continued to send me pigeons with updates, and I learned of Venka's pregnancy, leading me to suspect that the promised divinity lived within her."

"Where is Venka's child?"

"Sadly, she lost her infant at birth because of the plague, and her spouse blamed and abandoned her after," he sighed with sorrow. "The hunter wanted nothing from Molke, not even his clothes, and left naked to the Karekall, as a symbol of rejection and shame to his own people. Since then, he has not returned."

Marissa felt moved. She struggled to speak, wiped away a tear, and took a sip from his canteen.

"I got news from her situation and returned to Molke. . . to find her insane," Peken continued with sadness. "She was not the same Venka I have known, but I vowed to be near her. While I established myself as a trader of foreign items at Akiaba, Uskam took her to the outskirts for her protection."

"What led you to discover that Nehel was the true divinity?"

"I did not discover yet but my suspicions grew over time," the elf replied with a serious look. "I visited Venka and found her holding onto a rag doll made by Uskam and seeking solace in the shadows of her hut. It was the same every time. Since I was not on good terms with Uskam, I chose not to visit her for a period. It took a while, but I finally visited Venka again. To my surprise, I found her happily cradling a Casarak child, Lakia, in her arms, feeding her. The child's presence brought back memories of Sorceress Dalehel's words, which I could not come to accept them. I left for Akiaba, vowing not to encounter them for a decade. The ones who came to my hut were Uskam and Lakia after all that time."

"You knew about it, right?"

"I had no desire to know. But I was finally certain about her divinity when you plotted to execute Lakia back in the Black Forest. I have realized that those stories from the bygone world were real."

Brisel hissed, scared, attracting the attention.

Marissa wasted no time in grabbing the sword she had on the ground and positioning herself, observed her mantis pointing his head towards the tall grass close by the trees.

Slowly, Peken also drew his short blade.

With caution, Marissa advanced towards the sparse trees, using her sword to point, and her brown eyes caught sight of a crouched man hidden in the grass because of the strong sunlight. "Whoever is there, please stand with the hands raised in high!" she mandated firmly.

The suspicious man gradually rose and revealed his face.

With an ample smile revealing her white teeth, Marissa widened her eyes and hurled her sword. "Dessidere!" she exclaimed as she rushed to embrace him, unable to control her emotions.

After scratching his head, Peken returned the sword to its sheath.

Her sudden and unexpected reaction surprised the young man. However, her firm embrace and the hardness of her armor caused pain, prompting him to request some space.

"My apologies, Dessidere!" Marissa retreated, concerned. "Are you feeling right?"

"Aye! You are asking after you almost choked him!" Peken said in sarcasm, with crossed arms.

Casting an exasperated glance at the elf, she shifted her gaze to Dessidere, noticing him in an unfamiliar and simpler fashion compared to his usual attire from Casak.

"How did you track me down? What brings you here, so far from Tyza?"

"These people they call themselves... Vagrants? They let me know the route to find you after my disappointment at not being able to meet you. I had made it to the garrison close to the mountains..."

"Aye, Seled Post."

"They drew a map for me to locate you while an empress was traveling to Arrasem. . . The Plains?" Dessidere responded, confused, while recounting his story. "Anyhow. . . your mother, Lady Tasarissa, had sent me to look for you and also escape from being beheaded. . ."

"Beheaded? Why?"

"Lord Orssandro sought to have my head decapitated after he found out about my opposition to him and his search for the *Ykarte*."

Marissa's serious gaze fell upon Peken as she gathered the courage to reveal the truth to Dessidere, despite her reluctance. "My dear Dessidere. Have not you heard the news?" her voice quivered. "Orssandro fell in battle, and to make matters worse, the Korbas captured him. Archmage Missar is now the Head."

Dessidere took a moment to process the words she had mentioned. He shook his head and broke down in tears.

"No! Not my lord!" he yelled in surprising sorrow.

Alessandro had a new look thanks to the garrison's tailors, who made him new black clothes. He brought his enchanted greatsword in a unique sheath on his back and rode Nehel's chestnut horse named Twist, the same horse Marissa used at the Carretem jousting event, and gifted to Lakia by Laimet's captain.

Corr accompanied him on his gold stallion, Thunder.

On the flat landscapes of The Plains, both riders embarked on their solitary journeys along the ancient stone road. They were en route to the burgh of Arrasem, where they expected to encounter Nehel, her Court of Maids, the Artensens, and the Imperial Guard. There, they would speak about plans for the coronation procession from the Floating City of Dri to the Capital of Berrem Ri.

Alessandro, feeling thirsty from the sweltering midday sun, fetched a canteen from his saddle and drank water. He later tried to offer it to Corr, who refused. "How is it possible for you to consume plenty of brews, but not water?"

"As a slave, I could mostly survive without water, master," the feline, looking ahead, responded.

"Tell me. How Cassandro could live in these mines?"

Corr brought his stallion to a halt, with Alessandro stopping besides. His feline green eyes fixated on him. "Sweating and sleeping in these mines is tough for a Fennen, so you can imagine what it is like for a man like you."

"Please, Corr. Tell me, I deserve to know."

A peculiar sound captured the feline's attention, causing it to focus on the lone tree in the vicinity.

Alessandro, with one hand, carefully drew his greatsword from its sheath and began trotting towards the tree with Twist.

His eyes expanded in astonishment.

Fabehel hid behind. Tightly strapped onto Song, the mare, she revealed her tearful cheeks glistened as she stared intensely, shaking her head and swaying her long red braid. "Believe me. . . I tried. . . I tried to be away. . . but it hurts so much!" she said between sobs, finding hard to speak. "I yearn for your arms!"

Alessandro, still in disbelief, sheathed his blade again and moved closer to embrace her, offering his shoulder for her to cry on while he consoled her with soothing strokes on her back.

Discreetly, Corr rode on his stallion and gave back the handkerchief that Alessandro had thrown.

Alessandro used the handkerchief to clean her face with a smile.

"All is well. I am here now," he appeased sweetly.

Corr dismounted from Thunder and aided in unstrapping her legs from the saddle. That way, Alessandro could embrace her completely and both of them would descend from Twist.

Swiftly, he positioned her on the grass beneath the tree's shade.

Corr respectfully pulled all three horses aside and stood near the road, giving the couple their privacy.

Fabehel's composure returned, and she exchanged a tender look with Alessandro, her hazel eyes gleamed with moisture.

Alessandro tenderly grazed her flushed cheeks with a hint of uncertainty about holding her and closed the distance between their faces.

Their lips touched. They could finally reveal their loves in solitude and intimacy, with no interruptions.

No Gathering or dragoness would disrupt them any longer.

Nehel glanced back at The Plains panorama and smiled while shedding some tears.

Noticing her odd gesture, Juni asked.

"What had occurred, missy?"

"Uncle finally found Lady Fabehel, and Ser Marissa crossed paths with her childhood friend again. I made it possible and I sense them."

"How?"

"I have a strong desire to protect my loved ones from suffering, which is why I have used my blessings to intervene in their lives," she affirmed. "After all, they are my two Pillars of the Jyistereerk."

Although he did not approve of her actions, he understood her reasons and glanced ahead.

Juni, at her request, accompanied her, while a Court comprising hundreds of standing mystical maids surrounded them and diligently performed their customary tasks on board.

Nehel left Seled Post and made his way to the town of Arrasem. Instead of sitting on the elevated throne, she rested on the floating platform, which the people commonly referred to as the *Divine Flying Vessel*. Despite being an empress, she felt uneasy sitting on a throne, any throne.

As the empress made her way towards the Ri on a grand journey, her trusted sentinels flanked her, the Artensens, who escorted her vessel both ahead and behind. Accompanied by a massive crowd of hundreds of thousands, the procession grew larger than many who left the Seled Post and more joined in as the empress passed through different towns and burghs.

A maid approached Juni and Nehel, handing them cups with water. Upon her retirement, they thanked her.

Juni admired the vast expanse of tall, swaying grasses known as The Plains. He had visited these places countless times with her father and Jumeni during their travels in the wagon, but seeing the region from the platform's height was truly magnificent.

"This panorama is truly remarkable, missy!" he said in awe. "The Plains stand out as one of my favorite parts."

"The Plains will belong to the Jyistereerk, Juni," revealed with a gentle smile. "Berrem will be within my empire."

A wave of surprise took over Juni, and he shuddered as suspicions crept him.

31

TREATY

Alessandro, in complete solitude, rode Song at full speed on a road that was built directly on the water's surface. On behalf of the Empress Nehel, he had embarked on an arduous day of trip from Arrasem, in The Plains, to reach the Floating City of Dri on a vast lake in The Banks, an endeavor that was not exactly in line with his inclinations.

As an empress, Nehel held a position of authority that required him to follow her commands, even though she was his niece. By swearing allegiance and pledging to provide protection, service, and unwavering devotion, he has already shown his commitment.

Despite his opposition along with others, yet he had to obey her command.

Eventually, his dark eyes spotted the city on the horizon, its shining appearance stood out under the sun. Despite never having been to such an exotic city before, he could not have the excitement of arriving at a new place. His face remained somber and his heart raced without faltering.

He had with him a treaty, a questionable treaty.

A document to be signed with bitterness. . . and fear.

The burgh of Arrasem witnessed a momentous celebratory occasion as Empress Nehel and her people entered. The procession, which included hundreds of thousands of participants, multiplied the city's population by four.

The *Divine Flying Vessel*, along with the Artensens and most of the maids, stationed themselves at the boundaries.

Arriving first was Nehel along with her entourage of vagrants, and it was the Lady of Ten, representing The Plains lordship, who had the privilege of being the one to receive her. Despite the lady's generous offer to accommodate her and her companions in her palace, the empress graciously declined the invitation.

Opting for an alternative, the eldest Akhimeni, who held the role of overseeing the Court of Maids, asked the locals for advice on finding accommodations, and they were kind enough to point out a well-recommended large inn nearby. As per Nehel's request, in anticipation of the meeting, she reserved the entire venue, even including the tavern on the subfloor. For some days, the *Wind & Grass Inn* was the empress' home.

Whenever Nehel had to be in public, she would always choose to wear her white robes. However, after her second encounter with Ardek Korba, she took the preference to wear her leather clothes in private to remain being Lakia. That is the way she presented herself at the inn, once she cleansed in her private quarters upstairs, prior to her encounter with her people.

As Nehel descended to the tavern, she noticed Juni and Peken engrossed in a lively discussion.

The elf discovered her interrupting his chat and crossed his arms, showing an air of cynicism with his yellow eyes. Despite everything, he could not resist smirking when he caught sight of her appearance in her familiar leather garments, reminiscent of their previous journeys side by side. He noticed she had carefully braided her hair, looking more like a girl than a boy when disguised. "Coming to meet you was not in my plans, lass!" the elf exclaimed with a nod. "But I believe some mischievousness of yours caused my presence here."

Nehel chuckled.

Peken, who had once been a sorcerer's disciple, had a deep understanding of the intricacies of magic, and from his firsthand experience of traveling with the empress, he firmly believed that there was a hidden motive behind her attracting him to Arrasem.

She approached the elf and requested him to lean over so she could say something to him in his long, pointed ear. "*Lakia ish ke Peken, Gakia tu Korbeen, Nehel resh is Yukia,*" she whispered in Molkan.

Peken's face transformed into a grim expression, realizing Juni's curiosity as a witness.

Nehel's face turned severe. She knew his inevitability.

"Aye, Divine Empress. . .," replied as he left inside the tavern.

Marissa showed and saluted shortly after. "Nehel, we had just arrived moments ago," she pulled his hiding companion from behind a column. "This is my childhood friend, Dessidere, and Monitor to. . . my uncle, the Head Orssandro Vykar."

Trembling with a clear sense of insecurity, Dessidere showed a respectful gesture. "I am delighted to be in your presence, Divine Empress."

"The pleasure is mine." She held his hand with a smile to soothe his nerves. "Could you be my Herald?"

"Is. . . an honor!" he stammered in astonishment

Nehel's focus shifted when Alessandro showed up, bringing Corr along with him. With a look of exhaustion, he held Fabehel securely in his arms.

As the empress approached, a noticeable change came over her face—her smile faded away again, replaced by a solemn expression. She got closer, bringing her head to Fabehel's, gently closing her eyes to sense her. "Please, do not leave!" Nehel almost murmured, begging. "I urge you to stay with us, as both you and I rely on each other. My mother would have the heartfelt wish that her little sister remain associated with those who genuinely care for her."

Fabehel only nodded in response.

"I will be your protector, shielding you from any adversities that may arise!" determined, the empress assured.

Akhimeni herself took charge and made it her responsibility to arrange the tavern. In doing so, she discovered a large round table in a corner, which she promptly moved to the center of the place. She then arranged chairs around it and ensure proper illumination by using hanging lamps. Once the empress had confirmed all the required participants, she requested them to begin the meeting.

Akhimeni also considered the chair provided for the empress was too oversized for her.

The stewardesses had found a solution by retrieving the only tall chair with arms from the caretaker's chamber and adding extra cushions to accommodate Nehel's height.

The other chairs had no arms and no cushions.

It was the empress's first official meeting with the people she regarded as indispensable and urgent for the Jyistereerk, following her ascension. Despite not being as precise as desired and containing informalities, they had the meeting as hastily as possible.

The empress had something to say, and to act.

Alessandro took a seat on her right side while Marissa occupied the left, both as the Pillars. Corr stood for Fenn, next to the right beside Selee, representing Salter. Peken spoke for Molke and Dessidere in the role of the Herald. Fabehel, as a representative of the Arankans in exile, along with vagrant Keleana, who held the position of Imperial Guard Marshal. They completed the diverse group by including Juni, appointed provisionally for Berrem, and Akhimeni from the Court of Maids.

"The Guild!" Nehel exclaimed with emotion.

Keleana nodded, and a smile formed on her lips, which was uncommon in her. She had lost a guild, but she gained another one.

Seated near each other, Kekten and Jumeni found themselves in a corner at the same tavern, drinking sarsaparilla soft drink in their mugs.

Prior to the meeting, the Pillars had engaged in a discussion regarding the representation of both the Casakans and Kasnasgos. Selee, who had established a strong mystical communication with the Head Archmage Missar, emphasized the Casakan's vowed loyalty to the empress. Unfortunately, they revealed their inability to be physically present and represent themselves as their crucial tasks at hand involved managing the Casakan realm's devastation and facing the Korbas.

Despite this, Missar granted Alessandro the role of Casak's provisional voice.

Kasnasgar waited until the timing was right.

As the attendees selected their preferred beverages, the majority favored wine, prompting the stewardesses to bring bottles accompanied by wooden cups. There were also noticeable exceptions in beverage preferences. Corr chose brew, Peken, Juni, and Fabehel opted for rice milk, while Nehel stood out by solely consuming plain water.

The empress signaled to begin.

Nervous and quick, Dessidere extended a piece of papyrus he had gotten, along with a quill and ink, from the caretaker. He placed the papyrus on the table's surface, using two wine bottles as paperweights to keep it spread and ready to write. As his fingers trembled, Dessidere prepared to draft the first character.

As he announced the start of the meeting, the newly appointed Herald stammered. "In the eighteenth day of the Fourth Month. . . in the First Year of. . . the *Tikl the Third of the Gesha. . .*"

"Wait, lad," Selee, smiling, interrupted. "New times and hopes have ushered in a wave of changes, altering the face of Sankaris in just two months since the empress' departure from Molke. Do we still plan on utilizing that dire calendar that began with the obliteration of Aranka?"

"What do you suggest, archmage?"

"You are the expert, please, advise!" Selee insisted.

Unsure and quiet, Dessidere glanced at the empress.

With a subtle and gentle smile on her face, Nehel discreetly gave a nod at him, as if she already knew the answer.

He shifted his gaze downward onto the papyrus, then spoke once more, this time with confidence and no trace of hesitation. "In the First Day of the First Month in the First Year of the *Tikl the First of Nehel*, I officially begin this meeting!"

"New year, new tikl, new faiths," the archmage approved.

"What is the reason you wished to gather all of us?" Peken inquired, crossing his arms.

Nehel closed her eyes, allowing a somber expression to take over her face, before finally providing a reply. Subsequently, she unveiled her hazel eyes, seeing directly at everyone. "I have held my tongue for so long, please, I request your apologies," sighed. "Berrem's condition is more serious than you may realize."

"Would you care to explain?" Alessandro suggested.

"Do you recall the *Feast of the Dragoness*? It was no accident, but purposely done."

They suddenly filled the tavern with a ripple of chilling surprise.

"Aye," she continued responding. "Inside the Gathering, there is an infiltrator who has allowed the Korbas to blend in with the rest of the people. He already made a sworn commitment to serve Ardek, hence the reason for their presence."

"Pan Din!" Fabehel exclaimed in disappointment.

"I believe it was Tom Lai. After all, he was a demon before," Peken assured sure of himself.

"It is Lord Kong Rim," Nehel nodded. "He promised his allegiance with the Korbas for greater power."

"It explains why allegedly he could do nothing against the dragoness," Alessandro asseverated. "But the reason behind his decision to permit such many fatalities is still unclear to me."

"The dragoness was looking to infect as many as possible, but her rage did not allow to control her attacks and ended murdering the people. Someone provoked her," Nehel downed her head. "That is why I was absent after my confrontation with Ardek Korba. I was not yet ready to confront her as well as to Lord Kong."

"How is the *Feast of the Dragoness* related to Berrem's condition?" Corr inquired.

"In order to increase the number of Korbeens and expand the Korba Dominion to this side of the Karekall," she replied somberly. "Despite consistently respecting their boundaries for hundreds of tikls, something has recently motivated them to obliterate Aranka, unleash curses upon Molke, invade Casak, and expand their territories into Berrem."

"And soon Salter will fall," Selee asseverated.

"Hence, that is why you have arrived at this world in this precise moment, Divine Empress," Keleana claimed. "They have shattered the balance in Sankaris!"

"And the red mantises are Korbeens."

"By the goddesses!" Marissa exclaimed, stunned. "I came very close to becoming one of these damned!"

"I consider it necessary for us to take action and retake Berrem," Peken said with seriousness.

"Aye, you are right," Nehel nodded. "Before we move forward, I would like to attempt something—a treaty."

"What treaty?" Alessandro asked in surprise.

"I will request the Gathering to surrender Berrem to me!"

Murmurs of astonishment echoed throughout the room. Dessidere cut through the noise by forcefully banging the table with the bottom of a bottle.

"Let the Divine Empress to continue!" Dessidere demanded strictly.

"The last thing I want is a war that would tragically claim the lives of innocents. But if we do not get Berrem by the treaty, then I will begin the *Deken Karsaker*—The Reclamation War."

"No!" Alessandro disagreed, aware that the conflict would last for eighty years, as stated by the *Frelee Dee*. "You came to bring back a balance, not to start a conflict!"

"Aye, the balance. Keep in mind that I was born an empress because this is my stance! Despite my calm appearance, in order to stabilize Sankaris if the Korbas seek confrontation and malevolence, I must respond by fighting them!"

"Let us consider different alternatives instead of choosing between a war or a treaty!" Alessandro attempted to persuade her.

"Uncle, do not you comprehend?" she disclosed with authority, serene. "They are vicious mystical beings who do not understand humanity or reason. Their deepest craving is to devour the soul of every person inhabiting Sankaris. While I know you have dealt with negotiations before because of Lord Orssandro, but in this case involving the Korbas is useless."

"She is right, master," Peken seconded her. "They are creatures from the abyss."

"I still do not think it is important to claim Berrem or begin hostilities," Alessandro insisted with a negative shook. "Nehel, I wanted to share with you what I have learned about the situation in Casak. Unfortunately, we can not stand up against them. The Jyistereerk is just in the beginning and it is not well prepared yet."

"Advise then. What other options do you offer?" Selee insisted.

Despite his best efforts, Alessandro did not come up with another solution, not a clear one to him. With a face of shame, he ended by simply glancing at everyone and shrugging his shoulders.

The empress sighed. Although she appeared calm, deep inside, she experienced the immense pressure of a monarch.

"I wish to conclude that. . . either by treaty or conflict, I shall arrive to the Ri for the coronation," Nehel informed. "Despite my lack of appeal to be crowned, I find myself obligated to do so, as it is an essential step towards restoring balance."

The atmosphere in the tavern grew tense as everyone present, including the stewardesses and the caretaker, turned their gaze with expressions of concern and fear.

"Let us put it in a vote. . .," Dessidere said, swallowing his saliva. "If you are in favor of the treaty, please raise your hands."

Rapidly, those in favor lifted their hands. Corr, Fabehel, and Alessandro were in opposition. Juni abstained from the vote.

By the majority, the Guild had voted in favor of the treaty.

"It is because you follow master Alessandro, Corr?" Keleana inquired, pointing out the Fennen opposition.

"No, it is because my realm is already involved in a conflict to be involved in another one," the feline replied. "There is so much suffering in Fenn."

"And you, Lady Fabehel?" Selee asked.

"If the treaty fails, a war will complicate my search for those Arankans living in exile."

Silence.

Dessidere banged the table with the bottle.

"The Guild has endorsed the treaty, provided that a necessary conflict could occur!"

What began as a hopeful first Guild meeting ultimately concluded with a sense of sadness and concerns.

Silence again.

"I wish you to take charge of the treaty, uncle," Nehel mandated faintly. "You have my complete confidence."

The empress called a stewardess to assist her in descending from the chair, and departed, leaving the rest of the Guild behind.

After the meeting, with the help of Marissa and through meticulous planning, he used the knowledge he had gained while working with Orssandro for two years during his holidays, after turning fourteen, to write the treaty on a small scroll of paper. The empress reviewed and signed the scroll.

Alessandro bought a cage housing twelve pigeons after he contacted some breeders in Arrasem. And next morning the first ruby bird was used to include the treaty and sent to the Gathering in the Dri from the inn's rooftop.

A full day had gone by, he still had received no response.

Alessandro, being cautious and having false expectations about the Gathering by the sensitive nature of the treaty, took the precautionary step of making multiple copies. He expected a lack of replies and made sure that the empress signed all of them.

When the second day began, Fabehel met him on the rooftop, and Corr carried her upstairs. She observed Alessandro to launch the pigeon.

Not only did she have bread and cheese, but she also had grape juice to share with him. Taking a seat on the floor, they consumed their breakfast, securing to place a cloth beneath them.

Still no reply from the Gathering.

On the third morning, Nehel climbed up to the rooftop. She eagerly awaited to witness him sending yet another pigeon.

"What are you doing here, Nehel?" he asked with seriousness, with the bird in the hands, not paying attention to her. "Is your visit related to watching me perform my duties?"

"I. . . just wish to be with my uncle," she replied with a glimpse of uneasiness.

He heard her and let the pigeon go.

He invited her to sit together and observe the burgh on the rooftop. They gazed out at the magnificent view of the bustling Arrasem and had a conversation about the panorama, but curiously, they never spoke about the treaty.

Another day passed with no reply.

On the fourth morning, Corr accompanied him. They invested time in learning more about their past lives simply to have something to talk about and keep themselves occupied. They were indifferent to the light rain.

As usual, he let another bird go.

Just like always, there was no response for a full day.

As the fifth day approached, Alessandro made preparations by getting another pigeon ready. As he gazed at the cathedral towers in the northern part of Arrasem, shielding his eyes from the blinding rays of the setting sun in the east, he suddenly caught sight of a bird soaring, making its way towards him.

Having received the pigeon, he unfastened the small roll affixed to its foot. He read it.

Lord Bin Kam, who expressed a desire for a meeting at Dri to discuss the treaty and explore the option of surrendering Berrem to the empress, signed the message. In addition, he requested a personal meeting with Nehel.

The news of receiving a reply from the Gathering brought some relief to Alessandro, but the brevity of the message and the ease of the agreement raised his suspicions.

Upon being informed of the Gathering's response, the Guild strongly advised the empress to entrust arranging the treaty solely to Alessandro, because of concerns about her safety.

After agreeing, she sent Alessandro to Dri, accompanied by a small group of members from the Imperial Guard, specifically vagrants.

He had the official document of the treaty, properly endorsed by the empress, awaiting a signature from any of the Gathering.

With great haste, Alessandro swiftly departed to fulfill his task, to meet with the lords and take Berrem to the empress.

However, he had no trust in Lord Kong Rim. The mere thought of meeting him alongside the other lords caused a great deal of fear.

Alessandro brought himself to a halt on the road built on water, right in front of the gates of the floating city known as Dri, and he stood readily. The sentries merely stared at him with no discernible reaction.

He had commanded the vagrants to wait earlier, leaving them behind halfway, as he believed it would be more helpful for him to go alone.

His heart pounded in his chest, a combination of fear and apprehension ran through his veins, as he took the risk of his life to gauge the unknown reactions of the Gathering towards the treaty. The reply gave him bad feelings.

Finally, after a good amount of time had passed, the gates swung open, granting him access to a magnificent city built on water.

Alessandro mandated Song to enter and trotted at a slow rhythm, while eyeing the suspicious stares of the sentinels with crossbows as he crossed the gate. Nobody bothered to approach him or show the direction he needed to go, understanding that he had to find the Gathering on his own. While making his way into the city via the primary avenue, which was flanked by abandoned houses constructed on lands made on water, he could not help but notice the eerie emptiness of the entire city, making it impossible for him to inquire about directions.

He noticed from his mare a massive keep standing far away at the end of the avenue, and without hesitation, he decided it would be his ultimate destination. He also spotted the vastness of the city.

Maintaining his caution, he revealed the greatsword that he had been keeping at his back. The absence of any signs of life in the ghost city inspired him a serious lack of trust.

It took him a while, but he eventually arrived at the keep. The gates of the monolith were open, and just like the city, it was empty.

Not even guards.

Alessandro showed no signs of faltering as he held onto his blade and mounted on the back of Song. His dark and intense eyes meticulously scanned the surroundings for any potential threats that posed a danger, with no intention of entering the keep.

Startled by a noise, he spun his attention back to the gates. He heard the noise of dragged steps.

With his cane in hand, Lord Kong Rim made his way out from between the doors and halted at the stairs, showing no signs of descending. His scarlet fancy clothes were a distinctive of his usual appearance.

"Where are the others, lord?" From a distance, Alessandro, with utter distrust, inquired while tightly gripping the greatsword.

"It is only me, master," replied with a suspicious nod. "I am now the Gathering!"

Upon hearing him, Alessandro took a significant amount of time to process and comprehend the words. "What have you done to them?!" questioned, with both authority and alarm. "Where are the people in the Dri?!"

"Do you see the sun?" pointed to the horizon. "Can you tell me what time is it?"

"It is almost dusk. Why do you ask?! Why have you not answered to my inquires?!"

With visible exhaustion, Lord Rim carefully settled himself on the first step, taking a break and sighing. "I used to be a mage. I know you are aware of this. Regrettably, the sanctuary did not grant me the fulfillment that I had envisioned, thus I made the choice to resign, to pursue politics and be a part of the Gathering, and I accomplished that ambition, but it did not suffice to me."

"What were you searching for?"

"Absolute power over Berrem, master. I knew the Gathering would not allow me." the lord nodded. "With the obliteration of Aranka and the devastating state of Casak,

Berrem assumes the mantle of the most powerful realm on Sankaris, strengthened by the vast wealth flowing in from Fenn. And only one could give me what I wished for all these years."

"Ardek. . ." Alessandro murmured, disconcerted. "Could you not refuse him and follow the empress instead? She would have helped to pursue your dreams, lord."

"For what? So she can have total control over the realm?" he emitted a grin and chuckled. "Do you know, master? Once Lord Bin Kam received all the scrolls that you had sent, he ignored them. However, upon hearing from me about the deliberate and hidden Korba incursion into Berrem, he blindly agreed with the treaty and offered the entire realm to the empress."

"Answer to my inquiry! Where are the others?!" he demanded heatedly.

"It was necessary for me to make a substantial sacrifice for the sake of the realm. I still possess the power of magic within me, and I purposely caused an accident. Tragically, the fire rapidly spread throughout the Jarrdine Villa, leading to the loss of all the lords who were inside."

Alessandro was in disbelief upon hearing what he had just stated, causing his eyes to widen.

Using his cane, Lord Rim directed his gaze towards the sun as it descended on the horizon.

"It is almost dusk," he nodded with another grin. "The sentries that you have seen stationed at the gates are not ordinary beings, but shapeshifters. They are Korbas patiently awaiting the nightfall, to summon all the Korbeens—the now blessed former inhabitants of Dri."

Alessandro shuddered in panic. "What have you done, fool?!"

"Run if you can, master," Lord Rim said in sinister serenity. "Run! Because the focus is on the empress! As soon as the sun hides behind the horizon, they will be already on the way to Arrasem!"

Alarmed and scared, fully comprehending the seriousness of the situation, Alessandro urgently commanded Song to return as fast as she could to Arrasem.

As he passed through the gates after crossing the deserted city, he continued to hold on to the sword tightly while witnessing the gradual transformation of the sentries into menacing dragons. Despite this, he remained determined to keep running without interruption, not bothering to look back and see their striking change in Korbas.

As the sun gradually faded away, revealing the emergence of the nocturnal curtain in the sky, adorned with the presence of three moons—No Ta, No Sak, and No Nunn—Alessandro had his distressed focus solely on Nehel.

The document containing the treaty unexpectedly flew out from his clothes and gracefully descended onto the water's surface, becoming fully damp.

And so, the *Deken Karsaker* began.

32

HORDES

M arissa examined her feline companion as he indulged in his drink, marveling at his ability to consume copious amounts of brew without getting inebriated, as Corr appeared to be quite delighted by the moment
and also acknowledged the knight's fondness for the red
wine.

They both comfortably sat at a table.

"Do you genuinely savor your drink, ser?" in his usual
deep voice, he inquired.

"Aye, I find pleasure in drinking it, as you do with your brew," she replied with a nod. "Did you even try it?"

"We Fennens have a high tolerance for brew and other soft drinks, however, with wine, it burns in our throats."

She stood, her eyes widened in surprise at his unexpected response. The sight of the hundreds of maids congregating outside the inn diverted her attention from inside the tavern. She clearly saw them through the window and noticed every one of them holding a torch, casting a radiant glow that pierced through the dark of the night, resulting in a state of bewilderment and indecision among the members of the Imperial Guard that patrolled *Wind & Grass*.

The maids appeared strangely mesmerized.

"Something is transpiring. . .," Marissa stood up from her chair murmuring to attract Corr's attention. "We find ourselves surrounded by the maids!"

With a sense of alarm, Corr approached the window.

"Please summon the Guild!"

Nehel, in her leather attire and displaying a serious expression, caught them unaware as they turned their heads.

"Divine Empress," Corr had his concern. "Could you please tell us about the meaning of it?"

"The Korbas are drawing near, moving towards us like a windstorm," she nodded somberly. "We cannot delay any longer! We must reach the Ri and begin with my coronation before it is too late!"

After comprehending the situation, Corr wasted no time and, with haste, made his way to the upper floors in search of the Guild's members.

"Take Brisel and rescue my uncle with haste, Ser Marissa!" Nehel urged her. "He is in grave danger as he intends to come here followed by those dragons!"

With fright, Marissa gave her assent to the mandate. A sudden uneasiness crept over her as she placed her sheathed sword on her waist. "Where shall we meet you?!"

"Join us at the palace in the Ri."

In a rush, the knight left the place.

With keen observation, Nehel witnessed her knight's departure, first by the door and then through the window. She noted how fast she retrieved the mantis from the stables and mounted on its back, hastening away with great speed.

Standing, Nehel stood strained, her gaze locked onto the desolate table, where a mug of brew, filled by half, sat alongside a full cup of wine, next to an almost empty bottle. Noticing the wooden cup, she picked it up with care and took a moment to admire the wine contained within. She took a few sips, only to be met with a bitter taste in her tongue, causing her to ultimately decide against further consumption as she placed it back on the table with repudiation.

When she turned, Corr was standing behind, with Fabehel in his arms, and the reminder of the Guild with him.

"It is imperative that we depart hastily and reach the Ri with no delays! The Korbas are coming for us!"

"We are ready to fight against them, even if it means sacrificing our lives!" Marshal Keleana claimed.

"I urge you to not battle against them for my sake, as inevitably, you will meet a certain death!" Nehel demanded with authority. "Your focus should be on saving the lives of all those thousands who had put their trust in me."

"Aye, Divine Empress," Keleana agreed with hesitation. "Shall we take them back to the Seled Post?"

"Even you try. The crowd will follow me no matter where I go or if they lose their lives. They have a blind faith in me I never asked nor wished." she glanced at Selee. "Archmage, I implore you. I have word that you possess the ability to transport all of us to the Ri in an instant. Is it possible to make this happen?"

Selee, feeling startled and worried, responded with a doubtful nod, evading his usual smile. "While it is within my capabilities to accomplish this, it would demand the combined effort of hundreds of people in order to bring the thousands to the Ri."

"This is the main reason my maids are here!" Nehel replied, pointing to the window. "Have you forgotten about them?"

"Divine Empress, I have not forgotten. I believe it is not a good idea to use them."

"I know we prohibit to speak about important matters according to our rules. But could you make an exception this time, Divine Empress?" the head of the Court of Maids begged with calm in her intervention.

"You may speak, Akhimeni."

The eldest maid addressed Selee with a serious attitude. "Since our inception, we have devoted our lives to the Nehel's service. From the precise moment when the blade touched Kasana's neck, and we acknowledged her existence, countless maids that had sacrificed in seclusion for hundreds of tikls, and sadly, many never witnessed our precious jewel. Our generation, this generation, was fortunate enough to see and serve the Promise," she spoke with devotion. "For the Divine Empress, let us take part in your feats of magic as deemed necessary!"

"Very well. . .," the archmage finally smiled. "If the Divine Empress approves, let it be, then!"

"I do!" Nehel later glanced at Akhimeni. "Allow the maids to assist Selee, but I want you to bring my rod and stay by my side always."

The maid and Selee both agreed and left together.

Juni, observing her with growing concern, took a deep breath and approached, but the seriousness of the situation and the tense atmosphere impeded any effort to offer a comfort. A sense of confusion overwhelmed him, unable to understand her situation.

Following Fabehel's request, Corr positioned her on a chair next to the table he used to drink at. She noted the empress' shaking lips and reached out to hold her hands. "My dear, what is the matter?"

"I. . . am afraid. . .," Nehel reacted with widened hazel eyes.

Worriedly, Keleana shook her head and left to meet her vagrants before Peken's look, who was leaning on a column with crossed arms.

With a somber expression and shivering, Nehel glanced at the elf. "Do you feel them? The Korbas?"

"I do not, lass. But I might feel them later." That was the response he gave as he touched his chest to assure her.

Nehel clearly realized what was in store for him soon, but kept it to herself.

With the aid of the bleached No Sak, Marissa distinguished the road ahead amidst the darkness of the night. It was the only one of three moons that contributed to the panorama's illumination, yet the light was feeble, leaving everything cloaked in shadows and a faint darkness. Because of Brisel's exceptional speed, she did not carry any kind of torch that could have provided her with visibility ahead.

Despite facing challenges, she found the road from Arrasem to the Dri straight, leading her to believe that she would reunite with Alessandro in a relatively short period.

The crashing of the chilly wind against her face and the near-bleeding of her dry lips from biting them in despair did not matter to her. Although he loved another girl, she could not accept herself to lose him, as he was not only her best friend but also her intended life partner, with whom she had plans to wed.

Her feelings were still raw, and she did not accept the fact that she had already lost him. She admitted that without Alessandro, her life would be hollow and soulless.

On the way, her tears flew with the wind.

At his young age of eight, Alessandro felt confused, unattended, and overwhelmed with fear.

Lady Tasarissa did not comprehend how he had discovered solace in a young girl named Marissa, her daughter.

It was the morning after the Gesha.

Despite knowing him since they were both four years old, it was not until years later when the Gesha practically brought them together. They both met when Lady Tasarissa and Larissa Eskar, recently elected Head, became friends.

Before, Marissa had Dessidere, and Alessandro had Cassandro.

While nearing her destination on Brisel, she looked at the swarms of complete darkness engulfing the distant stars. These shapes were in a constant state of transformation, and she knew well that they were not simply clouds, but ominous hordes of Korbas disguised in shadows.

Invaded with panic, Brisel let out a hiss and gradually decreased his speed.

"Not now, Brisel!" she begged in despair. "Search his scent and find him! Do not vanish now!"

Hesitant at first, but in response to her plea, the mantis regained his speed and kept hissing out of fear. Then again, the velocity descended until he stopped somewhere.

The moldy smell suggested that they were deep inside somewhere with the road on the water.

Silence.

Marissa watched how the hordes grew bigger and threatened faster.

She heard a horse approaching.

She drew her sword.

She dismounted Brisel.

And readied for the worse.

In a sudden halt, the mare Song came to a stop and let out a surprised neigh, narrowly missing her with the hooves.

Alessandro controlled the mare, startled to find Marissa on the road. "What are you doing here?! These damn scourges are behind me!" in a state of surprise, he screamed and then dismounted from his horse in order to get a closer look at her in the mild darkness.

With terror in her heart, she constantly glanced behind him to notice the hordes moving near.

"Let us go with haste! Mount with me on Brisel!"

"Wait! What of Song?!"

Her face revealed sadness as she shook her head. "I am truly sorry. There is nothing we can do," responded apologetically. "I can not save both of you!"

Sorrow descended upon Alessandro and understood. He instinctively reached out to pet Song's head, gently planting a kiss on her. "My deep gratitude for all the things you have done for me. Thank you for being my constant companion," whispered with affection.

The mare neighed gently.

With tears in his eyes, he mounted behind Marissa on Brisel.

"If only Fabehel had the company of Song instead of a sure death. . ."

Amidst soft sobs, Marissa fixed her gaze on Song, her mind flooded with memories of the unforgettable moments she shared with her cherished stallion, Ghost.

They saw Song by last time. The mare appeared calm and peaceful, displaying a sense of tranquility, as she was aware of her fate and awaited it patiently.

Alessandro embraced Marissa tightly, burying his grieving face in the comfort of her back.

"Brisel. . . Take us away. . ."

Attentive to the surroundings, the mantis hastily responded by initiating his rapid movement towards the Ri by the west, successfully bypassing the malevolent hordes of Korbas that were traversing the area.

On the front of the *Divine Flying Vessel*, Selee held the Molkan Sorcerer's Staff in his hands as he meticulously scanned the path ahead, using the power of its sphere. His face took on a serious look as he gradually realized the hindrances ahead. "I do not believe that we could pass," he stated, after browsing the path with magic many times. "Hordes of Korbas lie ahead."

"There must be a way to pass through!" Nehel said in despair, as she leaned on her tall rod, wearing the white robe and her cloak.

"Divine Empress, we will not falter in our duty," Akhimeni, behind, assured.

"Are you sure?" Selee inquired in doubt.

"All you need to do is give us instructions on what needs to be done, and we will gladly provide you with all the help that you may need."

"Will you be able to bring all the people with us?" Nehel insisted, uncertain.

"Everyone!" the archmage nodded with a smile. "Except for the Artensens battling the Korbas, the survivors will join us at the Ri."

Once again, Selee turned and used the staff to scan the surroundings.

"If I may inquire, Divine Empress. Once we arrive at the palace, do you know who will be the one to crown you?" the elder maid asked.

"The Berrem's monarchs are the ones to give me their blessings once I sit on their throne," Nehel replied with seriousness. "Their voices have spoken to me from the afterlife, repeatedly conveying their desires for me to govern over this realm."

With a shudder of fear, Akhimeni made a startling discovery—the empress could communicate with the dead.

In a sudden appearance, Juni approached Nehel and startled her with a whisper in her ear. He requested her to accompany him.

Fabehel did not hide her concern while Peken tied her to the foot of the high throne. It was not just about ensuring her comfort and preparing her for transportation, with Jumeni by her side, but the elf's continuous shaking and profuse perspiration.

Taking her time, Nehel got closer to him and observed that he persistently clasped his chest, showing that he was experiencing considerable pain. As she shook her head, she could not accept the reason behind his suffering, something she was well aware of.

Jumeni stared at the elf in silence.

"Are you all right, Peken?" During the preparations, Fabehel shared her concerns with him as he assisted her, using the pillows he had set up to ensure a comfortable seating for both her and Jumeni.

"There is no need to worry. . ." Peken, gasping for breath, responded while ensuring their safety.

Juni noticed Nehel, and from her expression, he grasped the seriousness of Peken's condition. Aware of her unique abilities, he recognized the validity of her concern.

Distracted by the metallic sounds coming from the Artensens, Nehel noted their sudden dash towards the plains, continuing ahead until they vanished in the middle of the dark night. She also recognized the impressive ability of Keleana and her group of vagrants to gather a large crowd behind the vessel, as they displayed their fear in anticipation of the approaching, yet unseen, hordes.

Corr was within the crowd, riding on Thunder with Dessidere seated behind, both of them sharing the saddle.

With exceptional speed, the maids formed a chain surrounding both the vessel and the multitude. Instead of holding hands, they created distance between themselves by taking steps apart.

In a sudden burst of pain, Peken grabbed his chest and collapsed onto the floor, causing Juni to rush over to him in a state of alarm. Meanwhile, Fabehel, tied up, attempted to calm him down by gently touching his head.

Nehel, although lacking the power to heal, still wished to assist him. However, Selee called her.

"Me must leave now, Divine Empress!"

She approached the archmage, reluctantly entrusting Peken to the care of others.

"Are you ready?" she inquired with seriousness.

"Aye, the vessel will transport into the square, right in front of the palace, so you can promptly claim the throne before the Korbas arrive."

The faint sound of dragons caused a startle among all. The hordes were near.

"Do it now!" she mandated with apprehension.

The excruciating pain caused Peken to scream with no control on the floor. Fabehel, gripping by his arms, had to subdue him while attached to the base of the high throne, and Juni, who took the risk of not being securely restrained, also assisted in the effort of holding his legs.

Selee, using both hands, raised the Sorcerer's Staff, causing a powerful surge of white lightning to emit from it. The energy spread out, affecting all the maids and encompassing both the vessel and the crowd. The ground beneath us shook with such intensity that it felt as if the same Sankaris trembled, while a thick veil of darkness covered the night, causing the three moons that were once visible to vanish from sight.

In an unexpected maneuver, the *Flying Divine Vessel* swiftly took off and disappeared into the depths of a dark tunnel, causing Nehel to lose their balance and crash onto the floor. She had a mixture of emotions and mystical abilities that brought an indescribable trance state. Despite her condition, she still regained consciousness and grabbed the bottom of Selee's azure robes.

The archmage stood in complete stillness, like a statue, with the staff held high above his head.

Excruciating screams came from Peken. Despite the crashing wind, Fabehel and Juni remained resolute in their hold on him.

In fear, Jumeni instinctively clung to one foot of the high throne.

Amid the dark tunnel, everyone heard the terrifying screeches of the Korbas. Each shriek felt like a piercing knife, going straight into the empress's heart.

Inevitably, Nehel and the Korbas were linked, given that both of them shared the spilled blood of Kasana by the *Ykarte*.

As Nehel was in a trance, images of Venka, Natahel, and Dalehel crossed her mind.

Bursts of bright lights emerged, causing everyone in the tunnel to be blinded, extending from the vessel to the drifting crowd.

Intense brightness.

Nehel opened her eyes, startled to find herself on the floor with her rod lying beside her. She was conscious but struggling to catch her breath.

Her gaze landed outside the enormous circular palace, which seemed to have stood the test of time, now appearing more ancient than archaic, bathed by the light of the sun's first light. The giant wooden gates were open by a strange reason.

They had arrived at the Ri.

Instead of going inside the palace, Nehel turned her gaze and discovered a grim scene. In a distressing posture, Juni had knelt beside Peken's body, while Fabehel struggled to free herself from the bindings so she could go to the elf. Nehel ran beside him to find Peken dying but aware of his fate, yet she was helpless to take any action.

Fabehel crawled herself over to Juni's side and joined in the tragic moment.

The elf unveiled his yellow eyes and spoke frail.

"Lass. . . give me your blessing so I can go to the Gakia. . ."

"I will make sure of it, Peken!" she promised between sobs as her tears fell. "You will reunite with Venka!"

The elf gave a light smile and his eyes closed.

Nehel placed his hand on his chest, covered by his clothes, and took a moment to feel his beating heart and steady breath, until they ceased.

Peken, Uskam's disciple, traveler and trader, had died.

Nehel, same as Juni, sobbed.

Fabehel and Jumeni observed silently with sad gestures.

A shadow covered the empress, and she lifted to see with her wet eyes. "Take your rod and run to the throne! The Korbas are still coming!" Selee hurried her. "There will be time to mourn him!"

Nehel turned her head around to observe how the sky was becoming darker. The new day was transforming into the dim night. She nodded, and with determination, ran to pick up her rod. Afterwards, she jumped from the vessel.

The archmage used magic to slow her floating fall and land on the ground. Like a feather descending.

The sight of the approaching hordes of dragons was intimidating and overwhelming.

She kept running as the day shifted into darkness, and hastily entered to the palace.

At long last, she was on the way to her stance.

33
CORONATION

E mpress Nehel crossed the aisle with haste, her eyes caught sight of the expansive circular area, where she halted midway to ponder the nearly dim surroundings. The light was fading, but there was still enough visibility for her to observe the thousands of pedestals, holding gray statues representing the monarchs of Berrem that had ruled the realm for over two thousand tikls.

She heard a screech and, terrified, continued on her way.

As she moved closer steadily to her intended destination, she discovered an ancient throne positioned on a platform. The stone seat, which was quite large, featured an abundance of engravings that spanned across its entirety.

The screeching grew louder.

With determination, she sprinted and ascended the stairs leading up to the platform within that vast and desolate space. And gave the first steps to her throne.

As Nehel held onto her rod, she could not help but notice a certain atmosphere surrounding the area.

With all his fury, the giant black dragon entered, completely smashing the giant sturdy doors into countless pieces, and let out a thunderous roar that echoed throughout.

The empress closed her eyes with terror.

She knew who he was.

Ardek Korba with all his rage.

Somewhat, the dragon had gained more power, and Nehel knew she could not confront him. The power she possessed would not defeat him.

The giant monster gave the steps, making the ground to tremble, advancing with terror towards the platform.

The suspense grew as Nehel pondered her future, questioning whether she would perish or transform into a Korbeen.

Panic gripped her.

The wind rushed inside.

"Come here with us, little," a female voice said with sweetness. "Do not be afraid and take your stance!"

Nehel opened her hazel eyes.

A sight greeted her as she came to face with the ghostly figure of a woman. With a magnificent presence, she appeared as a queen from a bygone era as she extended her hand with grace.

"Fear not, and come to sit upon my throne."

Nehel nodded and let her guide towards the throne.

Taking her place in the seat, an extraordinary phenomenon unfolded—an immense multitude of spectral monarchs materialized, forming a captivating spectacle around her—. Every ghost extended their hands towards the empress, bestowing their blessings upon her.

Ardek Korba came to a stop, incapable of advancing any further as he found himself unable to step onto the platform. An invisible barrier, a mystical field, impeded his progress and he could not proceed.

By receiving an unconventional coronation ceremony from the deceased monarchs of Berrem, she could accomplish her purpose in her stance.

The balance.

And the Korba knew it.

Overwhelmed by an incredible surge of power in her inner, she locked eyes with the dragon, emanating an aura of eminent authority while gripping her rod with the Akareen star.

Unexpectedly, Empress Nehel's power surpassed that of Ardek in a sudden turn of events. In an instant, her strength grew.

"You know well that we can not have a conflict between us now," she made it clear.

The dragon aspect of the Korba underwent a trans-formation, shrinking in size until it transformed into the immaculate elder man of the Arankan aspect.

His eyes, regularly blue in human form, were red as he made a nod. "Very well, empress," replied with a grin. "You are naïve and small, yet you grew powerful in a short time. You were nobody, but in two months you were successful in building your Jyistereerk."

"Go back to your dominion!" she demanded with rigor.

"We will leave, but we will be stronger when you have grown enough. This balance of yours means a long war, and I guarantee it."

"I have established the *Deken Karsaker* for that reason. And I also assure that the Jyistereerk will be stronger to confront you."

Ardek Korba nodded and morphed into a flying black whelp, vanishing as he soared away.

Nehel sighed as sunlight streamed through the open entrance, realizing the retreat of the hordes.

The spectral monarchs vanished in front of her eyes.

Except one. A king stepped in front of her and nodded as a sign of respect and admiration.

Nehel answered the same way from her throne.

He was King Vihen of Aranka, her grandfather, who appeared alongside the Berremen monarchs.

He disappeared.

The empress was in solitude on her throne, but not for long.

An immense crowd made their way into the palace.

The vagrants fulfilled their duties as the Imperial Guard seized control of the ancient palace, primarily focusing on protecting the empress on the platform. The palace appearance amazed the massive crowd inside, having been closed since the end of the monarchies. Hundreds of thousands of people were a mix of visitors who followed the empress and locals who welcomed her.

The multitude was massive, that even half of them had to remain outside.

Keleana and Kekten assumed their positions on the sides of the throne.

With concern, Alessandro and Marissa navigated through the middle of the crowd on Brisel and reached the platform. Once there, they dismounted and approached the seated empress.

"I have failed, Divine Empress," Alessandro spoke with sadness. "There is no treaty. . ."

"I know, uncle," she replied with composure. "And is a fault of no one."

Corr and Dessidere made their presence on the platform, followed by Juni and his sister, Jumeni.

Selee was the last, carrying the Sorcerer's Staff.

In a matter of moments, a multitude of maids, with Akhimeni included, formed a ring around the crowd that had assembled inside the palace.

Drawing nearer to Dessidere, the archmage whispered in his ear.

With a nod, the Herald positioned himself at the front of the platform, ensuring his presence was visible to all. After making a request to an elder in the crowd for a walking stick, which he then used to beat the floor. "In the Seventh Day of the First Month in the First Year of the *Tikl the First of Nehel!* It is an honor to introduce all you, the Divine Empress Nehel of the Jyistereerk!"

"Nehel Hikis!" in unison, all the maids answered aloud from their places. The crowd was in awe at the salutations and reverences.

"*Nehel Jyistereerk*!" Dessidere continued with a firm voice.

"Nehel Hikis!"

"Divine Jewel!"

"Nehel Hikis!"

"Divine Empress of Sankaris!"

"Nehel Hikis!"

"Queen of Berrem!"

"Nehel Hikis!"

"Queen of Aranka!"

"Nehel Hikis!"

"Mystical Leader of the Kannestes!"

"Nehel Hikis!"

"High Sorceress of Salter!"

"Nehel Hikis!"

"We implore you to allow the Divine Empress to speak!" Dessidere concluded.

The crowd erupted with applause and shouts of joy.

Everyone on the platform fixed on Nehel as everyone eagerly awaited her response.

Despite her discomfort, the empress understood that delivering a speech was one of her responsibilities as a newly crowned empress, as her stance had not yet fully strengthened despite her recent encounter with Ardek.

With her rod in hand, she stood up and took a few steps forward, examining the silent and expectant crowd. "I am just a small girl with all the burden of an empire," she started, hesitant at first. "The much-anticipated balance has been restored. However, the consequences of this restoration are to be endured, as we have to face a major war on Sankaris. I am not finished with my task yet, and the Korbas are still on the other side of the Karekall. It is my duty to ensure this balance and oppose all evilness that could unbalance our world again."

Every single person, with no exceptions, was in awe of her words, as her remarkable wisdom left a lasting impression, even though she was young in age.

"I make a solemn promise that I and my future generations will preserve the balance and return the healed Sankaris to you until the Korbas cease to exist."

She concluded and returned to her throne.

Again, the crowd burst into applause and shouts of joy, creating a vibrant atmosphere.

But Nehel and the rest of the Guild were far from pleased.

It was only the beginning, the very beginning.

There were casualties.

And an uneasiness for the future under the *Deken Karsaker.*

OUTCOMES

Peken's lifeless remains were on a pile of wood while the Guild observed, silent and somber. His hands were on the chest that once was affected and poisoned by the evilness, and dressed him in new leather clothes alongside his blade and bag of belongings. With soft murmurs, Selee slowly approached the lifeless body and used his magical powers to ignite it into flames.

The smoke swiftly soared towards the heavens, symbolizing its last sendoff to the elf.

Nehel and Juni watched together, holding hands, sharing their sadness while they gave him farewells.

Marissa, while kneeling, paid her respects to the departed by placing her sword against the ground. Her tears drew her black cheeks while Alessandro touched her shoulders to give her solace.

"His death was certain, anyway." Alessandro whispered with prudence. "One way or the other, he would perish because of his tainted blood."

Corr placed Fabehel, who was sitting in her newly made wheelchair, ahead of himself and provided her with companionship.

Selee, Akhimeni, and Jumeni stood together in a small group, paying their respects at the funeral.

The sentinel found himself dashed to the ground with a sharp, ear-piercing buzzing sound and a flash of scarlet, as the red mantis lunged at his head with its elongated mandibles, simultaneously beating its wings in a rapid motion. The spines of the creature gripped him by his shoulders. Overcoming his fear, he bravely used his hands to push the creature away, even though it possessed immense strength.

In the end, the sentinel's capitulation allowed the vicious red mantis to execute him.

Once the creature had completed its mortal deed, it turned its attention to the Torret Post, already in Berrem.

The monster, along with a massive swarm, flew at high speed, starting their attack.

In her usual informal leather clothes, Nehel handpicked papyruses from a desk that was cluttered with various objects, while the sun's rays filtered through the window, providing ample illumination to the chamber she occupied. A document with a special request caught her attention.

"That is a request from the Breken Nation to join the Jyistereerk," Alessandro clarified, pointing to the papyrus she had seated beside her. "Father Orssandro, in his teachings, emphasized the need to exercise caution when dealing with requests from divisible realms."

"As is also Fenn. I truly feel sorry for Corr," she looked at him with a sympathetic stare. "You have counseled me to exercise patience in that matter, uncle. But I have an urgency to ease their sufferings."

He nodded with a light smile.

No matter how hard she tried, Nehel could not achieve comfort. In order to work at the desk's height, she required help from two thick cushions on a large chair.

Positioned at a corner within the same chamber, Fabehel was enjoying a book while sitting in a remarkable creation crafted by Jumeni and blessed by the empress herself, a new wheelchair, enabling her to maneuver in any direction with autonomy. Her purpose for being there was to be in closer proximity to Alessandro, the man who sought her affection.

Alessandro had the need for a brief respite from his work. He rose from his seat and made his way towards the window. Once there, he poured himself a glass of wine from a small table and sipped from it with enjoyment. Through the glass, his dark eyes observed how Marissa convinced Juni to take part in a bogus fight using wooden swords.

Juni had expressed his strong aspiration to become a knight at the service of the empress, and Marissa enthusiastically offered to instruct him in the art of swordsmanship.

"I do not comprehend it, uncle!" Nehel interrupted Alessandro, showing a specific papyrus. "It says something about a steam machine invented by some engineer. What is an engineer?"

He agreed with a nod and rejoined her to offer his continued help.

As Archmage Missar approached her bed, Carlissa turned her head to look at him. Through the lenses of her thick round glasses, she gazed at him.

The Head sighed, gasping for air, as he recently climbed the stairs. "Commandant Kartak is currently en route and will arrive soon! What is the message you wish to give?"

"Since the Divine Empress has successfully established her Jyistereerk, I need to go to her," she spoke in serenity.

"Despite this, I am refraining from giving myself to the empress until she reaches the proper age."

"Are you offering yourself as the same weapon you used to be?"

"I will give her a home and a motherland, which are what she needs."

Archmage Missar, while adopting a thinking posture and nodding, remained unable to grasp the meaning behind *Ykarte's* words.

To be continued in The Empress' Palace.

SAN LUIS POTOSI, MEXICO 1994

T his story was a product of a metamorphosis. I am 51 today when I finished *The Empress' Journey*.

Initially planned, it began as a vague idea from one of the many occurrences to write in the Science Fiction genre. At thirteen, I fell in love with Ray Bradbury's Martian Chronicles, and that's when my passion for English, Spanish, and Sci-Fi began as well.

Even at 22 years old, there was still much for me to learn.

Mars mesmerized and attracted me, and it still does. The works of Robert A. Heinlein, Isaac Asimov, Jules Verne, and H.G. Wells had an inspiring force on me while I practiced my English.

Also, writers like Pio Baroja, Gabriel Garcia Marquez, Octavio Paz, Juan Rulfo and Carlos Fuentes, gave me an early inspiration in the Spanish literature, especially Latin American authors. I was a fan of the *Magic Realism*.

Following many short stories, novellas, and drafts I have done as a hobby, I took on a bold literary endeavor. It felt like tossing a coin, unsure of my book's theme and its direction.

During that period, I was on summer break. In contrast to U.S. colleges, my Economics school was closed, resulting in a three-month wait to resume classes. I had friends, but they were busy on long vacations or working temporary jobs, just like me when I worked at a billiards saloon.

Anyhow, I had lots of time.

Despite the existence of the internet, it was not as advanced or accessible as it is today, making it complicated and expensive to get this service. All that, just for slow internet through dial-up and a phone line. The headache came from waiting over twenty minutes to download a simple JPG image, with the added fear of disconnection.

Cell phones earned the nickname "bricks" because of their bulky size, inability to fit into pockets, and limited functionality for calls.

Besides my writings, I used to collect comic books, play Nintendo and Atari, enjoy soccer and baseball, go to movie theaters, watch soap operas, and other various television programs. That was my carefree life back then.

Yet I had plenty of time.

The fabulous 1990s!

The original *Star Wars* had a big impact on me when my mother gifted me a remastered trilogy box set on VHS. Despite it, no, I am not a hardcore SW fan and never been, although I might have some lightsaber somewhere in the house.

I was drawn to write a Space Opera story just to experiment and enjoy with my writing. Here's when the spark for my life story was born in my mind. And though I planned it as a hobby, I didn't expect to make a whole series from it.

I wished to tell the story of an empire, but one benevolent, not evil. A sovereign of worlds—or planets—under one monarch. I remembered the Childlike Empress from *The Neverending Story* and pondered about making a different version to be the empress of all the worlds. The empress I made, or rather remade, was born on Earth but abducted as an infant by the Korbas, a type of extraterrestrial creatures. She became the ruler of an empire at the tender age of ten. Here's why my current story began with a ten years old.

My world building was made in ten sheets of letter paper, joined by pieces of scotch tape, and placed on my room's wall. My own *Frelee Dee*.

No, no lightsabers or Jedis in my story, neither a Sebastian nor a Falkor. From two stories, I wanted to make something different.

If I could call it "original". Duh!

As I previously mentioned, it was formerly a thing to fill the free time I had. It was fun to play and include elements from other media.

I continued adding characters from Earth—which I called our planet as *Casak*—, including Alejandro (Alessandro), Marissa, and Fabiola (Fabehel). Corr, Brisel, Selee, Uskam, and Kasana were the designated names for the aliens.

I made a first draft. The years passed and went to a second draft. In twenty years, I made six drafts.

I had generated sufficient elements for a world-building and cohesive narrative. Yet, there was something that didn't quite fit in the story. In fact, many things didn't match up.

The story lacked character, action, and emotional depth, which was embarrassing. It was like cooking a delicious meal with no salt or pepper on a boring paper plate.

When I moved to my new home, I realized that there were many tasks and responsibilities that I needed to address in order to establish an order and stability in my life. As a result, I underwent a significant transformation from the carefree and independent bachelor I was in college. I got married and now have three children.

It took about ten years of pause from writing.

Yet the story still bothered me. I wasn't happy with the way it was. I couldn't understand why I was so attached to it.

My half sibling, to whom I met twenty-five years of his life later, played a crucial role in introducing me to the world of fantasy, particularly *Lord of the Rings*. His fascination with Tolkien stories led me to explore the works of various authors, immerse myself in countless books, and even venture into the realms of the *World of War-Craft*—the books—and *Game of Thrones*. My intention was to enjoy from the stories, as I firmly believed that fantasy did not suit to my taste in writing.

During a discussion about fantasy with a friend, I linked it to my space opera novel and, much to my surprise, I saw where it went wrong.

I wrote it in the mistaken genre!

Hence, here is the result: *The Empress' Journey*.

ACKNOWLEDGMENTS

T here's only one person who had read all the six drafts and I owe her all my gratitude as she always lifted my spirits, believing in my gift to create unimaginable worlds. She was my number one fan, and my mother, now in heaven, always cheered me as she always enjoyed my stories. I won't never forget it. I am sure she still does from up there.

The warmth and love emanating from my family have helped to spark again my creativity for this narrative, accompanied by an inspiration.

In her own way, my treasured wife supported my endeavours.

To my three kids also witnessed me typing a story. Especially my daughter awaiting eagerly to read my book.

Also, to the main culprit who introduced me to fantasy, my half brother. If not because of him, I wouldn't have never written this story.

And to all the people who believed in me and worked altogether with me.

My deepest gratitude to all of them.